MW01139195

Cult Justice

A Marc Kadella Legal Mystery

By

Dennis L. Carstens

Previous Marc Kadella Legal Mysteries

The Key to Justice

Desperate Justice

Media Justice

Certain Justice

Personal Justice

Delayed Justice

Political Justice

Insider Justice

Exquisite Justice

email me at: dcarstens514@gmail.com

ONE

1987

Benjamin Sokol stopped typing, turned his head to the right, and looked out his dorm room window. Another Saturday night and here he was, alone in his room, working on a paper for a class. It was not due for another two weeks but with no social life, why not get at it? Graduation was barely three months away and the thought depressed him. Not because he did not want to graduate; he was already selected for graduate school. No, what depressed him was the belief he was going to be the only person in the history of the universe to go through four years of college and still be a virgin. Before he started college, Benjamin had been led to believe this was almost impossible.

Benjamin—Ben to the few friends he had—went back to his Commodore 64. The paper he was typing was for a history class. It was a brief history of the Great Purge of 1930 to 1938 in Stalinist Russia. To further the goals of the revolution, Stalin found it necessary to get rid of––purge—counterrevolutionaries plotting against him.

Ben's professor, a political liberal, was no fan of Josef Stalin. Of course, Professor Greer was also a hardcore Reagan hating pacifist. For Ben, the more he studied Stalin, the more he came to admire him. He also realized this would put him at odds with virtually all Western attitudes and ideals. His paper, to be graded by a weakling liberal professor, would have to be carefully written. Ben wanted a good grade and would play to Greer's bias. Stalin, the mad, paranoid, psycho tyrant would be Ben's official conclusion. Not Stalin the man who knew what he wanted and let nothing stand in his way to get it; that Stalin Ben could secretly admire.

Benjamin Hiam Sokol was the grandson of Jewish emigres who escaped from the Soviet Union in 1939. In fact, they were smuggled across the border into Finland on September 1, 1939; the very day Hitler unleashed World War II by sending his army into Poland. They were Levi and Hila Sokoloski, and Hila had been pregnant with Benjamin's father, Daniel.

Determined to have her baby in America, they arrived in New York in January 1940. Bigoted against Polish people, it was Levi's decision to Americanize their name to Sokol. This was easily done by using the name Sokol when they came through Ellis Island and claimed they were Russians.

Grandpa Levi was a business genius. Through hard work, connections in the Jewish Community of New York, and a gift for managing people and money, Levi managed to build a successful finance company. By the time Benjamin was born to Daniel and his wife Sara, the family was almost wealthy. Daniel completed the job of enriching the family under Grandpa Levi's tutelage.

Fortunately for Benjamin, he inherited his father's and grandfather's intelligence. Unfortunately, being the product of an East Coast liberal education, he was taught to be ashamed of their success, especially from leftist teachers with a not-so-subtle, anti-Semitic streak. By the time Ben enrolled at Princeton, he was thoroughly ashamed of his family's money, but not too ashamed to turn it down.

Engrossed in his writing, he failed to hear the lock being opened on the dorm room door. The next thing he was aware of was his roommate's voice.

"Hey, Benny," he heard his roommate say.

Christian Foster Evans was Ben's exact opposite. A person could not be more of a WASP than Chris Evans. He was a product of old-money Rhode Island aristocracy. Chris could even trace his lineage back to pre-revolutionary colonial days on both sides of his family. The entire extended family had so much money they were too embarrassed to talk about it. Except, of course, in the company of the correct East Coast political establishment. They paid for their guilt penance by contributing to the appropriate causes and politicians. Those politicians who wanted to use the government to take care of the less fortunate; people so less fortunate as to be arrested if they even drove through the neighborhoods where the political contributors lived.

Despite the burden of his sordid upbringing, Chris Evans was the most likeable person Ben had ever met. Partying his way through Princeton with a C-plus GPA for his criminal justice degree was Chris preparing for Yale Law School. For most people, a C-plus GPA on an Ivy League law school admission request would be laughed at. Chris was already accepted. The family tree had roots in the Yale Law garden.

"Hi, Chris," Ben replied as he turned around to greet him.

"I forgot my wallet. We're going to a party, a meeting actually…" Chris absently said as he searched through his dresser.

"Hi," the girl standing in the doorway said to Ben.

She was very pretty, as were all of Chris' girlfriends, with dark blonde hair over her shoulders.

Ben could not remember if he had ever met her and did not know her name. So, he decided to stick it to his roomie a little.

"Hi, Karen," Ben said and smiled.

2

"I'm Nicky," she replied. "Who's Karen?" she asked Chris with an evil look.

By now, Ben was laughing, and Chris said, "Thanks a lot, Benny." He then said to the girl, "He's just trying to get me in trouble."

"Uh-huh," she said with doubt in her voice.

"It's Saturday night, Benny. You need to get out. Why don't you come with us? We're going to some kind of political party meeting— a 'save the whales' deal."

Ben and Chris had only been roommates for senior year. This was the first time Chris, a notorious partier, had invited him to go out with him.

"I guess, sure, why not?" Ben replied.

"Lots of girls at these things," Chris said with a lecherous look.

"You are so bad," Nicky said. "What am I getting myself into?"

"It's our first date, Nicky," Chris said. "I haven't asked you to bear me a son."

"Ahhh! Stay away from me," Nicky mock-shrieked. "Don't you dare touch me!"

"See what I have to deal with?" Chris asked Ben.

"Yeah, beautiful girls that are after your family's money," Ben replied as he slipped on his coat.

"Don't tell him that," Nicky said. "He thinks we're after him because of his good looks and charm."

"No, he doesn't," Chris said. "I know better. We have to stop at the liquor store and bring some beer. Let's go."

"Reagan has been a fucking disaster for this country!" a frizzy-haired redhead girl sporting large, round wire-rimmed glasses loudly proclaimed.

"And for the environment," one of the boys chimed in.

"Worse for the environment. He'll destroy the goddamn planet," their host said.

Ben, Chris and Nicky were in a rental house a block off-campus. They were sitting together on the floor at the fringe of a large circle of young people, at least twenty-five of them, gathered for a leftist political discussion mostly about the Nazi Reagan and how to save the planet.

Their host was a thirty-four-year-old professional student by the name of Bentley Probert. Bentley had been in one school or another since he was four years old and had no intention of leaving. He had changed his graduate degree program so many times he could not remember them all. In order to keep his mother happy, Dad kept paying the tuition and his living expenses. Bentley surmised this was to keep Mom from digging into Dad's extramarital activities. This was fine with Bentley.

The thought of facing the adult world could send him into depression and bed for a week.

If Bentley had to guess what his political beliefs were, they would probably be libertarian. As far as saving the whales, and the planet, Bentley could not care less. He held these gatherings to make new customers and meet young girls. And seduce them with marijuana, alcohol and Quaaludes. The marijuana and Quaaludes were also his business product.

About a half-hour after arriving, a girl sitting a quarter of the way around the circle from him caught Ben's eye, at almost the precise moment he caught hers. There was a good reason for the attention. Her name was Abby Sentinel and she was the female version of Ben with a difference. Abby was seriously committed to the environmental cause and she was about as virginal as a dockside hooker.

She had started coming to groups like this about a year ago. At first, she came in hopes of losing her virginity before she finished school. After attending a dozen or so of them, she came to realize that at least half of the people who attended, both guys and girls, were there for that same reason: socially shy guys and girls looking for a date. Abby, having dispensed with losing her virginity to Bentley, also became a true believer.

They had been at the meeting for a little more than an hour when their host made an announcement.

"Hey," Bentley began, "what do you say we take a break and chill out a bit? If you need to use a bathroom, there are two upstairs and one off the kitchen."

Bentley, followed by about half of the crowd, went through a door leading to the basement.

Seeing the crowd follow him, Nicky asked Chris, "What's up with that? Where are they going?"

"Downstairs to Bentley's weed and 'lude sales emporium," Chris said. "You want some?"

"Uh, I don't know," Nicky said. "Do you?"

Chris leaned closer to her and asked, "Do you want some weed, yes or no?"

"Sure, if you do, why not?" she smiled.

"I'll be right back," Chris said.

When Chris left, Ben heard a feminine voice right next to his ear say, "Hi."

He turned his head to see the girl he had noticed looking right at him.

"Oh, uh, hi," he said back to her.

"Can I sit here?" she asked.

"Sure," Ben said, a little too quickly.

"I'm Abby," she said then held out her hand as she went cross-legged on the floor where Chris had been.

"Ben, Ben Sokol," Ben said. "This is Nicky," he added, pointing at her.

The two girls exchanged greetings while Ben sized Abby up. She was prettier than he had thought at first—long, straight, brown hair. A touch on the plump side, but then so was Ben.

"Would you like a beer?" Ben asked and offered her one of Chris' beers.

"Sure, want to smoke?" she asked, holding up a joint.

"Yeah, sure, why not," Ben said. He had tried marijuana a couple of times and was not impressed. But, at this moment, if this girl had asked him to go skydiving, he would have agreed.

Nicky's hand appeared in front of Abby's face holding a plastic Bic lighter. Chris returned and sat on the other side of Nicky.

The rest of the evening was the best time Ben Sokol had ever had. At least until he vomited four times on the walk back to the dorm. Fortunately, he was by himself. Chris and Nicky had gone off to her dorm and Abby went with the two girls she came with. But not before Ben and Abby had exchanged phone numbers and made a date for the next night.

TWO

As the New Jersey winter turned to spring, Ben and Abby became more and more inseparable. Of course, the "big event" happened after the obligatory three dates. The Friday evening after they first met at the pseudo-political party, Chris came back to their dorm room with Nicky. What he found astonished him.

Chris had stolen a Do Not Disturb sign from a local motel. He kept it in the room for use when either himself or a roommate, Ben, needed privacy. This was not to be used for studying; the sign was for bringing girls back to the dorm.

In the few months Chris had known Ben, Chris had never arrived back at the dorm to find the sign posted. In fact, it never occurred to him that it would be. But tonight, there it was, dangling from the doorknob warning him off.

The two of them, Chris and Nicky, silently walked to about ten feet from the door then stopped.

"You don't suppose they're in there going at it, do you?" he quietly whispered to Nicky.

"Well, duh," Nicky replied. "It's about time. I should have told you, Abby asked me for a condom. She was pretty psyched."

"Ben asked me for one, too," Chris said.

"Did you have to explain to him how to put it on?" Nicky asked.

"No, come on," Chris said trying not to laugh. "You didn't really tell her, did you?"

"Ssssh, yeah, I did," Nicky giggled. "I think she wanted me to believe she was a virgin. Don't tell Ben, but I've heard some things."

Chris held a finger to his lips then crept up to the door. As he did, Nicky tried to stop him but not too vigorously. When they reached the door, they both leaned up against it with an ear placed on it. They stayed this way for three or four seconds not hearing anything. Chris frowned, shrugged his shoulders and as he was about to give up, they heard Abby almost scream.

The pair of startled eavesdroppers jumped away from the door and sprinted down the hall. When they reached the stairs—they were on the second floor—they ran down the stairs and out the front door. Laughing hysterically, they ran and stumbled down the sidewalk and across the street.

When they stopped, Nicky, trying to catch her breath, spoke first. "Oh my god! I've never been so embarrassed. What if someone had seen us?"

"Ben, you stud!" Chris yelled toward the building. "I hope that was passion and not him strangling her."

"Shut up," Nicky laughed. "Let's get out of here."

"Where to? Your place?"

Nicky looked at him and said, "Are you kidding? After that, I can't even think about it. We'll get a beer. You can call Ben in a while then take me home."

Over the next three months, Ben used Chris' Do Not Disturb sign almost twice as much as Chris. In addition to a lot of sex, Abby was bringing him to political parties three and four times a week. At first, Ben was not very interested. He had never given social justice or the oppression of the less fortunate much thought. Gradually, by attending meetings farther and farther to the political left, he began to realize this philosophy was who he was. Ben also came to feel more and more guilty about himself, his family and their success and money. Of course, not so guilty as to decline the money his parents sent. Just guilty about his family's participation in oppressing so many groups.

Abby Sentinel came from a world of privilege and wealth that would make Ben feel inadequate. Her father was an enormously wealthy, managing senior partner of a mid-size New York investment bank. It helped that Grandpa Sentinel had founded the place. In addition to having significantly more money than Ben's family, she was also of a different religion. Abby was an Episcopalian who had been taught to hate Jews even more than Catholics by the time she was five.

After her sophomore year, an associate professor of sociology convinced her to do an internship of sorts. She volunteered at a Bronx food shelf. He was also a volunteer there and opened Abby's eyes to a world she had done her best to ignore.

"These last two meetings we went to," Ben said to Abby, "the one last night and on Monday, I think he was right, the professor, what was his name?"

"Webster Crosby," Abby replied. "He's an economics professor. I worked with him one summer at a food shelf in the Bronx."

Ben was tempted to ask if she had slept with him. He was afraid the answer might be yes and decided it was best to let it go. Besides, Ben was almost sexually smitten by the man himself.

"He's a gifted speaker," Ben said. "And I've been thinking about what he said, especially about our responsibility—the intellectual elites of society. We have an obligation to lead people to a better place. A more just society."

Abby smiled a Cheshire cat smile but said nothing.

"What?" Ben asked.

"Oh, nothing," she said. "It's just, well, I thought it would take longer for you to come to it. He is persuasive, though, isn't he?"

"Chris says he's an arrogant asshole. Says he's a bigot who blames everyone, especially the Jews, because he's not been anointed King."

"Chris is jealous because Webster gets more sex than he does," Abby said. "Besides, the more I have learned about liberal, social justice politics, the more I see he is right about the Jews. I don't think Hitler should have killed them all, but they are the worst of the capitalist oppressors. And they won't help anyone who isn't a Jew."

"He is really involved in saving the environment, isn't he?" Ben asked wanting to get the subject changed from Jewish oppression.

"He is," Abby said nodding emphatically. "He's right, too. If we screw up the planet, we'll all die. That dunce Reagan is too surrounded by greedy white guys to see that.

"I have to get back to this," she said, referring to her test studies. "More capitalist economics. The more I learn, the more I see how it has kept billions of people in poverty. But I suppose I better play the game and pass the test tomorrow."

"Me too," Ben agreed. "Then graduation next week."

"Why don't you want me to meet your parents?" Abby asked Ben.

They were in Abby's dorm room after making love. Abby was sitting naked on the bed; Ben was sitting at her desk wearing a white T-shirt and white boxers. Abby took a long hit off the joint and handed it to Ben. There was a small window fan in the window in front of the desk Ben was sitting at. The fan was blowing out to suck the smelly smoke out of the room.

"I told you," Ben impatiently said. "Everything has to be a big production with them. I don't need the hassle. They're driving down in the morning; they'll go to the ceremony and leave after I go to dinner with them. You go do the same with your family and we'll get it over with."

"You're ashamed of me. You don't want your parents to meet me," Abby said teasing him to get a reaction.

"Yeah, that's it. You happy now?" he asked, clearly miffed.

"You're right. I'm just teasing you," she said as he handed the joint back to her.

She was right, though. Ben did not want her to meet his parents. She had no idea he was a Jew and did not want her to find out. The people that she had introduced him to were right. The Jews were the worst of the oppressors and Ben could not be more ashamed. Just look at what they were doing to the Palestinians.

"Hi, Abby, Ben," Professor Crosby said. He smiled and shook hands with both then stood aside to let them in his house.

Crosby was a bit older than Abby and Ben in his mid-thirties. He was also charismatic, intelligent and photogenic. And a true-blue, socialist radical. Long, over the collar stylish hair and turtleneck sweaters with tortoiseshell glasses he didn't need.

A tenured professor by age 28, he was convinced capitalism was the death of civilization. The only way to save the planet and its inhabitants was through a centralized government run by the intellectual elites. Of course, Webster Crosby would have a prominent chair at that table.

"Where is everyone?" Ben asked when they got inside. Theirs was a small group, six including the professor. No one else had arrived yet.

"I wanted to talk to you alone before the others got here," Crosby said. "Let's sit down first."

They took seats in the living room and Crosby started again.

"I've had my eye on you, Ben, and I see leadership potential. But I need to know if you're in."

"Yes, definitely," Ben said. "In fact, we've attended other group meetings and there's no sense of purpose. No direction. It's just a bunch of spoiled brats whining that life isn't fair. Yet they don't want to do anything about it."

Crosby looked at Abby who was smiling back at him. "I'm glad, really glad, to hear you say that. Here's the deal and please, don't be offended. You're the last one I'm talking to about this because you're the newest."

"Yeah, okay," Ben said.

"It's time we stopped talking and started to act. We need to wake this country up before it's too late. Before it leads the world to its own destruction.

"There's a construction project starting in upstate New York. I'll tell everybody where later.

"It's on a beautiful lake which also has an Indian reservation near it. Right now there are small cabins around it, and it is very nice and well preserved.

"But local politicians have sold out to Jewish bankers and developers. They are in the process of buying up all the land around this lake. They have already obtained about half of it. And the local government is helping them because the Jews have them in their pockets.

"The plan is to bulldoze all of the property and build multi-million-dollar lake homes and very expensive condos around it. Ben, they're gonna destroy it, so the wealthy have one more playground for themselves."

"What can we do about it?" Ben eagerly asked.

"We're not gonna go up there and chain ourselves to trees. All that ever does is make the people who do it look like idiots," Crosby said. "A few years ago, there was a group called the Weathermen. Have you heard of them?"

"Yeah, sure," Ben said, eagerly nodding again.

"They had the right idea, just the wrong target. You don't get public opinion on your side by acting like a bunch of spoiled assholes and scaring the shit out of people. You need the right target. I believe the target should be rich people spoiling the planet for their own amusement. This, this is our target. This development."

"Want a beer?" Abby asked both men. She left for the kitchen to get them and while she was gone, Crosby let his sexist sideshow.

"We'll always need women around for sex and servants," he said with a wink.

"What do you have in mind, Webster?" Ben asked.

"I've been up there, and they have started construction. There must be twenty-million dollars' worth of equipment sitting around."

Abby came back and had a bottle for each of them. Crosby took a long swallow before continuing. He leaned forward, elbows on his knees and said, "We're going to blow it up. All of it. Then we're going to release a statement to the media with our manifesto to wake people up."

"Whoa, slow it down," Ben said, holding up his empty left hand. "I don't know shit about explosives and..."

"Don't worry about it," Crosby told him. "I've recruited a guy who knows plenty. Learned it in the Jew's army. He has taught me a lot. Believe me, it's not that difficult. You just need to be smart and careful."

"Okay," Ben quietly, cautiously said.

"And the best part," Crosby continued. "The name of the construction company is Rosenfeld Construction. They're out of New York. New York Jews."

"No one's going to get hurt," Abby added. "We've already worked it out."

"You knew about this and didn't tell me? Why?" Ben asked.

"Webster wanted to be the one to tell you," she replied.

"Okay, time for a decision, Ben. In or out," Crosby said.

"Is everyone else in?"

"Yes. That's why I kept this a small group. Once we pull this off, how hard do you think it will be to recruit others?"

"Good point," Ben agreed. "I'm in."

THREE

TODAY

Professor Ben Sokol, briefcase in hand stuffed with midterm exams to be graded, hesitated at the exit door. It was almost 8:00 P.M., and he was finished for the day. He watched the snow coming down in large, fluffy snowflakes, then pushed open the door.

Before reaching the bottom of the stairs, he pushed his hat down to sit more tightly on his head. There was already three or four inches of new snow on the ground and at least that much more on the way. Ben scurried across the common area of Midwest State-Minnesota University toward home. He had a modest, two-bedroom, two-bath, and brick exterior with fireplace two blocks off of campus. Comfortable and convenient.

Ben was angry with himself for forgetting to wear his galoshes. On his salary, new shoes were a luxury. He held his coat collar to his throat and hurried along. Fifteen minutes after leaving, he was stomping the snow off his shoes in the foyer of his house, angry again.

In fact, despite being a tenured professor of history at a nice, if modest, university, Ben was a man seething with anger, always boiling just beneath the surface. Ben, now age 58, was a lot like most people, although admitting that he was not much different than the bourgeoisie or worse, the unwashed masses, was not even a possibility.

Ben did not realize it, but when he looked in the mirror, Ben did not like what he saw. What he was looking at—like eighty to ninety percent of people—was failure. In the deep recesses of his mind, an area he kept repressed and refused to admit was there, Ben, also like most people, lacked accountability. The admission that the failure he saw in the mirror was the fault, deficiency and responsibility of the little man staring back was simply not in him.

Ben was not just an angry man. In his mind, he was a justified angry man. When Ben looked in the mirror, instead of a tenured professor of history at a small, Midwestern university, he saw unfulfilled greatness. Brilliance even. At 58, he should be an enormously well-acclaimed professor at a major university, Ivy League even, showered with awards, adulation by his peers and financial rewards. And what infuriated him, made him almost boil over, was the simple truth that it was not his fault.

No, he convinced himself as so many others do. *If I am not receiving the rewards that I am entitled to it cannot be my fault. It cannot be because of any lack of ability.* Ben had a borderline genius IQ. He had been showered with compliments about his intellect the entire time he

12

was growing up. This, he had convinced himself, was why he was not socially accepted as a kid in school. No, his lack of acclaim, adulation and financial rewards were not because of anything he did or didn't do. It could not be because of any mistakes, bad choices or errors Ben had made. Nope, can't be that.

Then what is to blame? He had begun asking himself this question a few years ago. It wasn't long before the answer became obvious.

As a true-blue member of the progressive wing of the Democratic Party and a self-made intellectual elite, what kept Ben back was the Great Oppressors. The angry, white, men of the Republican Establishment. The ones responsible for all the world's ills. The Great Oppressors: white men keeping everyone else down.

Ben hung up his overcoat and hat on the wall rack in the foyer. After dropping the briefcase in the living room, he went into the kitchen and microwaved his supper.

While watching a talk show on MSNBC, he ate his processed meal with vodka chasers. Halfway through the show, the host brought on a guest that almost shocked Ben out of his chair. There on the screen of his TV was the reminder of the night that changed him forever. A man Ben had kept track of for a while but eventually gave it up. A leading socialist intellectual and respected, almost revered, professor and darling of the uber left and closet anti-Semite: Professor Webster Crosby.

That summer between graduation and graduate school was the beginning of the awakening of Ben Sokol. Crosby and Abby Sentinel had him so thoroughly under their spell that he ignored it when he caught Abby coming out of Crosby's bedroom. A bit disheveled and flushed, it was obvious what she was doing. He had even heard Crosby's voice from the bedroom.

This had occurred about a week after he had been told about the explosives. As Abby walked by him away from the bedroom, he was unable to even speak let alone object or walk away.

The next evening, she called and when he heard her voice, he was happy she was not mad at him. Hoping she would at least apologize, she acted as if nothing happened.

"Tonight's the night. We're going to prepare the packages for delivery," she told him. This referred to the bombs they were going to make. "You need to be there. Wait until about ten o'clock, until after dark."

He had eagerly agreed. For the next few minutes, they chatted then Abby sweetly ended the call.

13

They were meeting at the rented home of the only black member of their little band of revolutionaries. A man named Tyrone Patterson. The house was located a couple of miles from the university in a quiet, if somewhat run-down, neighborhood.

Ben knew the drill. He parked his car two blocks away after arriving well past dark and then walked around a couple of blocks. Certain he had not been followed, he started toward his destination. When he was a half-block away, there were two explosions. It started with a small one that lit up the basement. It was quickly followed by a second one that was much louder and more destructive.

According to what the police would conclude, someone, there were five people in the basement, must have touched a wrong wire to an electrical charging device. That set off the first bomb. Within one or two seconds, this would set off a large cache of dynamite. The second explosion lifted the entire house three or four feet in the air. There were several witnesses.

The entire structure collapsed on itself and buried everyone in the basement. Or, what little was left of them. Between the explosions and the subsequent fire, it took almost four months to identify the victims. Included, of course, was Abby Sentinel.

The second explosion also knocked Ben onto the front yard of a house. By the time the first responders started to arrive, a shocked and terrified Ben was on his feet and hurrying away.

When Abby was finally identified by a few teeth and her glasses, the investigation finally got to Ben. His parents paid for an excellent lawyer, Ben admitted nothing, and the cops finally closed the books. It was ruled an accident, and that ended it.

It did not take long for Ben's professors to get word of his involvement with one of the victims. Despite his protests that he was not involved, the campus grapevine said otherwise. Ben was allowed to finish the second semester of graduate school then transfer. He was even provided with a letter signed by two of the history department associate professors. Despite misgivings, he acceded to his parents' request and enrolled at CUNY near their home.

Ben would finish his master's program early at CUNY. Primarily to get away from his parents, he applied for the doctoral program at the University of Minnesota and was accepted. Of course, dad's money didn't hurt to grease the skids.

Two years, a marriage and a child later, he finished his schooling. As is true with all too many naïve sheltered people, Ben expected the

14

world to come knocking on his door. To add to his burden of facing adulthood with a family, two months later, his father died.

His mother, with whom he had always had a strained relationship––Mom preferring his sister––made it clear the money spigot was about to be turned off. Dad's partner, who would take over the business and bankrupt it during the recession of 2008, agreed with Mom. No more money for Ben. The decision was made easier when the partner left his wife and moved in with Mom two weeks after Dad's funeral.

Fortunately, a teaching job opened at Midwest State. His graduate school mentor, Professor Lance Bary, helped get him the job. A grateful Ben moved the baby, Angela, and his wife, Kelsey, to Southwest Minneapolis. At the time, Ben believed he would work a couple of years here, publish something great then get back to the Ivy League.

Over the years he had managed to publish just enough to earn tenure but not enough to really overwhelm anyone. His students loved him because he entertained with silly skits ridiculing historical figures. He was very prone to using his morals and transplanting them back to previous eras. He would then condescend to critique those historical figures as morally inferior to himself. His students ate it up. Overall though, he was a slightly above average history teacher at a midwestern college and that was who he was. He would not admit it, but deep down he knew it, hated himself for it and carried a boulder-sized chip on his shoulder toward the world.

His family, wife Kelsey, daughter Angela and son Brody (who came along two years after Angela) settled into not-so-domestic bliss. Kelsey, a bar waitress he had met off-campus, expected bigger things. Barely a year after Brody was born, she began looking for greener pastures. After at least three or four affairs, she left him for a salesman when Angela was 10 and Brody was 8. The salesman, an abusive, drunken loser, would eventually kill himself.

Amazingly, after both kids were out of the house and he was finished paying child support, Kelsey came back. She had a sad tale of difficult marriages—two more—to abusive men. Of course, Ben knew all about this from his son and daughter. And, following his natural inclinations, he took her back. The second go-around lasted barely long enough for her lawyer to get her lifetime alimony.

Ben watched the rest of the interview of Webster Crosby almost seething with alcohol-induced anger. Crosby was peddling yet another book on the virtues of socialism. MSNBC was the only network willing to give him airtime and this was his fourth show of the day. The MSNBC people, especially the audience for this show, were certainly far left enough. The problem was they were not exactly big book buyers. But at campuses across America, liberal arts, humanities and social justice professors were eating it up. The book was already on the mandatory reading list of over 3,000 college courses. When he heard this, it was then that Ben-decided to get on the gravy train. Before the show was over, Ben was thinking, *I may be a slightly above average teacher at a midwestern college, but I know how to change that.*

FOUR

Professor Webster Crosby picked up his drink from the tray. The woman holding it was barely old enough to serve alcohol but that was not her primary responsibility. She was the latest plaything of Crosby's host, Tom Breyer.

Crosby watched the young woman's hips bounce as she walked toward the galley. He was sitting in the most comfortable leather chair he had ever known. Crosby was also on board Breyer's seventy-million-dollar G650 with Breyer and three others. They were on their way to a private get-away of political meetings in Jackson Hole, Wyoming.

"Forget it," Breyer told Crosby and laughed. "She'll be busy the next few days."

Thomas Breyer was a retired hedge-fund manager worth almost three billion dollars. He made his money the old-fashioned way, through massive amounts of insider trading, stock manipulation and outright bribery. He had started out in the coal mines of West Virginia using criminals to intimidate businesses into selling out to him, then making millions from it. Then he moved on to stock manipulation.

His retirement came about semi-voluntarily. Being a heavyweight political donor and fundraiser, Breyer was politely told by the SEC and DOJ that the posse was after him and it was time to step down. Having milked about as much as he could out of the business, and after screwing over his partners, investors and employees, he put on the platinum parachute and bailed out.

Since then, he had found a way to make even more money. Like a lot of wealthy people, he was scamming people with climate change lies. And now, what better way than to get on the socialist bandwagon. Tell everyone else, the little people, what they must do, what they must sacrifice, what changes they must make to save the planet. Changes in the lifestyles of the little people that won't be for the better. But changes the masses must make so Breyer and his rich, elitist pals won't have to change their lifestyles one bit. Especially the celebrities he liked to hang out with.

The luxury jet's bathroom door swung open, and another of Breyer's guests appeared. This one claimed to be a real socialist. Congressman Jacob Trane, the openly socialist representative from New York, came back into the cabin.

"Jesus, Jake," Breyer said, waving his hand in front of his face. "Close the damn door and leave the fan on. What the hell have you been eating?"

17

"Go to hell," the self-proclaimed "man of the people" growled as he reached back to shut the bathroom door.

Crosby was looking across the aisle at Breyer with his hand over his mouth and nose. He moved his hand and asked Breyer, "Is it safe to breathe?"

Breyer laughed and said, "Probably not. Give it a minute for the plane to circulate the air."

"Kiss my ass," Trane grumbled as he walked past. He flopped down in his chair between Breyer and Trane's campaign manager, Jarvis Goldblume.

The fifth and final passenger was an aide of Breyer's, Nash Brenner.

"Where's the girl with the drink?" Trane asked.

"Probably looking for a gas mask," Crosby said.

"Fuck you, schoolteacher," Trane quickly said, causing Breyer and Crosby to both laugh and Nash Brenner to cover a smile.

"I thought schoolteachers had a place of honor in your Utopia, Congressman?" Crosby asked. "As long as they know what to teach."

"Listen," Trane leaned forward and started to say, "we're going to make this world a more just and equitable place. Real equality, not just a Republican bumper sticker."

"You're on a seventy-million-dollar private plane, Jake," Crosby reminded him.

"I never said... thank you," Trane growled as the hostess brought his drink to him. "I've never said I wanted socialism for me. Socialism, true equality, is for the little people, the Masses. Someone has to still run the place. You can't leave that to the crooks who have been doing it."

"So, we need a new set of crooks," Breyer said, laughing uproariously at his own joke.

"It's inevitable that some people will be better off than others," Crosby said.

Trane's face had turned beet red at being labeled a crook. Although he was fortunate that most of the media were on his side, if anyone ever asked how he became a multi-millionaire on a congressman's salary, he would be hard-pressed to come up with a viable answer.

"What we're really after is social justice. The mass of people being treated equally," Jarvis Goldblume, Trane's campaign manager interjected.

"Exactly," Crosby said. "For far too long white people, especially the Jews who run the banks and own the financial industry, have oppressed people. People of color, women, other minorities..."

"You see many people of color or women on this planet?" Breyer asked.

"That's not the point," Crosby said.

"We've had this discussion before," Trane interjected. "The masses, the little people, are goddamn sheep, Tom. Always have been and always will be. There have always been elites. Now, more and more of the real elites, the intellectual elites, are seeing the injustice. We're evolved to the point where we understand that certain groups will always be dependent. Oh, sure," Trane continued waving his empty glass toward Breyer's mistress, "a few of them will rise up to where they can take care of themselves. Look at the coloreds, the black people. Thanks to us, some of them are doing quite well. But the vast majority are children. They can't take care of themselves; they aren't responsible for themselves and should not be held accountable. That's where we come in.

"Thank you, darling," Trane said to the younger woman. He sipped at his fresh drink and watched her walk away.

"Great ass on her," Trane whispered to Breyer.

"Now that the midterms are over, are you going to run next year?" Crosby asked the congressman.

"That's the main reason for this trip," Breyer said. "I've been lining up significant donors to set up a plan to funnel money into his campaign and make it look like it's coming from small donations."

"Why would rich people want to contribute to a self-proclaimed socialist?" Crosby asked.

"Because their money is safe," Trane said.

"Income taxes have already been paid on the fortunes of people like Tom," Goldblume said. "His lifestyle won't be affected one bit by a tax increase. We aren't talking about confiscating the money of the wealthy."

"These celebrities that are pushing global warming, climate change and the changes people have to make to fix it. The celebrities themselves aren't going to have to change anything. It's ordinary people whose lives are going to change," Breyer told Crosby.

"Yeah, I get that," Crosby agreed.

"When we talk about raising taxes on the rich to pay their fair share, it's mostly bullshit. Anyone with half a brain gets that," Goldblume said. "First of all, people at the highest end, the top ten percent, pay seventy percent of the taxes already. Raise their income taxes some more and it won't matter much. Plus, they make enough and already have enough so that even if they pay a little more…"

"I won't have to give up my private jet I hope," Breyer said and laughed again.

"What we need to do is raise taxes on people who work for a living, little by little so that they become dependent on government," Goldblume said.

"The idea is to get the vast majority of people in this country, people who work for a living, more dependent on government," Trane said. "Then we've got them."

"What about the banks?" Crosby asked. "They're the biggest problem."

"Have you heard of the Banking Act of 1933?" Goldblume asked. "More commonly referred to as Glass-Steagall?"

"Yeah," Crosby said. "Isn't that the law that says banks can't be securities investment firms and securities investment firms can't be banks?"

"Generally, yes. It's more than that, but that's the part that scares the hell out of Wall Street. It was repealed in the '90s when Clinton was president," Goldblume said.

"There was nothing money couldn't buy then," Crosby sourly said.

"Deregulation. Everybody was hot for it. It also created less competition, not more, and created too-big-to-fail investment and financial institutions," Goldblume said.

"We'll be fixing that," Trane assured him.

"We're also going to wake people up to the realities of climate change," Breyer soberly said. "We have got to start taking seriously the changes we need to make."

"You mean the changes the little people need to make," Trane said.

"Hey! I'll do my part," Breyer seriously said.

"What are you going to do, give up one of your homes?" Trane asked.

"You could give up one of yours," Breyer said.

"I only have three. What do you have? Six?"

"Hey, I own a hybrid. I encourage conservation," Breyer said. Even Breyer was having a difficult time not laughing at this.

"You have a Prius sitting in the driveway of your Brentwood home in case someone comes by to check. Your chauffeur drives you around in one of your Bentleys," Trane said.

"Someone has to live well," Breyer said as he raised his glass in a toast. "You said it. It might as well be us."

FIVE

"Oh, sorry, Professor Sokol, I didn't realize you were in already," the mildly embarrassed young man said as he opened Ben's office door without knocking.

"It's okay, Corey," Ben told him. "Come in. What can I do for you?"

The cheerful, almost jovial tone of the professor's voice caught the teacher's assistant a little off guard. Normally, Ben Sokol treated underlings with barely hidden contempt.

"Um, I, ah, was just going to drop off these papers I graded for you," he answered.

"Oh, great, thanks," Ben said. The TA was still standing in the doorway wondering what to do. Ben actually smiled and said, "Please, come in. Leave them on the desk."

"Yes, sir," Corey replied and complied.

He turned to leave when Ben said, "Hey, wait a second. I know this sounds a little weird, but I was wondering, do I smell okay to you?"

"Yeah," Corey slowly said. "I didn't notice anything."

"Good. Thanks," Ben answered. "I, ah, had a little too much to drink last night, at home watching TV. I don't know what got into me. Anyway, I was worried I might smell a little bit like booze."

"Oh, I see," Corey smiled and even chuckled a bit. "No, professor, you're fine."

A minute later, after leaving Sokol's office, Corey met up with another one of the History Department TA's, a young woman.

"I think an alien lifeform has taken over Sokol's body," Corey said to her.

"Is he worse than normal?" she asked, afraid the answer might be yes.

"No, he's actually quite pleasant."

"Wow, maybe he got laid," she said.

"Nope. He got drunk last night," Corey told her.

"Really? Maybe we should start spiking his coffee," she said with a laugh.

Ben boosted himself up onto the ledge where the classroom movie screen was. It was a few minutes before 9:00 A.M., the time for his first class to start. Ben taught three classes, one hour each, three times each per week. This morning's first class was Twentieth-Century American History. This morning's lecture topic was the beginning of the Great Depression. A perfect topic for Ben to begin his transformation.

The classroom was amphitheater-style with comfortable chairs, large enough for two hundred. Ben, primarily because of his cynical, sarcastic, attitude, was quite popular with students. He was viewed as having a great sense of humor. Little did they know his cynicism and sarcasm were genuine and not meant to be humorous. He was also an easy grader.

At 9:02, the eighty-odd number of attendees were seated and quietly waiting. While still sitting on the ledge behind the podium, a very unusual sight, Ben started his lecture.

"Good morning, everyone. Nice to have you stop in again," he said. This brought a smattering of light laughter as he dropped down to the floor.

In addition to a podium, next to it was a long table set up in the well of the classroom. These were both set back about ten feet from the first row of seats. All the front two rows of seats were empty.

Instead of standing behind the podium as he normally did, Ben stepped in front of it, into the space between the table and chairs.

"For more years than I care to remember, I have been teaching history to students, just like yourselves. But I've been lying to you and I think it's time I stopped.

"I have been teaching American and Western European History. But what I've really been teaching is the history that the ruling oligarchy wants you to be taught. Starting today, you're going to get the truth. And what better place to start than with the Great Depression of the nineteen-thirties.

"How many of you," he stopped his pacing, looked over his audience and asked, "have heard of the Great Depression before this class?"

Fewer than half of the students raised their hands. Based on his experience as a teacher, this did not surprise Ben at all.

"How many of you know what caused the Depression?" he then asked.

Ben counted the number of hands that were still raised. Six.

Ben then pointed at a young man who appeared to be a little older than the others sitting by himself.

"What was the cause? What caused the Great Depression?"

"The stock market crash in, I think it was October of nineteen twenty-nine," he answered.

"Anybody else? Anybody want to agree or disagree?"

A few heads nodded in agreement, but no one spoke up.

Ben looked at the student who had answered the question and said, "First of all, you're not alone. That is the myth that has been used for over eighty years now. But it's not true. It is the myth that the people who own this country, the banking industry, want you to believe to avoid their culpability.

"What triggered the Great Depression was not the market crash on October twenty-ninth, nineteen twenty-nine, which is generally blamed for the Depression. As I said, it's a lie perpetrated by the money industry of America and Europe.

"The market crash of October nineteen eighty-seven and the one we just went through in two thousand and eight were both worse than the crash of twenty-nine. Yet, no depression followed either. Yes, there was a downturn in the economy and the government bailed out a lot of rich people, but no depression.

"What caused the Great Depression of the thirties was bank failures. The banking industry basically crashed. Collapsed like a row of dominoes. And what caused that was what is called 'a run on the banks'.

"Let me give you an example. Hypothetically, let's say there's a man, a small business owner, who owns shares of stock in a bank. Let's call this bank the Bank of the United States.

"Now, again hypothetically, our small business owner in December of nineteen-thirty—this is more than a year after the market crash of twenty-nine— believing that the bank is having financial problems, goes to the bank with his shares of stock in the bank. He takes his shares to the cashier window and demands that the bank buy them back for cash which they had promised to do. But the bank refuses.

"Now let's say, hypothetically of course, that he leaves the bank and on his way out and when he gets outside the bank, he tells everyone he sees what happened. This starts a rumor that the bank is insolvent. It has no money.

"Within a couple of days, as the rumor spreads, thousands of depositors are demanding to withdraw their money. Hypothetically, because the bank does not have the money in its vaults, not everyone gets their money.

"Well," Ben continued watching his now enraptured audience, "within a few days of this, the bank's stock will collapse, it will no longer be able to get credit or pay its bills or employees and, hypothetically, the bank will collapse and go out of business."

Here, he stopped, paused, looked over the audience and said, "Hypothetically of course. Because we all know banks are safe. We've been told this forever. But are they?

"My hypothetical example is not hypothetical at all. In fact, that story is precisely what happened.

"One man trying to cash in his shares of stock triggered a cascade of rumor that crashed the banking system and brought on the Great Depression. And that's why the businesses that run this country, run the financial and economic world, pushed the lie that the Depression was brought on by the market crash of twenty-nine.

"The Bank of the United States in New York went down and the rest of them tumbled like dominoes. And now we are told these institutions, these banks that have their boot on the neck of our economy, are too big to fail. That no matter how careless they are, how much they gamble with our money, our lives, our economy, we have to keep them propped up."

"Questions?" he asked.

At least thirty hands went up. For the remaining hour of the class, Ben answered questions about the story. Mostly questions about why the truth was kept covered up and how culpable the government was.

Ben looked up at the clock on the wall and saw his time was almost up.

"Finish your reading about the Great Depression. Realize this: there are a lot of things going on now that are even worse than there was back then. For starters, what caused the crash of oh eight was Wall Street gambling. We were told there are sanctions in place to stop it, but it hasn't stopped. Why should it? Too big to fail and they know it. The big investment firms and banks, mostly the same people and companies, are holding us hostage.

"And one last thing to think about. The Soviet Union, the socialist country we have all been told was an evil empire, did not experience the Great Depression. The rest of the world did, but they did not. Socialism, which we are reminded almost daily as a failure and a horror, saved the Soviet Union from the ravages of the Great Depression."

The bell went off, but for almost fifteen seconds, no one moved. The entire class sat totally entranced.

Ben left school immediately after his two o'clock class on Nineteenth-Century Western European History. All three of his classes had gone the same way. Instead of his normal lecture, he had introduced his students to his version of real history. The capitalistic oppression of those less fortunate and the shared guilt that the privileged few must accept for it. And the lie that socialism cannot work.

The snowstorm from yesterday had moved on, and this afternoon was sunny and pleasant. Halfway across campus, he stopped and decided not to go right home. By the time he had walked this far, at least a dozen students had cheerfully greeted him and thanked him for his lecture. He decided to go to the student union and stop in the cafeteria for coffee.

The cafeteria was about three fourths full of students. As he made his way across the room, a noticeable buzz was following him, and a large number of the crowd was watching him. Ben had stopped here many times before, so his appearance was not unusual. Before today, he had never drawn any attention at all.

Ben bought a coffee and a piece of apple pie. He found an empty table with several sections of an abandoned newspaper on it. For the next thirty minutes, he sipped his coffee, ate the pie and read the paper. Gradually, it started with just one male student, the kids in the cafeteria came by, stopped at his table and thanked him for today's lecture. Several of them admitted they had not been there but had heard about it. They all asked if it would be okay to sit in and listen. Of course, Ben was delighted to agree.

One of them, the older student from his 9:00 A.M. class, sat down across from him. "Professor," he said. "I think you're onto something. We get hints of the harm of capitalism from other socially conscious professors. But what you did today was put it in a real, historical perspective. I think we need more of that."

"Well, thank you," Ben said. "I'm sorry, what is your name?"

"Luke, Luke Hanson, sir."

"That's interesting," Ben said. "I'll think about what you said. Do you think others feel the same way?"

"Absolutely, sir," Luke replied. "I feel like I've been lied to my whole life. Like democracy and capitalism have led to nothing but oppression to protect white privilege. Especially the privilege of the wealthy. Why did we bail out Wall Street a few years ago?"

"That's an excellent question. And the answer will be obvious if you put some thought into it. Let me put it this way. Millions, tens of millions of people saw their life savings disappear. Where was their bailout?"

"I don't know," Luke quietly replied.

"I don't either," Ben said.

SIX

Several months later, Ben Sokol was enjoying his elevated status as a campus celebrity. He took a short break from writing his latest project, a book about late eighteenth-century Middle European Socialism. Ben wheeled his desk chair closer to the window to stare out onto the campus grounds. It was the last week of finals for spring semester. By now, a significant number of students were already done for the summer. Because of this, the campus was almost empty. Despite the beautiful, early-June weather, there were very few young people around. Most were either indoors studying for tests or already gone. He missed the sight of scantily clad teenage girls out sunning themselves on the grass.

"Excuse me, Professor," he heard a voice coming from his open door say.

Ben spun around and found a young man, a student he recognized, but could not recall his name.

"Sorry, sir," the young man said. "I didn't mean to disturb you."

"It's okay," Ben replied. "What can I do for you?"

"Well, sir…"

"Please, call me Ben," he replied.

With his soaring popularity came an easing of his attitude. He was still angry at the world for his lack of acclaim, but he liked being treated as a sort of High Priest of the Left by impressionable students.

"Okay, Ben," the young man said a little hesitantly. "I just stopped to thank you for my grade. It's a nice A and I really enjoyed your class."

"I'm sorry, what's your name?"

"Gary Weaver," the young man replied.

Ben wheeled up to his desk, hit a few keys on his PC and looked over the list that appeared.

"Well, Gary. It says you earned a C. I must've screwed up."

"Really?" Weaver said as a rush of panic swept over him.

"No, I'm kidding," Ben said with a hearty laugh. He was even discovering a sense of humor, sort of. "You got an A and earned it. You don't need to thank me."

"Actually, Ben," a much-relieved Weaver said, "that's not why I stopped by."

"Have a seat, Gary. What's on your mind?"

He sat down and continued, "Well, Ben, a lot of us feel like we've had our eyes opened by you. Especially your waking us up to how the banks, Wall Street and big corporations are keeping so many people down.

"My father is a hard-core Republican," Weaver continued. "I was brought up to believe that capitalism is the best system there is; that capitalism is the way to give everyone the opportunity to improve their lives."

"That's what they want everyone to believe. It's how they keep the poor and working-class in line. The lie that if you work hard, you can make it big in America, it's bullshit," Ben said.

"The reason I'm here is, well, there's a bunch of us, at least a dozen, that are staying for the summer. Or live nearby. We've been getting together once or twice a week for, I don't know what you'd call it exactly…"

"A discussion group?" Ben asked.

"Yeah, that's probably it. Anyway, I was wondering, actually, we were wondering if you maybe could, you know, join us sometime?"

Ben thought about it for a moment then said, "I'd be delighted. When and where?"

Weaver happily wrote down the time and address of their next meeting; tomorrow night at a girl's apartment.

"Professor," he said after giving Ben directions to the place, "we'd really be interested in knowing your thoughts on global warming and climate change."

"That's a good idea since capitalism and destruction of the planet are closely tied together. In fact, they go hand in hand."

"Great!" Weaver said. "I'll spread the word. We'll have a good crowd on hand."

That was the beginning. Because of his growing reputation on campus, the attendance at this first meeting was almost twenty-five. They were so crammed into the small apartment that there was not enough room to sit. Instead of the usual hour to hour and a half, the discussion went on until almost midnight.

Ben arrived a fashionable fifteen minutes late to let the anticipation build. He also arrived carrying a case of beer. As the evening rolled along, a liquor store run was made and plenty of weed was rolled. Ben, wanting to fit in, even joined in as the joints were passed around. By the end of the evening, he was feeling pretty good.

He also carried the discussion and was the center of attention. There were several, at least a dozen, attendees who had been students in one of his classes. It was easy enough to sway them to his thinking since they were already with him before he arrived that evening. When the hostess finally called it a night, Ben had to stand at the door to shake hands and be thanked as each one left.

"Thank you, Professor," Gary Weaver, who was last to leave, said. "That was great. I'd like you to meet someone. This is Donna Gilchrist, my girlfriend," he added. Standing next to Weaver was a somewhat shy, pretty brunette.

"It's great to meet you, sir," the girl said shaking Ben's hand.

"It's very nice to meet you, Donna."

"Gary's told me so much about you…"

"Donna's not a student at Midwest," Gary explained.

"Oh, I see. Well, I'm glad you came. I hope you got something out of our discussion tonight."

The apartment's tenant joined them, and Gary introduced her to Ben again.

"Yes, I sure did," Donna said, answering Ben's question. "I had no idea how bad this country's system is. Why do they lie to us?"

"Money and power," Ben replied. "Greed. It's as simple as that. Politicians who will tell any lie to get elected and take money from people who use these political whores to line their own pockets."

"But they're destroying the very planet they are raping," Cindy, the apartment's tenant, said.

"They're not thinking that far ahead," Ben said.

"You're a great speaker, Professor," Cindy blurted out.

"Yes, I told them that," Gary said. "You moved us all."

"Well, that's very flattering," Ben said. He looked at his watch then said, "It's getting late. I should go."

Over the next few months, through the Summer semester, Ben continued to attend these meetings. What he found was a solid majority of young people desperately in need of someone to validate themselves. Give them something to believe in, a cause to join. And Ben was giving it to them. He was shoveling the inhumanity, destructiveness and oppression of the wealthy class down their throats. But not just those people with money. White male oppressors and white supremacists in general.

His message was clear and unambiguous. If you are not receiving what you are entitled to, what you deserve, it is the fault of someone else. Especially the banks with their usurious, capitalistic, crushing debt. Underlying all of it: The International Jew.

"Professor, I was wondering if I could talk to you for a minute," a young man asked Ben.

Ben was replacing his lecture notes in a leather folio. It was a Monday morning, the second week of Fall semester and his 9:00 A.M. class had just finished. The young man who had spoken was one of his students. He came down to the front of the lecture hall as his classmates, almost two hundred of them noisily filed out.

Ben looked up at the sound of the voice and saw the face it came from a few feet away. He looked like any of tens of thousands of kids his age. Probably six feet tall and thin with shaggy brown hair.

Ben smiled and said, "Sure. In fact," he continued as he put on his tan, wool, hooded overcoat, "walk with me. Do you have a class?"

"No, not till eleven," the young man said.

"You look familiar. We've met before, haven't we? Last spring as I recall. What's your name?" Ben asked as the two walked toward the exit.

"Yes, we did. Luke Hanson, sir," he replied.

"Oh, please, call me Ben. Everyone does."

"Ben, okay," Luke said.

They passed through the building's exit in silence. When they got outside, they both pulled the hood of their coat over their heads.

"Foul day," Ben said. "September in Minnesota is supposed to be nicer than this. Wet, cold, windy."

"Supposed to be nice by the weekend," Luke said.

"Yes, I believe you're right, Luke," Ben replied. "So, what's on your mind?" he asked as they hurried toward the student center.

"Well, sir, um, Ben," Luke started to say, "I really appreciate what you've been telling us. More people need to know how badly we are being held down.

"Anyway, it's about the banks. My grandfather, well, a bank stole his farm from him. He was seventy-eight and the farm had been in the family for over a hundred years. And they just took it from him."

"Geez, I'm sorry," Ben said.

"And a couple of months ago, Grandpa..." Luke paused and stopped walking, looked down at his feet then said, "He committed suicide. They kicked him off his farm, and he went back and hung himself from the rafters in the barn."

"I'm truly sorry, Luke," Ben said, placing a sympathetic hand on his shoulder.

"Thanks," he replied. "It's just, well, I'm so damn angry. That bank killed my grandpa. He was a great guy, a man I loved and admired. And now he's gone, and I'll never see him again. Never talk to him again or go fishing or well, just hang out with him."

They continued walking. Several students passed by and said hello to Ben. Twenty feet from the entrance to the student center, Luke muttered something that Ben was not sure he heard correctly.

"I'm sorry, what was that?" Ben asked.

"I said, 'I should rob the damn bank,'" Luke said. "Steal from them like they did my grandpa."

Ben smiled, patted him on the back and reached for the door handle. Just before he opened the door, Ben stopped, looked at Luke and said, "You know what? That's exactly what you should do. If you're really interested, let's do it."

SEVEN

"Your client is here," Marc Kadella heard Carolyn Lucas, the office's first sergeant, sweetly tell him on the phone's intercom.

"He showed up, huh? Great, lucky me," Marc replied.

"I'll let him know you'll be right out," Carolyn pleasantly replied so Marc's new client could hear her.

Marc Kadella was a lawyer in private practice. Most of his caseload consisted of criminal defense work. He was a sole practitioner renting space from another lawyer. Her name was Connie Mickelson. Connie is a crusty on the outside, marshmallow-soft on the inside, sixty-something lawyer. The building the office was in is the Reardon Building. It is ten minutes from downtown Minneapolis and is an inheritance of Connie's from her father. Connie has also made a lot of money from six almost successful marriages.

There are two other lawyers in the office. Barry Cline, who does some criminal defense work but mostly commercial litigation for small and medium-sized companies. The final renter from Connie is Chris Grafton. Chris is strictly a corporate lawyer with a very nice practice built up of small and medium-sized companies, the main source of Barry's litigation casework.

There are also three employees the lawyers share. The previously mentioned Carolyn Lucas, who is the de facto boss. Sandy Compton, an overqualified, underpaid legal assistant and a paralegal, Jeff Modell, who can research and write a legal brief better than any of the lawyers.

On the whole, it is a small, tight-knit group; a family that works well together and looks out for each other. Especially during the downtimes.

Marc slipped into his suit coat to meet his potential client and went out into the common area. There was only one man sitting in a waiting area chair whom Marc realized must be his prospective client. Connie Mickelson was standing next to Carolyn's desk, silently reading a letter.

"Mr. Flanders," Marc said loud enough to make sure Connie heard him. "Nice to meet you. Grab your stuff and come on back."

By "stuff" Marc was referring to a two-foot-high stack of papers, documents, legal pleadings, discovery, depositions and files piled onto a chair next to the man.

As soon as Connie heard Marc say the man's name, without looking up, she made a hasty retreat into her office and closed the door. Flanders was a favor Marc had agreed to look into for Connie. He was going through a very acrimonious divorce. The acrimony, according to Connie's friend, Flanders' estranged wife, was exclusively the fault of Harold Flanders.

Marc took his seat behind his desk and started reading the client intake form Carolyn had Flanders fill out. As he started this, Flanders dropped the two-foot stack of legal detritus in the middle of Marc's desk. It landed with a resounding thud.

Marc looked at the man, curled up his mouth in an insincere smile and said, "Don't do that again." He then turned back to the intake sheet while Flanders stared back at him.

"According to this, you're fifty-seven years old, married thirty-two years. No kids at home. You're an executive vice president of a manufacturing company in Excelsior. Your wife, Natalie, is a vice president at Lake Country Federal Bank. She's head of their mortgage department. You both make a good living, in fact, according to you, she makes more than you do. Is that correct?"

"Yeah," he gruffly admitted.

"So, spousal maintenance, alimony, is not an issue."

"A couple of my other lawyers said I might get some because she makes more than me," he said.

"They lied to get your money," Marc abruptly told him. "They told you what you wanted to hear. I will not do that so get it out of your head right now. You make a good living; you're a man and no judge is going to award you spousal maintenance. If she made a couple of million bucks a year, maybe. But not this."

"Well, you're pretty negative and abrupt. Whose side are you on?"

Marc stood up and picked up the pile of papers Flanders deposited on his desk blotter. He reached across the desk, handed it to Flanders and said, "Here, put this on the other chair."

While Flanders did this, Marc sat down, rolled his chair tight up against his desk and placed his arms with hands folded on the blotter.

"Okay, here it is," Marc began. "If you and I reach an agreement for me to represent you, I'll tell you right now I am not going to bullshit you. I'm not gonna blow a lot of smoke up your ass just to get your money. You're going to get the truth from me and not just what you want to hear. Are you with me?"

"Yeah, okay," Flanders quietly said.

"And I'll tell you something else," Marc soberly continued. "That," he said, pointing at the pile of papers placed on the other chair, "stops now. I am not going to let you use me and the courts to emotionally beat up your wife."

Flanders started to say something, and Marc quickly held up a hand to stop him. "I don't want to hear it. I don't know what's gone on up to now and I don't care. Looking at that pile next to you, I can guess pretty accurately what has gone on. As I said, that ends now. I don't care who's to blame for the divorce or if your wife has been screwing a ship full of sailors. I don't want to hear about it. Am I clear?"

"Who you gonna be working for?"

"You. How much have you spent on attorney's fees?"

"Almost thirty grand," he quietly admitted. "I owe about eighteen of that."

"And what have you accomplished? Why are you sitting here? Harold…"

"Hal," Flanders said.

"Hal, this is a nothing case. You gather all the financial documents, bank accounts, investments, property. You figure out what it's all worth and divide by two. It's arithmetic."

There was a silence between them for almost a minute while Marc's verbal bashing set in with Flanders.

"You want to keep doing this," Marc said, pointing at the papers again, "you'll have to find someone else. I'll tell you this. Whatever has been said in this room, no matter what, will stay in this room. But if you are ready to put an end to this, then I'll help you. It won't be that difficult."

"Yeah, I guess you're probably right. I heard you were a fighter. You've been in the papers, on TV…"

"If fighting is what's best for my client, yeah, I'll fight. If making a deal is what's best, we'll make a deal."

Marc opened the top left drawer and removed a single sheet of paper. "Here, read this first."

After he finished reading, Flanders asked, "Who's Connie Mickelson?"

"My landlord. She's the woman who was at the secretary's desk when you were waiting. I understand a friend of yours recommended me?"

"Yeah," Flanders admitted.

"Connie talked to him. She knows your wife, so she asked your friend to recommend me. There's no conspiracy going on. If you want to keep fighting, you can. If you're ready to put an end to it, I'm your guy."

"Yeah, okay. What do you need?"

"I need a check for three thousand dollars. I will bill against that at three hundred per hour. I think we can finish it for that amount if everybody wants to cooperate."

"You're even cheaper than the other guys," Flanders said as he pulled out his checkbook.

"Seriously? I gotta do a better job keeping up with what people are charging," Marc muttered.

"So, we're not going to court?"

"No, no judge would let us try this. He'd kick us out and tell us to settle it. I'm cheaper, really?"

"Yeah, a little," Flanders said.

"I'll need financials, bank accounts, the last three years tax returns, some recent paystubs," Marc said.

Flanders removed an inch-thick manila folder from the pile and handed it across the desk.

"All that stuff is in here," he said.

"Are you satisfied there has been full disclosure of assets? She's not hiding anything? You're not hiding anything?"

"No, everything's in there."

"How about a list of personal property of any value? Anything over a couple hundred bucks like jewelry, guns, whatever."

"Yeah, it's in there."

"Okay, I'll go through this and call your wife's lawyer. We'll meet them and put an end to this. I know her. She's reasonable and easy to work with. I don't see this taking long. But she is going to want a piece of her attorney fees paid by you."

"Screw her!" Flanders almost bellowed.

Marc pointed at the large stack of papers and court documents on the chair next to Flanders and said, "If she can convince a judge this is your doing, you will pay for it. It is your doing, isn't it?"

Flanders sat quietly in the client chair for a moment, unable to look Marc directly in the eye.

Marc finally said, "We'll see how it goes. I'll get back to you after I talk to your wife's lawyer and set up a meeting."

A short while later, Marc closed the exit door behind his new client. When he did, Connie opened her door a crack and asked if he was gone. She followed Marc back to his office and on the way, Marc asked Jeff Modell, the paralegal, to join them.

"What's up?" Jeff asked as he came through Marc's door.

"Here," Marc said, handing him the folder with the financials in it, the conflict disclosure form, retainer agreement and other documents for Flanders. "Go through the financials and get me some final numbers. Have Sandy or Carolyn open a case file for me, please and thanks."

"I'll do it. When do you need the financial information?" Jeff asked.

Marc, now seated, shrugged and said, "Couple days."

"Three, Monday, okay?" Jeff asked. Jeff Modell was normally the busiest one in the office.

"Four, Tuesday," Marc said.

"You got it, thanks," Jeff said, smiling.

Jeff closed the door as Connie asked, "How was he?"

"Grace is right," Marc said, referring to Natalie Flanders' lawyer. "I could see it in him early on. Right below the surface. He was seething."

"She's gonna want him to pay a good chunk of her fees," Connie said.

"Did she tell you that?"

"No, but because it's his fault the fees have gone so high..."

"I warned him about it but good luck to her," Marc said. "With the income Natalie has, I don't see it. The case is venued in Dakota County, not Hennepin."

"Oh, that's right. I forgot they live in Burnsville. Still..."

"Still nothing. If that's all they have. I don't think she would get much. I can make a good argument Grace could have and should have gotten this thing to court herself a long time ago. Besides, her client is probably so fed up with this she'll eat the fees just to get it over with."

"You're probably right," Connie conceded.

The door opened, and Carolyn was standing there. "Maddy's on the phone."

"Okay," Marc said.

Before he could answer the call, Connie asked. "How are things with you two."

Marc paused, then said, "When she spends the night, I wake up in the morning before her just to watch her sleep. Not because of her looks but because of the person she is. She's more amazing than I realized."

"That's sweet," Connie said. "Like, vomit level sweet."

"Cops and lawyers," Marc said. "The most cynical people on the planet."

Connie laughed and said, "You know we all adore her."

"What's the over/under for how long before she dumps me?" Marc asked.

Connie laughed again, then said, "Now that's cynical. Talk to your lady," she added as she stood to leave.

EIGHT

Marc Kadella was at his desk, his computer on Expedia while he worked through his finances. There was a knock on his door and Connie Mickelson barged in without waiting for a response.

"Hey, what are you doing?" Connie asked.

"Come in," Marc replied. "Oh, you're already in. Thanks for dropping by and put that chair back!"

Connie had picked up one of the client chairs and was carrying it to one of Marc's windows.

"Put that chair back and do not light that cigarette," Marc sternly told her waving a finger at her.

Connie raised the window, letting in some warm September air. She sat down in the chair, held up the cigarette she had and said, "If you're gonna be that way, maybe it's time we talked about raising your rent."

"Here, let me light that for you," Marc said reaching for her lighter.

"I thought you'd see it my way," Connie said as she fired up her lighter. "What are you doing?"

"I'm finishing paying for Maddy's Christmas present," Marc said.

"Already? What are you getting her?"

"A surprise vacation to London," Marc said. "Next June, eight days."

"No kidding? She'll like that. And, since it's not until June, she'll keep you around until at least then," Connie said.

"That's exactly what I'm thinking," Marc agreed.

Madeline Rivers, Maddy, was a private investigator and an ex-cop from the Chicago Police department in her early thirties. In her three-inch heeled, suede half-boots she liked to wear, she was over six feet tall. She had a full head of thick dark hair with auburn highlights that fell down over her shoulders, a model gorgeous face and a body worthy of Playboy. In fact, foolishly posing for that magazine was what led her to quit the Chicago PD.

Maddy and Marc met through another private investigator friend, Tony Carvelli. Carvelli had recommended her to Marc to help him on a highly publicized serial killer case. A friendship grew and from there, deep love developed between them. It came out when Maddy was kidnapped and almost murdered. Marc, in a panic over the thought of losing her, had finally admitted how he felt about her, and they had been lovers ever since.

"Has she ever been there?"

"No. In fact, I'm not even sure she has a passport. But this will give her time to get one."

Connie tossed the remnant of her cigarette out the window and quickly lit another one.

"Wait, what, you're gonna smoke another one? Stop!"

"Be quiet," Connie said, impatiently waving a hand at him. "I have something serious to talk about."

"Oh, no, no, don't tell me," Marc said, holding up his hands as if to ward her off. "The judge knocked you up and you're not sure what to do. I thought we had that talk."

"Close, smartass," Connie said, laughing and choking on the smoke.

There was another knock on Marc's door, it opened, and Barry Cline entered.

"What's going on?" Barry asked.

Before Connie could say anything, Marc said, "Connie's in the family way. Oops."

Barry stopped and stood perfectly still. He looked at Connie then at Marc and asked, "She's not claiming I had anything to do with it, is she?"

Marc looked at Connie, his eyebrows raised with an inquisitive look and asked, "Well?"

"You two are hilarious. We really do need to talk about raising the rent you guys pay," Connie said.

Barry picked up the second client chair, carried it to where Connie was sitting, sat down in it, took her hand and said, "What can we do to help? We're here for you. Whatever you decide, we'll stand by you."

Connie jerked her hand away and said, "Get away from me. Both of you."

While Barry moved his chair back, Marc asked, "Seriously, what's going on?"

Connie took a last, long drag on her second cigarette, tossed it out the window and said, "It's the judge. He's getting serious about this marriage business."

"No wonder, with all of your experience..." Barry started to say.

"Don't go there," Connie told him.

"Why not just tell him the truth?" Barry asked. "Do you want to give it another try?"

"No, not really," she said.

"Then tell him that," Marc said. "He deserves to know."

"I don't want to hurt him," Connie said.

"Nobody ever does," Barry said.

"That's not true. There were a couple of my exes I was delighted to kick to the curb," Connie replied.

Marc's intercom buzzed. He answered it, listened for a moment and then said, "No, I'll take it. Put her through." He covered the mouthpiece of his phone and said to Connie, "Grace Blaine, the Flanders divorce."

"Should I go?"

"Nah, stick around," Marc said.

"Grace," Marc said, "when can we get together?"

"I'm going to email a proposal to you. Your client won't like it, I can tell you that right now. But I called Judge Sloane…"

"Ex parte?" Marc asked.

"No, just listen. I asked him what his schedule was. He's in Apple Valley for the next two weeks. We don't even need to schedule a date. We can call and make sure he's there and just go out there any day he's sitting. He'll get us a conference room and we can work on it then."

"Why do we need Sloane involved?"

"Because your client's an asshole and it could come in handy to have the judge assigned to his case there to give him a little advice if he needs it. When he needs it. Advice from the judge himself."

"Grace, don't turn this more adversarial then it already is. I can get him to cooperate. But don't send a proposal you know my guy won't accept. What's the point in that?" Marc replied. He could feel the blood and heat rising in his face. He had believed this would be a simple division of assets. Now he was hearing his opponent tell him, probably not.

"Your client's been a jerk and his wife thinks he should pay for that. So do I," she replied.

"Grace, what's done is done. Put a stop to this. There is nothing for either to be gained by flogging a dead horse like this."

"My client's pissed. She's-"

"Then calm her down so we can get this over with. Do you know Mike Sloane?"

"No, not really."

"I do. I've known him for years. He's not gonna punish the husband to placate the wife. Trust me, he won't care."

There was a long pause, then Grace said, "Maybe I should file on him."

"This isn't Hennepin County. They don't punish men in Dakota County just because of their gender. Sloane's a reasonable guy. A good judge. Let's put an end to this."

There was another long pause while Grace thought about it. "You're probably right," she said with an audible sigh. "Just between us,

38

I'm getting a little tired of this case myself. Don't get me wrong, your guy is worse than her, but the wife's no princess."

"My calendar's good for next Monday. If Sloane's in Apple Valley, he'll be there all day handling the weekend arraignments. What do you think?" Marc asked.

"First thing next week? Yeah, if we can settle this, that will get my week off to a good start. What time? Nine?"

"Fine. Check with your client and let me know. I'll call mine and tell him. He'll do what I say," Marc said.

Marc was shaking hands with Hal Flanders in the courthouse hallway. It was nine o'clock on Monday morning. True to her word, Grace Blaine had emailed a settlement proposal late Friday afternoon.

"That settlement offer is bullshit," Flanders said. He had read it over the weekend and called Marc at home eight times while doing so.

"I know," Marc said. "Relax."

At that moment he saw Blaine come out of the courtroom and was walking toward them.

"Don't say a word," Marc forcefully whispered to his client.

"Morning, Marc," she pleasantly said as they shook hands.

"That settlement's bullshit," Flanders angrily blurted out.

"Come with me," Marc ordered him.

The two of them retreated about twenty feet.

"Sorry," Flanders said.

"You will speak only when I tell you to, understood? You cannot control your temper or your mouth, and that will not help."

"Okay, okay. You're right. I want this over."

"Relax. We'll make a reasonable deal. One your wife won't like," Marc said, a statement that made Flanders smile.

"I'm going to go see the judge; then we'll get started. Wait here," Marc told him nodding toward an empty, padded bench a few feet away. "Do not go in the courtroom. Your wife is in there. Stay out here."

Blaine was waiting for him, and as they walked toward the courtroom door, Marc said, "He's right. That proposal is bullshit."

Her only response was a sly smile.

"Hey, Marty," Marc said, shaking hands with a haggard-looking man at a table inside the court railing.

"Marty O'Gara," Marc said, "Grace Blaine." While the two shook hands, Marc continued, "Marty is with the Apply Valley City Attorney's office. He's here prosecuting misdemeanor cases."

"Wow," Marty said. "The great and powerful Marc Kadella is stooping to handle a misdemeanor today?"

"Nope, we're working on a divorce settlement," Marc said.

"You're still doing divorce work?" Marty asked.

"Whatever pays the rent, Marty."

A court clerk was sitting next to the empty judge's bench. Grace Blaine said, "I'll go talk to the clerk."

"Okay," Marc said. "Is Sloane in back?"

"Yeah, he is," Marty replied. "You got a divorce hearing?"

"No, we're going to try to settle it today. It's assigned to Sloane so, if we need the judge's advice, we can sneak in and talk to him."

Marc saw Blaine nod her head toward the back door indicating it was okay to see the judge.

"I gotta go. See you later, Marty," he said.

They checked in with Judge Sloane who told one of the court clerks to find a room for them. They gathered up their clients and went inside. Before they got started, Marc could literally feel the temperature in the room rising because of the level of animosity between two people who had once declared their undying love for each other.

"Okay," Marc began looking back and forth at each of them. "Let's get this over with so you can both get on with your lives. Set the anger aside and help us get this done. Agreed?"

"Sure," the petulant husband said.

"If he can," Natalie snidely said.

"Don't start, Natalie," Blaine said to her client. "Marc's right. Let's finish this today."

At 10:30 they agreed to take a break. So far, things had gone very smoothly. They had reached an agreement on all the large issues, the financial issues. Between the two of them, including a mortgage-free house, they had net assets of one and a half million dollars. Once it was agreed to sell the house and split the proceeds, everything else fell into place.

Following the break, the entire settlement almost collapsed because of the bickering over two things: personal property and the dog. Both insisted that the golden lab, a ten-year-old named after Natalie's dad, Barney, should be theirs.

It took until almost noon to get an agreement on personal property. The main sticking point was Hal's tools. He liked to work on cars and build furniture. Clearly out of spite, Natalie, who had possession of them while still in the house, did not want him to have them.

At that point, the tools still undecided, Barney came back into play. Marc became so frustrated he suggested taking a chain saw to Barney, splitting him down the middle and each have a barbecue of their half of

Barney. With that, a shocked and appalled Natalie agreed to let Hal have his tools in exchange for her keeping Barney.

The two lawyers, a tentative deal in hand, hurried back to see Judge Sloane. A court reporter was already set up in Sloan's temporary chambers. A half-hour later, after reading the settlement into the record and getting their clients to agree to it on the record, they were finished.

"I'm going to wait to write the Findings and Decree until everything is done," Blaine told Marc in the hallway after they finished. "I don't trust him."

"That's probably a bad idea," Marc said.

"Why? It doesn't matter. If either of them fails to perform, we're back here anyway," Blaine replied.

"I suppose," Marc said.

As they shook hands, Blaine said, "That splitting of old Barney. Very Solomonic."

"I meant it," Marc said.

On their way out to their cars, Marc and Hal Flanders walked together.

"Well, you got your tools but not the dog," Marc said.

"I didn't want the mutt anyway," Hal laughed. "I just wanted to take a last shot at her. I knew she wanted him. I just wanted to piss her off."

NINE

Luke Hanson parked his ten-year-old Ford van a couple of blocks away from his destination. The sun had set two hours ago, and the nearest streetlight was fifty yards away, across the street. Even if someone saw him, there would be no reason to pay any attention to him.

Luke retrieved a medium-sized, sturdy, dark green canvass bag from the back of the van. The contents of the bag weighed more than forty pounds. As he walked down the sidewalks, he occasionally shifted the bag from hand to hand. He reached his destination and impatiently rang the doorbell three times. Luke was about to ring it again when the owner of the house opened the door.

"Please, come in, Luke," Ben Sokol affably greeted him.

"Thanks, Ben," Luke said as he quickly stepped through the doorway.

Ben closed the door and said, "Come into the kitchen. Let's have a look at them."

Luke followed Ben into the small kitchen and placed the bag on the serving island in the middle of the room. He unzipped the bag and pulled the two sides apart.

"Wonderful," Ben said, looking down at a dozen 9mm semiautomatic handguns. He picked one up, a Smith & Wesson, and looked it over. Ben held it up, pointed it at the wall and looked down the sights.

"I've never even fired a gun let alone owned one," Ben said.

"Really? If you want to, we can go down in the basement and set up a target. I'll show you how. There's nothing to it," Luke said.

"What if someone hears it?"

"I doubt anyone will. But even if they do, there's nothing illegal about target shooting in your own basement," Luke said.

"Really? Are you sure?"

Luke laughed, then said, "This is Minnesota, not New York. Nobody starts weeping at the mention of a gun. Come on, let's try it out."

Using cotton balls for earplugs and a couple of telephone books as a target, Luke taught sheltered, city-boy Ben how to load, aim and shoot. When they were done, Luke quickly swept up the empty cartridges and they went back upstairs.

"That was fun," Ben said. "I can see why a lot of people like shooting."

"You did pretty good," Luke said.

Ben replaced the gun in the bag with the others.

"You got these from a guy down in Waseca?" Ben asked, referring to a small town in southern Minnesota.

"Yeah, a guy a friend knows."

"They can't be traced to you?"

"He doesn't even have my name. No receipt, no bill of sale, no registration. Nothing. Cash exchange and they're all stolen."

"And how many of these clips did you get?" Ben asked holding one up.

"Magazines," Luke corrected him. "They're called magazines. Two dozen. Two for each gun."

"Okay," Ben said. He went to the refrigerator and came out with two bottles of beer. He handed one to Luke, held his up in a toast and they clicked bottles together.

"Here's to the completion of stage one," Ben said. Each man took a large swallow.

"I have a place in the attic to store these," Ben said, referring to the contents of the bag. "Now, stage two. Recruits."

Luke set his beer next to the bag, reached in his pants' pocket and pulled out a folded piece of paper. "Here's a list of six names I think can be recruited," he said, handing it to Ben.

Ben read the names, recognized two or three, then handed it back to Luke. "Have you talked to them?"

"Yeah, all six. I've checked out a few more who are good possibilities. But these," he continued, holding up the list, "are solid. A couple of them are fanatics. This chick, Sherry Toomey, she thinks anyone who doesn't believe in climate change and global warming should be put in prison or a re-education camp. She's in your class and believes all banks should be abolished and Jews rounded up."

Ben smiled but said, "I'm not sure we want someone that nuts. Is she controllable?"

"I don't see her as a leader," Luke said after thinking over the question for a moment. "But she'll be in, I know that."

"The first time they're told what to do, well, we'll see. Do they know I'm involved?"

"Not yet, no," Luke answered. "I thought we should meet with each one individually and bring them in slowly."

"Good idea. We can start tomorrow night. If you're sure enough about them, we'll meet them here or my office. Schedule an hour for each. We'll start by telling them we want to get serious about doing something. Not just talk. Talk is getting us nowhere."

"Yeah, I know. I'll set them up. I'll try to get Sherry first. She's pretty hot, too," Luke said.

"She's not a lesbian, is she? No lesbians, no gays. They have their own agenda. We want sheep. We want political sheep, not deep thinkers. Not people who are too prone to think," Ben reminded him.

"How do I find out if she's a lesbian?"

"Try asking," Ben said.

Luke paused while thinking about it, then said, "Yeah, that should work."

An hour after Luke left, Ben was relaxing in front of the TV. He was sipping his second inexpensive brand of scotch—the really good quality scotch was over his pay grade which added to his bitterness—watching a movie. It was about two brothers who were on a bank robbery spree. They were robbing different branches of the same bank to get the money to save the family farm. This was at least the fourth time Ben had watched it, enjoying the delicious irony; using the bank's own money to stop that bank from foreclosing on their home.

At 3:15 A.M. the sound of the TV woke him up. The ice had melted in his fourth glass of scotch and a movie he did not recognize was on the screen. Ben was still sporting a slight buzz as he staggered up the stairs.

"Come in," Ben replied to the knock on his door. It opened and Luke entered followed by a twenty-year-old girl dressed in black half-boots, jeans and a black leather coat. She was tall, in her boots almost six feet, with her brown hair pulled back in a ponytail. She was attractive in a serious, severe looking way and Ben assumed this was Sherry Toomey.

While Ben and Luke greeted each other, the girl took a few seconds to look over Ben's office. Luke introduced Sherry and Ben to each other.

"Do all professors live in a cluttered office of books and papers?" she asked with a fetching smile.

Ben laughed and said, "Yeah, it's part of the job description. Close the door, please," he told Luke. "Have a seat," he politely told her.

"No, I'm not a lesbian," she said as she sat down.

"Sorry, did that offend you?" Ben replied.

"No, not all. Just curious why you would ask it?"

"Did Luke tell you why we want to talk to you?"

"A bit, yeah. Something about getting serious. Starting a real movement. Whatever it is, I'm in. I've been at some of your meetings and even sat in on a few of your class lectures. My dad, my family was destroyed by capitalist pigs. They toss people aside like they're trash."

For the next hour, Ben and Luke quietly indoctrinated Sherry into what they had in mind. The more they revealed, the more enthused she became. Obviously, she wanted in.

44

Her father had been a minimally educated working man who had gone through a dozen jobs in barely fifteen years, mostly after buyouts and takeovers, layoffs and downsizing would occur. And as more and more plants and jobs were shipped overseas, employment became harder and harder to find.

"His last job was delivering pizzas. A fifty-year-old man with a family," Sherry told them. "That was the best he could find. All to put a few more bucks in the pockets of rich people.

"He was drinking heavily then one night he drove his car in front of a train and that was that," she finished as a single tear trickled past her nose.

"Fifty-year-old men with a family should not have to deliver pizzas."

"No," Ben quietly agreed.

"Are you willing to commit to something? Something that might get you killed? Or sent to prison?" Luke asked.

"Depends on what it is," Sherry replied.

"Something bigger than all of us. Something important," Ben said.

"Sherry, the vast majority of people in this country are not getting the life they are entitled to. Oh, sure, the oppressors will tell you the lie that this is America, the land of opportunity. That you are free to go as far as your ability and ambition will take you. But is it? Is that true?"

"Of course not," Sherry vehemently, angrily replied.

"Even if you do work your ass off your entire life, they'll still take it away from you any time they want," Luke interjected.

"That's for sure. Whatever it is you're up to, I want in. I didn't realize it before, but this is what I've been looking for. Something to give my life a purpose. I don't want to be a slave to convention. Marriage, two-point three kids, a big-ass mortgage, a husband I'll hate in ten years…"

"Sounds exciting," Ben said, drawing laughter.

"We're putting together a small group to start off. You're the first recruit. We have to be careful," Luke said. "The thing is, there can only be one leader and that's Ben. He's our decision maker. Can you live with that?" Luke asked.

"No problem. One question. Why did you want to know if I'm a lesbian? I'm not interested in being someone's sex toy."

"No, that's not it," Ben replied. "Lesbians come with a cause of their own. As do other people. We want commitment. One cause at a time."

"Have you ever handled a gun?" Luke asked.

"Yes, sure. I used to go hunting with my Dad. Guns don't scare me."

"What do you think?" Luke asked Ben.

Ben looked at Sherry and said, "Don't be in a hurry. What we're doing is going to require keeping calm and cool."

"Tell me you're going to rob banks," Sherry said with a determined look. "Tell me we're going to shake them up."

"I guess she's in," Ben said to Luke.

"I guess she is," Luke answered.

Over the next several days, Luke brought an even dozen prospective recruits to meet Ben. Luke would interview them slyly without them knowing they were being recruited. All twelve were good prospects. They selected five more for now with the idea that others might join later.

Ben's cult of angry radicals was set to begin.

TEN

The slender blonde girl, after patiently waiting her turn, stepped up to the teller window. With her was a young man. He was wearing glasses, a baseball cap and a heavy beard.

"Hi," the girl said to the older woman behind the counter. "I don't have an account here, but I was wondering if I could get a cashier's check?"

"Sure," the teller pleasantly smiled. "How much do you want it for?"

"It's only twenty-five dollars, but they insisted on a cashier's check. It's for something for my mom's birthday," the girl said.

"No problem. Just give me a minute. We'll need cash for it plus there's a two-dollar charge."

"Two dollars? It's only for twenty-five and..."

"Just give her the two bucks," the young man with her said, smiling at the teller.

"You're right, sorry," the girl said.

While the teller started to type in the information to print off the check, the girl placed twenty-seven dollars on the counter.

"Who do you want it made out to?" the teller asked.

"Oh, jeez. I left that at home," she said.

"I told you to bring it," her companion said. He looked at the teller, pointed a finger at his own temple and rolled his eyes.

"Shut up," the girl said and lightly elbowed his arm.

The teller smiled and said, "It's okay. You can fill it out yourself."

She then handed the girl the check and a carbon copy. The couple thanked her and left.

"How did it go?" Luke asked as he pulled away from the curb. The two bank customers had walked a block away from the bank then got in Luke's van. There was a girl in the front seat with Luke. The new arrivals from the bank got in the back.

"Piece of cake," she said as she pulled off the blonde wig and shook out her brown hair.

"Did you get everything?" Luke asked the guy in the back seat.

"Oh, yeah," he replied. "It's not that complicated. I'll draw a perfect floor plan. Only one guard." He slapped his hands together and howled. "God, this is gonna rock."

"You two are not going in, Neil," Luke said.

"I know," Neil replied. "I get it but still..."

"We'll get our turn next," the now brunette girl said. "Calm down."

47

"I know, Cindy," he irritably replied.

"Did you get a look at the back exit?" Luke asked.

"Yeah, it's down the hall on the right-hand side where the restrooms are. It's got an emergency exit bar on it to open it," Neil replied.

"I checked the back of the building," Luke said. "There's a small parking lot that looks like it's used for employees. The back door has one of those locks that you have to punch in a code to unlock and get in."

"What do you think? Should we have someone back there?" Jordan, the girl in front, asked.

Luke thought about it for a moment, then answered. "Maybe, but I think the fewer people the better. We'll talk about it."

The following evening all seven members of their little club, including Ben Sokol, got together on campus. Ben knew of a room attached to the music department that was usually empty. Using the underground walkways between the buildings, Ben walked to it from the inside. When he got there, he waited five minutes to see if anyone had noticed him. Satisfied that the building was empty, he opened a back door to the room and let the others in.

Neil and Jordan had described the layout of the bank almost to perfection. This was used to make a 4 x 8-foot poster board drawing. The group used that to mark the floor of the empty room to closely approximate where everything was in the bank.

Over the next two hours, with Luke as the team leader, they rehearsed. The seven of them all brainstormed and critiqued every aspect of it they could possibly think of.

At first, their inexperience was obvious. It was agreed that the entire show must be no longer than a minute and a half to two minutes. The first rehearsal took over three minutes.

"This isn't going to work," Neil said. "We're too new to this."

"Are you committed or not?" Sherry Toomey asked him. "Well?"

"Yeah, sure. I'm just worried about what amateurs we are."

"We'll get it," Ben said. "Here's what we'll do. We'll get a police scanner. Cindy, you and Jordan will be parked a couple blocks away with it. Two girls sitting in a car won't draw any suspicion. Find a parking lot with a lot of cars. As soon as you hear the call go out, you call Neil in the car in front of the bank.

"Reese, you go in with a phone bud in your ear. When Neil gets the call from Cindy and Jordan, you start your timer. Thirty seconds to get out money or no money. Let it go and get out. Understood?"

"Yeah, got it."

"Neil, if you see a single cop car on the street, you call Reese again and let him know. Then drive away."

"What? Just leave them…"

"Yes," Ben continued. He was walking around now, and he pointed to where the back door would be.

"Reese, if you get that call, you yell at Luke and Sherry to get out. Go through the back door. Gary will be waiting there in Luke's van."

"That's good," Luke said. "You can drive out a back exit onto a residential street and calmly drive away."

The room went silent as they all thought it over. Several heads started nodding in agreement while Ben looked them over.

"No one said this would be risk-free. There are no traffic cameras and the freeway entrance is less than half a mile. If you have to leave the money, do it," Ben said.

"What if they stop me?" Neil asked.

"Let them. You haven't done anything," Ben replied. "The most important thing is for Luke to get to the manager as quickly as possible. Stick a gun in his face and don't let him press the alarm. And the tellers and guard," he told Sherry and Reese. "Get those hands up and get them and any customers on the floor. Remember, Luke, tell that bank manager what his kids' names are. He'll cooperate."

"You know the names of his kids?" Cindy asked.

"We did a little research," Luke said. "The manager is James Barron, wife is Holly and the kids are Jimmy Jr., age fourteen and Claire, age eleven."

"You're not going to hurt them…" Cindy started to say.

"Of course not!" Ben replied. "We'll just use their names to make sure the manager cooperates."

"Okay," Luke said. "Let's keep at it. We have to get this down to a minute and a half."

Two hours later, satisfied that everyone knew precisely what they needed to do, they called it a night. The last five practices were brought in under a minute and fifty seconds.

"Okay everyone, tomorrow we go out to Willmar. One last thing. Make sure you pee before you leave and don't drink anything until it's over," Luke said.

This brought smiles and nervous laughter.

"I'm serious. We're all gonna be a little nervous. The last thing we need is for someone to be hopping around cause you gotta use the bathroom."

Millie and Margaret Herron, eighty-two-years-old, never married twin sisters and lifelong residents of Willmar, Minnesota, were finished with their weekly bank trip. Thanks to their father's success as a farmer and the sale of the land he acquired, the elderly women were jointly worth millions. And it was all safely deposited in the Willmar branch of Lake Country Federal. Once a week, like clockwork, the two drove themselves to the bank to check on their money. Unspoken was a secret each held: each of them was waiting to outlive the other.

As they went through the bank's front door, a nice-looking young man held the door for them. For at least the next month, the two women would bicker back and forth about what he looked like. There would be at least thirty calls to the police with updates on what they believed. At one point, Millie even thought that he was a black man.

Luke Hanson, wearing a black windbreaker, jeans and black sneakers held the door for two elderly women exiting the bank. He smiled at them through his newly pasted on beard and mustache, then entered the bank. Luke also was wearing a dark wig with a Twins baseball cap covering a black stocking cap with a face mask.

To avoid the cameras, he kept his face pointed slightly downward as he walked quickly to the office of the branch manager. Before he reached the door—the man was sitting at his desk looking at Margaret and Millie's accounts—Sherry and Reese, stocking caps pulled down, entered the bank.

Luke walked through the manager's open door and pulled his stocking cap down over his face as he entered. When Jim Barron looked up, all he could see was the barrel of Luke's 9mm handgun pointed straight at his forehead.

"Don't," Luke growled, disguising his voice. "We know where Jimmy Jr. and Claire go to school. Don't press the alarm."

By now Barron's hands were up, his eyes looked terrified and he was already starting to sweat. Luke could hear Reese and Sherry loudly ordering the guard, tellers and customers to get down on the floor.

"Please, don't hurt my kids," Barron pleaded.

"Cooperate, and we won't hurt anyone," Luke said. "Get up and get the safe open."

Barron nervously unlocked the door leading to the vault. The vault itself was open and the two of them went in. Luke pulled a folded cloth bag from his coat and handed it to the frightened man.

"Fill it. Twenties and fifties only," Luke said.

While Barron filled the bag with cash, Luke took a peek at the timer on his wrist. Less than a minute had gone by. He saw Barron sneak a peek at him.

"Don't be a hero," Luke said as he held his gun to the man's head. "Jimmy and Claire need a live dad, not a dead hero. It's not your money."

"Okay. Okay, here, it's full," Barron nervously said.

"Let's go," Luke ordered.

As the two men walked through the outer vault door, Luke heard Reese yell, "Time."

Barron was put on the floor with the others and his wrists and ankles were quickly handcuffed with plastic zip ties by Sherry.

The three of them pulled off their stocking caps as they climbed into Neil's car. It was a twelve-year-old tan Toyota. It was about as commonplace and non-descript as could be found. When the police questioned four witnesses who might have seen it, they got four different cars and four different colors—all wrong.

"No cops," Neil said.

"Give me your phone," Luke said from the back seat. "I'll call Cindy."

While Luke did that, Neil asked Sherry, who was in the front seat with him, "Did you leave it?"

"Yep. They can't miss it." Sherry said.

What she left was a two-page manifesto about the crushing oppression of capitalism and the glorious, social justice system of socialism.

ELEVEN

They were all crammed into Ben's laundry room in the basement of his home. The kids were all wound up with an adrenaline rush, each talking over the others. They were also on their third or fourth beer.

Ben mostly ignored them. Wearing thick, rubber, cleaning gloves that went up to his elbows, he carefully removed each bundle of money from the bag. Ben had half-filled his sink tub with water and was gently placing them one-by-one into the tub.

"What are you doing, Ben?" Cindy asked.

"I saw this on TV," Ben replied. "I hope it works."

"Saw what?" Reese asked.

The bundle that Ben had just placed in the tub exploded with a large red bubble. A startled Ben jumped back and waited for the water to calm down.

"That," Ben said. "I saw the dye pack burst open when exposed to a tub of water. Grab that garbage bag please, Reese," Ben said.

Ben reached in the tub, pulled the plug and waited for the water to drain. He then placed the wet, red-dyed packet of fifty-dollar bills in the garbage bag.

It took the better part of an hour to check all the money for more dye packs. The one that went off in the sink was all they found. While Ben was washing the cash, Luke was drying it in a small microwave oven in the laundry room. By the end of the evening, the money was dried, counted and stacked. One hundred sixty-five-thousand dollars.

Ben's basement was unfinished with cinder block walls and a bare, concrete floor. The only enclosed room was the laundry/furnace room. In the middle of the other part was a table with a dozen folding metal chairs. The seven of them were seated at it, staring at the neatly stacked piles of cash.

"A hundred-sixty-five grand," Neil Cole said several times. "No way did I think we could get that much. Most bank robberies get what, ten to fifteen?"

"Less than five," Ben replied.

"That's because some junkie goes up to a teller, takes what he can get, then runs out," Luke said.

"Okay," Ben said from his chair at the head of the table. "What did we do right and what did we do wrong?"

"I thought it went well," Sherry Toomey said.

"No shooting, no one got hurt…"

"We got lucky," Luke said. "The guard was watching the customers. Plus, there was only one guard."

"What do we do if there is more than one?" Ben asked.

The table went silent while everyone looked around at each other. It was Sherry who first spoke up.

"First, we drive or walk by to check it out. If there is one close to the door, one of the entry team members puts a gun to his head and orders everyone on the ground."

"Are you prepared to shoot the guard?" Ben asked.

This question brought silent introspection from everyone at the table. This question had been mostly ignored up to now, except everyone knew it was hanging out there and needed to be addressed. How far was this little band of revolutionaries willing to go? The Rubicon, so to speak, was in front of them.

"What are we here for?" Luke spoke up and asked. "We robbed a bank and got away with it. This is not a game. Everyone here was selected because we all agreed that going to leftist-socialist political candidate rallies was a waste of time. The politicians are all in it for themselves. Why are we here and how far are we prepared to go?"

"The bank guards wouldn't hesitate to shoot and kill any one of us," Jordan Simmons said. "I don't speak for anyone else, but I'm not here for the money or the thrill. The planet is being destroyed and no one is doing anything about it except talk and push idiotic ideas that won't accomplish anything."

"I'm with Jordan," Gary Weaver said. "I think what we are is the start of something. Once our manifesto is made public, we will see our movement grow…"

"Especially among people our age," Jordan interjected. "Older generations are too complacent. They have theirs, but they're destroying our chance."

"They don't want us to have our chance," Reese said.

"Could you shoot and kill someone, Sherry?" Ben asked, looking down the table at her.

"Yeah, I could," she replied without hesitation. "I've never felt so, I don't know," she hesitated then said, "useful, I guess. This is what the Sixties must have been like. But better. We're going to save life on this planet. What could be better?"

"No, we're not," Luke said. "But in a hundred years, they'll look back and say we began the salvation."

"Yeah, that's it," Gary Weaver said.

"And there won't be a Jew left alive to start it up again," Ben said.

"We're not going to do this without casualties," Luke said. "Be ready for it."

"What about the money?" Reese asked. "Don't we need to launder it? How do we do that?"

"How many casinos are there in Minnesota, western Wisconsin and the Dakotas?" Ben asked.

The others all looked at each other and shrugged. A couple of them said, "I don't know."

Cindy said, "At least a dozen."

"There are twenty in Minnesota alone," Ben said. "Over the next two weeks, we each take three or four thousand in cash, go to a casino, buy chips with the cash. Hang around for a while then cash them in and get a cashier's check for most of it and cash for the rest. Have the cashiers make the checks out to XYZ Plumbing. I have it incorporated. I have a dozen different bank accounts for it.

"We deposit the checks into the corporate accounts then transfer the money onto the internet for Bitcoin and other cryptocurrencies. We can then pull it out via PayPal and voila, laundered and it didn't cost more than a few bucks."

"If you want to gamble a little bit, get small denomination chips. Tens and twenties. Don't get carried away. Don't lose or win more than two or three hundred bucks," Luke told them.

"We're going to use this money for the cause," Sherry said. "Not to party on."

By now the heads around the table were bobbing up and down like a CNN panel discussion. There were even a few high fives that took place.

"If everyone can get a car, we can convert this in three or four days," Ben said. "Go to several different casinos and cash three or four thousand in each one. That won't raise suspicions and we can get it done quickly."

"If there is only one cashier and it's a small place and not very many people, keep it under eight hundred. Don't raise any flags. Get a little and move on. Pay with casino cash for meals and motel rooms. Don't leave a paper trail with your name on it," Luke said.

"What about the next job?" Reese asked.

Luke looked at Ben, who said, "Go ahead and tell them."

"St. Cloud," Luke said, naming a small city about an hour north of the Twin Cities. "I've already been up there checking it out. They have a Lake Country branch even better than Willmar's. Better access and better getaway."

"When?" Reese asked.

"Why another Lake Country?" Sherry asked. "You got some personal hard-on for them? And is that a good idea?"

"We'll do one more of theirs then something else," Ben said.

"You do have something personal with them though, don't you?" Sherry persisted. "Let's hear it."

"Look, there's another bank in St. Cloud just as good. St. Cloud State. We'll do that instead if it looks as good. The Lake Country bank has only one guard. Same exact set up as Willmar."

"What do you think, Ben?" Sherry asked.

"Check out both, then we'll decide."

"Why don't you come with me, Sherry?" Luke asked. "We'll check them together."

"Okay," Sherry agreed. "Sounds like a plan."

"Let's meet back here tomorrow night. I'll have money allocated and casinos assigned for everyone," Ben said.

The plain-looking young couple waited patiently in line for an open teller. The girl was an unnoticeable, average looking late-teen; a brunette with large, out-of-style glasses that dominated her face. Her companion of roughly the same age was even less conspicuous than her. Frizzy dark hair, a scraggly beard and sunglasses. Gary Weaver's own mother would not recognize him.

"I need to open a joint account for my mom," the girl told the teller when they reached an open spot. "She's not really good with money and she needs my help."

Sensing that this young girl and her shabby friend might be scamming the mother, the woman behind the counter stopped it.

"Geez," the teller said. "I'm sorry but for a joint account, you'll have to bring your mother in. She'll need to go over the paperwork and sign a few of them."

"Okay," the girl cheerfully replied. "What should she bring with?"

"Well, you'll both need a picture ID and you'll need at least twenty-five dollars for a deposit."

"That's all? Okay. I didn't know so I'll talk to her and we'll be back. It won't be for a few days. She's at my aunt's in Duluth," she told the teller who was now thinking the girl might be legitimate.

"Okay, let's run through it," Ben said.

They were back in the empty room in the music building, preparing for a rehearsal. The Lake Country branch in St. Cloud was an exact duplicate of the one in Willmar, with one notable exception. There were two armed guards.

Jordan Simmons and Gary Weaver had been the recon team. Gary had also gone to the men's room by the back door and counted the paces. While Jordan waited in line, she had spotted the manager's office and vault room. Same exact place as Willmar. The problem of the two guards had become an issue that Luke solved.

"Look," he said to the group, "we can't be sticking guns in the faces of armed guards. Sooner or later someone is going to get shot."

Murmured agreements went around the small group.

"Okay, what do you have in mind?" Sherry asked.

"Tasers. Give me a day to run down a guy I know who can get us some. Let me get two or three…"

"Get at least five," Ben said.

"Okay, five. We'll tase the guards and use plastic ties on them," Luke replied.

They practiced for a half-hour with Luke again going after the branch manager. Only this time, he had to stroll past the second guard and put him down. It was obvious this was a problem. It was Sherry who was the first to see it.

"If Luke has to hit the guard and drop him, if the other guard sees him do it and I'm not on him perfectly, he could pull his gun and shoot Luke."

"Not likely, but it could happen," Gary agreed.

"And," Sherry continued, "with his door open, the manager could see it and hit the alarm. We need a second guy going in with Luke. Actually, we should use one of the girls, Cindy. Put a brunette wig on her, sunglasses, a fake tattoo on her face. They walk in together. When they get by the guard, Cindy casually steps over and hits him."

"I got a better idea. She opens up her blouse an extra button or two and we put the fake tattoo on one of her boobs. He won't see anything else," Jordan said.

This brought a laugh from everyone, including Cindy whose face had turned red.

"She's got the rack for it," Sherry agreed.

That was exactly how it went. Luke and Cindy strolled into the bank and headed toward the manager's office. Cindy stopped, turned to the guard, said, "Excuse me, sir" and he turned to her. While he looked at the fake butterfly tattoo on her right breast, she pulled her hand out of her jacket and put him down.

Like clockwork, before Cindy's guard hit the floor, Sherry tased the one by the door while Reese covered the tellers and both customers. Again, in under a minute and forty seconds, they were out the door leaving everyone unharmed but zip-tied on the floor. This time the sidearms the guards had gone with them. No alarm had been set off.

The four of them piled into the back of Luke's van. The bag with the cash went into a large, black, plastic lawn bag in case a dye pack went off. They were northbound on I-94 in less than thirty seconds.

Waiting for them at the first rest area were Jordan and Gary in their separate cars.

The bag of money went into Jordan's trunk. Jordan and Cindy would head south on I-94 back to the Cities. The cops would be looking for four people in a van, not two girls in an Audi. Gary and Reese would drive Gary's Chevy east to I-35 then south to the cities with the guns and disguises in their trunk. Luke and Sherry would drive the van a hundred miles toward North Dakota before turning and going back. The guard's guns would be tossed into a river by Gary and Reese about two miles down the road. They would all meet up at Ben's that night.

The take this time was over two hundred twenty thousand and no dye pack was found. The bank manager, terrified after Luke mentioned his kid's names, knew which bundle it was in and deliberately left it out.

TWELVE

Tony Carvelli parked the Camaro in a ramp on Fourth Avenue and Sixth Street in downtown Minneapolis. Despite the beautiful October weather, he took the skyway across Fourth into the Hennepin County Government Center.

Carvelli was a retired Minneapolis detective. His last three years were spent in the Intelligence Department. Because of this, Carvelli knew just about everything and everybody in the seedy underside of the entire Metro area.

In business for himself, he had become a successful investigator for local corporations. His current assignment was tracking down a hijacked eighteen-wheeler, bound for Best Buy, with a load of 88-inch, top of the line, Samsung HD TVs, each one of which retailed for twenty-thousand-dollars. The World Corporate Campus of Best Buy was situated less than ten minutes from where Tony was currently located.

Carvelli had received the job from an old friend, a VP in Best Buy's security department, the day before. By midnight, Carvelli had located the truck and turned the MPD robbery division onto it. They agreed to sit on it for a couple of days to bust the hijackers and the fence. In the meantime, Carvelli kept the news from his friend at Best Buy to justify his five-thousand-dollar retainer and the ten-thousand-dollar reward from the insurance company. All, sort of, more or less, legitimate under the guise of helping law enforcement.

Carvelli went out the front of the Government Center and hurried across Fifth Street and the light rail tracks. He went in the back entrance of the Old City Hall and sweet-talked his way past the female guard into the police headquarters.

As he strolled through the homicide division toward his destination, he heard his name called out.

"Nice job on the Best Buy hijacking, Tony," he heard one of the detectives say.

"How do you know about that, Flaherty?" Carvelli asked.

"It's all over the department," the detective replied.

By now there were another seven or eight detectives listening, all of whom nodded in agreement.

"Great, now I gotta call Earl and let him know," Carvelli muttered. More loudly he sincerely said, "Thanks, Ron."

He knocked on the door of the man he was there to see and began opening it before he heard a response. It was the office of an old friend, Detective Lieutenant Owen Jefferson. The front wall of Jefferson's office was half-clear glass windows and Jefferson had seen him coming. Carvelli could also see his friend at his desk as he walked toward him.

Jefferson was, as usual, buried in paperwork. He looked up as Carvelli came in.

Jefferson tilted his head to his left to look behind Carvelli then said, "Is Maddy with you?"

"Ah, no, she's not."

"Then why would I want to see you? I'm busy. Go away or come back with Maddy!"

Owen Jefferson was an eighteen-year veteran of the Minneapolis Police Department. He was also a rising star and had been since joining the department. A six-foot-five-inch black man with a sweet jump shot, he was a one-time University of Minnesota, All Big Ten shooting guard. A brief NBA career was cut short by two knee surgeries. Tony Carvelli had known him since he was a rookie.

Carvelli ignored him and sat down in front of Owen's desk.

"Have a seat, Tony. What can I do for you?" he said with faux pleasantness.

"Hang on, I gotta make a phone call," Carvelli said while scrolling through his phone.

"By all means. Come on in. Have a seat. Use my office to make a personal call," Jefferson sarcastically said.

While the phone rang, Carvelli moved it from his mouth and said, "It's a business call...Hey, Earl," he said when the man answered.

"When you gonna tell me you found our truckload of TVs?" his Best Buy VP friend asked.

"That's why I'm calling," Carvelli said.

"You found it last night. Where is it? We want it back," Earl said.

"MPD has it staked out. It's not going anywhere. Give them a day or two and they'll bust the crew and maybe the fence, although I'm pretty sure they know who that is, and they won't get him."

There was a pause then Earl said, "Okay, we can live with that. How did you find it so fast?"

"I, ah, I'm not gonna tell. That's what you pay me for; my brilliant investigative skills. Give Bob Everson a call. He's in charge for MPD."

"Okay, I will," Earl replied. "And, just so you know, everybody's pretty happy with you."

"So, Best Buy's happy, Earl Thomas is happy, you're happy and now you're gonna make me happy," Jefferson said.

"Making you happy is not my job. I stopped by cause I'm hearing rumors about a series of bank robberies. Specifically, mostly robberies of Lake Country branches outstate. What's going on?"

"Stay out of it," Jefferson said. "The Feebs have it."

"I'm not in it," Carvelli said. "At least not yet."

"You know people at Lake Country corporate?"

"I know people everywhere," Carvelli said. "I'm very popular."

"Oh man, now I gotta get my feet off the floor."

"Come on, tell me what you know," Carvelli said.

"Okay, this will be public knowledge tomorrow anyway," Jefferson said. "They're very good. Very quick, very smooth. In and out in under two minutes. The Feebs say three, sometimes four of them with outside help. People driving and monitoring. And get this, they think it's a gang of kids. Or at least young adults."

"Seriously?"

"Yeah and the thing is, they leave a typed statement behind. A manifesto of some bullshit about capitalist oppressors, corporate greed, power to the people, that kind of thing."

"I thought the sixties were a bad memory."

"Guess not," Jefferson said. "Must be the grandkids. So far, no one's been hurt at least."

"How many banks?"

"They think seven. Six of them were Lake Country branches. Every branch in Minnesota is being staked out by private security," Jefferson said.

"Every branch of Lake Country?"

"Right," Jefferson replied.

Carvelli pulled out his phone again and scrolled through the directory. When he found the number he wanted, he pressed it and asked Jefferson, "What are you doing for lunch?"

"You buying?"

"Hello, Bob," Carvelli said into his phone while nodding at Jefferson. "Tony Carvelli here. What are you doing for lunch?"

"You buying?" the Lake Country executive vice president asked.

"I thought you had one of those big corporate expense accounts," Carvelli said.

"We gonna talk business?"

"That's why I'm calling," Carvelli answered.

"Yeah, I was gonna call you anyway. I assume you've heard," Bob said.

"I'm sitting in the office of an MPD lieutenant. He looks hungry," Carvelli said to which Jefferson smiled and nodded.

"Bring him along. I'll get us a table at Ruth's Chris on Ninth and Second. Noon?"

"See you then," Carvelli replied.

Carvelli looked at Jefferson and told him where they were having lunch.

"These guys eat lunch here?" Jefferson quietly asked Carvelli.

"Yeah, nice life, huh?" Carvelli answered.

"I took my wife there for our anniversary a couple years back. I about choked when I got the bill. I must admit, the food was great," Jefferson said.

They were in the restaurant's foyer and Carvelli was looking for his friend. He saw the man from Lake Country Federal and they went to where he was seated.

Carvelli introduced the two men by bluntly saying, "Owen Jefferson, Bob Olson."

Bob Olson looked like a banker. At sixty-two, he had a full head of silver hair. A two thousand-dollar Brooks Brothers suit and one look at the man you would immediately think: bank exec.

"You're a lieutenant with the MPD?" Olson asked.

"Right, homicide," Jefferson replied. "How do you know this rogue?" Jefferson asked, referring to Carvelli.

"My home was hit by burglars back when he worked for the cops. He actually solved the case and retrieved some family heirlooms which was much appreciated. Mostly my wife's family. I've been able to toss some work to him from time-to-time. So far, he hasn't made me regret it."

"Give it time," Jefferson said and literally stabbed Carvelli with an index finger.

"I'm in the wrong business," Jefferson said while looking over the dining room. "This is where you eat lunch, huh?"

"Oh, no," Olson said with a laugh. "Maybe once a month. If I ate here more often, I'd weigh three hundred pounds."

A waiter came by and Olson suggested a lunch entrée. They agreed and as the waiter walked off, Carvelli got down to business.

"What's up with these robberies, Bob? Somebody out there got a problem with you guys?" Carvelli asked.

"I don't know, maybe," Olson replied. He looked at Jefferson and asked, "What have you guys heard?"

"The guys in robbery don't know much. The FBI has it and they don't share. Rumor has it that it could be young kids. Twenty-somethings."

"That's what the thinking is. They've left a typed statement at each bank. Some half-assed socialist manifesto about corrupt banks and how we're oppressing people and destroying the planet."

"How is robbing you going to save the planet?" Carvelli asked.

Olson shrugged, sipped his coffee and then said, "Don't know. They haven't gotten around to explaining that part of it. We're not polluting but we are evil capitalists that employ thousands of people."

"Actually, you are cruelly oppressing all of those employees," Jefferson sarcastically added.

"We've hired a security firm to monitor our branches twenty-four-seven," Olson said. "And it's costing us a fortune." He looked at Jefferson and said, "I thought that's what we pay police for."

Jefferson's eyebrows shot up, but before he could say anything Carvelli intervened.

"Don't even go there, Bob. You know they can't sit on every business that might be robbed."

"You're right and I apologize, Lieutenant. It's just getting frustrating and expensive. Cops can't be everywhere."

"Tell me about the robberies," Carvelli said.

"Well, from what we've seen on the videotapes, they are very well planned. These are not some junkies walking in and shaking down a teller…"

For the next fifteen minutes, pausing only while their food was being served, Olson continued to explain how the robberies occurred.

"No forensics of any kind. No hair, no fingerprints, no fibers-"

"There're a million prints and fibers. Try sorting them out," Jefferson said.

"That's what the Feebs are good at," Carvelli said. "But I'll bet you a dinner here that they won't find them in their database. These aren't street crooks. These guys are radicals. And they're smart and careful. Anyone hurt?"

"We've had a few guards hit with Tasers but they're all okay. Other than that, no one. Not even a single gunshot. They go right for the manager. Stick a gun in his face and scare him by using the names of his or her kids," Olson said.

"Their kids' names? Where do they get that?" Carvelli asked.

"Online. Do a Google search of someone and see what you get," Jefferson said. "Plug your own name in sometime and see what you come up with. You must still be using that guy that no one admits to knowing or what his name is for your internet needs."

"In and out, two minutes and they're gone," Carvelli said, ignoring Jefferson. "And they only take twenties and fifties. Small denominations easy to launder."

"Yeah," Olson sighed. "What do you think, Tony? You want to look into it?"

"Oh, yeah, that's a good idea. Snoop around an FBI investigation," Jefferson said. "In fact, that's right in your wheelhouse, Tony."

"See how much fun you can have by retiring and going out on your own?" Carvelli replied.

"I'll stay where I am, thanks," Jefferson replied.

"Can you put me on a payroll?" Carvelli asked.

"How much?" Olson asked.

"Four grand a week plus expenses," Carvelli answered. "I'll be splitting that with someone. Give us a couple of weeks and if we don't have anything, you drop us."

"Who are you bringing along?" Olson asked.

"Maddy?" Jefferson asked.

"Yep. A woman I know. She's really good," Carvelli replied.

"You know her?" Olson asked Jefferson.

"Oh, yeah," he replied, nodding and smiling. "Trust me, four grand a week. You'll think that's a small price to pay just to meet her."

"Oh?" Olson said, raising his eyebrows.

"She's involved with a good friend," Carvelli said.

"She is terrific," Jefferson politely said. "You won't be sorry."

THIRTEEN

"Let me see your boots!" Sandy Compton exclaimed. Sandy was one of the two legal assistants, along with Carolyn Lucas, in Marc's office. She was at her desk leaning over to get a look at Maddy Rivers' new half-boots.

Maddy had met Marc for lunch at a restaurant across Lake Street. She decided to stop by the office afterward and say hello to everyone. Whenever Maddy dropped in, work came to a halt.

Maddy stepped closer to Sandy and lifted the left leg of her boot cut Levi's. The boots, Maddy's favorite style of shoes, were a tan suede with double buckles and three-inch wooden heels.

"They're gorgeous!" Sandy almost squealed. "Where..."

"Macy's at MOA," Maddy said, referring to the Mall of America. "You should go. They were on sale. Eighty dollars. And they are so comfortable."

Marc had been walking toward his office when this started. He turned to watch as Connie Mickelson came out to say hello to Maddy.

"Oh, I like them," Connie said. "Very sexy."

"Michael Kors," Jeff Modell said.

"You know who the designer is?" Marc asked Jeff. "You're starting to worry me, Jeff."

The women laughed. Jeff turned red then explained. "This girl I've been out with a few times wears them."

Connie looked at Marc, looked down at the shoes then back at Marc, and very quietly mouthed the words "high maintenance." Except she said it just loud enough for Maddy to hear it.

"I am not high maintenance!" she almost yelled. "Am I?" she asked, looking at Marc with her eyes narrowed into a sever expression.

"I didn't say it!" Marc protested, raising his hands.

By now the other two lawyers, Barry Cline and Chris Grafton, had come out of their offices.

"Maddy, if you need any help with maintenance, just let me know," Barry said winking at Marc.

Maddy looked at Barry and said, "I'll keep it in mind."

"Don't those heels make you taller than him?" Connie asked, referring to Marc.

"Sssh, you know how fragile their egos are," Maddy replied. She bobbed her head back and forth, then quietly said, "A little."

"Just keep talking about me like I'm not here," Marc said.

Maddy's phone rang and she retrieved it from her purse. She looked at the ID and then answered it by saying, "Hey, goombah, what's up?"

"Is that Carvelli? Say hello for everyone," Connie said when Maddy nodded her head.

Tony Carvelli and Owen Jefferson had left the restaurant a couple of minutes ago. They were walking down Second Avenue to go back to City Hall.

"Hey, kid, what are you up to?" Carvelli asked when Maddy answered her phone.

"I'm at Marc's. Why? What's up?"

"His office or home?"

"Office," she replied.

"Can you stick around there for a while?"

"Sure, why?"

"I'm into something and I need your help. I'll see you in about a half-hour and tell you all about it."

When the conversation ended, Jefferson said, "You two are gonna get your ass in a sling with the Feebs. They don't even like local law enforcement messing around in their investigations."

"Good thing I'm not law enforcement and I don't care. Besides, after I handed them Damone Watson and that mess, they owe me."

"Oh, yeah," Jefferson said. "I'm sure they'll see it that way. Can you say impeding a federal investigation?"

"Relax, Owen. The feds have more of a sense of humor than you give them credit for," Carvelli flippantly said. "Who's in charge of their investigation?"

"I don't know. I know better than to pay attention to what they're up to. It's never good for my career prospects," Jefferson replied.

"Chief Owen Jefferson," Carvelli said. "Has a nice ring to it, don't you think?"

Jefferson smiled, looked down at the shorter private investigator and said, "You know, I think it does."

Both men laughed but also realized it was likely to happen.

Carvelli took the old wooden backstairs of Connie's building two at a time. When he reached the top, he was not breathing the least bit faster than normal.

"Not bad for a fifty-four-year-old man," he said to himself.

Carvelli entered the suite of offices and drew almost as much attention as Maddy did. After saying hello to the staff, he cautiously opened Connie's door and stuck in his head.

"Hello, beautiful," he said to Connie. "I'm still holding out for you."

"I've told you a dozen times, you don't make enough money," Connie looked up and said.

"Money isn't everything," Carvelli replied.

"Really? I'll have to bring that up at synagogue next time. See what they think," Connie replied and then leaned back roaring with laughter.

"That is so bad," Carvelli admonished her while trying not to laugh.

"What are you up to?" Connie asked when she finally got ahold of herself.

"You don't want to know," Carvelli told her. "It's serious and could get me in trouble."

"Now, I have to know," Connie said rising out of her chair. "Can it get you thrown in jail?"

"Ah, yeah. There's a fairly good chance of that," he replied.

"Good! Let's use the conference room. Maddy's in with Marc," Connie said as she hurried across the office to Marc's closed door.

She stopped at his door, put her left ear to it to listen and then looked at Carolyn. "Any, you know, kind of noises coming from the inside?" she quietly asked.

"No," Carolyn replied and laughed. "I think you're okay."

Connie knocked on the door and waited for a response. She heard Marc say come in and opened it.

"Hey, Carvelli's here. Let's use the conference room," Connie said.

"Okay," Marc slowly replied. "I didn't know you and I were invited."

Marc looked at Maddy who shrugged and said, "Let's find out."

As the four of them filed into the conference room, Carvelli looked down at Maddy's feet and asked, "New shoes?"

"See," Maddy said pointing a finger at Marc. "Even Tony noticed. Why didn't you?"

Marc looked at Carvelli, rolled his eyes, shook his head and said, "Thanks."

"I do that just to stick it to you a little," Carvelli replied.

"Thanks, again. Is that why we're here?"

They all found seats at the conference table, Maddy sitting across from Marc in a feigned huff. While the others listened, Carvelli told them about his lunch with Owen Jefferson and Bob Olson.

"I've heard about these bank robberies," Connie said when he finished.

"They've been in the news," Carvelli agreed. "From what Owen and my guy at Lake Country told me, this gang is very smooth. In quick, out quick."

"And no one's been hurt, so far," Marc said.

"Olson wants the two of us to start snooping around?" Maddy asked. "The FBI is gonna love that," she added with mild sarcasm.

"Olson's the executive vice president of a significant bank. If he isn't happy with the progress the Fibbies are making they have every right to look into it themselves," Carvelli said.

"And when they come knocking on our doors, that's our story," Maddy said.

"After you call your lawyer," Marc added.

"Where do you want to begin?" Maddy asked.

"Well, I thought we'd go around to the usual suspects, at least to start off. Jefferson's gonna get a new, updated list of robbery assholes in the metro area from MPD robbery and intelligence," Carvelli answered. "Their list will be better than what the Feebs have."

"Why won't the FBI have the same information as local cops?" Connie asked.

"Because too many of the Fibbies think the words local and yokel are synonyms," Carvelli said.

"Jeff Johnson isn't like that," Maddy said referring to a senior local FBI agent. "And he owes us," she added referring to the agent running the investigation. Carvelli was given Johnson's name by Bob Olson at lunch.

Carvelli and Maddy arrived for their first meeting in Carvelli's Camaro. Before leaving Marc's office, Carvelli had made a phone call and the man he spoke with was waiting for them. Carvelli pulled in next to a new Lexus 350 parked alongside the restaurant.

"If I had known we were coming here I wouldn't have eaten lunch," Maddy said.

"Great burgers," Carvelli said. "We can share some onion rings."

They were about to enter the Sixty-Two Club, named for the Hennepin County highway it was near. From the outside, it looked like a seedy, sort of low-life place. From the inside, it looked like that as well. But the food—American comfort—was outstanding.

When they got inside, they both needed a moment for their eyes to adjust to the low interior lighting. Carvelli spotted the man they were meeting sitting at a table in the farthest corner away from the door.

"Tony Carvelli, as I live and breathe," the man said, extending his hand to shake with Carvelli without getting up.

"And who's the lovely lady?" he asked.

"Maddy Rivers, Noah Hemmer," Carvelli said, introducing them.

Hemmer extended his hand to Maddy palm up, so she had to put her hand in his palm down. For a brief moment, Maddy thought he was going to kiss the back of her hand. She did her best to hide her revulsion at the thought.

Noah Hemmer weighed at least three hundred pounds, all rolled fat. He was also quite bald with a face so fat the rolls of it almost covered his eyes. He was also, now that he was out of prison and back on the streets, the premier conduit of stolen property in the Upper Midwest. It was Noah, with one phone call, who had tipped Carvelli to the truckload of Best Buy's stolen expensive televisions. It was a message to the hijackers to use Noah to move swag and not one of his competitors.

The waitress appeared with Noah's afternoon "snack"; a twelve-ounce sirloin with all the normal side dishes. It was his third meal of the day.

Carvelli and Maddy ordered drinks; a vodka tonic for Tony and a Diet Coke for Maddy. Fat Noah watched the teenager walk away and then turned to his guests.

"And what can I do for you, Detective Carvelli?"

"Have you heard about these outstate bank robberies?" Carvelli asked. "Outstate" meaning outside of the Twin Cities metro area.

"I have, indeed," Noah replied as he began to eat.

Maddy silently watched the man eat, a little bit amazed. Despite his girth and obvious appetite, Noah Hemmer ate with the level of delicacy of a princess. He noticed Maddy watching, smiled and put down his knife and fork.

"Food is life's great gift to be savored and enjoyed. I should know," he said with a chuckle. "I certainly get my share."

Maddy snapped her fingers and said, "I know who you remind me of..."

"Sydney Greenstreet," Noah finished.

"Yes, the fat guy from the Bogart movies."

"I take it as a compliment. He was a great actor who loved life.

"Now, back to your question, Tony. Yes, I have heard about these bank robberies. In fact, there is a buzz about them throughout the Cities."

"And?" Carvelli asked while Noah ate some more. "Thanks," Carvelli said to the waitress as she dropped off his and Maddy's drinks.

"And nothing," Noah finally replied. "They are new or not from around here. From what I've heard, I tend to admire them. In and out. Get what they can. No one gets hurt.

"There is a strange rumor going around about a copy of some political statement they leave behind. A 'down with the banks and capitalist oppressors' kind of thing. Is it true?" Noah asked.

Carvelli took a sip of his drink to think about his answer. He set the glass down and then said, "Yes, that's true. What do you make of it?"

"It could be a smokescreen to confuse law enforcement..."

"That's what they think," Carvelli said.

"…or it could be legitimate," Noah continued. "There's a lot of socialist brainwashing taking place on college campuses."

"You think college kids could be pulling this off?" an incredulous Carvelli asked.

"Why not? Think about it. Most bank robberies are not well-planned military-type occurrences. Normally, it's some guy with a gun who sticks it in a teller's face, gets what he can and runs out the door.

"These robberies take planning, recon and intelligence. College kids who buy into this nonsense aren't necessarily stupid, they're just childishly naïve. They could very easily have the intelligence to do this. What most of them lack are the balls. One strong charismatic leader filling their heads could change that."

"It's a theory," Maddy said.

"Yeah," Carvelli agreed. "And if it is true…"

"They could be very difficult to identify," Noah said.

The two of them stayed for another fifteen minutes kicking the story around while Noah finished his meal. Noah insisted on getting the check while waiting for dessert.

"How did you find this guy?" Maddy asked Carvelli as they walked to his car.

"I put him in prison a couple of times," Carvelli answered.

Maddy stopped at the passenger door and asked, "And he cooperates with you?"

"We're friends. Besides, Noah doesn't really mind prison. He's strictly a fence. No violence. He goes to the medium-security joint in Lino Lakes. Not hard time like Stillwater or Oak Park Heights," Carvelli answered, talking to her across the roof of his car. "While he's there he meets a lot of future customers. And he gets protection inside from current customers. All the while his money that we can't find is earning eight to ten percent."

"Crime can pay," Maddy said.

"Crime can pay pretty well," Carvelli agreed. "Especially if you avoid the violent end of it."

FOURTEEN

Professor Webster Crosby was standing at the window of his hotel room staring through a telescope. He was in the Presidential Suite of the Edgewater Hotel in Madison, Wisconsin. A perfect Upper Midwest October day had brought out hundreds of college girls in shorts and light blouses to enjoy the seventy-degree sunshine. Crosby, now pushing sixty, was looking forward to treating himself to a young, barely legal girl after this evening's speech.

The more naïvely impressionable they were, the easier to get in the sack, he thought, smiling while watching through the telescope. He took a minute to raise the telescope to look out onto Lake Mendota. There were dozens of boats of various sizes cruising the lake. With the lake bordering UW, there was no shortage of young girls in bikinis on the boats.

"You're a dirty old man," Crosby muttered to himself. "Yes, you are, and I'll enjoy it as long as I can," he said out loud as if answering himself.

The Presidential Suite was part of the standard contract Crosby had for making campus appearances. His two-hundred-thousand-dollar fee, he believed, was a bargain. Especially when he was doing three evenings of two-hour appearances.

Crosby's personal cell phone began to ring, and he went into the living room to answer it. He checked the caller ID and pressed the talk button.

"Hello, Tom," Crosby said to the multi-billionaire, Tom Breyer.

"How are your lectures going?"

"Just fine," Crosby said.

"No protest, no trouble, no…"

"Of course not," Crosby said. "Why would there be? Republicans don't have the balls to protest. They think they can win by appealing to people's intellect. We're appealing to the emotions of their children. That's why we will win. We'll get their children."

"I know, I know," Breyer agreed. "Where to next?"

"The University of Michigan," Crosby said.

"Great. Well, I just called to check in, see how you're doing," Breyer said.

"Have you talked to our socialist representative lately?"

"A couple of days ago. My God, that man is a self-righteous, insufferable fool. There are times when I think he actually believes his own bullshit," Breyer answered.

"He does. But he's useful. He also knows this is about power, money and control. Anyway, I have to go, Tom. I need to make a few revisions to my lecture before the limo gets here to take me. I'll call in a couple of days."

Ben Sokol, Sherry Toomey and Luke Hanson were seated at a small table on the balcony of Shannon Hall. The three of them had the same basic view of Lake Mendota as Webster Crosby, just not as high up as he was. Crosby was the reason the three of them were in Madison. They were there to attend Crosby's lecture in Shannon Hall at the Wisconsin Memorial Union on the campus of the UW Madison.

The sun had gone down a short while ago, and the balcony lights were on. Ben checked his watch and looked at the people already entering Shannon Hall. The lecture was scheduled for 7:00 P.M. but Ben knew Crosby well enough to know that would not happen. Due to his ego and vanity, Professor Webster Crosby of Princeton University never started a lecture on time. He was not fashionably late; he was egotistically late.

"What time do you want to go in, Ben?" Luke asked.

Ben was sitting on one side of the round red table by himself. Luke had moved his chair so close to Sherry that the arms of their chairs were touching. Ben had noticed signs that Luke was becoming a little too smitten with Sherry Toomey of late. The problem was, what to do about it?

Each of them had a glass of some local micro-brewed beer they were trying to choke down. All the glasses were still half-full, which, because of the taste, was the pessimist's version.

"In a little bit," Ben replied. "We have reserved, aisle seats in the center of the main floor. We won't have to trip over anyone."

Sherry took a small sip of her beer, made a nasty face and then asked, "What do they do, strain this stuff through somebody's dirty jockstrap? Who thinks these yuppie beers are good? Give me a cold bottle of Bud or Miller every day."

"It is pretty bad," Luke agreed. "I think this particular trendy glass of pisswater is made from bacon grease, brussel sprouts and hemlock."

The applause started on the left-hand side of the audience and grew as Crosby quickly crossed the stage. He stood at the podium for about thirty seconds, enjoying the adulation that poured over him. Ben, who did not applaud at all, checked his watch and chuckled. Right on time; 7:25 for a 7:00 start.

For the next hour and ten minutes, they were treated to the same basic lecture Ben remembered Crosby giving when Ben was a graduate student.

"I've noticed something," Sherry whispered to Ben. "He seems to live pretty well for a socialist."

Ben whispered back, "The people like him, these self-appointed elites, they never mean socialism for themselves. They're pushing socialism for everybody else. But we may be able to use him."

There was a Q & A session following the lecture. A long line of students queued up at the microphone. The microphone was set up almost close enough for Ben, on the aisle seat, to touch it. All three of them opened a small notebook. As each questioner spoke, they all wrote down names and notes with their impression of the questioner.

The first twenty or so did little more than gush over Crosby and his brilliance. A few of them tossed softball questions at him. Mostly it was a line of drooling admirers. There were two students who did not join in the lovefest; a young man and a woman, not together and both in their late twenties, who asked real questions. The man asked Crosby about the failure of socialism and the millions of people starved and murdered by socialist governments.

Of course, Crosby had a ready answer for this. These were gross exaggerations by capitalist imperialists who used scare tactics to keep control. The questioner was roundly booed by almost the entire audience. Along with the booing were several dozen chants of "racist."

Crosby had a little more difficulty with the young woman. When she had her turn at the microphone, she was prepared with a list of uber-left-wing politicians, academics and celebrities who were living extremely well, including Crosby. She read off his demands for "speaking fees and creature comforts" including the Presidential Suite at a five-star hotel tonight.

"Are you and your benefactor, the multi-billionaire hypocrite Tom Breyer, going to give all of this up to bring about your Utopia? How about your pampered celebrities? Are they going to give up their lifestyle for the greater good?" she asked.

By this point, the audience had grown totally silent. Their hero was squirming and having problems with his answers.

"How about the great socialist from New York, Jacob Trane? Is he going to give up his three homes, or should I call them 'dachas'? And how did he become a multi-millionaire on a congressman's salary? Is he going to live with Medicare for all, or will he continue to let the rest of us pay for his health care?"

"This will all be worked out when we crush the oppressors and move to a more socially just society," Crosby managed to say. "I'm sorry but my time is up," he quickly added and then fled as he waved to a silent audience.

"I think he recognizes you," Sherry said to Ben.

The three of them had a table at a bar in the Memorial Union. It is a popular place named Der Rathskeller. This being Wisconsin, a German motif was quite popular. They were several tables away from Webster Crosby who was sitting at a table by the fireplace almost surrounded by adoring fans. Crosby had glanced toward Ben at least three times. Even though the bar was quite crowded, he seemed to have a look of recognition on his face.

"Maybe," Ben replied. "It could be that he sort of recognizes me but can't place me. He'll remember when I tell him who I am, I'm sure."

Once again, Luke had his chair pushed up against Sherry's. Ben again made a mental note to talk to Luke about this. With the business they were in, emotional attachments were to be avoided. Plus, Ben knew with certainty that Sherry was not interested.

A young couple sitting close to Crosby stood up together to leave. Ben saw this and decided to grab the opportunity. While the two kids were shaking Crosby's hand, the girl practically drooling over him, Ben quickly made his way through the crowd.

Crosby's attention was directed at a very pretty, young blonde girl sitting to his right. He failed to notice Ben slip into one of the chairs the couple had just vacated. Ben leaned forward, elbows on the table, and waited for Crosby to notice him.

"Hello, Webster," Ben said when Crosby finally looked at him. "Ben Sokol, I'm sure you remember me."

Crosby's eyes bulged with recognition as he visibly sucked in a large breath of air and sat silently for several seconds. Finally, having collected himself, he said, "Um, it, ah, sounds familiar."

"Get a grip, Webster," Ben said. "I just stopped to say hello. Get rid of the kids."

"You know," Crosby said, waving a finger at Ben. "I do remember you. You were a student from what, twenty years ago?"

"Close," Ben said.

"Would you excuse us?" Crosby said to the small crowd hovering around him. "I'd like to catch up with Ben, please."

While the students were leaving, the nightmare of the explosion at Princeton when Abby Sentinel and the others were killed replayed itself in Crosby's mind. Certain that Ben was here about that, Crosby's hands started to shake and sweat formed on his forehead.

Ben waited for the kids to leave, enjoying the look on Crosby's face. After fifty years of being a nerdy, insecure wimp, Ben was reveling in his new-found confidence. A year ago, the thought of confronting Webster Crosby would have left him a quivering jellyfish.

"Relax, Webster," Ben said. "I'm not here to drudge up old memories or events from the past. I never blamed you for what happened. Although, I was a little pissed that you were screwing my girlfriend. Do you even remember her name?"

"Abby," Crosby quickly replied. "It was her idea, Ben. She seduced me."

"Stop," Ben told him. "It's water under the bridge, to use a tired old cliché. Plus, I know you're lying. Abby was pretty insecure.

"No, I just stopped to say hello and let you know what I've been up to — at least some of it. And to let you know that I want in on the national campaign to save this country from itself. To help take it back for the people."

The two of them, after Sherry and Luke joined them, discussed the cause until after midnight. The only thing Ben kept from him was the bank robberies. All in good time.

Crosby could be a source of money and political recognition. Ben and his merry little band of admirers wanted more than just local attention. This business was making Ben's ego grow in leaps and bounds. Never in his previous wildest dreams did he believe he could achieve such power.

The three of them, Ben, Sherry and Luke, took a cab to their hotel. They had three separate rooms, and after Ben went in his, Luke took a shot at Sherry coming with him. She politely declined, and a chastened Luke went in his room by himself. Ten minutes later, after climbing into bed, Luke heard a noise in the hall. He got up, went to his door and looked out into the hallway. Just in time to see Sherry use a card key to enter Ben's room.

FIFTEEN

Tony Carvelli and Maddy Rivers had spent the previous evening cruising the Twin Cities underworld. Working together, they had covered the northern half of Hennepin County and the western side of Anoka County. They hit mostly biker bars and assorted asshole hangouts. Even the far-out, outlaw gangsters would soften up and talk to Maddy.

They were at it until well past 2:00 A.M. when Carvelli dropped Maddy at her downtown condo building. It was after 3:00 by the time Carvelli crawled into bed. For their efforts, in search of the bank crew, they had come up with nothing. Everyone had heard about it, but no one knew anything.

Carvelli's brain registered a noise that caused him to open his eyes. He was lying on his side, facing his bedroom alarm clock that read 6:26 A.M. He lay still staring at it for a few seconds wondering why he woke up. His eyes started to close again as he began to drift off back to sleep. The second he did so, he heard the pounding on his front door again.

"Sonofabitch," he quietly growled.

Carvelli tossed off the blankets, rolled out of bed and sat up. He stood up, picked up a pair of gray sweatpants and struggled into them as he walked out of his bedroom.

"Yeah, yeah, I'm coming," he grumbled when he heard the pounding again. He was in his empty dining room when he detoured to his left to go into the kitchen. The coffee maker was set up, so he hit the start button.

"What?" he loudly said as he opened his front door. "What is wrong with you people? Don't you ever sleep?" he continued, glaring at the man in the off-the-rack blue suit and dull tie.

"Why can't you just call, Jeff?" he asked. "Hi, Tess," Tony politely said to the woman standing behind her partner with an amused look.

"Morning, Tony," Tess Richards quietly replied.

"We need to talk," FBI Special Agent Jeff Johnson said with his stern FBI facial expression.

"By all means," Carvelli replied. "Please come in," he said as he stood aside.

"Why thank you, Tony," Johnson said with the same insincere, smartass attitude Carvelli displayed. "Mind if we look around?"

"Of course, I mind," Carvelli said. "You can sit on the couch and don't move.

"The coffee will be ready in a minute, Tess," Carvelli said. "Make him get his own. I gotta use the bathroom."

"Why won't you let us look around?" Johnson asked. "What are you hiding?

"Bodies in the basement," Carvelli replied as he walked away.

Two minutes later, Carvelli returned, his face washed, and hair combed. There were three cups of coffee on his coffee table. He took a chair and looked at his unwanted guests.

"Is this in the Fibbie manual of How to be a Pain in the Ass? Show up at six in the morning when people are still in bed? You didn't bring a couple of dozen SWAT guys with you, did you?"

Johnson looked at Tess and said, "Damn, we forgot the HRT guys. Well, next time…"

"What do you want, Jeff?" Carvelli impolitely asked, sipping from his cup.

"What do you think we want, Tony?" Johnson said mimicking Carvelli's question.

"Let's see, you're selling Girl Scout cookies. No, that's in February. You're collecting for…"

"What the hell are you doing stomping around a federal investigation? You looking to get your ass thrown in jail?" Johnson said, cutting him off.

"Oh, that," Carvelli said. "You mean, why am I trying to solve the case for you?"

"You're admitting it?" Tess asked.

"I'm on retainer with Lake Country Federal," Carvelli told them.

"You could get yourself seriously jammed up," Tess told him.

"You two heading up the investigation?" Carvelli asked.

'That's none of your business," Johnson said.

"Lake Country has a lot of political juice. They asked me to check around. If you don't like it, take it up with them. Besides, Jeff," Carvelli quickly continued when he saw the look on Johnson's face, "if I get anything, you'll be my first phone call. I swear. You can always arrest me later."

Johnson hesitated and then said, "That's a good point. How do I know I can trust you?"

"Damone Watson," Carvelli said, referring to a huge drug, political corruption and money-laundering case Carvelli had all but dropped in his lap.

"Good point," Tess said.

"Okay, I'll keep the handcuffs in my pocket, for now. What do you have?"

"The same thing you do," Carvelli said as he stood and walked toward the kitchen. "More coffee, hang on."

Before Carvelli reached the coffee maker, the phone he had left on the kitchen table rang. He looked at the ID, recognized the number and answered it.

"You're up?" the caller asked.

"Don't ask," Carvelli said. "What's up and why are you up?"

"I keep strange hours," Noah Hemmer replied.

"Yeah, I'm sure," Carvelli said more quietly so his guests couldn't hear him.

"I have something for you," Hemmer said. "It may be something, it may be nothing."

"Okay."

"There's a gun dealer down around Waseca. His name's Kenny Wrangler, like the jeans. Anyway, I heard he sold a dozen nine millimeters to some kid a few weeks back. Also threw in magazines and bullets."

"I'll check it out. Thanks."

"Don't mention it and I mean, don't mention it."

Carvelli returned to the living room with the coffee pot and filled their cups.

"What was the phone call?" Johnson asked.

"None of your business," Carvelli replied. "Not everything I do is related to your investigation."

"Uh-huh," Johnson skeptically said. "Okay, so what did you find out?"

"The same thing you have. No one out there seems to know anything. Could be young kids, college kids, on some half-assed crusade. You've read their manifesto. 'Down with the capitalist oppressors,' 'Power to the people,' the usual bullshit. Now, your turn."

"You know what we have."

"Squat," Tess added.

"Why do I doubt that?" Carvelli said.

"Because we're the Feds and we don't share with the other kids because we don't have to," Johnson said. "You can't put us in jail if we don't cooperate, but we can put you in jail for obstruction."

"You know, your attitude at this time of the day really sucks," Carvelli said.

"Listen, Tony," Johnson quietly and sincerely said, "I'll give you some rope because I know you. And yeah, I kind of owe you for Watson. That and I know you have connections we don't. Keep us informed, or I will slap your ass in jail. And Maddy Rivers, too."

"Jeff, I'm shocked. Shocked to think you might have concerns about me not sharing. Sharing is my middle name."

Even Johnson, along with Tess Richards, had to laugh at this statement.

"Stay in touch," was the last thing Johnson said before they left.

Carvelli tried going back to bed but the information he received from his fence/snitch, Noah Hemmer, kept him awake. At 9:30, he was in the back booth of his favorite restaurant; Sir Jack's on Fiftieth and Chicago. Knowing he was looking at a long day, he had just finished ordering a big breakfast when his phone rang. Carvelli had left a message on Maddy's phone, and it was her calling back.

"You're up," Carvelli said.

"Yeah. Marc called to check-in. He was wondering if we found anything last night. What's up?"

Carvelli quickly told her about the visit from the FBI and his phone call with Noah Hemmer.

"You didn't tell Jeff and Tess about the gun dealer, did you?"

"Well, um, I figured we should check it out first," Carvelli said.

"You're gonna get us both in trouble," Maddy said. "But then again, we know some good lawyers. I'll see you in half an hour."

Five minutes later, while reading the paper and waiting for his food, Carvelli got another call.

"Did you forget something?" Carvelli answered the call.

"It looks like they hit again," Jeff Johnson said. "At least we think it's them. It wasn't a Lake Country bank. It was a branch office of First State Bank of Duluth."

"In Duluth?"

"Yeah. Same M.O. Quick in and out. Tasered two guards. Snatched what they could from the vault. Left the tellers and cash drawers alone. Left everybody zip-tied on the floor. No one was hurt."

"How much?"

"Not sure, exactly. They think between sixty and eighty. Only this time, they didn't leave their political manifesto. They just grabbed the money and fled."

"Copycat?"

"I don't think so. Maybe, but they did some of the same things that weren't released to the public. We're on our way up there now."

"Later," Carvelli said.

"You Carvelli?" the lone man, an obvious plainclothes cop, asked Tony. They were in a booth in a Denny's restaurant in Waseca,

Minnesota. Waseca is a small city about 75 miles straight south of the Twin Cities. The man who asked was a local investigator with the Waseca County Sherriff's office, Tom Haig. Carvelli had called in a favor with Owen Jefferson. Jefferson had called Waseca and asked the sheriff to have someone meet Carvelli and Maddy.

"Yeah. You Tom Haig?"

"Yeah," the detective answered, shaking Carvelli's hand.

"Maddy Rivers," Carvelli said, introducing Maddy.

Haig looked at Maddy, then back at Tony, then almost dislocated a vertebra snapping his head back to Maddy.

He took Maddy's hand in both of his and said, "Nice to meet you. Welcome to Waseca. If there's anything you need, just let me know."

"I like your wedding ring," Maddy said. "How long have you been married?"

"Oh, um," he stammered, letting her hand loose while trying to remember how long he was married. "Um, ah, a long time. Almost nine years." By now the poor guy was a nice shade of scarlet.

Haig sat down, took a breath and asked Carvelli, "So you're looking for Kenny Wrangler?"

"Yeah, you know him?"

"Everybody knows Kenny. A first-class asshole. Badass crook, fence, gun runner, you name it. He and a couple of other assholes are trying to be real gangsters. I guess they pretty much are."

"You know how to find him?"

"Well, I know where he has his sort of base of operations, if you want to call it that.

"He's got a few acres on an uncle's farm outside of town a few miles. We can run out there and see if he's around. We've searched the place a few times. He's a smart guy. Doesn't keep anything there. The other two guys are Dwight and Davy Cook. His cousins. There are usually other assholes out there hanging out. Bikers mostly. What do you want with him?"

"We think he sold some guns to some college kid a few weeks back. I'm trying to ID the buyer."

"Kenny isn't going to tell you squat," Haig said.

Carvelli smiled and replied, "You'd be surprised at what people will tell Ms. Rivers when properly motivated. We'll see."

"Is that it?" Carvelli asked.

They were in Haig's unmarked car stopped on a dirt road about a quarter mile from their destination. There was a horseshoe-shaped grove of trees around two houses and a large garage. The south side, facing the road, was open where the driveway met the county road.

Haig was driving, Carvelli in the front passenger seat and Maddy in back. Haig was looking at the buildings through binoculars. He handed them to Carvelli who put them to his eyes.

"Are they home?" Maddy asked.

"Looks like it," Haig said. "I counted three pickups and a couple of motorcycles."

"Let's go say hello," Carvelli said as he placed the glasses in the glove compartment.

By the time they turned onto the driveway, there were four men in the parking area. All four wore surly expressions and were holding AR-15s.

"They're probably full auto," Haig said, referring to the rifles. "Keep your hands visible."

"I thought that was illegal," Carvelli said. "Should we arrest them?" he asked very sarcastically.

Haig stopped his car about fifteen feet from the men and got out with his hands held out.

"Didn't you see the 'No Trespassing' sign?" one of them asked.

If there were a stereotype for Aryan Nation, bikers and idiots, these four would be it. Long, stringy hair, wife-beater tees and prison tats, including a couple of visible swastikas.

"What do you want, Tom?" one of the others asked.

"Got a couple people here from the Cities would like to have a word with you, Kenny," Haig answered the man.

By now both Carvelli and Maddy had exited the car and were watching. Kenny, the obvious leader, looking at Haig while the other three had their eyes glued on Maddy.

"Tough shit," Kenny said. "Get lost."

Maddy put up her hands and started walking toward the men. Kenny was holding his rifle across his body in a relaxed posture. The other three were pointing theirs at Maddy.

"What the hell are you doing?" Carvelli whispered to himself.

Maddy stopped a few feet from Kenny, looked at the others and said, "What are you gonna do? You gonna shoot me? I don't think so. Now, relax."

She looked at Kenny and said, "We're private investigators. We have a couple of questions for you, alone. Then we'll go."

Kenny looked at her for a moment, smiled, revealing a full set of teeth and said, "Okay sweetheart. But just you."

Maddy turned around and saw Carvelli watching her, his eyes almost horrified. She smiled, winked and nodded.

"Okay, big boy. Let's go," she said.

80

"Don't hurt him," Carvelli said loud enough for everyone to hear.

The three thugs got a chuckle out of this until Carvelli said, "Hey, I'm serious."

Maddy followed the man for about twenty feet for their private chat. With his AR-15 still held loosely across his chest, Kenny stopped and turned.

"Well, what?"

"We're looking for information only," Maddy started by saying. "You sold some nines to a college kid a few weeks back…"

"Don't know what you're talking about."

"Don't. Don't insult me like that. Here's the deal. I know a shitload of feds. Jerk me around and I'll have the FBI, DEA, ATF and anyone else I can think of crawling up your ass. How long will it take them to come up with enough to send your ass to Atlanta?" Maddy asked, referring to the federal prison in Georgia, probably the nastiest place in the federal prison system.

Kenny stood silently for a moment contemplating his life. He finally replied, "Okay, hypothetically, I might know something about that. Hypothetically."

"Who was it? A college kid?"

"Don't know his name, but yeah from what I heard, he could've been a college kid."

"You didn't get his name?"

"No, you know, don't ask, don't tell," Kenny said.

"Ah. Big believer in gay rights, are you?"

Kenny smiled and snorted a sort of laugh.

"Who brought him to you?"

"You mean, who did I hear about this from?"

"Yeah, yeah, whatever," an impatient Maddy said.

"A guy named Terry. Don't know his last name. He's from the city of Waseca. He buys dope sometimes. Weed and oxy. Sometimes sale weight." He then gave her a brief description.

"That's it?" Maddy asked.

"Yeah, that's it. Hypothetically."

Maddy pointed at the swastika on his left shoulder and asked, "So, when's the next meeting of the Aryan Supremacist Moron Club?"

"Why, you want to come? We'd show you a good time…"

"I doubt it. Thanks," she said, then walked back to the car.

"Terry, huh?" Haig asked.

"Yeah," Maddy said from the back seat. They were back in Haig's car heading back to Waseca.

"He claims that's all he has. He did say this Terry guy buys sale weight from them."

"So, he might be a dealer," Carvelli said.

"Weed and oxy," Maddy added.

"I'll check around for you and see what we can come up with. That's all he had for a description? White guy, twenties, brown hair, maybe five-ten?"

"Kenny's not enrolling in Harvard's medical school any time soon," Maddy said.

"He's smarter than you think. Plus, Terry might not be his real name. Weed and oxy dealer. We've got our share. I'll let you know if I find anything."

SIXTEEN

It was late, after 8:00 P.M. and it had been a very long day. A tired Natalie Flanders turned the corner onto the street where her house was located. As soon as she did, she saw the white Ford SUV in her driveway. It had been backed up, and the back end was a foot from her garage door.

"Sonofabitch," she snarled.

Natalie pulled onto the driveway and parked her new BMW up against the SUV's bumper, blocking it in. She went in through the front door. Moving quietly, she went through the house, into the kitchen to the door to the attached garage.

"What the hell do you think you're doing?" she screamed from the doorway.

Her husband, Hal, from his knees, jumped almost a foot off the ground. Holding a hand to his chest, he turned his head around to look at her.

"Goddamnit, Natalie, you just took five years off my life," he said.

"Good! Now get out!"

Hal stood up and looked at her.

"I have every right to be here. This is still my house, too."

"Bullshit! Go to hell! Die soon, asshole," she screamed.

"Hey! I've left five messages for you telling you I wanted to stop by and get my things," he yelled back, now a little hot himself. "Things you agreed I could have."

For the next fifteen minutes, the two of them stood in the garage, screaming at each other. With Natalie doing most of the screaming. It stopped when Natalie heard the front doorbell ringing.

"Who's that?" Hal asked, his breathing heavy, his face red.

Natalie turned from him and stomped off into the house. From the kitchen, she could see the officers in their uniforms through the window alongside the front door.

"I'll fix your ass," she quietly said.

She quickly locked the garage door, then hid behind the refrigerator. The doorbell rang another two or three times as she did this. Instead of going to it, she slapped herself on the right side of her face five or six times as hard as she could. She then grabbed her left blouse sleeve and almost ripped it off.

"Please help me," she sobbed after tearing open the door. "He's in the garage. He's crazy. He's gonna kill me..."

Natalie collapsed into the arms of one of the cops. The other one pulled his gun and asked her who was in the garage.

"My husband. He came for some things and…well, he's got a temper and…we're getting divorced…"

"Is he armed?" the cops asked.

"Um, maybe. I don't know. Please help me…"

The cop holding Natalie helped her into the living room and laid her down on a couch. The other one went to the garage door.

He opened the door a crack and yelled, "This is the police. Get down on your knees, hands above your head where we can see them."

"Okay, okay," Hal yelled from inside. "I'm not armed. I'll do it."

By now his partner had joined him at the garage. The two officers cautiously went in, guns pointing at Hal on his knees in the middle of the garage.

"What? What's wrong? What did that bitch tell you?"

"Hands behind your head, sir," one said as he put the cuffs on. While his partner held his gun on Hal, he continued, "You're under arrest. You have the right to remain silent…"

"That goddamn bitch," Hal quietly muttered while shaking his head.

"Hang on, son, I have another call coming in," Marc Kadella said into his phone.

Marc and Maddy were on his couch watching television. Marc was on a call with his grown son, Eric, when the call waiting kicked in. He looked at the number, then spoke to Eric again.

"It's the office after-hours answering service, Eric. I better take the call. Tell your sister to call me. I've left a couple messages, and she hasn't called back."

"She's got a new boyfriend, so we're not high on her list. I met him. He's okay. No purple hair, earrings or tattoos," Eric replied.

"Well, that's a step up. I gotta go. Love you, son."

"Love you too, Dad."

Marc switched to the incoming call as Maddy asked, "How's Eric?"

"Marc Kadella," he said into the phone. Marc looked at Maddy and mouthed the word "okay."

"Mr. Kadella, this is Carmen from your service. We received a call from the Burnsville Police Department. A man gave his name as Harold Flanders. He said it was…"

"…an emergency," Marc said.

"Well, extremely urgent is the way he put it. He was very agitated and wants you to call right away," Carmen said.

"Give me the number," a very unenthused reply came back.

She read him off the number and Marc repeated it while Maddy wrote it down. He pleasantly thanked the woman before ending the call.

84

"What?" Maddy asked as she handed him the note with the phone number.

"A divorce client," Marc said. "He's in jail in Burnsville."

"You're not going out tonight, are you?" Maddy asked.

"I hope not. Let me call him and find out what's going on."

An extremely agitated Hal Flanders answered on the first ring. As soon as Marc identified himself, Flanders started screaming that he did not touch his lunatic, bitch wife.

"Shut up, Hal!" Marc shouted back. "Now calm down and tell me why you're in jail and keep your voice down."

"She had me arrested. Domestic assault. I swear, Marc, I didn't touch her. She's crazy. I…"

"All right, listen," Marc said. "There's nothing I can do tonight…"

"Get me out of here!"

"Shut up, Hal, and listen. They'll take you to court tomorrow. Either in Apple Valley or Hastings. I'll find out when and where and meet you there. Until then, they are going to keep you. And, keep your mouth shut. Is the arresting officer or his supervisor near you?"

"There's a sergeant here," Hal said.

"Let me talk to him."

A moment later, Marc heard a woman's voice say, "Sergeant Sheffield. May I help you?"

"Sergeant, my name is Marc Kadella. I am Mr. Flanders' lawyer. You are now officially notified that he is represented. No questioning without me there."

"No problem," she said.

"Are you taking him to Hastings?" Marc asked, referring to the county jail.

"No, we'll keep him here, then take him to Apple Valley in the morning," she replied.

"Good. Thank you, Sergeant. Let me talk to him again."

Flanders got back on the phone and Marc explained what was going on. An angry Hal Flanders demanded that Marc find a judge and get him out now. Marc calmly explained that was not going to happen and again told him to keep quiet around the cops or any cellmates.

The next morning, because Marc knew the judge, the prosecutor and, more importantly, the court clerk, Marc and Flanders walked out of the building before 9:30, a $15,000 bond having been posted.

"Do you have a way to get home?" Marc asked.

"No, I, ah, hadn't thought of that. I guess I could get a cab or Uber," Flanders said.

"I'll give you a lift," Marc said. He handed Flanders a slip of paper and said, "This is where your car is."

"Great. What's that gonna cost me?" he asked. "I'll get my son to take me. Thanks again for getting me out. I…"

"Stay away from Natalie," Marc said again.

"I will."

"Call me and make an appointment for either today or tomorrow."

"I will. I gotta get my car, so probably tomorrow."

SEVENTEEN

Gary Weaver turned the corner on the street where Ben's house was located. He was two blocks away, looking for a parking space. It was agreed that none of them should park any closer than that to Ben's house so his neighbors would not notice them.

Despite the lateness of the hour and the darkened street, Gary could see Neil Cole's old Toyota a couple houses up from him on the opposite side of the street. He saw Neil get out of his car and Gary hurried to join him.

"Hey," Gary said when he caught up to him.

Neil returned the greeting, then asked, "You think Ben would let me have a few bucks to get my car fixed? It's gonna need a transmission pretty soon."

"I don't know," Gary replied. "We sort of decided to only use the money for climate change and social justice causes. Not for personal things."

"Yeah, I know, but I gotta live, too. I'm working part-time at a box manufacturing company making twelve bucks an hour. I can barely pay my rent."

"Twelve bucks an hour?" Gary asked. "Are they looking for people?"

"Always," Neil said. "They only hire part-timers 'cause they don't want to pay benefits. I think a lot of the workers are illegal immigrants. I'm not even sure they make twelve bucks. They like hiring single, college kids because they're more dependable. No sick kids or other personal bullshit to deal with. I'll get you the address. It's not hard work, and they treat us pretty good. They'll hire you right away."

"What the hell is that?" Gary asked, looking at a car parked in front of Ben's single car garage.

Ben's garage was built a decade or so after the house. It was set up in the backyard with a single-car driveway. The driveway was made up of two brick-lined paths and a grass center-strip.

Neil and Gary walked back to the car which was illuminated by a single light fixture above the garage door. The car was a shiny, black, BMW 550i and looked showroom new.

"Nice," Gary said.

An annoyed Neil said, "If he can buy this, I should be able to get my transmission replaced."

"Hey, he's a college professor. They make good money. He may have saved up and bought it himself," Gary said.

"Yeah, maybe," Neil quietly replied. "Let's go find out."

"I have a list here to pass around of all the places we have sent anonymous donations to," Ben announced.

The seven of them were seated around the table in Ben's basement. Ben handed a single sheet of paper to a sullen Luke Hanson who barely looked at it. He gave it to Reese Fallon to begin its passage around the table.

Before the accounting document reached him, Neil asked, "Where'd the car come from, Ben? The new Beemer in your driveway?"

"That's none of your business," Sherry quickly snapped at him.

"No, no," Ben said, holding up a hand. "I've got nothing to hide," he continued looking at Neil. "I've recently been given a raise, and I've been saving. Plus, it's not new. It's a used car, and I got a good deal on it."

"Okay," Neil quietly said. "Sorry. It's just well…"

"Tell them," Gary prodded him.

"My car needs a new transmission, and I don't have the money."

"Say no more," Ben said. "Does anybody have an objection to using some of the money to get Neil's car fixed?"

Everyone, including Luke, looked around at each other, shook their heads and muttered no.

"Okay. Tell you what, Neil," Ben continued, "get it looked at, and an estimate then let me know. Your car is used for our work so it's only fair we get it running well for you. Fair enough?"

"Um, yeah sure," Neil happily replied.

"Good, now I'll turn the meeting over to Luke. Luke, Reese and Jordan went on a recon mission and came up with a new target," Ben said, happy to change the subject before someone noticed he did not deny using robbery funds for the car. In fact, he had not been given a raise, and he only used one hundred dollars of his own money for the purchase, enough to avoid totally lying.

Luke stood up and went to an easel that had been placed behind Ben. He lifted the first sheet of paper on it to show the particulars of the bank.

"It's a branch of Lake Country in Grand Forks, North Dakota," Luke began.

"Another Lake Country. Why them?" Gary asked.

"They do a ton of farm loans in both North Dakota and Minnesota," Ben answered. "They also have a very high foreclosure rate."

"They foreclose on small, family farms, kick them off of the land they've been farming for generations, then sell the property to large, agribusinesses," Luke said.

88

"We're going to add some language to our manifesto about this," Ben said. "It's a travesty, and it needs to stop."

"This branch is a little bit bigger than the others," Luke continued as he flipped over another large sheet of paper on the easel. The next page showed the floor plan of the bank.

"It's not much bigger and, as you can see, it's the same basic layout; tellers to the left as you walk in. There are some private offices past the tellers along the left and three more to the right, then the hallway on the right to the back exit past the bathrooms.

"The good news is," Luke continued, using a pen as a pointer, "the branch manager's office is here, the first one after the tellers. The other offices are used for making loans. The door for the vault is in the same place as the others right here," he continued, again pointing with the pen, "in the middle against the back wall."

"There are two guards. Here, in front of the vault door and at the front door. The usual places.

"There is more risk to this one. It's these loan offices. If there are employees in there, the two on the left or the three on the right, they could be a problem. We checked the place out Friday and Saturday. Friday afternoon, the place was empty."

"Which probably makes sense," Ben interjected. "Who goes to the bank for a loan, especially a farm loan, on Friday afternoon?"

"But, on Saturday, especially in the morning, the place was very busy."

"So, we go in Friday afternoon," Sherry said.

"We go in Friday afternoon," Luke said more or less ignoring Sherry. "At three o'clock. We saw a delivery of money at two. Check cashing day, probably.

"The police department is on the other side of town," Luke said, flipping another page on the easel. "The bank is here, on University and South Washington by the U of North Dakota campus. The police department is over here, almost at the river between North Dakota and Minnesota. We clocked it. If they get an alarm, they can be at the bank in a little over two and a half minutes."

"That's cutting it close," Neil said.

"There are two escape routes. One north to U.S. Highway 2 then east into Minnesota. The other, University to Interstate 29, south to Fargo," Luke said in conclusion.

"We need to go in with five people," Jordon Simmons said. "Cindy with her boob tattoo for the guard by the vault door. Sherry and Reese for the front door guard and tellers, I'll go in for anyone in the loan offices to the right and Luke for the branch manager."

"Whose name is Mike Farin, forty-two years old, married, three kids. He'll cooperate," Luke said.

"This is really risky," Gary said. "If the cops get an alarm, they'll chase us all over the country. There's no place to hide up there."

"Any rest areas we could use to switch cars?" Sherry asked.

"No," Luke said. "The nearest one is about thirty to forty miles north of Grand Forks on 29."

"How about the U?" Cindy asked.

"There is a possibility. There is a parking ramp along University," Ben said. "I'll go up there and set up in the lot below the ramp. We'll use walkie talkies. I will monitor the cops. If I hear them coming, I will contact Gary driving the van. He will pull into the ramp and so will I. We ditch the guns and money in my car. They won't be looking for a fifty-year-old professor driving a BMW. Neil is in the ramp waiting. Two of the inside people get in with him and drive off. I can take Sherry with me. Luke and Cindy can wander off and look like students walking around campus. We'll figure out what to do about the van later."

"We can come back and get it," Luke said. "Even if they stop us, so what? They won't find anything. We can just tell them we're thinking about attending North Dakota and we're just checking out the campus."

For the next two evenings, they used the storage room of the music department for rehearsals. On Friday afternoon, they pulled off their best job yet.

Within a minute, the entry team had the tellers, two customers, the guards and a loan officer face down on the floor, gagged and secured with plastic ties. The manager, at the sound of his children's names, was completely cooperative.

Holding his gun to the man's head, Luke ordered him to skip the money packets with dye packs and fill the bag. When they finished in the vault, the manager was secured on the floor and they were in the van under two minutes.

They had decided ahead of time, cops or no cops, to do the car ramp exchanges. It all went smoothly. The next evening, Saturday, they got together and counted their score. Almost two hundred thousand dollars.

The kids were becoming professionals and a little too ballsy.

EIGHTEEN

Marc was seated on a barstool at the serving counter in his kitchen. It was a few minutes past 7:30 A.M. He was already dressed for a court hearing, reading the paper while waiting for Maddy. Five minutes with the sports page was enough to make him throw it in the trash. The Vikings were probably a playoff team but going nowhere. The Timberwolves, with a two-win and eight-loss start, were, for all practical purposes, already out of the playoffs. The Wild, Minnesota's NHL team with, what Marc believed, the worst nickname ever, were already settled into eighth place. And finally, the Twins' season was at another merciful conclusion.

Marc tossed the sports page aside and sarcastically muttered, "The Twins will probably expect a parade for coming in short of their normal ninety-loss goal."

Marc picked up the A section and on the front page, below the fold, saw the story. He was about halfway through it when Maddy joined him.

"Morning," she said with a contented smile then leaned down to kiss him.

"Hi, babe," he said.

Maddy went into the kitchen while Marc continued reading. She poured herself a cup and brought the pot to Marc and also filled his cup.

"Who called?" she asked, referring to a phone call Marc got a short while ago.

"Jessie," he replied without looking up.

"And?"

"Oh, um, she's fine," he said as he set the paper down. "New boyfriend. He sounds like he's a closeted Republican. He has a job, working his way through school toward an engineering degree."

"You mean a degree where he'll have a job and earn a living when he's done?"

"Yeah," Marc replied, obviously impressed. He handed the section of the paper he was reading to Maddy and pointed a finger at the story.

Maddy started reading and quietly said, "Another one."

When she finished it, she asked, "Where is Grand Forks, North Dakota?"

"It's up on the border, on the Red River, between Minnesota and North Dakota," Marc answered. "It's the garden spot of North Dakota."

Maddy's phone rang. She retrieved it from her back pocket, looked at the ID, then the clock and said, "Tony's up already."

"Have you heard?" Carvelli asked her.

"I just finished reading about it in the paper. Why?"

91

"Johnson called…"

"Already?"

"Yeah, I don't think he sleeps. Anyway, he went up to Grand Forks and he said there was something new. He said they added something to their political manifesto. A couple of lines about greedy banks throwing people off their farms so they could sell out to agribusiness corporations."

"Why is the FBI so willing to share with us?" Maddy asked. "That's not like them."

"He asked if I'd ever heard of anything like it before."

"And?"

"Told him, no, I hadn't. But we've all seen this stuff from radical leftist groups. Save the trees, save the whales, save the chipmunks and the cockroaches. Whatever. It's like these kids read about the Sixties and feel like they missed out."

"That's pretty cynical," Maddy said. "I think they really mean well but are going about it wrong."

"Fortunately, no one was hurt. But it's only a matter of time. I got some ideas about some guys to check with today. Meet me at Sir Jack's in an hour," Carvelli said.

"Leave your cynicism at home," Maddy said.

"You'll get there, too. Especially if you hang around that lawyer long enough."

"I can't help it, he makes me feel good," Maddy replied.

"He's sitting there?"

"Yep."

"Say hello. See you in an hour."

"Where are you off to today?" Maddy asked Marc.

They were in the living room, getting ready to leave. Marc was putting on a trench coat while Maddy snapped a holster with her gun in it to her belt.

"I told you about Hal Flanders, the divorce client who called the other night from jail?" Marc asked.

"Sure," Maddy replied as she went through her usual ritual of straightening his tie and fixing the knot.

"His wife got a temporary restraining order, and the hearing is today to make it permanent."

"Good luck, I think," Maddy said as she kissed him.

"Hey, goombah," Maddy said, sliding into the booth opposite Carvelli. He was reading the same story in the same paper about the Grand Forks robbery.

92

"Hi kid, how's the lawyer?"

"He has a name and he is a friend of yours," Maddy admonished him.

"It's a cop thing. Okay, how's Marc?" he asked when he saw the look on her face.

"He's fine," she answered. "Besides, I know you love him, too, even if your macho cop thing won't get you to admit it."

"You got me," Carvelli laughed. "Listen, on the way here I got a call from that guy in Waseca; Tom Haig. He thinks they have that guy, Terry, that we're looking for."

"Let's go!" Maddy almost yelled.

"He's in jail and not going anywhere. I need to eat."

The waitress arrived, and Maddy ordered orange juice and a muffin.

"That's it? That's all you're eating?"

"The jeans are getting a little tight. I need to cool it."

"Yeah, you're expanding like a blimp. We'll be painting Goodyear on your side and slapping a wide-load sign on your ass."

"Really?" Maddy asked with a distraught face.

"No, you look fabulous."

Two hours later, Carvelli and Maddy were waiting patiently in the entrance to the Waseca Police Department. There was an armed receptionist sitting behind bulletproof glass. She had called back to Tom Haig to let him know his visitors were here. Both had left their guns locked in Carvelli's trunk.

"Never ceases to amaze me," Carvelli said. "Our police stations are filled with armed, trained police officers and they are harder to get into than schools. Something's out of whack there."

"You know, you're right. Why is that?" Maddy replied.

Before Carvelli could answer, a door to the interior opened and Haig came through it.

"Hello, again," he said while holding the door open. "Are either of you carrying a piece?"

"No," Carvelli replied. "We left them in the car."

"Good. Come on back. He's waiting for you."

Carvelli and Maddy followed Haig as he led them back toward a secure conference room.

"His lawyer is with him. A local guy acting as a public defender. He's okay, but I called the county attorney. Someone is coming over. We may need her," Haig told them.

As they approached the room, they could see through the window a scruffy looking young man in his early twenties dressed in an orange jumpsuit. He was at a table with a fifty-something, almost bald man in a suit.

"Thanks, Al," Haig said to the uniformed cop who had been in the room. He left and Haig introduced Maddy and Carvelli to Terry Nagan and the lawyer.

Carvelli sat across from Terry, Maddy across from the lawyer whose name she could not remember, and Haig sat at the end of the small table.

Carvelli looked the young man over and smiled. Terry Nagan was, maybe, twenty-two, skinny, bad complexion, straggly, brown hair, and had a cowed, feral cat look on his face.

"What's he charged with?" Carvelli asked, even though he knew. He asked so Haig would say it for Terry's benefit.

"Drug sales, Opioids and three illegal guns in his possession," Haig said.

"Allegedly," the lawyer chimed in.

"Fine, Eddie, allegedly," Haig said to the lawyer.

"Sounds like Stillwater," Carvelli said, referring to a maximum-security prison.

"Okay, any more of that and this is over," the lawyer said.

"Any more of what, Eddie?" Haig asked. "He's right. It is Stillwater this time. This is number three for him."

"What do you want, dude?" Terry asked Carvelli while looking over Maddy.

"You introduced a buyer to Kenny Wrangler a couple of months ago. Wrangler sold him a dozen stolen handguns, nine millimeters and…"

"I don't know what you're talking about," Terry said.

"…and," Carvelli continued, "we want to know who that is."

"And my client gets what for this?" Eddie asked.

"A big jar of KY jelly to lube up with for the boys in Stillwater," Maddy said with an evil grin.

"That's not funny," Terry squeaked.

"Who's laughing?" Maddy replied.

"All right…" Eddie started to say.

There was a knock on the door, and a woman stepped in. She was barely five feet and weighed maybe a hundred pounds with very curly, dark blonde hair and tortoiseshell glasses on a chain.

"Hey, Kathy," Haig said to her.

"Eddie," she said nodding at the lawyer. "What's going on?"

"Let's step outside," Haig said to Carvelli and Maddy.

In the hall, Haig introduced everyone. Kathy Marlys was an assistant county attorney for Waseca County. It took about two minutes to explain what was going on.

"So, you think these guns might be tied to these bank robberies," Kathy said, a statement more than a question.

"Maybe. What can you give him to help us out?" Carvelli asked.

"I suppose we could give him immunity on setting up the gun sale with Wrangler. Although I'd love to nail that asshole," Kathy said.

"He's gonna want more than that." Haig said.

"How about recommending Lino Lakes?" Maddy asked.

"He might go for that," Haig said. "She just put the fear of God into the little shit about going to Stillwater."

"Okay, I don't have a problem with that. But then he pleads to the drug sales and guns."

"If you have to, drop the drug sales and make him plead to the guns. That way, if the liberals take over, they can't release him as a non-violent offender," Carvelli said.

They went back in, and when the haggling was finished, they had a deal. Terry would plead to the sale of opioids and one-gun charge for immunity on a potential conspiracy charge for the sale of guns by Kenny Wrangler. The county attorney would let the judge sentence without a recommendation. The county attorney would recommend the medium-security facility in Lino Lakes.

"Okay, name?" Carvelli asked.

"The guy's name was Luke, and that's all I know. He was introduced by a guy I knew in middle school. I won't give him up. He's clean. And anyway, he's in college back east somewhere; I don't know where. I don't know how he knows this Luke, but it's not from around here."

"Bullshit," Carvelli snarled.

"Hey, that's it. That's all I got," Terry protested.

"What's Luke look like?" Maddy asked.

Terry thought for a moment then gave up a good description of him.

"He was wearing a long sleeve shirt, a Twins' hat and glasses. The shirt was maybe to cover up tattoos. It was a hot day. At least that's what I thought at the time. He was definitely from the Cities. Minneapolis, I'm pretty sure."

"How do you know?" Carvelli asked.

"'Cause he mentioned something about the drive back to Minneapolis and being careful he didn't get stopped."

"Do you guys have a sketch artist you can put him with?" Carvelli asked.

"Yeah," Haig answered. "She's not on staff, but we can get her in here today and have something for you later. I can email it to you."

In the hall, Carvelli said to Kathy, "If this is him, or if we find him at all, you might be able to use this Luke character as a way to get at Wrangler for conspiracy."

"Maybe, if Kenny doesn't scare the hell out of him first," Kathy said.

Before they left the parking lot, Maddy asked, "Do we have anything?"

"Don't know," Carvelli said. "Maybe, if we can find this Luke guy. We'll see."

"We have a name," Maddy said.

"Yes, we have a name," Carvelli agreed.

"And a description."

"And a description. And, hopefully, we'll get a reasonable drawing of him."

Maddy looked across at Carvelli and said, "But we have no idea if it's right or if this is involved with the robberies."

Carvelli paused for several seconds, looked back at her, nodded and said, "No, we don't. But it feels right. You know what I mean."

"Yes," Maddy emphatically agreed. "It does feel right."

Halfway back to the Cities Carvelli decided to make a call. His driving normally made Maddy nervous. After digging out his phone, while scrolling through the numbers, Maddy closed her eyes and turned her head to face away from him.

"Hey, Jeff," Carvelli said when the FBI agent answered. "We may have something."

It took him almost two minutes to explain the gun sales and how they came up with Luke's name, description and sketch artist drawing. Maddy opened her eyes, looked through the windshield to find the car straddling the road's solid yellow line.

"Tony?"

"Huh? What?"

"Get over. Get back in America. We don't drive on the left."

"Yeah, yeah," Carvelli muttered.

"Is that Maddy?" Jeff Johnson asked.

"Yeah."

"Give her the phone."

Maddy took the phone with a sigh of relief, said hello and heard, "Hey, kid. Tell me, what do you think about this name you came up with?"

"It's something. It kind of feels right. How else would college kids––if that's who we're looking for—get guns? What do you have from the Grand Forks robbery?"

"They're very good. The locals and state patrols, both North Dakota and Minnesota, had the area shut down within ten minutes. They had a witness sighting of an older model Ford van, brown or tan. They threw a net over the area and searched every van they came across and found nothing."

Maddy thought for a moment and then said, "They switched it out. They stopped somewhere and emptied the van. I'll bet the van drove through the net and even got searched."

"Could be, but we're back to looking for a needle in a haystack," Johnson said.

"Tell him to run the names 'Luke' and 'Lucas' through DMV for car ownership. See if they can find one that owns a Ford van or any van," Carvelli said.

Maddy passed that along and Johnson said, "Will do."

Unfortunately, Luke's van was in his mother's name for insurance purposes.

NINETEEN

While Maddy and Carvelli were in Waseca, Marc was in a courtroom in Hastings. Hastings is a city southeast of St. Paul and the county seat of Dakota County. Dakota is one of the seven counties that make up the Twin Cities metro area. His evidentiary hearing for the restraining order was scheduled for 9:00 A.M. in the courthouse in Hastings. It was now past ten and Marc and Hal Flanders were still waiting.

At 9:15, the judge's clerk had told them they had received a call from Grace Blaine, Natalie's lawyer. They were on their way but obviously late.

"How long do we have to wait?" Flanders grumbled. "This is bullshit. If she can't get her ass in here…"

The hallway door opened, and Natalie Flanders came in following her lawyer, Grace Blaine.

"I'm really sorry, Marc," Blaine sincerely said. "A little car problem."

"These things happen," Marc replied. "Let's go back and let them know we're here."

Before they did, Marc whispered to Hal Flanders, "Face the other wall. Do not even look at Natalie. If she speaks to you, ignore her."

Blaine knocked on the clerk's door and opened it when she heard the clerk answer her knock. Standing next to the clerk's desk was Judge Deann Peterson.

"Well, you made it," Peterson said with a warm smile.

"Yes, your Honor. I'm truly sorry," Blaine apologized.

"Don't give it a thought," Peterson said with a flip of her hand. "We'll be right out."

Deann Peterson was the now ex-wife of a former governor, which is how she got appointed to the bench. A die-hard feminist, she had a well-deserved reputation as a ball-buster of defense lawyers, especially the male defense lawyers.

On their way back to the courtroom, Marc thought about his first encounter with Judge Peterson. He was in court for a first appearance, felony DWI case. There were least a dozen other defense lawyers with cases on her docket.

One of the lawyers, a man Marc knew whose office was at least forty miles away, was ten minutes late. Peterson ripped the man a new ass in open court for it. Quite a difference from the way she had treated Grace Blaine.

The hearing started with Blaine making a brief statement before Natalie Flanders took the stand. Her testimony was that she came home and found Hal in her garage going through personal property. She politely questioned him about it and he immediately exploded.

For the next fifteen minutes, he ranted and raved at her calling her a long list of vile names. When she tried to calm him down, he became more enraged, and that's when he attacked her. She testified he slapped her several times and dragged her around the garage almost tearing her blouse off.

Blaine used this testimony to introduce four photos of Natalie's swollen face and torn blouse.

Natalie then testified that a neighbor called the police. She heard the doorbell ring, and when Hal heard this, he stopped which allowed her to escape and flee for her life.

Blaine introduced a copy of the police report into evidence which drew an objection from Marc. This should be done with one of the police officers, and Peterson should have sustained the objection.

"Have you seen the report?" Peterson asked Marc.

"Yes, your Honor," he replied.

"Do you doubt it's accuracy? Do you believe the officer would testify differently if he was here today?"

"I have no idea, your Honor," Marc said. "How would I know what he would say under oath."

"I'm going to overrule your objection and allow it into evidence," Peterson almost flippantly ruled.

"Mrs. Flanders," Marc said, beginning his cross-examination. "Your testimony was that you heard the doorbell, broke away and ran to the front door. Is that an accurate summation of your earlier testimony?"

"Yes, it is," she agreed.

"When you're in the garage, can you clearly hear the doorbell?"

"Oh, yeah, the bell itself is in the kitchen right by the door to the garage," she replied.

"Is it safe to say you went to the door on the first ring?"

Becoming a little leery of why Marc was asking this, she hesitated.

"You just said you can hear the front doorbell very clearly from inside the garage. So, you must have heard the ringing right away?"

"Um, yeah, sure. It's pretty loud," she said.

"You also testified that when you got home, you saw your husband's car in your driveway. You parked your car, went into the house and found him in the garage, is that accurate?"

"Yes, it is."

"And he was going through some personal items. Were those the tools you had agreed he could have?"

"Maybe, I don't know."

"And, then you politely asked him what he was doing?"

"Yes," she answered but visibly squirmed in her chair.

"And he immediately lost his temper and started screaming at you, which eventually became physical?"

"Yes, absolutely."

"You didn't yell at him or do anything to provoke him?"

"No, absolutely not."

Marc, still seated at the table, made a point of fumbling through his notes.

"Do you have anything else, Mr. Kadella?" Peterson impatiently asked.

"Oh, yes, your Honor. One last thing. Did Mr. Flanders ever call you to make an appointment to drop by and get his tools, the tools you agreed he could have in the divorce settlement?"

"Irrelevant to the issue before us today," Blaine objected.

"Goes to credibility, your Honor," Marc replied without taking his eyes off Natalie Flanders.

"Overruled, I'll allow it," Peterson said.

"No, not that I'm aware of."

"Never left a message?"

"No."

Hal Flanders took the stand and spent fifteen minutes telling his side. Or, at least the side Marc wanted him to tell today. He told the truth but not necessarily the whole truth.

Blaine, knowing the judge would extend the restraining order, did not bother to cross-examine him.

The lawyers each gave a very brief final argument. Peterson adjourned and told them to wait in the hall. Before Marc went into the hall, he talked to the court reporter. Marc gave the man one of his cards and the reporter gave Marc his.

Ten minutes later the judge's clerk appeared with fresh copies of a signed two-page restraining order.

"How the hell could she write this in ten minutes?" Flanders asked Marc as they walked toward the parking lot.

"Easy. She wrote it before we showed up. Probably had her clerk do it from the affidavit Natalie gave when she got the TRO," Marc replied.

"You mean this was a waste of time. She had her mind made up."

"She had her mind made up, but it wasn't a waste of time," Marc said. "I knew we were going to lose today. All they need to do is show proof by a preponderance of the evidence. For a restraining order, all she needs to do is claim she's afraid of you. That's enough. She claims you hit her and tore her blouse. Any judge is going to give her the restraining order, especially since you're already living apart.

"What I'm concerned with is the criminal charge. The domestic assault charge. I got Natalie on the stand and nailed down her lies, under oath, on the record.

"Remember, she said she ran to the door after the first ring. But you heard it ring at least three of four times before she left to answer it. And, she was gone for almost five minutes before the cops came into the garage. Where was she?

"Plus, I didn't tell you this, but I had an investigator talk to the two cops. They told her they rang the doorbell at least four times before she showed up. Cops don't lie to my investigator.

"And, she talked to the neighbor who made the 911 call. The neighbor, right next door..."

"Mary Compton," Hal said.

"Yeah. She said it was Natalie she heard yelling and screaming at you first. That's why I talked to the court reporter. I told him I was going to need a copy of his transcript."

"Good old Mary Compton, the nosy old bag. She always did try to stick her nose into everybody's business. I don't know how Ralph puts up with her."

"Anyway, we've got a good shot at keeping the domestic assault charge off of your record."

"I could lose my job, and the bitch knows it," Hal said.

They arrived at Hal's SUV, and he asked, "Now what?"

"I sent you a letter with the date and time for a pretrial conference on the domestic assault charge. Did you get it?"

"Yeah, it's on my calendar. Tomorrow, nine o'clock at Apple Valley," Hal said. "Do we need to meet before that?"

"No, that's just a settlement conference to see if we can work out a plea," Marc replied. "You're not going to plead to anything."

"Will Natalie be there?"

"She'll get an invitation to attend, but she doesn't have to. Normally, if a plea is made, they'll call the victim and tell her what it is. They have to find out if it is acceptable to the victim."

"What happens if it isn't?"

"They'll talk her into it. Most of these domestic assaults get taken care of at the pretrial. Usually because the victim is there telling the prosecutor how sorry she is to have wasted everyone's time because she doesn't want to go through with it. All the while the boyfriend who beat her up is sitting in court with a pissed off attitude because he thinks she made him hit her and now he has to be in court while she begs the court to let him walk.

"Go down to Hennepin County and see for yourself. It looks like a biker convention. The victim looks sorry, is hanging all over him while the asshole sits there in his biker leathers with an attitude. It's disgusting."

"Anyway, I'll see you tomorrow," Marc said. They shook hands and parted.

Back in court the next day, Marc whispered to Hal Flanders, "Oh, shit, I was afraid of that."

The two of them entered the courtroom at the Dakota County court in Apple Valley. Marc had stopped when he saw who the prosecutor was. Displeased with what he saw, he looked for a place for them to sit. As he did, he noticed Grace Blaine with Natalie Flanders, seated behind the prosecutor's table in the front row.

"What?" Flanders asked Marc.

"I'll tell you in a minute. Have a seat. I'll be back."

Marc nodded toward Grace when he passed through the gate. He walked up to the court clerk and informed her they were here and checked in. On his way back to his client, the prosecutor and a defense lawyer walked by him on their way to go back to the judge. The prosecutor looked at Marc and gave him a very disapproving scowl.

"I saw the look that guy gave you. What's up with that?" Hal asked.

Marc took a breath and said, "His name is Edsel Lacey and he's the Burnsville City Attorney. He's pissed off at the world in general..."

"With the name 'Edsel' I can see why," Flanders said.

Marc smiled, then continued, "And defense lawyers in particular. He's a born-again Christian type who thinks he's doing God's work by smiting the wicked scofflaws. Defense lawyers should be banned. They try too hard to keep him from his holy task."

"And he doesn't like you," Flanders said.

"No, I beat him at trial once. That's the unforgivable sin. Don't worry about it. We're not looking for a deal anyway. In fact, I'm going to intentionally piss him off and then we're leaving."

About ten minutes after the two lawyers came back and the defense lawyer abruptly left with his client, Edsel Lacey looked at his list of cases, then said, "Mr. Kadella, would you care to join me?"

When Marc reached the prosecutor's table, without so much as a hello or handshake, Marc said, "Let's go see Judge Connelly."

"Why? We haven't even..."

"You'll see," Marc said as he walked away.

"I'd like this on the record, if you don't mind, your Honor," Marc said when they were seated in front of him. A court reporter was set up in the room and ready to go.

"No problem," Connelly said. The judge read the case name and court file into the record then told Marc to say whatever was on his mind.

"I'm making a formal statement, a warning to Mr. Lacey. His complainant, Natalie Flanders, is lying and I'm going to prove it. If they go through with this prosecution, she will have to get on a witness stand and commit perjury if she tells the same lies she has told so far. If she does, and I believe she will, a solid case of subornation of perjury can be made against Mr. Lacey."

"That's outrageous! How dare you..."

Connelly held up a hand to stop him, and Marc continued.

"You've now been notified," he said, looking at Lacey. "I realize prosecutors, even the Attorney General's office, believe they have no obligation to make sure their witnesses are telling the truth. I had a case with the AG's office, and one of her lawyers literally told me that.

"Anyway, I believe you do have an obligation to investigate your case and make sure, to the best of your ability, that you are not involved, even inadvertently, with perpetrating a fraud on the court. Willful blindness should not be a defense," Marc concluded.

"You know, I think he has a point," Connelly said.

"Your Honor, this is absurd. How am I supposed to...""?

"Strap her onto a polygraph," Marc said. "You'd sure as hell do it to a defense witness if you could."

"Your Honor!" Lacey almost screamed.

"Calm down, Mr. Lacey. Do your job the way you see fit. I can't tell you how to do it," Judge Connelly said.

"You've been warned," Marc said. "I'll see you at a prelim to set a trial date."

Marc stood up, looked at Connelly and said, "Your Honor, nice to see you again."

When Marc went back into the courtroom, Lacey did not follow him. Instead, he walked up and down in the back hall to calm down.

"We're done," Marc told Grace Blaine. "But I'd like a word with you before we leave."

Outside the courtroom, Marc stood with Hal silently watching an angry Natalie stomp off. He then told Hal what happened in chambers.

"You threatened him?" Hal asked with a laugh.

"Now I'm gonna have a little chat with her lawyer. I'll stay in touch and let you know if I hear anything."

"What's next?"

"A trial date. Edsel's pretty pissed. We'll see what happens. I gotta go talk to Grace. I'll see you later."

"What happened?" Grace asked Marc.

"I told him we weren't going to plead to anything. No deals."

"You're really going to take this to trial? They have the cops and photos of her injuries," Grace said.

"Grace, your client's lying. There are serious holes in her story. I'm going to shred her on cross if we go. You may want to have a little chat with her."

Grace's eyebrows shot up, and she said, "You're getting pretty close to witness tampering."

"Oh, I am not," Marc said, waving a dismissive hand. "I'm talking to her lawyer. Just thought I'd warn you."

Grace sat still for a minute, they were on a bench in the hall, thinking over what he said. "Between us, I suppose I have an obligation to pass this along, but it's not my problem. Edsel Lacey represents her in this business, not me."

"We still okay on the divorce settlement?" Marc asked.

"She wanted to cut your guys balls off, but I calmed her down. The settlement is okay."

"Why is it women always want to mutilate significant body parts?"

"Because you guys ask for it," Grace laughed.

TWENTY

Natalie Flanders inhaled a long drag of the marijuana cigarette and then handed it to her boy toy lover. They were in his bed at his South Minneapolis apartment coming down from their sexathon, a word he had made up. The bedroom was a bit stuffy and reeking of sex and weed. Kent had a fan in a window pointing out to remove the marijuana smell but not very effectively.

Natalie, at forty-eight, smiled once again at God's little joke; giving men a sex drive peak of eighteen years old and women at forty. At forty-eight, Natalie had peaked a little late. Fortunately, her featherhead personal trainer lying next to her was very accommodating and had the stamina of a male gorilla.

"I have to go," Natalie said, looking at the bedside clock which read 12:10. "I have an early meeting," she lied. Spending the night with Kent was more than she could bear. The few times she had done so had caused her almost to run screaming from the apartment. The dolt was good looking and had a great body but was not someone she wanted to wake up with. In the morning, she would have to try to converse with him. Almost impossible.

"Do what you gotta do," Kent replied.

Natalie, naked, climbed out of bed, gathered up her clothes and went into the bathroom. While she was in there, Kent again found himself thinking—if what went on between his ears could be called thinking—*How am I gonna get out of this? At least she doesn't want to sleep here.*

A couple of minutes later he heard, "I'll call," as he saw Natalie leaning against the bedroom door frame.

Kent looked her over and again was impressed at what she did to a tight pair of jeans. At the ripe old age of twenty-four, he had trouble coming to grips with a woman his mother's age looking this good.

"Yeah, do that, soon," he replied.

Kent's apartment building was one of a four-building complex. There were four rows of open parking spaces close to the buildings. Then there were two rows of single-car garages. Behind them were two more rows of open parking spaces. Natalie always parked in back behind the garages. She did not trust her husband not to have her followed. Parking in back would make it harder to find her car and figure out which apartment she was in, or so she thought.

105

There were very few cars and little light in the back part of the lot. She hit her key fob when she was about ten feet from the car. It unlocked, and the interior lights came on.

She never saw it coming; never knew what happened. One second she was reaching for the door handle of her car, the next second, she was face down on the asphalt. Natalie Flanders never even heard the shot or felt the bullet. One shot, one sharp, loud, bark of the pistol. The bullet hit her in the brain stem, went into her brain and it was lights out.

Her shooter had stalked Natalie for over a week. Three nights ago, followed her to this exact location and then decided this was the spot. This was where Natalie Flanders would be so deservedly taken.

Kneeling down, the shooter took a small, penlight-type flashlight from the windbreaker's pocket. After finding the spent cartridge, removed Natalie's phone from her purse. All her cash and her watch were also removed from her wallet. There was a horizontal board privacy fence at the property line; the shooter was over it in two quick steps and gone. The phone and watch would go down a sewer a block away. The two-hundred-forty-dollars from her billfold would be kept. Cash being tangible.

Lt. Owen Jefferson parked his department-issued Chevy Impala behind the apartment complex's rows of garages. Jefferson got out of the car and casually strolled the hundred feet to the crime scene. As he passed under the yellow tape, a female detective started walking toward him.

"And what brings you out on this crisp, autumn morning, boss?" Marcie Sterling asked.

"I didn't have much going on this morning," Jefferson replied. "Gives me an excuse to get out of the office. What do we have?"

Marcie opened her case notebook and started to recite for him. The body had been found a little before seven by one of the tenants, a man who was patiently waiting. Marcie pointed him out to the lieutenant.

"Natalie Flanders," Marcie said. "White female, age forty-eight. Looks like a single GSW to the back of the head."

"Professional?" Jefferson asked.

"Well, at this point, looks like a robbery, although I'm a little skeptical. No cash in her wallet. Her phone is missing, and there is a fading tan line where a watch would be. No ring and no tan line for one."

"But?" Jefferson said.

"But, I'm not so sure. A robber hanging around back here after midnight. He just happens to catch a victim to rob in the bank of this parking lot? More likely it was made to look like a robbery."

"She lives here?"

"No," Marcie replied and read Natalie's Burnsville address to Jefferson. "We're canvassing for whoever she was visiting."

By now, the two of them were behind Natalie's car watching the medical examiner look over the body.

"Hey Nick, get your hand off that woman's ass," Jefferson said to the M.E., Nick Pham, a Vietnamese pathologist with Hennepin County.

"Gotta get it where you can, Owen," Pham answered back.

"You guys are disgusting," Marcie said to both.

Dr. Pham stood up and joined them.

Owen asked, "What do you have?"

"Looks like a single GSW to the spinal column and into the brain. She probably never felt a thing. Time of death between midnight and two. It was a little cool last night so that's about as close as I can get at this point..."

"Oh, my God! That's Natalie," they heard a man's voice say.

The three of them looked and saw a well-built, young man dressed as if he had just gotten out of bed. He was with Marcie's partner, Detective Gabe Anderson, and a uniformed officer.

Natalie was still lying face down, but Kent Stone recognized her anyway. Gabe Anderson told the uniform to take him away but keep an eye on him. Gabe joined Jefferson, Marcie and the M.E.

"Who's he?" Marcie asked Gabe.

"The boyfriend," Gabe said.

"Boyfriend?" Marcie asked a little disapprovingly. "He's barely old enough to vote." She was the senior of the two detectives and would take the lead in the case.

"Anyway," Gabe said, ignoring Marcie, "he says she left his place around 12:15 or so. No later than 12:20."

"There's your T.O.D.," Pham said.

"It's the husband goddamnit," they heard Kent yell. "He's an asshole. It's him."

"Great, there's a husband involved in this," Marcie quietly said. "Let's go, Gabe."

"I'll get him in the car," Gabe replied.

Marcie turned to Owen and asked, "You want to do me a favor? Call the Dakota County Sheriff and get a search warrant for her house in Burnsville."

"Sure, you go downtown and find out what this guy has to say," Owen said.

"He's a suspect," Marcie said.

"You really think he screwed her then sneaked down here after her and shot her in the back of the head?" Dr. Pham asked.

"Thanks for pointing out the likely absurdity, Sherlock Pham," Marcie said. "I'll keep it in mind."

"Just giving you the benefit of my years of wisdom," Pham said.

"You're younger than I am," Marcie replied.

"Look at this," Gabe Anderson said to Marcie. They were in the home of Natalie Flanders conducting a search for evidence. It was the afternoon of the same day of her murder. Anderson had been in the den. He was walking toward Marcie while holding up several documents. Marcie was in the dining room supervising the search.

"What?" Marcie asked.

"Husband's name is Harold Flanders. They're going through—or have recently gone through—a divorce. Here's a recent restraining order against the husband."

"Let me see it," Marcie said.

Gabe handed it to her, and she quickly skimmed through the factual part. This was where the judge writes out the facts to back up the issuance of the restraining order.

When Marcie finished, she looked at Gabe and said, "Looks like a suspect. We need to find out where he works and lives…"

"It's right here, in the divorce papers," Gabe said. "He works at Ericsson Manufacturing in Excelsior."

"Got an address?" Marcie asked then noticed Owen Jefferson enter the house.

Gabe wrote down the address as Jefferson joined them.

"What did you find?" he asked.

"An acrimonious divorce," Marcie said. "We're gonna drive out to Excelsior and tell the husband."

Gabe told Jefferson where Hal worked, then Jefferson asked about the victim's employment.

"She works for Lake Country Federal," Gabe said, reading it off the divorce papers.

"Where?" Jefferson asked.

"Lake Country…"

"Federal," Jefferson said. He looked at Marcie and asked, "Is that a coincidence?"

Marcie shrugged and answered. "Probably, but we better check it out."

"What?" Gabe asked.

"The bank robberies," Marcie said. "Most of them are Lake Country branches."

"Yeah, well, my money is on the husband," Gabe said.

"Ah, ah," Jefferson said, wagging a finger at him. "Keep an open mind, detective."

"Sure, I will," Gabe said. "You know," he continued as he started flipping through the divorce papers. "We can see who his lawyer is…"

"Stop! Don't look. We don't need to know," Marcie said as she snatched the document away from her partner. "Leave it alone. These guys can finish up here. Let's go."

"Are there any messages on her phone?" Jefferson asked.

"Not on the phone here in the house," Marcie said. "The shooter took her cell, we think."

"You mind if I tag along?" Jefferson asked.

"Yes, but you will anyway," Marcie said with a smile. Owen Jefferson was her first partner when she became a detective. They had been good friends ever since.

"True, I was only asking to be polite," Jefferson replied.

On the drive out to Excelsior, a suburb west of Minneapolis, Gabe looked over the divorce papers. Everything except the pages where the lawyers' names were written.

"Oh, will you look at this?" he whispered to himself.

Marcie, who was driving trying to keep up with Jefferson, said, "What?"

"This is a list of personal property they each get," Gabe said. He looked at Marcie and added, "There's a nine-millimeter handgun on the list. It's listed in his name, but she gets it."

"Call the house and see if they found it," Marcie said.

A minute later, Gabe ended the call and told her, "No gun. They'll keep looking."

TWENTY-ONE

Marcie showed her shield to the receptionist at Ericsson Manufacturing. Jefferson had wandered off to look at photos of machine tools in the reception area. Gabe Anderson stood behind Marcie with a grave face in place. A cop's face.

"We're here to see Harold Flanders," Marcie politely said.

"Um, let me, ah, call back and tell him…" the woman nervously said.

"No, don't do that," Marcie said. "We just have some news for him. So, we'll go back. Does he have an office?"

"Yes," the receptionist replied, obviously relieved that they were not there to arrest him. She gave Marcie directions and the three of them went up a flight of stairs to the second floor. They found Flanders' office, knocked, and went in when he answered.

Marcie showed him her shield and introduced the three of them.

Flanders was standing at a design desk working on a drawing. Annoyed, he tossed his pencil on the drawing board and sat down at his office desk.

"What does that lying bitch claim I did now?" Flanders asked.

"I'm sorry?" Marcie said, a puzzled look on her face. "What lying bitch are you referring to?"

"My soon-to-be ex-wife, Natalie. What is she accusing me of now?"

"May I sit?" Jefferson asked.

"Sure."

Jefferson and Marcie took the two chairs in front of Flanders' desk. Gabe Anderson sat down on the stool next to the drafting table.

"I'm afraid we have bad news," Jefferson said. "Your wife, Natalie, was found dead this morning. I'm very sorry."

Flanders sat still for a full ten seconds while the news hit home.

"What? I mean, how, what are you talking about? How did she die? Oh shit, I've gotta tell the kids. What happened?"

"She was murdered," Marcie said, leaving out the part that it may have been a robbery, which none of the cops believed anyway.

"Where was she found?" Flanders sat up and sharply asked.

"In the parking lot of an apartment…" Marcie started to say.

"Where a guy by the name of Kent Stone lives?"

"Yes, how did you…"

"I knew she was banging that guy, that kid. The lying, cheating bitch," Flanders said.

"I think it's time we continued this discussion downtown," Jefferson said.

"I'm not going anywhere with you people," a now visibly angry Hal Flanders said.

"Where were you last night shortly after midnight?" Marcie asked.

"At home in bed," Flanders answered.

"Alone?"

Flanders realized she was looking for an alibi that he did not have. "Yeah, alone," he softly said. "I'm still not going…"

"Yes, you are," Marcie said, pulling out a set of handcuffs as she stood up. "We can do this easy or hard. We don't want to embarrass you at work, but we will if we have to."

"Can I call my lawyer first?" Flanders asked almost pleading.

"Sure, go ahead," Marcie said.

He had called Marc's office enough times to have him on the speed dial of his personal phone. He dialed, and a familiar female voice answered.

"Um, Carolyn, it's Hal Flanders," he nervously said. "I need Marc right away." When Jefferson heard him use the names Carolyn and Marc, a bell went off in his head. Before he said anything, Flanders' call was answered.

"The cops are here in my office," he blurted out. "Natalie was murdered at her boyfriend's apartment last night. They think I did it and they want to take me in for questioning."

"Keep your mouth shut," Marc said. "Who's the senior cop? Let me talk to whoever that is."

"Ah, here," Flanders said and handed the phone to Jefferson.

"Mr. Kadella, it's Owen Jefferson, sir. What can I do for you?"

"Hey, Owen. How've you been? Listen, are you taking him in?"

"Yes, we are," Jefferson replied.

"Okay. You're on record notified he's represented. No questions, no nothing until I get there. Are you taking him to the City Hall building?"

"Yes, we should be there in about thirty minutes."

"Okay, I'll see you then. Let me talk to him."

Jefferson handed the phone back to Flanders, who heard Marc say, "Keep your mouth shut. I told Lieutenant Jefferson they are not to question you."

"I have to go with them?" Flanders asked.

"Yes. I'll meet you there."

Marc shook hands with Jefferson, Marcie and Gabe Anderson in the hall outside the interrogation room. Marc could see a very distraught

Hal Flanders inside through the window in the interrogation room door. Hal was sitting by himself at a table with six cheap, government-issued chairs around it. While he waited, he glanced up at the wall clock every few seconds.

"What can you tell me about Natalie Flanders?" Marc asked Marcie.

She looked at Jefferson who simply shrugged, nodded and said, "Go ahead, tell him. He'll find out anyway if we charge the husband."

"All we know, so far, is she was shot in the back of the head and was probably dead by the time she hit the ground. By the boyfriend's statement, between 12:15 and 12:30 last night in the parking lot of his apartment. Your client admitted he knew the wife was seeing this guy and he has no alibi."

"What's the boyfriend's name?"

Marcie checked her notes then said, "Kent Stone, age 24..."

"How old?" Marc asked.

Marcie smiled and continued by giving Marc Kent's address.

Marc looked at Jefferson and said, "Twenty-four? We're too old for women pushing fifty. When did this happen?"

"I'm staying married," Jefferson said. "And you should kiss Maddy's toes every day. You're the luckiest dog I know."

"I gotta buy her a new car or something," Marc said as he started to open the door. "Give me a few minutes with him."

"Am I glad to see you!" Flanders said. "I'm sick about this. I mean, yeah, things were pretty bad, but she's the mother of my kids. I didn't want this," he quickly blurted out with an almost pleading look on his face.

"Sit down, Hal," Marc said. He sat next to Flanders and removed a tablet of paper to make notes on.

"I didn't say anything, I swear, Marc," Flanders said.

"That's not quite true," Marc replied. "They know you have no alibi and they know you knew about the boyfriend. What else?"

"Oh, shit," Hal muttered. "I think I gave them the impression I knew where he lived."

"Perfect," Marc said. "Well," he continued, looking up at the wall past Flanders while saying, "this is gonna be a short interview. You're already suspect number one, and until I am convinced there's nothing more you can say to help them, you're not talking."

While Marc was in the room with Hal Flanders, Marcie took a phone call.

"You're sure? You've gone through the place and didn't find it?"

"No," the caller said. "I even had one of my guys go to the impound lot and search her car. No gun."

"We'll see about getting a search warrant for his place," Marcie said. "I'll get back to you."

Jefferson was already on his phone calling the county attorney's office. It was almost 6:00 P.M., but there were always a few lawyers working late. He got one he knew and quickly gave him the factual basis for the warrant. From the divorce papers, they had the address for Hal's townhouse in Minnetonka, Hennepin County. He had moved to be much closer to work.

"Let's go in," Jefferson said when he finished the call.

When the three police officers were seated, Marc asked, "How did you find out where he worked?"

"We're the cops," Marcie said. "We know everything."

"Bullshit," Marc said. "You searched the house and found the divorce papers. We're leaving," he added, standing up.

Marcie removed a document from a file she was carrying and slid it across the table toward Flanders.

"Explain this," she said.

Marc glanced at it and immediately knew what it was; the restraining order.

"Marcie, he doesn't have to explain anything," Marc said.

"Hey, I can explain it," Hal nervously said.

Marc sat down again, looked at Flanders and seriously said, "No, I told you, these people are not your friends. If you talk to them, they are not going to say, 'Sorry to have bothered you,' and let it go."

"He's not leaving, Marc," Jefferson said.

"And why not?"

"We can hold him and..."

"You're getting a search warrant for his house," Marc said. "Why? What are you looking for?"

"Firearms," Jefferson said. "Specifically, a nine-millimeter, semi-auto Browning. It's listed on the divorce papers as personal property..."

"That's Natalie's gun..." Hal said which drew a 'shut your mouth' look from Marc.

"It's registered to you," Gabe said. "I checked, it's your gun."

"Can I explain?" Hal asked Marc.

"Come here," Marc said, gesturing toward a corner in the room.

"I bought it for her, I don't know, four or five years ago," Hal whispered. "She was working late, or so she said, and I thought she should have some protection. I think she was screwing one of the guys who she worked with. Anyway, she kept it in her car, in the glove

113

compartment. I haven't seen it since I gave it to her. If they want to search my place for it, let them, I don't have it."

"You're sure?" Marc asked.

"Yeah, I'm sure. I have my guns, two shotguns, two rifles and a Colt forty-four, but no nine-millimeter."

"Okay," Marc said.

Knowing they were going to get a search warrant no matter what, they went back to the table and Marc told Marcie, "You have his permission to search his townhouse for a nine-millimeter, semi-automatic, Browning handgun."

Marc looked at Gabe and said, "I assume you have the serial number."

"The search warrant will read search for firearms," Jefferson said.

"He has two shotguns, two hunting rifles and a Colt forty-four. Do you have medical or forensic evidence she was shot with one of those?"

"No," Marcie admitted. She looked at Jefferson who added, "Okay we'll restrict the search to nine-millimeter, semi-auto handguns. Nothing more specific than that."

"Let's go," Marc said.

By nine o'clock that evening, the search team had gone over every inch of Hal's townhouse. No nine-millimeter was found. Both Marc and Hal Flanders were on site while they searched.

As they were leaving, Gabe Anderson received a sharp lesson about why cops hate lawyers.

"Make sure your client stays in the jurisdiction," he told Marc while poking a finger at him with his best tough guy cop look. Marc noticed both Marcie and Owen Jefferson cringe before replying.

"Really?" Marc said with a flat, bored, inflection. "Do you have some judicial order giving you some power to restrict my client's right to move about the country? Has the Constitution been amended recently, and I missed it? That might work on TV, but show me the court order, Detective Anderson."

"Hey, he's a suspect in a..."

"Then arrest him and we'll set bail. Oh, by the way, a judge does that, not you."

A red-faced Gabe Anderson stomped out the door. Marc looked at Marcie and said, "If you need to talk to my client, give me a call."

He handed her his card, and she said, "Will do.

TWENTY-TWO

Maddy Rivers was getting tired, hungry and crabby. She had been wandering around the Humanities and Liberal Arts buildings at the University of Minnesota for most of the day. Maddy was carrying copies of the artist's sketch of the Waseca gun buyer named Luke. She showed it to students, hoping someone would recognize him.

Most of the guys hung around her 'checking out the picture' a lot longer than necessary. So far, no luck identifying him.

"Hey kid, how's it going," she heard Carvelli say coming up behind her.

"This is stupid and a waste of time. You know how big this campus is? I could be here until spring," Maddy snapped back at him.

"Hey, I tried calling, but your phone goes right to voice mail. You got it shut off," Carvelli said.

"Really? Shoot," Maddy said. "Why did you call?"

"I talked to Johnson. He agrees we should put this on TV and…"

"Now you tell me! Let's go. I need to get some food," Maddy snarled as she stomped off.

"Maybe you can call Gabriella," Carvelli said as he hurried to catch up with her.

Maddy turned on her heel, jabbed a finger into Carvelli's chest and firmly said, "I suggested that in the first place. You didn't want to. You thought it would elicit too many false leads. You thought it was a bad idea," she said, jabbing him once more with her finger.

"Sorry," Carvelli quietly said. "I was, ah, I was, um…."

"Wrong?" Maddy narrowed her eyes to tiny slits and leaned toward him.

"Um, yeah. I guess."

"Say it."

"Okay, I was wrong," he muttered,

"I didn't hear you."

"I was wrong. Okay? You happy now?"

"No, I want it in writing so I can post it on the internet for the whole planet to see.

"I'll call Gabriella. You're taking me somewhere nice and expensive to buy me lunch," Maddy said, then turned and walked off.

Gabriella Shriqui was a TV personality with Channel 8 News, the local Fox affiliate. She had worked her way up to where she now hosted her own afternoon show, *The Court Reporter*. She had also been in the right place at the right time to take over the show. The woman who had originated it was a brash, abrasive, arrogant type who had the misfortune to anger a serial killer. After her body was found, Gabriella took over. Gabriella also happened to be Maddy Rivers' best friend.

"Oh! You brought the Italian Stallion with you," Gabriella said, arms extended as she walked to Carvelli. They were in the lobby of the Channel 8 building.

"No, I brought Tony," Maddy replied. "What's this Italian Stallion business?"

"I thought you'd calm down once I got you fed," Carvelli said after hugging Gabriella.

Maddy poked him in the shoulder and said, "Not by a long shot, buster. You're still on my shit list."

Gabriella looked back and forth at them, then said, "What's going on? Did I get in the middle of something?"

"No, let's go back. We need a favor," Maddy replied, still snarling at Carvelli.

"I'll have to run this by Hunter," Gabriella said, referring to her boss, Hunter Osgood. Osgood was head of the news division. They were in Gabriella's office, and Maddy had given her a copy of the drawing of Luke Hanson and told her what they wanted.

Gabriella picked up her office phone, dialed an internal number and waited. Osgood answered, and she quickly explained why she called.

A few minutes later, Hunter Osgood knocked and entered Gabriella's office. He had met both Maddy and Carvelli on several prior occasions, so introductions were unnecessary.

"This is rare. Normally I get summoned to his office," Gabriella said, teasing her boss.

"Don't get used to it," he growled, shaking Maddy's hand. "Actually," he continued as he pulled up a chair and sat down, "I've been in that office all day. I needed to get up and walk around for a while. So," he said, looking at Carvelli, "what's up?"

Carvelli took a couple of minutes to explain what they wanted and why.

"The FBI is okay with you two poking around in an ongoing investigation?" Hunter asked.

"Sort of," Carvelli said. "We're working for the bank. That stays in this room along with our involvement," he added, looking at Gabriella.

"Let me see the drawing," Hunter said.

He looked it over then asked, "You think this guy is involved with this?"

"We don't know," Carvelli admitted. "It's a long shot…"

116

"But it feels right," Maddy said.

"Cop's intuition?" Hunter asked, smiling.

"Call it what you want, but it feels right," Maddy said again.

"And we've seen the videos from the robberies, and it looks like the kind of guns the gang is using. Nine-millimeter, semiautos," Carvelli said.

"Are you taking this to other stations or the papers?" Hunter asked.

"Not yet. If it's okay with you we thought we'd run it with you guys first and see what we get," Maddy answered.

"The Feebs want to see what kind of response we get," Carvelli added.

"He looks like everyone's twenty-something neighbor," Hunter remarked, referring to the drawing. "Pretty common looking."

"Yes, but we have a name: Luke," Gabriella said, reminding everyone.

"That should help if it's his real name," Hunter replied. "Go ahead, put it on the air," he said, handing the picture back to Gabriella. "Get copies to the news producers. I'll shoot them an email to run it at 5:00, 6:00 and 9:00."

Ben Sokol was relaxing in his new recliner admiring the two-thousand-dollar Brooks Brothers suit he had picked up that afternoon. Once again, he laughed to himself at buying such a petty bourgeoisie article of clothing. He had only dreamt of buying such an ostentatious suit, but with his little gang of revolutionaries bringing in bags of money, why not indulge himself? Of course, he had to be careful about where he would wear it.

Ben picked up the crystal brandy snifter with three inches of Courvoisier in it. He held it under his nose for a few seconds enjoying the fine aroma. Ben took a large swallow, smacked his lips and said out loud to himself, "It's nice to have money. I could get used to this."

Ben checked his watch, a new eighteen-hundred-dollar Movado, then turned on the TV. 9:00 P.M. and time for the news. Of late—ever since the robberies started—he had made a point of watching news shows. Especially local ones.

Ben settled back, took another sip of the Cognac while the show's intro was playing. The female anchor started off saying something about the robberies. This caught his attention, causing him to sit up a bit just as the sketch artist's picture of Luke Hanson appeared on the screen.

For the first few seconds, Ben was frozen with panic and fear. His hands were shaking so badly he was barely able to take another swallow of his drink before kicking down the chair's footrest. The fear eased enough for him to listen to the anchor. When she finished and switched to her male partner, the picture came down as they transitioned to another story.

Ben hit the mute button on the TV's remote. He wanted to keep an eye on the screen to see if Luke's picture came back while he tried to calm down and think. As he stared at the TV screen, he quickly downed the rest of the sweet, expensive brandy. He stood up, went to his cupboard and half-filled the glass. For the next several minutes, he paced in front of the TV while pouring down more Cognac and thinking.

At some point, he realized what he had to do. He was refilling his glass when his phone rang. Ben sat down again, picked up the phone from a side table and looked at the ID.

"I just got a call from Neil," Ben heard Sherry say when he answered the call. "He said he saw Luke's picture on Channel 8 News. What the hell..."

"I know," Ben calmly said. "Relax, I saw it too. I know what to do. I'll call him and we'll take care of it."

"Call who?" Sherry asked.

"Luke. You call Neil and everybody else. Tell them you talked to me and..."

"They're all out of town, doing, well, you know, business in Wisconsin," Sherry said, reminding Ben. They were all at Wisconsin casinos washing the proceeds of the Grand Forks job.

"I know," Ben said. "Relax. Call them anyway and explain what's going on. They probably haven't seen it. I'll call Luke. By this time tomorrow, you won't recognize him.

"Okay, okay," a much-relieved Sherry said. "That should work. You saw the picture?"

"Yes," Ben replied. "It was him, but it could be hundreds of guys his age. Don't worry about it."

"How did they...?"

"I don't know," Ben said. "The reporter didn't say. Just asked people to call the FBI if they knew him, said his name is Luke and put an eight hundred number on the screen. They'll get a ton of calls and will be chasing their tails for weeks. Okay?"

"Yeah, okay. I feel better already," Sherry said. "Hey, um, can I come over tonight?"

"Ah, I'd love that, but probably better cool it for a couple of days. I got an idea for a job. I'll check it myself and give you a call," Ben said.

"Shit," a disappointed Sherry said. "Okay, you know best."

Channel 8's newscasts were picked up by small stations throughout Minnesota, Eastern North and South Dakota and Western Wisconsin. Ben nailed it when he told Sherry the FBI would get a ton of calls. In fact, more than three hundred including a call each from Winnipeg and Thunder Bay, Canada. Jeff Johnson, Tess Richards and a dozen other FBI agents would spend the better part of two weeks running them all down.

A few days after Sherry Toomey's call to Ben following the viewing of Luke's picture, the group got together. The cash from the Grand Forks job was safely sitting in an internet account in Bitcoin and other cryptocurrencies. In a few days, it would be withdrawn in small amounts into several bank accounts only Ben knew about.

The meeting took place in Ben's basement. When everyone but Luke was present and seated at the table, Ben opened the utility room door. A man walked out, and the other five looked at him with perplexed expressions.

Luke Hanson's hair was gone, replaced by a shaved, completely bald head. He had a very good start on a mustache and goatee, was wearing rose-tinted, gold-rimmed glasses with a small diamond earring in his right ear. He looked nothing like the sketch shown on TV.

Luke stood at the head of the table and after ten seconds or so, asked, "So, what do you think? Like the look?"

"Yeah, I do," Cindy quickly blurted out. "It's hot in a cool, bad boy way."

"Cool," Luke said. "When we do a job, I take off the glasses and take out the earring. The glasses are plain glass anyway."

"Wow, do you look different, dude," Neil said.

"Okay, let's get the meeting started," Ben said.

Two hours later, Neil and Gary were walking together back to their cars.

"I think Ben's spending money on personal shit," Neil said.

"Naw, I doubt it," Gary replied.

"Yeah, he is," Neil insisted. "And I know for a fact him and Sherry are sleeping together."

"How do you know that?" Gary asked.

"Ah, I'm not saying," Neil said. "I just know it's true. I'm not sure I care about that. I know Luke was hot for Sherry, and ever since they came back from Madison, Luke's been pretty cool toward her."

"She's a little 'out there' for me," Gary said, making air quotes with his fingers. "Know what I mean?"

"Oh, yeah," Neil replied. "I bet she's wild in the sack, though. I'm pissed about the money. We're trying to do something to save the planet and Ben's using the money for personal shit. And, I'll bet Sherry's getting some too. That ain't right. Ain't fair. I want mine, too."

"What are you gonna do?" Gary asked. They were stopped next to Neil's Toyota.

"I don't know yet. Let me think about it."

TWENTY-THREE

"Sorry to keep everyone waiting," Steve Gondeck said to the small group. Steve Gondeck was the head of the Felony Division of the Hennepin County Attorney's office. He was entering a conference room at the county attorney's offices to discuss a homicide case. In the room were Owen Jefferson, Marcie Sterling and Gabe Anderson from the MPD. Also in attendance were the two prosecutors assigned to the case. The first chair was Jerry Krain, a/k/a the Nazi. The second chair and furious about it, was Jennifer Moore.

It had been almost two weeks since the murder of Natalie Flanders. In that time the investigating detectives had put together, they believed, a solid circumstantial case.

Gondeck sat down at the conference room table across from Jefferson. He had a leather folio with a legal pad in it that he would use to take notes.

"Okay, what do you have?" he asked Jefferson.

"Marcie," Jefferson said.

"First of all," Marcie began, "this is the only case Gabe and I have. We've turned over every rock, talked to everyone who knew the victim and/or the husband. Even the husband's friends admitted he was a hothead asshole. He was furious about the wife's infidelity or infidelities.

"The murder weapon was a nine-millimeter. State records show he purchased one a few years ago which is now missing. He claims it was for his wife and she kept it in her car. We have not been able to find anyone who can verify that.

"Our techs have recovered voice mail recordings from her home phone—her cell is missing—of the husband threatening her."

"To kill her?" Gondeck asked.

"Not specifically, no. But things like 'You fucking, cheating bitch. I'm gonna get you yet. I'm gonna make you pay. You're gonna regret this.' A lot of stuff like that."

"Are you sure it's him?"

"Yeah, he left his name on a couple of them, and the techs ran voice analysis. They're all from the same guy," Marcie answered.

"Then there's the restraining order where he physically assaulted her," Marcie said in conclusion. "And we have him admitting to us he knew the boyfriend and had no alibi for the time of the murder. And, we have been over every aspect of their lives and can find no one with a motive or link to any evidence."

"What about the boyfriend?" Gondeck asked.

"Too stupid and no motive. He had nothing to gain. Plus, he has a romp between the sheets with her and follows her out to her car and pops her? I don't see it."

"Jerry?" Gondeck asked, looking at the lawyer who had taken the chair at the head of the table.

"It's enough for an arrest warrant for second degree. We can then put it to the grand jury. I'm positive I can get a couple counts of first degree. Premeditated lying in wait and domestic abuse," Krain replied.

"Doesn't domestic abuse murder need to be done while committing domestic abuse and causing death with a history of domestic abuse?" Jennifer Moore asked.

"I'll convince them that shooting his wife in the back of the head is committing an act of domestic abuse," Krain condescendingly replied.

Jennifer glanced at Gondeck who, almost imperceptibly shook his head at her to stop her. He then said to Krain, "Okay, Jerry. Write it up and get an arrest warrant."

Gondeck looked at Marcie and asked, "When are you going to serve it?"

"Tomorrow morning at six o'clock," Krain quickly said.

"Is that necessary?" Jennifer asked.

"No, but it sure is fun. And it lets the scumbag know who's in charge," Krain said.

"Steve," Jennifer said to Gondeck, "his lawyer is Marc Kadella. We can call…"

"All the more reason to roast his ass first thing in the morning," Krain said.

"If you're going to make this a personal thing between you and Kadella, I'll give it to someone else right now," Gondeck told Krain.

"No, that's not it. You know the drill, Steve. If we rattle his cage first thing in the morning, he may say some things we can use."

"All right," Gondeck said. "It's your case. I'll let you guys figure it out."

With the meeting over, as everyone filed out of the conference room, Steve Gondeck walked as fast as he could toward his office. Jennifer Moore had to half-run, half-walk to try to catch up with him.

"Steve," she almost yelled at him, "I want to talk to you."

"No! I don't have time," he yelled back.

He was at his office door when he said this. Turning the doorknob to go in, he heard Jennifer say, "Good, we'll use your office."

Gondeck tried to close his door, but she pushed her way through.

"Doesn't anybody in this office understand the word 'no' anymore?" he asked as she closed the door behind her.

"Shut up," she said. "We need to talk. You've been avoiding me…"

"Yes, I have! Take the hint," Gondeck replied as he sat down behind his desk. "I know what you want, and the answer is no."

Jennifer sat down in front of his desk, leaned forward and placed her forearms on the top of it.

"What did I do to you to make you want to punish me like this?" she asked with her best sad, hurt, little girl look.

"Don't look at me like that; it won't work. I want you on this case to try to rein him in," Gondeck said, referring to Jerry Krain. "You know Marc, I know Marc. He will get under Krain's skin and have fun doing it."

"Then you take it," Jennifer said.

"I can't. Seriously. I'm up to my ass in alligators now. I don't have time to…"

"Bullshit. You just don't want to risk losing to your pal again."

"Okay, there's that too. You and the Nazi can handle this just fine. Besides, Krain will get under Kadella's skin, too. It will be fun for you to watch them. Jennifer," he continued more softly, "I need you on this, and I'm not changing my mind."

"I'll go to Felicia," Jennifer said, threatening to go over Gondeck's head to his boss, Felicia Jones, the Hennepin County Attorney.

"An empty threat," Gondeck said with a smile. "She'll toss your ass out, and we both know it."

Jennifer sighed, sat back and gave him a serious look. "Okay, you win. But," she continued poking a finger at him, "you owe me big time."

"Deal. I owe you, and I'll regret saying that."

At 5:55 A.M. the next morning, Jerry Krain strolled up and down the street in front of Hal Flanders' townhouse. In two of the homes across the street, there were lights on, and the occupants opened their doors for a quick look at the mob in the street.

Krain acted as if he was directing a movie or leading the landing on Omaha beach. He was even dressed for the occasion. He wore hunting boots, camo cargo pants and shirt, and a duck hunter's vest. Arrayed around him were a dozen members of the MPD SWAT team in full battle gear. There were four sheriff's deputies and the Hennepin County Sheriff herself. And to be sure the invasion of the Flanders' townhouse would be preserved for history, Krain had a camera crew from the local NBC affiliate on hand.

Also in attendance was a seriously furious and thoroughly embarrassed Marcie Sterling with her partner, Gabe Anderson. Marcie was three houses down, leaning on her car trying to keep calm and wondering if she should call Owen Jefferson. Deciding he could do nothing about this fiasco, she opted to wait.

At precisely six o'clock, Krain took up his position in the middle of the street in front of Hal's home. Trying for his best George Patton stance, he checked his watch then blew a whistle to get the action started.

Two SWAT members, AR15s at the ready, started pounding on Hal's front door. The camera crew's lights came on, and the other cops took their assigned positions, guns drawn ready for combat.

"Are we gonna go down there?" Gabe asked Marcie.

Marcie gave him a look that almost made his knees buckle. While the pounding on the door continued, she continued to glare at him for several seconds. Finally, she exhaled and said, "Sorry. I guess we better. I have the arrest warrant. Unless the Nazi brought another one."

"He has the search warrant," Gabe said as they walked toward the townhouse.

By now there were lights coming on in quite a few of the homes and more people looking outside. When Marcie and Gabe reached Krain, she looked at him standing in the street, feet apart, fists on hips, a stupidly serious look on his face. Seeing this, Marcie lost it.

"Are you out of your goddamn mind?" she yelled, intentionally loud enough for the news crew to pick it up. "What the hell's the matter with you? Who do you think this guy is, John Dillinger?"

"He has guns in the house," Krain yelled back.

Marcie shook her head, turned and walked toward the front door.

"Hopefully, you're the first one that gets shot you asshole," she whispered. At that moment, Hal's front door light came on and he opened the door. Before he realized what was happening, the SWAT guys had him face down on the walk-in front of his house.

By now, four more SWAT members were with them all pointing their AR15s at him. One of them knelt on top of Hal, cuffed him and frisked him.

All the while Hal kept repeating, "What did I do? What are you doing?"

Marcie and Gabe had hustled up to join them and to stop them from getting too carried away. The man who had cuffed and frisked him stood up and announced, "He's clean."

"No kidding," Marcie said. "He's wearing a t-shirt and boxers. Where did you expect him to hide a gun?"

"Come on, Mr. Flanders," Gabe said, helping the terrified man to his feet.

"Harold Flanders," Marcie formally said. "You're under arrest for the murder of Natalie Flanders. You have the right to remain silent, anything…"

While Marcie finished reciting the Miranda warning, Flanders' only comment was to say, quite loudly, that he wanted to call his lawyer.

"Take these off of him," Marcie said to the SWAT guy, referring to the handcuffs.

"Not a chance," she heard Krain say from behind her.

"Yeah, it's safe now. You can come up," Marcie said for the cameraman and reporter who had followed Krain. "Get them out of here," Marcie said, looking at the other SWAT guys referring to the news people.

While the SWAT people hustled the reporters away, Marcie lit up Krain some more.

"This is my arrest, and we'll do it the way I say. You got it? I said take the cuffs off now. The man needs to get dressed."

While the cuffs were being taken off, Marcie told Flanders about the search warrant. Since Flanders did not live in Minneapolis, the Hennepin County Sherriff's deputies would have to be on hand for the search.

Marcie looked at Krain and said, "If your tiny, little head is going to explode, go do it somewhere else.

"Gabe, you and the officer take Mr. Flanders upstairs and let him get dressed. Then we'll take him downtown."

"I want to call my lawyer," Hal repeated for at least the tenth time.

"When we get downtown," Marcie assured him.

While Gabe and the SWAT cop led Flanders inside, an apoplectic Jerry Krain snarled, "I'll have your ass for this, little girl. I'll…"

"Yeah, yeah, yeah," she replied, waving a hand as if chasing off an annoying fly. And then she did something she would brag about for years and would make her an MPD legend. She quickly stepped up to get in Krain's face, reached between his legs and grabbed him by the testicles.

"And if you ever call me 'little girl' again, I'll turn you into a eunuch." She squeezed a little harder, Krain's pained expression worsened, and she said, "Do we understand each other?"

"Yes," he croaked.

Marcie, a smug, satisfied look on her face, let go of him and walked away. As she did so, Krain dropped to one knee and choked down vomit from the pain.

TWENTY-FOUR

A furious Marc Kadella burst into the interrogation room, slammed the door and went right to a seated Jerry Krain.

"Are you out of your goddamn mind?" Marc practically screamed, his face less than a foot from Krain.

Marc continued to glare at him, and it took several seconds for a very startled Jerry Krain to gather himself. When he did, his natural arrogance kicked in.

"I don't have to account to you or any other scumbag, defense lawyer," Krain said.

While Marc continued to stare, Krain looked at the cops in the room, Owen Jefferson, Marcie Sterling and Gabe Anderson. "Get him out of my face," Krain squealed, his hands shaking and forehead perspiring.

The three cops looked on impassively for another four or five seconds until finally, Jefferson quietly said, "Marc, it's over. He's not worth it."

Marc stood up straight, placed his leather satchel case on the table and then sat down as far away from Krain as he could get.

"Lieutenant, I would've thought better of you," Marc said.

"I had no idea what he was up to," Jefferson quietly said. "But," he continued leaning on the table and looking at Marc, "of all the defense lawyers, I probably respect you the most."

"Huh," Krain snorted.

"…and I like you personally. But we don't make decisions on arrests by what defense lawyers want. Mr. Krain overreacted, a little."

"A little?" Marc asked.

"But your client does have guns in the house."

"That's weak, Owen. This is Minnesota. Almost everyone has guns in their homes," Marc said.

"It's over and done with, Marc. Let's move on."

"It's not over and done with, Owen. Channel 6 is gonna run that film all day. They've already called me."

Marc looked at Krain and said, "When I leave here, I'm going right to their studios and I'm going to rip you to shreds."

"I'll sue you…"

"Please, that's empty nonsense and you know it. I can't imagine Steve Gondeck and Felicia Jones are gonna be very happy with you. Are you running for County Attorney next year? Look in the mirror. This is Hennepin County. You're a white man and a Nazi. Forget it."

Marc stood up to leave, then said, "I'll be back at one o'clock this afternoon for the arraignment. You might want to let Jennifer handle it."

Krain gave him a puzzled look to which Marc said, "Yeah, I know Jennifer Moore's been assigned to this case. I talked to your boss a few minutes ago. Like I said, Steve's none too pleased with you. By the time I'm done at Channel 6 and 8, you're gonna look like the asshole you are."

When Marc finished saying this, he looked at Krain as if seeing him for the first time. He stared for several seconds, then said, "What are you doing? You going duck hunting? Is this how he was dressed for the big arrest?" he asked looking at Marcie who was having trouble holding back a laugh.

Marc looked back at a red-faced Jerry Krain, shook his head and left.

Marc entered Judge Kyle's courtroom on the twelfth floor of the Hennepin County Government Center. It was a few minutes past 1:00, the start time for afternoon felony arraignments. The judge was already on the bench handling an in-custody defendant. Marc took a seat in the semi-crowded gallery and looked for either Jennifer Moore or Jerry Krain, neither of whom was present. Puzzled, Marc waited for the judge to finish with his current case.

"Mr. Kadella, nice of you to join us," Judge Kyle said when the defendant was being led away. "Come up, please."

Marc went through the gate and quickly went up to the bench. Judge Kyle leaned forward and covered the microphone with his hand.

"Your case has already been assigned, Marc," Kyle said. "It's with Judge McVein in 1458. They're probably waiting for you."

"Thanks, your Honor," Marc replied.

Instead of waiting for an elevator, Marc took the stairs the two floors up. When he made it, he again silently vowed to get back in the gym. A vow he knew would be difficult to keep.

Marc found 1458 and went into an empty courtroom except for Jennifer Moore patiently waiting.

"Hey, Jen," Marc said as he approached the bar.

Jennifer gave him her best displeased-mother-look and tapped her watch.

"Really? For the first time in your career, you've had to wait for a defense lawyer, and you're annoyed? Try it from our side. We're always waiting for prosecutors."

By now, Jennifer was laughing and managed to say, "Hi, Marc. Let's go see the judge."

"Do you know him?" Marc asked.

"Yeah, he's…" she paused and said, "okay." Then she stood up and whispered, "Just between us he's not the brightest bulb on the tree."

McVein's clerk led them in, and Marc walked right up to the judge, introduced himself and apologized for being late. "I was downstairs in Judge Kyle's courtroom."

"It's okay, have a seat," McVein said.

The judge was maybe forty years old and looked younger. He had been appointed two years ago, and this was Marc's first case with him.

"Your client's in a holding cell," McVein said. "I'll have my clerk tell the deputies to bring him in," he continued, looking at the woman waiting by his door.

"Do you need some time to talk to him?" McVein asked Marc.

"No, I saw him this morning. We went over everything."

"Should we do it in here?" McVein asked, looking at both lawyers.

Both nodded their approval before Marc said, "I'll go back out and come back with Mr. Flanders."

When Marc reached the courtroom, Hal Flanders was there. He was in an orange jumpsuit with his ankles shackled together and a waist manacle attached to each wrist.

"Take those off," Marc said to the two deputies.

"I don't think so…" one of them started to say.

"Now or I get the judge out here," Marc barked at the two men.

With an annoyed, lawyers-are-assholes look on their faces, they unlocked the hardware. While they did this, Marc spoke to Hal.

"We're gonna do it in chambers. It's the same thing, just a little more comfortable."

There were three chairs in front of the judge's desk. Marc took the one in the middle, Hal the one to his left, Moore to his right. The deputies took up places by the door.

McVein asked the court reporter if he was ready, then read the case name and court file number into the record. The lawyers noted their appearance and that the defendant was in attendance.

"We're here for the arraignment of the defendant, Harold Flanders, on the charge of second-degree homicide in the death of Natalie Flanders. Is that correct?"

Both lawyers responded affirmatively.

"Your Honor, the defense will waive reading the complaint. We are prepared to enter a plea."

"Very well," McVein said. "Harold Flanders, to the charge of murder in the second-degree, how do you plead?"

"Not, ah, not guilty," a nervous Hal Flounders managed to say.

"Bail, Ms. Moore?"

"Remand, your Honor," Jennifer replied. "We are presenting this case to a grand jury and expect multiple first-degree charges will be forthcoming."

"Your Honor, this is, at best, a weak circumstantial case. A no-bill from the grand jury is just as likely. Mr. Flanders has strong ties to the community, limited resources, and as an innocent man, has no reason to flee. He is not a danger to others. Has never...."

"I beg to differ," Jennifer said, interrupting.

"...been charged with a crime let alone convicted."

Judge McVein looked at Jennifer and said, "Ms. Moore."

"Your Honor, we have already found several witnesses who know the defendant and say he has a violent temper and..."

"No charges, no arrests, no convictions..." Marc interjected,

The two lawyers went back and forth at each other for another minute or so. McVein finally stopped them when he realized neither had anything new to offer.

"Bail will be set at five-hundred thousand dollars, cash or bond," he ordered. "We'll reserve any additional bail request until you hear back from the grand jury.

"Anything else?" he asked.

"Yes, your Honor. Mr. Flanders has access to assets he would like to use to pay a bondsman and use for his defense. Specifically, the homestead," Marc said.

"Any assets in the wife's name are frozen until the case has been adjudicated," Jennifer quickly said. "He cannot financially gain from a murder he committed."

"Except," Marc jumped in and said, "the house is in joint tenancy, and he has a sole interest in half the equity. He should be allowed to get at that for his defense. The pending divorce settlement specifically states the house was to be sold and the proceeds divided."

Marc had removed the written settlement agreement from his leather satchel and handed it to Judge McVein.

"Page three, your Honor. I've highlighted it," Marc said.

McVein read the appropriate paragraph then looked at the signature page.

"It's not signed, and it was never accepted by the court. Do you have case law on point?" McVein asked Marc.

"Well, not specifically but..."

"Not specifically means no. Sorry, he'll have to look to other assets. Does he have any?"

"Well, he has some retirement accounts solely in his name..."

"There you go, use those."

"It won't be enough, especially after taxes and penalties are taken into account."

"Sorry, Mr. Kadella. I'm not going to let him use any assets that have her name on them. That's final."

Before he left, Marc went into a conference room with Hal.

"What are my options?" Hal asked.

"Use your 401k or stay in jail," Marc said.

"Shit," Hal muttered. "Let me ask you, and no bullshit. What do you think of my case?"

"I don't know everything they have," Marc replied. "I was told they found some telephone recordings of you threatening her life. Is it true?"

"That was months ago. And I didn't know where the boyfriend lived. I told them I knew about him but…"

"They'll claim you followed her. We'll see. I think we can shoot down the restraining order. And, if what you say about the recordings is true…"

"It is, I swear it."

"…we can punch holes in that, too."

"How long before we go to trial if I stay in jail?"

"A couple months. Maybe a little longer. It usually works in the defense's interest to stall. But, the longer we give them, the more time they have to dig around and investigate."

"You think the grand jury will go for first-degree?"

"Yes, it looks like whoever did this was waiting for her. That's pretty obvious premeditation."

"Shit," Hal said again. "Should we push it?"

Marc thought about the question before answering. "It hurts us also in my preparation time. Plus, I won't be getting paid."

Hal started to say something, but Marc held up his hand to stop him

"I can take a lien against your house, your townhouse, your 401k, whatever you have. I'll get paid. Don't worry about it.

"I think going to trial as soon as possible wouldn't be a bad idea," Marc said.

"I agree!" Hal replied. "Plus, if they find me guilty, what's a couple of months waiting in jail for trial compared to what I'll get nailed with."

"That's optimistic," Marc said with a touch of sarcasm. "Okay, let's get started."

Both men stood up to leave, and Hal grabbed Marc's arm.

"Marc, I swear on my children, I didn't do this. I did not kill Natalie," he said pleading with him. "I had no reason to. The divorce was done."

"I know," Marc quietly said while patting his hand. "We can use that to show that motive is pretty weak."

TWENTY-FIVE

The Gulfstream's wheels hit the runway with a very light bump. Tony Breyer's pilots were well paid and earned their money.

From his luxurious, comfortable leather chair, Professor Webster Crosby, the radical left's social justice guru, looked out the plane's window. There was a light rain gently falling at the airport in downtown St. Paul. Crosby did not even notice the rain while he again thought about the reason for his visit.

Breyer's comely hostess came back to his seat while the jet rolled up to the terminal.

"How was the landing?" the pretty brunette politely asked. "Everything okay?"

"Just fine, Cheryl," Crosby answered.

"The pilot has confirmed your car is here and ready for you. It will only be a minute or two."

Crosby watched her walk away, a nice sight to watch for the sixty-year-old letch. At that moment, the plane was stopping, and Crosby saw his ride. He frowned at the Lincoln Town Car, much preferring a Cadillac limo. Crosby proclaimed himself to be a socialist but even socialists, at least those at the top, like to travel in style. Some people are, indeed, more equal than others.

Crosby was about to exit the plane when he paused to speak to the pilots.

"This shouldn't take more than a couple of hours," he said.

"Take your time, Professor," the captain replied. "Mr. Breyer made it clear. We're at your disposal."

"Great. I'll call if it's going to be longer," Crosby said.

"That will be fine, sir."

At the bottom of the stairs, the chauffeur was waiting with an umbrella. Top tier socialists must be protected from the rain, too. Especially by a member of the working class.

"Is it safe to talk in here?" Crosby asked Ben Sokol.

They were in Ben's office at the university about to deal with the purpose of Crosby's trip. Not wanting to give Ben any more warning than necessary, Crosby had called him yesterday to make an appointment with him.

"Yes, of course," Ben answered. Ben was behind his desk, wondering what Crosby wanted.

Crosby removed his two-thousand-dollar Burberry raincoat, a gift from Tom Breyer, and tossed it on a chair. He looked around at Ben's cluttered office—to Crosby the size of a broom closet— and remarked, "Plush digs."

"So, what do you want, Webster?" Ben asked.

Crosby could look out one of Ben's windows and see the Town Car waiting for him. He turned back to Ben, sat down in one of the chairs, the one without the coat on it, and picked up his briefcase. He placed it on Ben's desk, snapped the latches open and removed two documents.

"We received a copy of this from a media source," Crosby said, handing one of the documents across the desk. "Myself and several others of our political persuasion read it with a great deal of dismay. When I first read it, something in the back of my mind started to nag at me. There was something familiar about it," Crosby said.

Ben had scanned the document, immediately recognized it, then tossed it onto the desktop. While Crosby spoke, Ben leaned back in his chair, folded his hands across his stomach and listened with an indifferent expression.

"A couple of days later, it hit me. I thought I remembered where I had seen this before. So, I dug around for a while in my stored papers. It took a while, but I eventually found it." Crosby then handed the second document across the desk. Curiously, Ben leaned forward and took it. As soon as he saw the title, he knew what it was.

"Yes," Crosby said, seeing the recognition on Ben's face. "It's a paper written many years ago by a college student who proudly gave me a copy of it.

"The first one," Crosby continued, pointing at the document on Ben's desk, "is some half-assed radical manifesto that a gang of bank robbers is leaving at banks they've been robbing. You, of course, recognized it immediately. The second one is a paper that you wrote roughly thirty years ago."

"I had forgotten all about it," Ben replied.

"That's odd since it is almost a word-for-word statement of what is in the bank robbers' manifesto. Care to comment?"

"Sure. What possible business is it of yours?"

"What the hell has gotten into you? What have you been thinking about?" Crosby leaned forward and almost yelled.

Again, Ben leaned back, folded his hands across his stomach and slightly smiled.

"Do you not understand what your reckless behavior can do to our movement? Don't you get it? We can't have this. It's this type of nonsense that scares people. That makes ordinary people, the drones we need, believe we are all a bunch of anarchists."

Crosby paused and stared at Ben for several seconds. Finally, Ben replied, "Are you listening to yourself? Do you really believe your own bullshit? If you really want social justice, if you really want to transform society, you're going to have to shove it down their throats."

"We're going to do it by beating them at their own game. By winning at the ballot box," Crosby said.

"With whom? That senile old fool from New York, Jake Trane?"

"The kids love him," Crosby said. "They believe his bullshit about making everything free. And it was Hitler who said to an older opponent, 'What do we care about you? You are old and will die. We have your children. They are the future, and they are ours.' Hitler knew what he was talking about.

"And you need to wake up and grow up," Crosby continued. "This has never been about social justice. That's pablum for the idiots. It's about power. Getting it and keeping it. We're just using Trane and his nonsense to take over.

"Do you think Lenin and Stalin gave a damn about social justice? Or Mao or Fidel? Wake up. It's about power. And money."

"That is really cynical," Ben quietly replied.

"No shit? Now you're starting to get it. And it's about human nature. Why do you think socialism always fails? Trane really believes because it was never done correctly."

"He's right!" Ben said. By now, Ben was also leaning on the desk. The two of them were face-to-face barely two feet apart.

"What childish, naïve nonsense," Crosby said with a laugh. "To believe that you must believe people are all altruistic do-gooders out to help their fellow man. They're not. Socialism always fails because it kills the human spirit. The desire to strive and improve one's lot in life. And it lets those who have no real interest in education, work or putting an oar in the water to help row the boat, sit on their ass and take."

"I don't believe that," Ben quietly, weakly replied. But he knew in his heart Crosby was right.

Crosby sat back, looked at Ben and respectfully said, "Ben, I appreciate your zeal. I really do. Running around robbing banks and terrorizing people is not the way. Convincing them that the current system is corrupt and needs to be brought down by them at the ballot box is what needs to be done."

"Now who's being naïve?" Ben asked. "People are complacent sheep. At least two-thirds of them would rather eat their young than allow a rational thought into their tiny, little heads. Watch TV news if you don't believe me. How much reasoning goes on in those heads? Especially those on the left, but the ones on the right aren't any better."

"Good. In fact, so much the better. Look at how easily manipulated they are. Ben," Crosby said, "for God's sake, more people vote for the American Idol contest than for president. They care more about their beer, Barcaloungers and football than who's running the country and how much they're paying in taxes."

"Your way will take too long," Ben replied. "Jacob Trane will never be president. Even the masses of America aren't that stupid. People generally know nothing is free."

"He's a means to an end. Even we don't want him to win the White House. The man's an idiot. He's never accomplished anything in his life."

"Who is 'we'?" Ben asked.

"You don't need to know that, yet. Just cut out the terrorism; kids playing with guns. It's amazing no one's been shot," Crosby replied.

"I'll talk to them," Ben said.

Crosby stood up, reached across the desk and shook Ben's hand.

"Good," he said. "Do this, and I'll get you inside. Then you'll see who the 'we' are. You'll be impressed."

"Okay," Ben said.

A minute later Ben was standing at his office window watching the chauffeur hold the door for Webster Crosby.

"You phony, hypocrite sonofabitch," he muttered quietly to himself.

Ben picked up his personal phone, scrolled through the listings and made a call.

"Have you finished your recon?" Ben asked when the call was answered.

"Yeah, it should be no problem," Luke replied.

"Okay. But I've been thinking. Maybe it's time we did one a little closer to home. Here, in the Cities," Ben said.

"Okay," Luke cautiously replied. "Anything in mind?"

"Yes, a couple of possibles. Come by the house tonight, and we'll talk about it."

"Okay, see you around eight."

After he ended the call, Luke thought he should have asked if Sherry would be there. He was still having problems with that.

135

TWENTY-SIX

"What do you think?" Sherry Toomey asked.

She was in the back of Luke's van, leaning forward between the two front seats. With her in the back were Jordan Simmons and Neil Cole. Luke was in the driver's seat and Cindy Bonn in the passenger seat.

They were parked across the street from a Lake Country branch in a St. Paul suburb. To be a little more cautious, they had conducted two inside recons and two others from across the street where they were now, a Holiday Inn parking lot. Based on what they found, a Thursday afternoon was the quietest time of the week. Today was the day.

"Relax, Sherry," Luke sharply said. "We go in another fifteen minutes."

"I am relaxed," Sherry barked back at Luke, then under her breath, she added, "Asshole."

A moment later, Luke's handheld radio buzzed. He held it up, made a one-word response and received a one-word reply.

"They're set," Luke announced referring to Ben, Reese and Gary.

Luke checked himself in the interior mirror once more. He was sporting a fake beard and black, wrap-around sunglasses. He had a black ball cap on with a face-covering ski mask under it. No earring or any distinguishing marks. Everyone was very careful about that. Almost all of them had a tattoo—Sherry had several—and they were careful to cover them up.

"We need a new van," Cindy said. "This one has been used too many times."

"Talk to Ben," Luke said with obvious annoyance. "He controls the money. Right, Sherry?"

"Stop whining, Luke. Ben knows what he's doing," Sherry said.

"Yeah," Neil said, "driving a hot Beemer, he knows what he's doing."

The van went silent as the time got closer, and the anticipation grew. Luke looked at the clock on the dashboard for the tenth or twelfth time, then said, "Okay, everybody. Ready?"

Luke started the van as the others answered affirmatively. Thirty seconds later, he parked in front of the bank.

Luke and Cindy, also in disguise, went in first. From their recon, they were expecting two guards. There were times when only one was on duty, but normally there were two. Today, there was only one. He was casually standing by a pretty, young teller flirting with her. There were no customers at all.

136

Having discussed this contingency—only one guard—ahead of time, Cindy stood by a customer table while Luke continued on through the lobby. The guard, preoccupied, paid no attention to Luke at all. By the time Luke reached the manager's office, Sherry, Neil and Jordan were inside and the bank.

As soon as Cindy saw the others coming in, she made three quick steps to the guard and hit him with her taser. Cindy waited for the others to get everyone on the floor then bolted for the van. Since they no longer needed her, she would drive.

Once the guard was down, everything went quickly and very smoothly. A minute after going into the vault, Luke came out with a bag of money. He gagged and tied up the manager, then dropped the bag in the garbage bag Neil was holding.

Luke went out first, followed by Neil and then Sherry. As Jordan turned to leave, they heard three shots in rapid succession. They turned back and saw Jordan on the floor and a second guard, gun drawn, by the hallway to the restrooms.

Sherry was the first to react. The glass interior doors had closed behind them. Without bothering to open one or take a moment's hesitation, Sherry raised her gun and shot back. The guard, a look of terror on his face, was in a shooter's stance when Sherry's first shot blew out the glass door. She fired another ten times spraying bullets all over the bank. One of them found it's mark. It hit the second guard squarely in the chest and dropped him flat on his back.

"Come on, come on, come on," Luke screamed at Sherry as he knelt down next to Jordan.

Jordan was face down on the floor, blood coming out of a hole in her upper thigh. She was writhing around and making squealing sounds but obviously still alive.

"Come on," Luke yelled again at Sherry who was still waving her gun around looking for targets.

"Help me get her up. We gotta go!" Luke yelled again.

Neil was standing behind Sherry dumbstruck, trying to understand what was happening.

By now, the people on the floor Neil was looking at, were screaming in terror, sure that they would be next.

Finally, after the third time, Luke yelled, Sherry came to and went to his aid. They each took ahold of Jordan under an arm and pulled her up.

"I'm okay, I'm okay," Jordan kept repeating over and over.

"Come on, we'll get you out of here," Luke calmly said.

They started toward the door when Sherry saw something on the floor. "Her gun," she said. "She dropped it."

"Leave it," Luke said. "It's nothing. We have to get out of here."

By now Jordan was helping by limping along on one leg. Neil was watching the inside of the bank behind them and holding the doors open. When they got outside, Luke reminded Neil to lock the entryway doors. Neil put a bicycle lock on the two door handles and rushed to get in the van with the others.

"Holy shit! What happened?" a terrified Cindy yelled several times as she drove.

"Shut up and drive," Luke calmly told her.

Jordan was lying face down in the back of the van on top of a couple of plastic garbage bags. Luke had managed to stay calm enough to do this to keep the blood off the van's floor.

Neil, scared numb, was sitting in back in a corner as far away as he could get. Sherry was opening a first aid kit they kept in the van. She found a pair of surgical scissors and carefully sliced open Jordan's jeans to get a look at the wound.

"It's seeping blood, not spurting. That's good. It must have missed an artery," Sherry announced. She reached a hand under Jordan's leg, trying to find an exit wound.

"No exit wound in front. The bullet's still in there, I think," Sherry said.

"Okay, get some gauze on it, and we'll tape it up. That should keep the bleeding down," Luke said.

A very nervous Cindy hit a pothole and sharply bounced the old van. Jordan let out a yelp and Luke yelled at Cindy to watch the road.

"Is it bad?" Jordan asked for at least the tenth time.

"No, it's not," Sherry assured her while Luke taped the bandage in place.

When he finished, Luke retrieved his radio from upfront and buzzed for Ben. He was in his car waiting for them a mile from the bank. The plan had been to put the money, Sherry and Jordan in Ben's car. Cindy along with Neil and the guns would go with Reese while Luke drove off down 35E into St. Paul.

"We got a problem," Luke said into the radio. "We're gonna have to beat it to your place. We've got an injury."

"Okay, see you there," Ben said.

Luke gave Cindy directions to the nearest freeway, then looked at Sherry.

"I shot a guard," Sherry said. "Where was he? What if he's dead?"

"He must have been in the men's room," Luke said. "We finally had some bad luck."

"What if he's dead?" Sherry asked again.

"We can't worry about that now," Luke coolly answered.

To Luke, Sherry seemed very concerned and quite upset. But on the inside, the thought that she may have shot and killed a man gave her a weird rush.

Tony Carvelli pulled the Camaro into a parking space across the street from the Lake Country Federal Bank branch. By coincidence, it was the exact same parking spot in the Holiday Inn lot that Luke had parked the van before the robbery.

Along with Maddy Rivers, Carvelli hurried across the street toward the bank. They were stopped by an Eagan police officer before they reached the bank's parking lot. While Carvelli was explaining who they were to the obviously unimpressed cop, Maddy spotted Jeff Johnson.

"Jeff!" she yelled at the FBI agent. She waved at him, and a moment later, he joined them.

"It's okay, officer, I'll take it," Johnson told the cop.

"What can you tell us?" Carvelli asked.

"Same gang," Johnson said. "Only this time there was a shootout. One of the guards was in the men's room sitting on the..." he said, then hesitated for Maddy.

"On the toilet," Maddy said.

"Anyway, he didn't hear a thing that was going on. He came out just as they were leaving. He pulled his piece, yelled and started shooting. He hit one of them, a girl..."

"How do you know that? How do you know she was a female?" Maddy asked.

"I'll get to it," Johnson said. "One of the others opened up on him from the doorway. Sprayed eight or ten shots all over the place. Hit the guard with one in the chest."

"Is he..."

"He'll be fine. The bank has provided all the guards with Kevlar vests. He was wearing his," Johnson said. "Knocked him down and maybe fractured a couple ribs but he'll be all right. The girl went down, and they heard one of them, a male's voice, tell the one who did the shooting to help him with her, the one on the floor. Plus, there's blood from her. We'll have DNA in a couple days."

"So, it finally happened," Carvelli said, "and one of them got shot."

"We've got an alert out to all of the hospitals, clinics; you name it in the five-state area. If she turns up, we'll get her."

"What if she doesn't turn up?" Maddy asked.

"She has a bullet in her. We think she got hit in the upper thigh from behind. We haven't found the slug. It's probably still in her leg. They need to do something to get it out.

"Why are you two here?" Johnson finally asked.

"I got a call from my guy at the bank, Bob Olson. They're getting pretty pissed. Especially now that one of their people almost got killed. In fact, Olson doesn't know he's okay. I'll give him a call in a minute. Anything worth seeing in there?" Carvelli asked.

"No, and our forensics people are in there now anyway," Johnson replied.

"These kids have been playing with fire, and they just got burned," Maddy said. "Now what do they do?"

Twenty minutes after leaving the bank, a much calmer Cindy turned the van onto Ben's driveway. She parked it almost against the garage door as Luke got out. A moment later, the garage door opened, and she drove in. Luke closed the door and got back in the van.

"What are we going to do with her?" Neil asked nervously, looking at the other three; Ben, Luke and Sherry. Reese, Cindy and Gary had been sent home. Jordan was in the basement lying face down on the table, a blanket keeping her warm. They were in Ben's kitchen to discuss what to do.

"She needs a doctor," Luke said. "We need to drop her off at a hospital."

"Yes, you're right, that's what we should do," Ben agreed.

No one said a word. They all avoided eye contact trying to not say the obvious. Finally, after more than a minute, Sherry spoke up.

"We do that, and we're screwed. The cops will be on her in a minute. I like Jordan, but she's not tough enough. None of us are. She'll talk, and we all go to prison."

"At least the guard's not dead," Neil said. They had seen a news report earlier that evening.

"So, what are you saying?" Luke asked.

"We have a decision to make," Sherry said. "I don't know about the rest of you, but when I got in this, I knew the risks. We got in this as a revolutionary cause. Remember? We are all expendable. The cause is what's important. We're out to start the process to bring the world back from the brink of extinction. Do you still believe that?"

Slowly, the other three nodded their heads in agreement.

"Who's gonna do it…" Luke started to ask as Sherry walked away into the living room. When she returned, she was carrying a small pillow from the couch. She opened the door to the basement and looked at the others.

"Let's go," she said.

"She's in shock," Ben said as he leaned over Jordan to examine her. "Sepsis may be setting in."

Jordan was unconscious but quietly moaning, still in pain. Her hair was matted by sweat to her head, and her face was very flush.

Ben stood up and looked at Neil and Luke. They were standing at the foot of the table watching Ben.

"I hate to say this, but we could probably wait a day or two…"

At that moment a muffled gunshot went off behind Ben. While he was looking at the two young men, Sherry took care of it. She covered Jordan's head with the pillow and fired one shot through it into the side of Jordan's brain.

Despite seeing her do it, Neil and Luke were both taken completely by surprise. Ben jumped at least a foot, turned with his hand on his heart to see what had happened.

"Waiting a day or two would have been cruel. This had to be done."

"You crazy bitch!" Luke screamed. "What the hell is wrong…"

Before he could finish, Sherry clamped a hand over her mouth, ran into the laundry room and vomited in the sink.

An hour later, Luke and Neil carried Jordan into the garage and put her in the van. She was wrapped in several layers of black plastic lawn bags and secured with duct tape. This was done while they all wore surgical gloves and even surgical masks to avoid leaving any forensic evidence on the bags. They had also stripped Jordan naked to dispose of anything that might be on her clothing.

"You sure you know where to go?" Ben asked Luke for the fourth or fifth time.

"Yes, Ben. I know a place. We get rid of the van tomorrow. While we're gone, you two get the money ready to be laundered," Luke replied.

Unspoken was the Rubicon they had crossed tonight. Ben Sokol was no longer completely in charge. At least a couple of the kids were growing up.

The next morning, dressed in a silk robe, Webster Crosby stared out the window of his two-bedroom suite, looking at the Golden Gate Bridge. He was in San Francisco, Tom Breyer's guest, enjoying the luxury of the Mark Hopkins Hotel. Crosby heard a knock on the door and went to let room service in with his breakfast.

For the next ten minutes, while enjoying a leisurely meal, Crosby perused a copy of the Chronicle. On page five of the A section he saw the story. Another bank robbery in Minnesota by a radical environmental, climate change group. By the time he finished reading the story, he was so furious he almost had steam coming out of his ears.

TWENTY-SEVEN

Marc stepped off the elevator, made two quick right turns and walked toward Judge McVein's courtroom. Halfway there he saw a man seated on a padded bench stand up. As the man approached, Marc stopped. For a brief moment he thought about fleeing but that would only encourage the little pest.

"Philo Anson, as I live and breathe," Marc said as the StarTribune reporter came closer. "To what do I owe the pleasure?"

"I saw you on TV a couple days ago with that hot chick babe, Gabriella Shriqui," Philo replied.

"Put that away," Marc said referring to the handheld recorder he was holding.

"Come on, Marc. I thought we became friends," Philo said. He was still holding the recorder and pointing it at Marc who silently stared at it.

"Okay, I'll put it away," Philo glumly replied as he placed it in his coat pocket.

"Shut it off first," Marc said.

"Oh, gee, did I forget to do that," Philo said. He pulled it out of his pocket, held the device up, pushed the button to shut it off and said, "See? Okay, now tell me about your case."

"My client's been falsely accused of murdering his wife," Marc flatly said.

"Is it true he was a cuckold and caught her at her lover's and that's where she was killed?"

"No comment except, again, he didn't do it. Why are you interested in this? Shouldn't you be in New York winning awards for the Times?"

"Soon," Philo answered. "But right now, things are kind of slow. A juicy love-triangle murder might be fun to cover. What's going on today?"

Marc hesitated then said, "I guess I can tell you. You'll find out anyway. They got an indictment for first degree. This will be the first appearance on it."

"The rule five and rule eight hearing?" Philo asked.

"You've been studying criminal procedure," Marc said. "Yes, and, so you know, we're not going to waive a speedy trial. My client's in jail and you can use this. The judge denied him access to assets he could use to make bail. I have to go. Come in and watch."

"I hear the Nazi is prosecuting this case. And, I hear you have an acrimonious history with him," Philo said as they walked toward the courtroom.

"Off the record, everyone has an acrimonious history with him, even the people on his side," Marc replied.

As Marc started to open the door to go inside, Philo asked, "How's Maddy?"

Marc looked down at the much shorter man and said, "She's wondering why you haven't called."

"Really?" Philo said, a look of wonder on his face with his mouth hanging open. Marc turned to go in, and Philo grabbed his arm and asked, "Do you have her number?"

Marc looked at him again and replied, "She's in the yellow pages and has a website."

"Hey, thanks," a beaming Philo said.

While Marc walked up the center aisle to the gate, he thought, *I'm going to be sorry I did that.*

The courtroom was empty except for a deputy standing by the jury box and the judge's clerk. Marc checked in with the clerk then looked at the deputy.

"Your client's in holding," the deputy said. "Whenever you want to see him, let me know."

"Thanks, give me a minute," Marc answered as he watched Jennifer Moore come through the back, hallway door.

"Hi, Jenny," Marc said when he saw her.

"No, I wasn't back in chambers ex parte," she replied.

"I trust you so much I wasn't even going to ask," Marc replied.

"Yeah, right. That's pretty funny," Jennifer replied.

The two lawyers went to their respective tables and dropped their briefcases on them. Jennifer walked over to Marc.

"You got a copy of the indictment, didn't you?" she asked.

"Yeah," he replied. "My client hasn't seen it yet."

"So, go show it to him," she said. "Is your guy planning on making bail?"

"Are you going to ask for more?" Marc asked instead of answering.

"Sure, and McVein will give it to me. You going to waive speedy trial?"

Marc smiled and said, "I have to go see Flanders."

As Marc walked toward the door being held open by the deputy, the clerk said, "The judge told me to let him know when you're ready."

Before following the deputy, Marc noticed that a half dozen spectators had entered and sat down. Philo Anson was sitting in the front row behind the prosecutor's table.

Marc patiently waited while Hal Flanders scanned the indictment. When he finished, Hal handed it back to Marc.

"Seems a little thin on evidence," Flanders said. "Since I didn't do it, I'm not surprised."

"Hal, it's a solid circumstantial case, I'll move to exclude the audiotapes of you threatening her and I can handle the restraining order but..."

"Will the judge keep out the tapes?"

"Nope," Marc said. "Shows intent."

"Great," Hal glumly said. "Did you see my kids out there? My sons and daughter?"

"Ah, I didn't really look for them," Marc replied. "How are they taking this?"

"They believe me," Hal said. "They're pretty upset with their mother's death and her cheating, but I convinced them I didn't do it. I had no motive."

"That might be our case," Marc said. "You sure about staying in jail and not waiving a speedy trial."

"Absolutely," Hal said. "I'm doing okay here and the more I think about it, the better I like the idea of not giving them more time to come up with anything."

"What else could they come up with Hal? Tell me now if you know of something."

"No, I don't. I swear."

Marc was looking him squarely in the eyes for any sign that he might be lying. They stayed like this for a few seconds without speaking.

Satisfied, Marc finally said, "Okay. Today, we'll go through another first appearance on all three charges. Two first-degree and one second. She's going to argue to increase bail which I'll oppose, of course."

"Will he increase it?"

"Probably," Marc answered. "Then I'll demand a speedy trial and an omnibus hearing."

"What's an omnibus hearing?"

"It's the same thing as what they call a pretrial hearing on TV. The state will have to present sufficient evidence to create probable cause that you did this. If the judge decides they don't have the evidence, he can dismiss the case."

"What are the odds of that happening?"

"Somewhere between none and zero," Marc said.

"Is there a jury?"

"No, no jury. And the omnibus hearing has to be done within twenty-eight days of today. We'll set a trial date then, too."

"When will that be?"

"Well, you don't want to drag it out so, I'll insist on it being sixty days from today. But the judge can extend that if he finds cause. The prosecution will object but I don't think they have adequate grounds. Stalling to find more evidence is not sufficient grounds."

Marc and Hal, along with two deputies, entered the courtroom together. Seated in the front row were three young adults, a girl and two boys, Hal's daughter Melanie and her two younger brothers, Brian and Kyle. Teary-eyed hugs took place, and they exchanged greetings while they all waited for the judge.

"Are you sure you will not waive your right to a speedy trial? Are you confident your lawyer, Mr. Kadella, will have sufficient time to prepare your defense in sixty days?" Judge McVein asked Hal.

"Yes, your Honor," Hal replied. "I have complete confidence in him."

"Mr. Kadella, you have thoroughly discussed this with your client?"

"I have, your Honor," Marc answered.

"Your Honor," Jennifer Moore interrupted, "again, the people strongly object. We are concerned that the defendant will try to claim he did not receive a fair trial on appeal. He'll claim it was his lawyer that rushed him to a fast trial…"

"No, I won't," Hal said. "It's my idea entirely."

"The state cannot possibly prepare for a…"

"Then you should not have brought charges until you were ready, Ms. Moore," Judge McVein said. "It's not your right to a speedy trial I'm interested in. Plus, you just requested an increase in the defendant's bail. Do you want to allow the defendant to be released without bail?"

Jennifer thought about the question for a few seconds before answering. "If I can be assured the defense will waive a speedy trial, I'll run it by my boss."

"Mr. Kadella?" McVein asked Marc.

"Ask me again after they agree to it," Marc answered.

"No deal," Jennifer said when she saw the smile on Marc's face.

"Okay," McVein said. "I'm satisfied the defendant understands what he is doing."

He looked at his calendar and said, "We'll do the omnibus on Thursday, November fifth at nine A.M. How long will you need?"

"One day should do it," Marc said.

"Yes, I agree," a clearly annoyed Jennifer Moore said.

"Good, I want my calendar cleared before deer season begins on the seventh of November. I'll be gone that week," McVein said. "We'll set a date for trial, motions, witness lists and anything else then."

Hal was finished with his kids and was being led away. Jennifer Moore had taken a couple of minutes seated at the table to calm down. When she had, she packed up to leave then stepped over to talk to Marc.

"Wonderful, I barely have two weeks to prepare for the omnibus. On top of it, he denies my request for a bail increase. Thanks a lot," she said.

"Where's the Nazi? Let him do it," Marc replied as his phone vibrated in his coat pocket.

"Unlikely His Highness can be bothered," Jennifer said while Marc read a text message he just received.

"Oh shit," he muttered. "You think you have problems. Maddy sent me a text. Philo Anson called her and asked her out to dinner."

"Seriously? What possessed that little troll to do that?" Jennifer asked.

"Oh boy," Marc said, still looking at his phone. He looked at Jennifer and said, "It was something I said to him. I sort of, ah, jokingly told him to call her."

"Really?" Jennifer asked and laughed. "Tell her to call me. I want to know how bad she rips your ass. That could make up for what you did to me today. Good luck."

"Thanks," Marc said.

As she went through the gate, Jennifer looked back and asked, "Is she going out with him?"

"Smartass," Marc replied. "Actually, she didn't say."

Jennifer laughed all the way into the front hallway.

TWENTY-EIGHT

Starting as early as 5:00 A.M., the morning after Jordan's death, Ben began receiving text messages. Cindy's was the first and worst. She went into a long, dramatic ordeal about her night. No sleep, near panic, terrified the police were going to be at her door any minute. On and on. Finally, she got to the point. How is Jordan? By 7:00, the others had checked in as well. None of them knew the truth, yet.

Ben sent back a short answer to their inquiries to stop texting and meet at the music hall at twelve that night.

Ben and Sherry arrived at the music hall storage room a full half-hour before the others. Ben had intentionally avoided all contact with all of them except Sherry. He left a brief message on her phone to come early. The two of them needed an explanation for what happened to Jordan the night before.

"I think we should tell them the truth," Sherry said. "Why hide it? Jordan became a liability and had to go. We need to stop coddling them. This isn't a game. It's likely none of us, the original members, will survive. It's the movement that's important."

Ben stared at her for several seconds, all the while thinking about what she said. Did he still believe it himself?

"Of course," he finally said. "You're right, but I'm not sure they're ready for that."

"Tough shit! Besides, they're gonna know. They're gonna figure it out."

"Okay, so they do. Then what? We wait to see how they respond. But we don't need to tell them the whole truth. We say she went into shock, probably from sepsis or some other infection. Her temperature skyrocketed, and her heart must have stopped."

Sherry sat down on a metal folding chair, thinking this over. Last night, what she did, had shocked her and made her sick. But today, she was feeling very differently. Ambivalent, but not guilty. She convinced herself that shooting Jordan was both necessary and merciful. Taking her to a hospital would have been a disaster. She would not have held up for ten minutes under the questioning by the cops. So, what was the alternative? And, Sherry admitted to only herself, she was quite proud of herself. Someone had to have the balls to do it. In fact, it took a while to admit it, but she got a rush out of it — pure power.

"Okay, we'll go with that. Did you square it with Luke and Neil? Did they…"

"No, not yet. When they left last night, I told them to keep quiet, don't say anything to the others and I'd think of something. They'll go along with it."

"Where did they take her?" Sherry asked.

"Luke knew a place where he used to go hunting. Some deep woods where no one will find her. They didn't get back until early afternoon."

"What about Luke's van? That's gotta go," Sherry said.

"We took care of it. It's been put through a car crusher at a salvage yard."

"Are you sure?"

"Yeah, we waited and saw it done. We paid the guy an extra hundred bucks to do it right away."

"He'll know!" Sherry said.

"He'll know what? That the van may have been hot or used in a crime? So what? It's a block of scrap metal on its way to being recycled. It's gone. Then we got Luke a really good, used SUV. A Chevy Tahoe. Dark blue. There's a million of them in this state," Ben said then stopped when he heard pounding on the door.

"What happened to Jordan?" Reese asked. "I've been worried all day."

"Me, too," Gary and Cindy agreed.

"Come in, have a seat," Ben told them.

They were all together, including Luke and Neil. There were metal folding chairs set up in a circle, and everyone took a seat.

Ben started out by sadly telling them the story that she died of shock and heart failure. Luke, Neil and Sherry all sat impassively while he did this. The other three looked at Ben with horror on their faces.

Cindy looked at Luke, and calmly asked, "Is that what happened?"

"Yeah, yes it was. We were trying to figure out where to take her, what hospital to take her to. All of a sudden, like Ben said, she went into convulsions from the shock. She felt really, really hot then her heart must have stopped."

Cindy Bonn, the brunette with the fake boob tattoo she used to distract guards, was considered the mental lightweight of the group. But Cindy was no featherhead. She was a follower but not an idiot. While Luke confirmed Ben's story, she watched him carefully. Especially his eyes. There was movement in them. Not much, and if you were not looking for it you would probably miss it. Cindy saw it and knew he was lying. And she knew what really happened.

"I've been thinking," Ben said, continuing, "we should take a break. Go quiet for a few weeks. What do you guys think?"

The idea was kicked around for a few minutes without any dissent. The events of yesterday's job and Jordan's death had rattled everyone.

"We're going to continue. We set out on a crusade. This was never a game," Sherry said then silently looked each of them in the face. "Let's not lose sight of why we're doing this. Anyone have a problem with that?"

All of them, including Ben, shook their heads to agree with her.

"What about yesterday's money?" Luke asked.

"I went through it and did not find any dye packs," Ben said. "I threw it in the dryer then counted it — a hundred and twelve thousand. I suggest we wait a few weeks before we wash it. Any objections?"

"I need some money, Ben," Luke said. "I'm barely making ends meet."

"Back to my question," Ben said. "Any objections to waiting a while on yesterday's score?" While he was saying this, he was holding up an index finger toward Luke to indicate they would talk money in a minute.

When no one objected, Ben said to Luke, "You could all use some. I've got ten grand in clean bills for each of you. Will that do it?"

With a relieved look, Luke agreed and each, in turn, did the same.

"But, don't be stupid with it. Spend it carefully. If you need it to catch up on some bills, go to a Walgreen's or a post office and buy money orders. Don't go to banks. Be careful," Ben said.

"What's with the new truck for Luke?" Gary asked. "I could use new wheels too."

"One thing at a time," Ben said. "We had to get rid of the van."

"Yeah, okay, for now," Gary said.

"Get the guns back to Luke," Ben started to say.

"They have," Luke told him.

"Okay," Ben stood up and said, "That's it for tonight. Get new burner phones and get the number to everyone. Cool it on the texting; it leaves a trail. Stay in touch and keep a low profile."

Reese, Gary and Cindy had arrived in Gary's Chevy. Two minutes after leaving in it with their money, but without a word being spoken, Reese broke the silence.

"I'm just sick about Jordan. I really liked her. She was a great chick and…"

"She killed her," Cindy impassively said. "Sherry killed her," Cindy repeated. "Sherry shot her and killed her."

Cindy was in the front passenger seat when she said this. A shocked Gary looked back and forth at her three or four times without saying anything. Reese unbuckled his seat belt and leaned forward between the front seats.

"What do you mean?" Reese asked. "Why do you think that?"

"Because they were lying," Cindy calmly, flatly said. "I could see it in Luke's eyes. Sherry did it. I know her. She's a psycho bitch. She loved shooting that guard. She got off on it."

"What do we do?" Gary asked.

"I don't know," Cindy replied. "Let me think about it."

She turned back to Reese and told him to sit back and put his seatbelt on before a cop saw him and stopped them. They drove on in silence.

Ben had received a phone call the previous evening a few hours before their group meeting. The caller ID read Anonymous. Normally, like most people, he would have simply ignored it. This time a little bell seemingly went off in his head, and he knew who the call was from. Expecting an explosion from him, Ben smiled in anticipation while answering the call.

Instead, it was now the next day, and Ben was in the back of a Cadillac limousine at the St. Paul airport. He checked the time on his watch then looked down the runway to watch the Gulfstream cruise down for a smooth landing. His next ride had arrived.

A few minutes later the executive jet's engines whined down as it stopped near the limo. Ben waited in the car for the plane's door to open and stairs to descend. When it did, he was surprised to see Webster Crosby himself come down to greet him.

Ben had a small suitcase with two days of clothing with him. The chauffeur retrieved it and carried it on board. After greetings were exchanged, Webster affably led Ben on board. Before the pilots started moving the luxury aircraft, Webster gave him a complete guided tour. This was not just the nicest, most plush and opulent plane he had ever seen; it was better than any room or home he had been in, and Ben literally became lightheaded at just being a guest here.

TWENTY-NINE

The flying time from Minnesota to the Jackson Hole Airport in Wyoming is a few minutes more than two hours. They had left St. Paul at brunch time—intentionally scheduled by Webster Crosby—to allow for a superb breakfast to be served and enjoyed.

They could smell the eggs benedict being prepared in the galley by a male chef. The hostess served it along with orange juice and champagne. When she had finished clearing the table, a special blend of coffee was served.

"This is really great coffee," Ben said while Webster refilled his cup. "But please don't tell me it's that cat shit stuff from Asia. Even if it is, I don't want to know."

Webster laughed and said, "Kopi Luwak from Indonesia and no, this is not that. I can't bring myself to drink cat shit coffee either."

"Where are we going, Webster?" Ben asked.

Every time Ben, a former acolyte and student, called Webster Crosby by his first name, Crosby felt a twinge of annoyance. And Ben Sokol being a professor at, what Crosby considered, a third-rate college in fly-over country, did not help the matter.

"Jackson Hole, Wyoming," Webster replied. "Ever been there?"

"No, I haven't."

"Great place. Beautiful. A little jewel tucked inside the Teton Mountains."

"Oh, damn. I didn't pack my climbing gear."

Webster smiled despite being unimpressed with Ben's attempted witticism. "You won't need any," Webster said. "We're going there to introduce you to some people. Very influential people."

"Okay. Is that where I get the intervention? You and your rich pals gonna sit me down and jump down my throat for being a bad boy? For not doing what you say?"

"You know, Ben. It's interesting," Webster replied, ignoring the sarcasm, "I remember you as being, well, for lack of a better word, a bit of a wimp. A follower, certainly not a leader nor someone I would have expected such confidence from. What happened?"

Annoyed with Webster's condescension, Ben said, "I guess I grew up a bit and realized that a professor's title from an Ivy League school isn't as impressive as the titleholder thinks."

"Touché," Webster said with a laugh. "To answer your question, no, we're not going to an intervention.

"You seem to be able to connect with young people on a certain level. I have that gift myself if I can say so without sounding too arrogant.

I have convinced some people that you can be an asset—someone who can work with us. We want the same thing, Ben. So, please keep an open mind, hear what we have to say."

"And?" Ben asked.

"And you could move into this world," Webster said, holding up his arms to indicate the luxury of the jet.

"I really am a believer in saving the planet and bringing about a more just society," Ben replied.

Webster leaned forward, poured more of the expensive coffee while saying, "Believe it or not, Ben, so are we. Someone has to do it. It won't happen by screaming, sign-carrying kids or self-involved politicians. It will require real leadership. People out for the global good."

Webster sat back, crossed his legs, sipped his coffee and looked at Ben for a reaction.

"Will Jacob Trane be there?"

"No," Webster replied. "Between you and me, that man's a fool. Oh, he's a useful idiot, I suppose. But never forget, when he talks about the wonders of socialism and his utopian dreams, he doesn't mean for himself. No, the wonders of socialism are for everyone else. He'll still take in millions.

"Have you noticed; he's stopped complaining about millionaires now that he is one? Now it's just billionaires who are greedy. Apparently, it's okay to be his level of greedy but no more than that."

The hostess appeared and told them they were heading into their approach and to please buckle up.

A Tom Breyer limousine was waiting for them at the Jackson Hole Airport. The two men made innocuous small talk and shared a drink during the thirty-minute ride to the hotel. When the car parked in front of the Four Seasons Teton Club, Ben—not entirely sober—did his best to remain calm. As impressive as the building's exterior was, the interior made Ben feel out of his depth. Modern, rustic, five-star luxury would be the best way to describe the place.

"They'll take care of your bag," Crosby assured Ben. "There are some people who are waiting to meet you."

"Thank you," Ben said to the desk clerk as she handed him his card key.

He looked at Crosby and said, "Well, okay, sure. Lead the way."

Crosby had the card key to the private penthouse elevator. It went directly to the ninth floor, and the doors opened at the suite's entrance.

Before they stepped through the elevator doors, a smiling, casually dressed Tom Breyer arrived to greet them.

Crosby introduced Breyer to Ben who managed to mutter something about the room.

"It's fabulous," Breyer beamed as if he had designed it himself. "I get it whenever I'm in Jackson Hole. Have you been here before?"

"Ah, no, I haven't," Ben managed to coherently reply.

"Let me show you around," Breyer said lightly taking hold of Ben's right arm. "Webster, the others are in the living room. Go ahead and join them for a drink. We're having a lunch served whenever we're ready."

"Will do, Tom," Crosby replied. "Enjoy the tour, Ben. It's quite a place."

It took Breyer almost a half hour to conduct the tour. The suite had five bedrooms, each with its own full marble bath and balcony. There was a family room, living room, dining room for ten, and a private, gourmet kitchen. Over four thousand square feet of elitist luxury, all being displayed to impress a nobody professor from a second-rate Upper Midwest university. And Ben was very impressed, especially with the other guests.

In the living room, enjoying the best liquor money could buy were four men, besides Webster Crosby. Breyer introduced Ben to the other guests. One was the head of the Republican National Committee; another a senior Democrat U.S. Senator; the majority leader of the U.S. House and two billionaire pals of Breyer's from Silicon Valley.

"What can I get you, Ben?" Breyer asked, referring to a drink.

Realizing he was in some pretty exalted company, Ben knew he needed to keep a clear head. "I'll just have water," he replied. "At least until I get some food in my stomach."

Breyer brought Ben a bottle of Evian and a glass filled with ice. Everyone found a chair. Breyer sat directly across from Ben.

"Ben," he said, "I'm going to be blunt, totally honest with you. All of us here approve of your zeal and commitment. We all want the same thing," he continued as the others solemnly nodded their agreement.

"But…" Ben said.

"But we can't have this. We can't accomplish what needs to be done with a bunch of kids running around with guns robbing banks," the senator said with an attitude bordering on abrasive.

Breyer held up his left hand to stop the normally belligerent senator from going further. "What the senator means is, Ben, while what you're up to makes a point, it scares people."

"Who says I'm up to anything?" Ben asked, looking directly at Webster Crosby.

"Don't go there, Ben," Crosby said. "We're all friends here. We're all working toward the same thing; an egalitarian society. This country cannot continue down the path it is on. The world can't do it. We're going to destroy ourselves. Sensible people need to step up."

"That lunatic bully in the White House may win a second term and then what?" the head of the RNC chimed in.

"We've got to plan for when he is gone, and we can bring this country back together," Breyer said. "And deal with social justice, income inequality and, most importantly, climate change. Someone is going to have to lead these people to the lifestyle changes they have to make."

So, you don't have to make any changes to your lifestyle. It's the little people who need to change their lifestyles so you guys can continue to live like royalty, Ben was thinking.

"We're all on the same page here, Ben. We need to cool it on the violence. Hell, a bank guard almost got killed the other day. You want that?" asked the senator.

"Of course not," Ben replied.

"Let's have some lunch," Breyer announced to calm things down a bit.

Lunch was a six-ounce filet mignon and four-ounce lobster tail. Of course, accompanied by cheesy bacon ranch potatoes and sautéed garlic asparagus. Probably the best meal Ben had ever eaten.

When the meal and chocolate mousse dessert was finished, the RNC chairman said, "It's a good thing I don't eat like this every day, I'd weigh four hundred pounds."

The rest of the afternoon was spent with a limo tour of Jackson Hole and Teton National Park. It included viewing some of the most beautiful mountain scenery in the world. The topper was the four grizzly bears they saw: a mother and three yearlings.

When they arrived back at the hotel, Ben begged off another meal and more alcohol. Before the tour, he had changed into jeans and casual clothing in his room. Now, he wanted to get back there and drop on the bed, relax and sort out his feelings. Was entrée into this group what he wanted? Was this what they had in mind? Would this rich bunch really admit him or were they just out to stop his group? He would probably find out more tomorrow.

Ben had guessed correctly. The next day he was treated to more of the same. Political ideology layered with the lavish lifestyle he would enjoy. All he had to do was disband his merry little radical group and join the club.

In midafternoon the cherry on the sundae arrived. Ten of some of the best-looking women Ben had ever seen were ushered in. He would find out later they were top-grade prostitutes flown in from Las Vegas. The rest of the day and evening was spent in an orgy of debauchery to rival the Roman Emperors. The only exception would be when the guests chose to enjoy the girls' services, they had the good manners to do so privately.

Ben, being the guest of honor, was hustled off by two of them to his room. When he awoke the next morning, the girls were gone. The memory was still there as was the hangover headache.

"How are you feeling this morning, Ben?" Breyer cheerfully asked,

Ben was back on the ninth floor in the Penthouse working on a perfect Bloody Mary. Food was available, a brunch having been set out. Food was the last thing Ben wanted to even think about.

"Have a good time last night?" Webster Crosby asked.

"You know I did, Webster," Ben quietly said.

"That wasn't even a party," Breyer said. "That was just a last-minute thing I threw together."

"Where is everyone else?" Ben asked.

"Had to leave early," Breyer answered.

"What we have in mind for you, Ben," Webster said, finally getting down to it, "is to do what I do. Get you on the college speaking tour. You'd be good at it, and you can use the same scheduling agents I use. You'll make more money in a year than you have in your life. Plus, you'll be doing a helluva lot better to fight for climate change, corruption and for social justice than sticking up banks with a bunch of kids."

Ben had expected something along these lines. Confronted with the reality he had to admit to himself he was certainly tempted.

"That's very, ah, interesting, appealing, Webster," Ben replied. "I'd have to say I'm probably ninety percent in, but I'd like to think about it a bit. I'm very loyal to my people, and I'd like to see how this will affect them."

"Of course," Breyer said. "I admire your loyalty. But, in the meantime, the bank robberies have to stop."

"Sure, okay," Ben agreed, knowing they had already called for a moratorium.

Webster looked at his watch and said, "I need to get going, Ben. I have a meeting with people later today in Pennsylvania."

Ben placed his empty Bloody Mary glass on the end table next to him then stood up. "I need to go pack. Won't take long. I'll meet you in the lobby in what, fifteen minutes?"

"That will be fine," Webster said.

After the "nice to meet you" lies Ben exchanged with Tom Breyer, he left to go to his room and pack.

"What do you think?" Webster asked Breyer when Ben left.

"He's certainly nothing special. And a Jew on top of it. We'll use him as long as he delivers, but he'll never get in on the real inside. Do I make myself clear, Webster?"

"Absolutely," Webster replied while thinking Ben Sokol would not see many more birthdays.

THIRTY

Hal Flanders was escorted into the courtroom and led by two deputies to the defense table. Hal took a couple of minutes to meet and greet his sons and daughter. Then Marc stood and shook hands with his client again. He had already met with him earlier while bringing a suit for Hal to wear to court. With the guard watching over them and Marc running late, they did not have time to talk until now.

"Okay, so what's going on here today?" Flanders asked.

"It's basically a pretrial hearing. The prosecution needs to show the court that there is sufficient probable cause to support the charges for a trial. We could really piss off the prosecutor and jerk his chain by demanding he read the full indictment."

"Why would we do that?"

"For the fun of it. But it's pointless, and the judge won't like it. If he asks, we'll admit we got a copy and move on.

"The judge will then tell the prosecutors to put their witnesses on. It gives us a chance to see their witnesses and gauge the strength of their case."

"Will we see all of it?"

"Maybe. They might just put on enough to show probable cause and hold back some things. We'll see."

"Can we stop it here?"

"No," Marc replied, shaking his head a couple of times. "Your threats and the gun you bought are probably enough."

"Can we put on witnesses? Should I testify and explain things?"

"Yes, we can put on witnesses, and no you're not getting on that witness stand," Marc replied. "The only witness that we might have that would help is an alibi which you don't have."

Flanders exhaled a deep breath, and sullenly replied, "So, I'm screwed."

"Relax, Hal. I told you, this is just the beginning."

Judge McVein started on time at 9:00 A.M. The prosecution again argued for an increase in bail which, this time, McVein granted. He raised it to an even one million dollars. Since Flanders could not or would not pay it, it made little difference.

By two o'clock and without a lunch break, the prosecutor, Jerry Krain, had made quick work of the probable cause hearing. Having done dozens of them, Krain was very prepared.

He started with Marcie Sterling because she was the lead investigator. She confirmed how Natalie was found and where. An element of the charge of murder required the homicide to have occurred in Hennepin County.

An efficient parade of witnesses testified to the cause of death and gun type. A crime scene tech introduced the tapes of Flanders' threats. And, one of the responding Burnsville police officers testified about the domestic assault call that resulted in the restraining order.

Marc knew ahead of time that McVein would find probable cause. Mostly because there, in fact, was probable cause. He had decided to hold his case back and did not bother to ask a single question. When it was over, Marc took Flanders into a conference room to discuss it.

"Why didn't you ask any questions?" an angry Flanders asked.

"I didn't want to give anything away," Marc replied. "Yes, I could have gone after his witnesses and maybe even poke some holes in his case. But, finding probable cause is a pretty low threshold. I would not have been able to prevent it. All I would have done is show my hand, so to speak, and Krain would know what he needed to fix for trial. They do have some holes. Better to show them to a jury than give Krain a chance to fix them. See what I'm saying?"

"Yeah, sure. Makes sense. Okay, now what?"

"I have to go back in chambers. They're waiting for me," Marc said as he stood up. "We'll set a trial date. Oh, yeah, that's another thing. Even if I had won today and the judge turned them down for a finding of probable cause, that would not have been the end of it."

"What about double, you know, ah…"

"Double jeopardy?"

"Yeah, that."

"Doesn't work that way. That attaches when the jury is sworn in. If we had won today, they could continue to investigate and if they found new evidence, they could charge you again. This way we get a look at their case and their witnesses."

"Why did you object to all of their testimony and the evidence they have?"

"To preserve it for a possible appeal. If you don't object, you can't complain about it later."

"Lawyers," Flanders said shaking his head in disgust. "What a clusterfuck you people have made out of our court system."

"That's why we get to charge so much money," Marc said. "We made the mess, and we get to profit from it. Sweet deal. Come on. We have to go."

Marc led Hal back into the courtroom and turned him over to the deputies. He then noticed that annoying little man sitting in the front row.

"I'll come over and pick up the suit," Marc told Hal.

As Hal was being taken back, Marc spoke to the reporter.

"Hey, Philo, what's up?"

"Got a minute? I need a quote," Philo Anson, the Star Tribune reporter, replied.

"Beware of gin-soaked barroom queens from Memphis. She'll try to take you upstairs for a ride," Marc said.

"What!?"

Marc started laughing then said, "You wanted a quote, that's a quote. Not a Rolling Stones fan, I guess. That's a paraphrase of the opening lyrics of Honky Tonk Women. Look it up."

"Your brain is turning to mush. What is Maddy doing to you?"

Marc laughed again, then said, "I need to see the judge to set a trial date. Stick around, and I'll talk to you."

"Sorry, your Honor. My client had a lot of questions," Marc said, apologizing for keeping him waiting.

"It's okay, have a seat," McVein said.

Marc sat down, looked at Jerry Krain and said, "I trust I won't have to bring an ex parte complaint against you."

"Your Honor!" Krain protested.

"All right, that stops now. I'm told you two have a history and I'm not putting up with it. Do I make myself clear?"

"I don't understand," Marc said, trying to look as innocent as possible. "I've always had the greatest respect and admiration for Mr. Krain."

Returning Marc's sarcasm, McVein said, "Really? That would make you the first defense lawyer with that attitude. Now, knock it off.

"Trial date?" McVein continued. "Since you won't waive time, we have about forty-five days to get this to trial."

"Sixty days, your Honor," Krain said. "Sixty days from the first appearance which was today."

"Nice try," Marc said. "Sixty days from the first, first appearance. Which means, now that it's November fifth that would make day forty-five four days before Christmas Day, a Sunday," Marc said.

"Thank you for giving me cause to extend the trial date through the holidays," McVein said, then glanced at a grinning Jerry Krain.

"Ooops," Marc said out loud. "We could go earlier," Marc suggested.

"I'm not going to risk making a jury sit through Christmas," McVein said.

"I'm willing to," Krain said.

"Yeah, knowing they'll likely blame it on my client," Marc said, looking at the calendar on his phone, "How about January fifth? It's a

Monday. We should be able to get done by Friday, the tenth. One week should be plenty of time. They barely have a case."

"Your Honor this is a first-degree case. Jury selection will take at least three days," Krain said.

"He's right, Mr. Kadella. Block out time through the following week. If we finish early, so much the better.

"I want discovery done by December fourteenth. Witness lists by the twenty-first and all motions heard no later than December twenty-eighth. Understood?

"Yes, your Honor," they both said.

When they left McVein's chambers and went into the back hallway, Marc asked Krain, "Where's Jennifer? I expected her today."

"Not that it's any of your business, but I decided to handle all of the preliminary matters myself," Krain replied.

"It's always a pleasure, Jerry," Marc said.

Krain had been walking away when Marc said this. He turned, looked back and almost snarled, "I'm not here to make friends…"

"…and you're doing a splendid job of it."

"I'm here to put scum in prison."

"And because you take it so personally," Marc said with sincerity, "you pretty much suck at it."

"Yeah, we'll see about that. Tell your client to get used to jail. He's gonna be there for most of the rest of his life. Besides, you want to see my won/lost record?"

"Not interested. Like all prosecutors, it's inflated because you won't go to trial with a case you can't possibly lose," Marc said knowing his needling would get under the Nazi's skin.

Krain turned on his heel and stomped off.

While Jerry Krain used his prosecutor's hall pass to sneak off through the judges' back hallway, Marc went into the courtroom. Hoping to find Philo impatiently gone he was able to mask his disappointment.

"You going to give me a few minutes?" Philo asked while Marc packed up his briefcase.

"Sure, Philo," Marc replied. "We'll go out in the hall."

The hallway was deserted, so they found an empty bench to do the interview.

"Tell me something, Philo, what's your interest in this case? It's a run-of-the-mill domestic homicide. I realize Minnesota doesn't get many of them, but you don't strike me as a champion of feminism. What's going on?"

"Hey, these things create interest."

161

Marc looked at Philo's shifty eyes, smiled and said, "I'm not buying it. Be honest, or I walk."

Philo paused for a moment, thinking over his answer before replying, "Okay, I'll come clean. I met a hot, feminist chick at a 'Down with Domestic Abuse' rally. I'm trying to, you know..."

"Get in her pants," Marc said.

"Well, yeah," Philo replied. "Anyway, she called me when your guy got arrested. She told me she would take it as a personal favor if I covered the case. Give it appropriate publicity, was the way she put it."

"How cynical are you? I thought lawyers and cops were bad, but this is low even for journalists."

"Hey! I'm doing a public service," Philo protested.

"Philo, domestic abuse is a serious matter. You've been trying to use it, and a murder case on top of it, to score with some woman."

"Well, uh, yeah, I guess, but..."

"And you're not going to be objective. You're going to write what you think she wants so you can get her in the sack."

"Not necessarily. I'll be professional and give your guy a fair shake," Philo protested.

"Uh, huh. Look, here's your quote. Hal Flanders is innocent. He did not kill his wife."

"That's it?" Philo asked.

"You're going to have to attend the trial and see for yourself. I hope she's worth it."

"Well, she's not Maddy but..."

"That reminds me," Marc said as he picked up his briefcase. "Stop calling her. I was jerking your chain. She's not interested."

"I figured that when she told me about the gun," Philo said to Marc's back.

Marc turned around and replied by saying, "Don't take it personally. She reminds me about the gun at least two or three times a week. See ya', Philo."

THIRTY-ONE

Tony Carvelli and Maddy were standing alongside Carvelli's Camaro. For early November, the weather was a bit cool but not unpleasant. The sun was shining, no clouds, no wind. In fact, most of the trees still had their leaves.

They were at Firehouse Park in Brooklyn Center, less than half a mile from the local FBI offices. Parked off the street by a vacant ball field, the pair of them were waiting for their FBI friends.

"How did Marc's hearing go yesterday on the Flanders' case?" Carvelli asked.

"About the way he expected," Maddy replied. "They set a trial date for early January."

"How's it look?" Carvelli asked. He looked up at the clear, bright blue, sunny sky and deeply inhaled. "I love this time of year," Carvelli said.

"You know Marc. All he ever says is 'we'll see.' So, I guess we'll see. He's gonna want me to do some footwork on it," Maddy replied.

Carvelli looked at his watch and grumbled, "The only time Feebs are on time is when they knock on your door at six in the morning."

"This is them now," Maddy said watching an obviously government-issued car come toward them.

Because offices tend to have ears, it was best for them to meet clandestinely. It would not be a good career move for Johnson and Tess Richards to have to explain Carvelli's involvement.

They parked next to the Camaro, and the four of them gathered at the back of the agent's car.

"Any news on the forensics at the last bank job?" Carvelli asked.

"We have DNA on the wounded girl, but she hasn't turned up," Johnson said.

"You don't suppose they…" Maddy started to ask.

"Killed her or let her die?" Tess finished for her. "Who knows? They might have access to a doctor who removed the bullet and patched her up. We can only hope."

"What about ballistics?" Carvelli asked.

"Nothing. We recovered ten slugs all together, including the one that hit the guard. All from the same gun but not a match with anything on file," Johnson answered.

"So, unless the girl turns up," Maddy said.

"We have evidence if we can find any of them," Tess said.

"What about the search for our mysterious Luke, the gun buyer?" Carvelli asked.

163

"We've narrowed it down to a half a dozen possible. Three look pretty close to the drawing and have no alibi. The other three we have not contacted," Johnson answered. "I've got people still looking for them and investigating the three we found. So far, they don't look too good for it. And we have other cases and, to be blunt, this isn't our highest priority. Don't say it, Carvelli!"

"Say what?" Carvelli said, trying to look innocent.

"Don't say what?" Maddy asked.

"Still wiretapping Republicans?" Johnson said doing his best Carvelli voice mimic.

"Would I say that?" Carvelli innocently asked while Maddy and Tess laughed.

"Every chance you get," Johnson replied.

"What about the other gun found at the bank?" Maddy asked. "Find anything there?"

"Damn," Tess said. "We forgot about that entirely. Did you hear back from ballistics on that one?" she asked Johnson.

Johnson was already on the phone to their local lab as she asked. It rang several times before the head of their lab answered.

"Artie, it's Jeff Johnson. I'm calling about the Lake Country robberies. I didn't get a report on the gun found on the floor of the Eagan branch. What's the deal?"

"I don't know, I'll have to ask Bill Swenson about it," Artie answered, referring to the ballistic guy.

"Hey, Bill," Johnson heard the man yell. "Come here a second."

A minute later he could hear Artie asking the man about the gun found at the bank. He then heard a man's voice say, "Oh shit," then some muffled talk.

"He'll get right on it and have a report this afternoon," Artie told Jeff Johnson.

"Great. Good work," Johnson sarcastically replied.

"The gun was never fired. It slipped through the cracks. We'll fix it," Artie said. Johnson did not hear the last part since he had already ended the call.

"They'll get right on it," Johnson said to the others.

"Relax," Tess said. "We forgot about it, too. Besides, do you really expect to find anything?"

"That's not the point…"

"Let it go," Tess told him.

"Now what?" Maddy asked. "They seem to have gone underground."

"For now," Johnson said. "I don't think they're done."

"Anything new on the manifesto they leave? Prints, DNA?" Carvelli asked.

"No, nothing. I'll say this; they're smart and careful. Our lab guys have been over every one of them. So far, all they can tell us is they'll probably be able to match the printer if we ever find it. Although they do admit, the last two were done on a different printer than the first ones."

"Printers are cheap. You can get a good one at Best Buy..." Carvelli said.

"Or anywhere else," Maddy added.

"...for a couple hundred bucks,"

"What about the money? Have you seen any significant donations to environmental groups or other leftist organizations?" Maddy asked.

"Those groups are not exactly eager to share," Johnson said. "But we have put out the word to the banking world to keep an eye out for that."

"But banks aren't exactly eager to share either," Tess said. "They'll report anything over ten grand, and that's about it."

"You think that's where the money is going?" Johnson asked Maddy.

"It's what they claim. Everybody knows about the ten grand reporting requirements. If they donate in smaller amounts..."

"We'll not be able to trace it," Tess finished for her.

"We'll keep snooping around, but the criminals in the Cities don't know anything either. Except they seem to admire this gang," Carvelli said.

"Stay in touch," Johnson said as the two agents got back in their car.

Jordan Simmons' roommate, Patti, heard a loud, almost demanding knock on their apartment door. It was unexpected and startled her for a moment. She was in her bedroom getting dressed after a shower and struggled into a pair of jeans while hurrying to check it out.

A step before she reached the door, whoever it was gave three or four more loud raps. Patti put her eye to the keyhole and saw two people, an older white man and a younger, Hispanic woman. Both were dressed in office-type clothing except the man's suit was obviously an inexpensive, off-the-rack one. *Cops*, Patti thought as she unlocked the door. She opened it but kept the chain lock in place.

"Can I help you?" she asked, looking at them through the partially open door.

The man held up a Minneapolis detective shield and politely said, "We're with the Minneapolis Police. We've had a report of a missing young woman, Jordan Simmons. Her mother gave us this as her address. Do you know her?"

"Um, yeah. Jordan's my roommate," Patti nervously replied.

"May we come in?" he asked.

"Uh, yeah. Ah, sure," she answered. Patti closed the door, removed the chain and showed them into the apartment.

The men standing in the living room introduced themselves as Detective Mel Lewis and Officer Olivia Nunez. They had decided ahead of time that Nunez would question the roommate. Jordan's mother had told the police who she was.

"May we sit down?" Nunez pleasantly asked nodding at a somewhat shabby couch.

"Oh, sorry, yeah, sure," Patti replied, then scooped up an armful of laundered clothing from the couch. She tossed the clothes into her bedroom then went back and sat down facing the two police officers.

"I haven't seen Jordan for, I don't know, at least a week," she quickly said before being asked.

"Are you Patricia Munson?" Nunez asked, looking at her notebook.

"Oh, yeah, sorry. I'm a little nervous. I don't have much to do with police."

"It's okay," Nunez said with a smile. "We're here because Jordan's parents are worried about her."

"Her mom," Patti said. "She doesn't talk to her dad. She says he's an asshole. Sorry, I mean…"

"It's okay," Nunez said again. "Did she ever say anything about her dad hurting her?"

"No, no, nothing like that. He's just, I don't know, pretty conservative and doesn't approve of her degree program. She's in school at Midwest going for a degree in environmental studies. He wanted her to do something more practical. She says they argue about it a lot. He's paying for it."

"She's been gone for a week, and you didn't call her parents or anyone else?" Lewis asked a little roughly.

"It's not unusual. I just met her a couple of months ago. We run in different circles. Different friends. We don't have the same schedule at school, and we both have jobs. She answered an ad I put in the school paper for a roommate. So, we can go days without seeing each other. She paid her share of the rent for November."

"You don't know who any of her friends might be?" Nunez asked.

"Not really. I know she was kind of hot for a guy she knew. She never told me his name. I thought, maybe, and please don't tell her mom this, maybe they hooked up and went somewhere," Patti replied.

"But you don't know his name?"

"No."

"How about others?"

"No, not really. Like I said, we pretty much had separate lives."

"You mind if we look in her room?"

"No, sure, go ahead. I didn't know her before she moved in but she's really a nice girl. Whatever I can do to help."

The two MPD cops took a half-hour going through Jordon's bedroom. They were careful but also thorough. The only thing of interest was found by Detective Lewis. In a shoebox tucked away under other things in her closet was a diary.

"Can you look at this for me, Patti?" Lewis asked.

He showed her the diary and while he held it, asked her to look through it but not read it.

"Do you recognize the handwriting?"

"Yeah, it's Jordan's. I've seen enough of it. This was written by her."

Lewis and Nunez wore surgical gloves. Nunez held open a clear plastic evidence bag, and Lewis put the diary in it.

"We're going to take this and go through it," Nunez told Patti. "We will protect her privacy, but there could be information in it to help us find her."

"Sure, okay," Patti said.

"I'm going to seal this door with this warning sign," Lewis said, referring to the red paper with the Do Not Enter warning on it he held in his hand. "Don't let anyone come in this bedroom…"

"What if she comes home?"

"Then have her call us," Nunez said.

The officers gave her their business cards and asked her to call if she thought of anything. And of course, if she heard from Jordan or anyone calling and looking for her.

THIRTY-TWO

"I hope my daughter doesn't write this kind of crap," Detective Mel Lewis said to Olivia Nunez across their desks.

Olivia looked up, laughed and replied, "You don't want to know everything that Laurie's up to." She was referring to Mel's sixteen-year-old daughter. They were both reading through copies of Jordan Simmons' diary. They had copies made, and the diary itself sealed in an evidence bag to preserve it.

Mel held up his copy and asked, "Is this the kind of stuff you were into at her age?"

"Not as a teenager, but as far as college goes, I plead the fifth," Olivia replied.

"Hookups means sex, right?" Mel asked.

"Again, I plead the fifth," she replied. "Weren't you ever young and doing things you probably shouldn't have?"

"I was in the army back then fighting Desert Storm," Mel answered.

"That lasted what, a hundred days?"

"That's my story, and I'm sticking with it," Mel replied. "This is some kind of code," Mel continued getting back to the diary. "We need to figure out who L is, and S and B and the others. She is in some kind of group. Sounds like a climate change or environmental thing."

"Especially this L guy she has hot panties for," Olivia said. "We need to get over to Midwest State and find some people who know her. Let's set this aside for now."

"Yeah, good idea. Let's see if we can track them down."

"I'm not sure if I can give that to you," the woman behind the counter told Mel and Olivia with a touch of arrogance.

Sensing her impatient partner was about to light up the female clerk, Olivia took over. "Look, Sharon," she politely said using the name from the plaque on the desk she was sitting at when they arrived. "We have a missing girl here. Her parents are extremely worried. She's been gone for over a week, and we're just trying to find her."

"I don't see how her class schedule could help. If she was in class, she wouldn't be missing, now would she?" the woman said with a smirk on her face as if to convey her superior intelligence.

Olivia grabbed Mel's right hand under the counter and squeezed it to stop him.

"We're looking for people who know her who might be able to help us find her. People who might have some information about where she might be," Olivia replied.

"So, you want to hassle innocent people and use them as informants…"

"What's going on, Sharon?" they heard a man's voice ask from off to the side and out of sight. A moment later he appeared.

"This is Dean Campbell," Sharon said to the two cops. She had a smug look on her face as if to say: *Now you'll find out who's in charge.*

Campbell was a late thirties person dressed casually with a warm smile.

"Alan Campbell," he said, introducing himself. "What can I do for you?"

Olivia and Mel showed him their shields as Olivia said, "We have a report that one of your students is missing. We're trying to locate people who know her and might be able to help us."

"We just want a copy of her class schedule so we can talk to teachers, students and anyone who might know her," Mel said.

"Oh, sure. No problem," Campbell said. He turned the computer monitor so he could read it and asked, "What's her name?"

"You're going to simply give it to them? How do we know…"

"Yes, Sharon," he replied. "I'm going to give it to them. It's not a state secret, and they're not the Gestapo."

"Very well then, I suppose," Sharon said then stomped off.

"You can't fire anyone these days," Campbell said to Mel. "Ordinarily she's very efficient. She's just protective of her turf."

"And desperately needs to get laid," Oliva said.

"That too," Campbell chuckled.

The two cops spent the next two hours tracking down professors. Most of them had classes with too many students to know any of them very well. One of them, a woman in her late-forties dressed like a 60's hippie knew Jordan. The woman, a full-time lawyer and part-time adjunct professor, taught environmental law.

"I was wondering where Jordan has been," she said. "I don't think she missed a single class before this. That's not good, isn't it?"

"We'll see," Olivia replied. "Let's not get ahead of ourselves."

"Now I'm worried," the professor said. "She's a bright kid and was even thinking about law school."

"We certainly need more lawyers," Mel said.

"Ah, there's a cop. Never miss a chance to take a shot at lawyers," the professor replied, but she was laughing when she said it.

"Sorry," Mel weakly said.

"It's okay, Detective. I don't like most lawyers either. But if you want to buy me dinner, I might be able to change your mind."

"Ah, I ah," a shocked Mel Lewis started to stutter.

"He'd have to get permission from his wife," Olivia said.

"You guys should wear rings. Anyway, I can think of a couple of people for you to check with."

She gave them the names of five students, three young women and two guys. The two cops were able to track down all five of them before calling it a day.

"You're pretty quiet," Olivia said while starting their car, "What gives?"

"That last one. I'm certain he was lying. Why would Professor Saunders give us his name along with the others? All four of the other kids admitted knowing her. And I think they were honest when they said they didn't know where she could be. The last one..."

"Denied even knowing who she is. Yeah, I caught that, too," Olivia said.

"We need to check him out a little more. Something's not right there," Mel said. "Gary Weaver," Mel continued looking at his notes. "Why did he lie to us?"

"There's a G in Jordan's diary she refers to quite a few times," Olivia said.

"Yeah, you're right, there is."

"Could be anyone," Olivia said.

"Yeah, it could," Mel agreed.

"The cops just talked to me about Jordan," Gary said. He was on the phone with Luke, having called him as soon as he got away from campus.

"What did they want?" Luke asked. "What did they ask you?"

"If I knew her," Gary quickly replied.

"Calm down..."

"You calm down. The cops found me," Gary almost yelled.

"How did they find you?" Luke asked.

"Ah, Professor Saunders. The hippie who teaches environmental law gave them my name. She knows we knew each other."

"And you lied to the cops about it," Luke harshly said.

"Hey! I, well, yeah, I guess I did," Gary meekly admitted.

The phone went silent for a few seconds, then Luke said, "Did you get a business card from them?"

"Yeah, I did. From both," Gary admitted. "A man, a detective and his partner, a chick."

"Okay, tomorrow morning call them back. Call the chick. Tell her you were nervous. Tell her you just got scared because you never had to deal with cops before..."

"I have a couple times," Gary said.

"Okay, then tell her you've had a couple of bad experiences with cops and you just got scared. Then answer their questions. You haven't seen Jordan and have no idea where she is. Do you have Jordan's name and number in your personal phone?"

"No, I'm sure of it."

"Okay. Relax and call them back tomorrow then call me and let me know what happened."

"Will do," a much calmer Gary said.

"Guess who I just talked to?" Olivia said to Mel as he walked to her desk.

"Here, take this, it's hot," Mel said, holding a ceramic coffee cup for Olivia.

"Thanks," she said. "So, guess who?"

"I'm very bad at that," Mel said as he took his chair across from her.

"Gary Weaver," Olivia answered sipping her coffee.

"Oh? And what did he have to say?"

"He admitted he lied yesterday. Gave me some BS about having been hassled by cops and was nervous," she answered.

"And he knows her but has no idea where she might be. Hasn't seen her and so forth," Mel said.

"You got it."

"In fact, barely knew her. Just to sit by in class and say hello to," Mel added.

"Were you listening in?"

"There's a reason he lied, and it isn't because he was nervous about talking to cops," Mel said. "He knows something. Did you get his phone number?"

"Yeah," Olivia answered. "You want me to run it?"

"Yes. Let's do a search and find out how many times he called this girl he barely knew. Jordan's phone number is in the file."

"I know, her mother gave it to us. I'll get right on it."

When Gary told Luke that Jordan's name and phone number were not listed in Gary's phone, he was telling the truth. What he did not tell Luke was that Gary had simply deleted her name and number from his listings. A phone company tech could retrieve his calls.

By midafternoon, the tech guy doing the call search for Olivia was finished. He emailed a list of all of Gary's calls for the past year. There were over a hundred of them to Jordan's personal phone. Gary Weaver, even though he was involved with Donna Gilchrist, had a secret crush on Jordan.

That same afternoon, Jeff Johnson's boss received an email. Attached to it was the ballistic report for the gun Jordan dropped when she was shot. Johnson's boss, the Special Agent in Charge (SAIC) of the Minneapolis field office, was a woman with a rather well-known name: Taylor Swift. Other than musical talent, the main difference between this Taylor Swift and the better-known one was this Taylor Swift was an African American.

Agent Swift read through the attached ballistics report of Jordan's gun. When she finished, she quietly said to herself. "Interesting. Wait till she sees this."

She clicked on the 'forward' selection on the email and typed in the address. She also wrote a quick note to her good friend, Felicia Jones, the Hennepin County Attorney. Taylor Swift, the SAIC, was normally a very sharp, efficient woman. This time, she made a mistake. She neglected to send the report to her agents, Jeff Johnson and Tess Richards.

THIRTY-THREE

Billy Clark was crashing through the forest's underbrush toward the sound of his friend. He was making enough noise thrashing about to scare off every deer within a half a mile. Billy was not the least bit concerned with that.

Twenty minutes ago, Billy had shot a trophy buck. The deer dropped on the spot, but by the time Billy climbed down from his tree stand, it was gone. He was sure he hit the big boy because of the blood trail. Billy and his two friends had tracked it for a couple of hundred yards, then lost him. They had spread out to try to pick up the trail and a minute ago, the man in the middle of the three of them, Nick Santos, had yelled out that he had found it.

"You got it?" Billy yelled at Nick as soon as he saw him standing among the trees.

"Yeah, yeah," Nick yelled back waving at him. "Right here."

Billy joined up with Nick, and a few seconds later, the third man, Paul O'Brien followed.

"Oh, yeah," Billy said. "That's gotta be him. Fresh blood. Let's go."

"Looks like he's losing more blood," Paul said as they started off.

Less than five minutes later, it was Nick who was the first to see the buck.

"There! There he is," Nick excitedly said.

The deer was quite visible, lying on its side in a small opening among the brush. They started running as best as they could through the undergrowth toward it. Paul got to it first. Billy next and then Nick stepped on a slight, short mound on the ground and fell face first almost landing on the dead deer.

While his friends laughed, Nick stood up, brushed himself off, then picked up his rifle.

"I stepped in something," Nick said as he went back to the mound of brush, leaves and dirt.

He knelt down to examine the indentation made by his foot. Nick started moving aside the detritus to get a better look, even digging up the dirt around his footprint.

"Never mind that," Billy said. "Give us a hand with this monster. We got lucky. The road is less than a hundred yards away."

Ignoring his friend, Nick continued to dig with his hands where he had stumbled. About a minute or so into his excavation, Nick muttered, "What is this?"

173

Working more quickly, he expanded the hole and his two companions joined him, stood behind him and watched over his shoulder.

"What is that?" Paul asked. "It looks like a plastic bag," he added, answering himself.

Nick took his hunting knife from its sheath and gently sliced open the plastic. He replaced the knife in its sheath then, using two fingers of each hand, pulled the plastic apart.

"Holy shit!" Nick yelled, fell backward onto his butt and scrambled backward away from what he had seen.

"Is that…" Paul started to ask.

"It's a body," Billy quietly said.

They all stepped back and silently stared at the discovery. Not quite sure if it was a body or what to do, they stood silently for several moments.

"We gotta check it," Paul said. "We need to make sure."

"Go ahead," Nick quietly said.

"Come on," Billy said. "Whatever it is, it won't hurt us," he continued as he slowly walked toward it.

Several hours later, the deer still lying unattended, the body of Jordan Simmons was carefully removed from her shallow grave. The Aitkin County Sheriff's deputies had the area sealed off, and a team from the state Bureau of Criminal Apprehension had arrived.

Aitkin County, along with several others in Minnesota, did not have its own medical examiner. They used the Ramsey County—St. Paul—M.E. That is why it had taken so long to remove the body. Everyone had to wait for the M.E. to arrive.

The three hunters, having calmed down from the sight of their discovery, were standing on the road cradling their rifles. They had been questioned by the sheriff and then held for the BCA people from St. Paul. It was the BCA who were the ones searching the area for evidence.

"Say, uh, Sheriff," Billy asked, walking over toward the sheriff.

"I guess you boys can go," the sheriff replied.

"So, is there any way I can get my deer out of there?" Billy asked.

"Too late now anyway, son. The meat's gone bad by now," the sheriff said.

"I don't care about the meat. I want the trophy. That's a ten or twelve-point buck."

"Sorry, son. It's a crime scene. We can't have people stomping around in there."

"Next time I'm in Aitken, can I stop by your office and get a look at it since it will be mounted on your wall?" Billy asked.

174

"You can go now, smartass. There's a dead girl in there," the sheriff seriously told him while thinking, *That's not a bad idea. It will look good on my wall.*

Detective Mel Lewis and Officer Olivia Nunez waited patiently to view the body. They were at the Ramsey County medical examiner's office with a recent picture of Jordan Simmons. As a routine part of their job with the MPD missing persons unit, they checked the notices of discovered bodies every day. That was how they found out about the discovery of the dead girl in Aitkin County.

Jordan was found naked with no identification on her. The decomposition would normally make fingerprinting very difficult. Even so, Jordan, having never been fingerprinted, was not in the FBI's database, AFIS. The two MPD police officers would view the body for a possible identification.

They had been waiting for about ten minutes when a white-coated technician came for them. She led them back to the autopsy area to view the body. Nunez held the photo of Jordan while they looked at the girl's face. Decomposition made it more than a little gruesome, even for veteran cops.

"It's her," Mel Lewis said.

"You sure?" the pathologist asked.

"Yeah," Nunez answered. "We'll see about getting dental records from the parents, but I'm convinced."

"C.O.D.?" Lewis asked, referring to the cause of death.

"Unofficially, she has what looks to be two gunshot entry wounds," the pathologist said. "One on the back of her right leg, upper thigh. Another one in the right side of her skull. That's probably the one that killed her."

At that moment, the lab's door opened and a man in a suit entered.

"Kevin Turner, BCA," the man said introducing himself to Lewis and Nunez, both of whom reciprocated.

"Is she your case?" Turner asked.

Nunez handed him the photo while saying, "Yeah, we're pretty sure."

Turner looked her over, compared it to the photo and agreed.

"Where was she killed?" Turner asked.

"Was it where she was found?" Lewis asked him.

"No. There's no indication of that. Besides, why shoot someone up in the woods then wrap her up in plastic to bury her?"

"Very little blood inside the plastic bags they wrapped her in," the doctor added.

175

"So, she was moved," Lewis said.

"Doctor you said she was shot in the back of the leg," Nunez said.

"That's right. We'll get both bullets, the one in her leg and the one in her head."

"What are you looking for?" Turner asked.

"The Eagan bank robbery a couple weeks ago," Nunez said. "One of them was shot. A female shot in the back of the leg. Remember?" she asked Mel Lewis.

"That's right," Lewis said. "Good catch. Be careful with the bullets, Doc. The FBI will want them for the bank robbery."

"No problem."

"Minneapolis want jurisdiction?" Turner asked, referring to the investigation.

"For now, sure," Lewis answered. "We have the missing person case. Odds are she was killed in Minneapolis or, at least, Hennepin County.

"When's the autopsy?" Lewis asked the pathologist.

"I was going to do it this afternoon. You want to be here?"

"Someone will—either us or MPD homicide. We'll go inform the parents and find out who her dentist was," Lewis replied.

"Unless you want to," Nunez said to Turner.

"No, thanks. I've done my share of that. Worst thing ever."

"Informing parents their child is dead. Horrible," Nunez added.

"Here," the doctor said to Lewis. He was holding a business card out to him. "If you find the dentist, have him email the x-rays. My address is on the card."

"Good, I'll do that."

The four men sent to attend Jordan's autopsy leaned against various tables in the lab. They were patiently waiting for the pathologist after they had introduced themselves to the doctor and each other.

In attendance were two homicide detectives from Minneapolis; Jack Menke and Cliff McNamee. Both in their fifties, they had been partners for over twenty years. They were also the least productive team in the MPD Homicide Division. Both were treading water, waiting to max out their pensions. The pair were known as the M and M boys. An ironic reference to Mickey Mantle and Roger Maris. They were also called this because like the candy, they were hard on the outside and soft on the inside.

The other pair were two FBI agents. A black man with twelve years as an agent, Terrell Jones. With him was his younger and much greener partner, Elliot Douglas.

176

Having expected Jeff Johnson and Tess Richards, the MPD detectives were abruptly informed by Jones that Johnson and Richards had been reassigned. When Menke inquired as to what Johnson and Richards were reassigned, he was told, somewhat arrogantly, the Bureau's business was not public information.

"Before I get started…," the doctor started to say.

Before he went further, the lab door opened and Marcie Sterling, by herself, came in.

"What are you doing here?" Menke asked, clearly annoyed.

"Jefferson told me to come over here and observe," Marcie said.

She opened her small purse and removed a bottle of VapoRub. Like the others, she applied a generous amount under her nose to block the smell.

"As I was saying," the doctor continued. "I received a set of dental x-rays. I ran a comparison and verified the woman's identity as being Jordan Alison Simmons."

The doctor held up a small, plastic bottle and said, "I have already removed the bullet from her leg. The wound was starting to show signs of infection. Given that, I can estimate she was alive eight to ten hours after she was shot in the leg. That wound was definitely not the cause of death. Who wants it?" he asked, referring to the bullet.

"We'll take it," Special Agent Jones quickly said. He stepped up to the table, reached across the body and snatched it from the M.E.'s hand.

"You gonna just stand there and let him take it?" Marcie asked the M and M boys.

"They'll send us the ballistics report," McNamee replied. "Right?"

Before Jones could answer, Marcie said. "This is a local homicide case…"

"It's part of a federal bank robbery investigation," Jones said. "We take precedence."

"Great, we're going to have a jurisdictional mine's-bigger-than-yours case," Marcie said.

"We'll work it out, Marcie. Relax," McNamee said.

The pathologist started by cutting a Y incision the length and width of her abdomen. For the next three hours, he methodically opened her up, removed and weighed internal organs and found nothing out of the ordinary—a healthy, young, twenty-one-year-old female.

At one point Marcie asked after he had cut open and examined her pubic area, "Was she pregnant?"

"Why would we care about that?" Jones asked.

"Motive," Marcie replied. "You don't do very many homicides, I guess."

"No, she was not pregnant."

Finally, the pathologist opened the skull. As he examined it, he continued to record into a microphone.

The bullet entered the right side of her skull three centimeters above the right ear. It passed through both halves of her cerebrum doing massive tissue damage to the brain.

He closely examined the entry wound and carefully removed twenty-seven pieces of, what appeared to be brown cotton fibers.

"A pillow?" Marcie asked.

"Likely," the doctor replied. "The lab will examine them more carefully and thoroughly. It looks like whoever shot her, placed a pillow on her head and shot through it. There is also gunshot residue on the wound but not nearly as much if the shooter had placed the gun against her head."

It took him another half-hour to carefully examine and remove the brain. During the course of this, the doctor retrieved the bullet. Despite having gone through the skull, it was still in good condition. This one was also taken by the FBI.

A half-hour after leaving the M.E. lab, Marcie stormed into Owen Jefferson's office.

"Come right in, Marcie. I always appreciate that you don't feel the need to knock first," Jefferson said before Marcie had a chance to speak.

Marcie took a deep breath, pursed her lips together, gave her boss a nasty look and said, "Fine!" She then went out, closed the door, knocked once and went back inside.

"Okay, what's wrong?"

"You screwed up giving this case to the M and M's," Marcie said. "The FBI is going to run all over them and it's our case."

"How'd the autopsy go?"

"Two bullets. One in the upper thigh, back of her right leg. The next one was roughly eight hours later through the brain. We, I mean the Feebs, got both bullets."

"Jeff Johnson…"

"Jeff's been reassigned," Marcie said. "We got two other guys. I know one of them, Terrell Jones. He's an arrogant, by-the-book guy who acts like local cops are too stupid to be in the FBI. The other guy I don't know."

"You think this is the girl from the Eagan bank robbery?"

"Probably."

"That's their case, anyway," Jefferson said, referring to the feds. "And there's not much I can do about it now. It will work out. Besides, you have enough to do."

"Can I keep an eye on it?" Marcie asked.

"Discreetly," Jefferson answered.

THIRTY-FOUR

"In case any of you haven't heard, the police questioned Gary about Jordan," Ben announced to the group.

They were gathered in Ben's basement a week after Gary spoke to the police. It was also the same day Jordan's body was found although none of them knew this, yet. Luke and Ben had decided it was time to cool it for a while longer. At least for a couple of months, because of Jordan. Ben reminded them of this.

"What did you tell them?" Cindy asked Gary.

"They wanted to know if I knew Jordan and have I seen her or talked to her lately. I told them that I knew her, but I had not talked to her and had no idea where she might be," Gary replied.

Luke stood up from where he was seated next to Ben, and said, "No one outside of this room knows anything about what happened to her. If we stick together and everybody keeps their mouths shut, we'll be fine. Even if they ever find her, which is highly unlikely, they have no evidence of anything and won't find any."

Luke sat down again as Reese asked, "What about money? Can we still have some to help us get through?"

"Ben, we'd like another accounting," Cindy said. "Not that we don't trust you..."

"Absolutely," Ben said, interrupting her. "I'm sorry, I should have prepared one for you tonight. I'll have one the next time we meet. And Reese, yes, we have money to get us through for a while. Is another five thousand okay on top of the ten I gave you before?"

"How long are you thinking we need to cool it?" Sherry asked.

"At least until after the first of the year. January, maybe even February. Give the cops a chance to move on to something else," Ben answered.

"Everybody okay with that?" Luke asked.

All their heads bobbed up and down along with a few quiet "yes" and "sounds good" being said.

Ben passed out more cash, and the meeting broke up. It was after midnight on a weekday which meant the neighborhood was asleep. As they were starting to leave, Luke pulled Neil aside.

"Hey, I need a new job. My new appearance is a distraction at the grocery store where I am now. Is that place you work at looking for people?"

"Always. I'll call you with the information. They'll hire you in a heartbeat," Neil replied.

"Good, thanks. I'll talk to you tomorrow."

"Is that a good idea? You, me and Gary all working in the same place?"

"It'll be okay," Luke said.

"If you say so. I'll call tomorrow."

After everyone had left, Ben and Luke were upstairs having a drink.

"What did Neil say about the job?" Ben asked.

"He said it shouldn't be a problem," Luke replied.

"That's a good idea, you get in there and keep an eye on Gary," Ben said.

"It's either that or we deal with him the way Sherry wants to," Luke said.

"Only as a very last resort."

"You need to stop sleeping with her," Luke unexpectedly said, catching Ben off guard.

"What? I don't know..." Ben tried to protest.

"Don't go there, Ben. Everybody knows, and it's a bad idea."

"It's also none of your..."

"Yes, it is, and drop the bullshit," Luke demanded. "It puts us all at risk."

"How?"

"It stops, now," Luke told him, making it sound like an order, which it was.

Ben sat sullenly for several seconds, watching Luke's unwavering eyes. He then meekly replied, "Okay, if you insist."

"I do," Luke said. "Cindy's right, we need an accounting. I don't care what you show them, but I want the real one. I know you've been spending our money on personal things..."

Ben opened his mouth to deny it, but Luke verbally slapped him down again. "Don't bother denying it. Don't treat me like an idiot. I want to know where the money has gone."

"Okay," Ben docilely agreed.

The group's power dynamic had permanently shifted.

"I'm telling you, Boss, we've been on this Weaver kid like white on rice," Jack Menke said.

The M and M cops were sitting in the chairs in front of Lt. Owen Jefferson's desk a week after Jordan's autopsy. Jefferson was looking for a case status report on the murder of Jordan Simmons. He was getting heat from on high about the case. Even though the Feds had stolen the case, it was still an MPD case. The Feds could suck eggs. But by now both the state BCA and the Hennepin County Sheriff's Office were sticking their nose into it. If the MPD did not come up with some evidence soon, they might take the case, and as usual, the Feds were not sharing.

"Weaver hasn't done anything to draw any suspicion that he knows what happened to her," Cliff McNamee added.

"Have you come up with any evidence she was murdered in Minneapolis?" Jefferson calmly asked.

"The van they drove away from the Eagan bank job was seen heading toward Minneapolis," McNamee replied. "The girl lived in Minneapolis."

"It was seen driving west on 494," Jefferson said. "It could have gone anywhere."

"We got a couple people who saw a brown Ford van right after the robbery heading north on Hiawatha," Menke reminded Jefferson.

"It's as likely she was murdered in Minneapolis as anywhere else in Hennepin County and even the BCA admits she was transported to Aitkin County. Tell the BCA to pound sand," McNamee said.

"What about the diary?" Jefferson asked.

"We showed it to everybody we could find who knew her except the Weaver kid, including her roommate. We didn't want to spook Weaver," McNamee replied. "None of them could tell us who the initials in it belong to. Could be anyone."

"Any other numbers this Weaver called that might be them?"

"There were about a dozen calls to a Midwest State professor, a Ben Sokol," Menke replied. "Weaver made other calls to other professors at the school. Not as many as Sokol but a couple of them have either first or last names starting with letters in the diary."

"What are the Feds thinking?" McNamee asked Jefferson. "She was involved in the bank robbery so why can't we get the ballistic reports on the two bullets found in her?"

"You don't have them?" Jefferson asked.

"No, we haven't heard a thing. We've asked a half dozen times, too."

"I'll go upstairs and see what we can do. With the Feebs, information is too often a one-way street," Jefferson said.

"How about we pick up this Weaver kid and lean on him?" McNamee asked. Cliff McNamee was never shy about using extralegal persuasion of a physical type.

"No, not yet. You have any reason to believe he knows something?"

"He lied to Nunez and Mel Lewis," McNamee reminded him.

"At first. Plus, he's a college boy. Odds are he'll scream to his mom and dad for a lawyer, and that will be that. Let me see what the Feebs are up to. In the meantime, you have other cases."

While the M and Ms were meeting with Jefferson, Tony Carvelli was sitting down with two executives from Lake Country Federal. One was his contact, Bob Olson and the other was their head of security, Randy Townes, a man Carvelli knew well. They were in Olson's office. Carvelli and Townes on a couch; Olson a matching armchair with an expensive glass table between them.

"Nice view of the new stadium," Carvelli said.

"Haven't you been up here since I got the new office?" Olson asked. "Thanks, Dorothy," he said to his assistant who had brought in coffee for them.

"No, I haven't," Carvelli said.

"Lifestyles of the rich and pampered," Towne said taking a little shot at his boss.

"Here we go with the class warfare," Olson shot back with a smile.

"Anyway, Tony," Olson said. "Getting on with the show. What are you hearing from the Feds?"

"Nothing. My two contacts have been taken off the case. I was very rudely told to get lost. Your phone call to the SAIC, Ms. Swift, didn't mean much."

"Randy?" Olson asked Towne.

"There's a new sheriff in town in Brooklyn Center," Towne replied referring to the location of the FBI headquarters.

"Goddamnit it's our bank," Olson snapped. "What the hell..."

"Oh, they'll keep us informed," Towne said. "At least as little as they can get away with. Trust is not a word they often use. And they won't let Tony snoop around anymore. In fact, they could throw his ass in jail and charge him with impeding a federal investigation, obstruction of justice and probably a few other things."

"I think with the news that the girl's body was found..." Carvelli started to say.

"You think she was a member of the gang?" Olson asked.

"I heard that the bullet they pulled out of her leg was one shot from the guard's gun. The other one, my source didn't know about," Carvelli said.

"The other what one?" Olson asked.

"The other bullet. She was shot twice. Once in the leg, then several hours later, someone shot her in the head."

By the time Carvelli finished reminding Olson of this, Olson was nodding his head, then said, "That's right, you told me that before."

"I think they've gone quiet," Carvelli said. "Maybe even decided to stop."

"What about their manifesto to save the planet from all of us greedy capitalists?" Towne asked.

"Getting somebody killed..."

"Or more likely doing the job themselves," Towne said.

"...probably scared the hell out of them. These aren't professional criminals. They're more like cult members," Carvelli said.

"That's what all of these tree-hugging, save-the-planet nitwits are," Olson said. "Not a rational or independent thought in their heads."

"Anyway, as I said, I think they've stopped. At least for a while. But, I'm out of it, Bob. I like you, but not enough to face federal prison time. You're gonna have to deal with the Feds."

"I appreciate all you've done, Tony. We've received more information from you than the FBI. Get me a bill, and I'll see to it you get paid."

"How's Ms. Rivers?" Towne asked Tony.

"Maddy? She's good. She was very helpful," Carvelli replied.

"Did you get to meet her, Bob?" Towne asked Olson.

"No, I don't think so," Olson said.

"You'd remember," Towne told him.

THIRTY-FIVE

Marc Kadella had his desk chair turned around to the window behind his desk. He had the window open and was leaning on the windowsill watching the traffic on Lyndale. The snow was coming down in large, fluffy snowflakes, rapidly piling up below on the streets and sidewalks.

Marc stuck his head completely out of the window then looked to his right at a city bus on Lake Street. He deeply inhaled a large breath of the cool, fresh air. He heard a single rap on his door, then Connie Mickelson entered his office.

"Don't do it! Don't jump, Marc! You've got a lot to live for," Connie facetiously yelled.

Marc pulled his head in, spun his chair around to look at her and said, "It's only the second floor. I'd probably just break a leg. Oh, don't do that…" he added as Connie moved a client chair to the other window. She opened it, sat down and put a cigarette in her mouth.

"Why do you have to do that here?" Marc asked as she fired up her plastic lighter.

"It's too smoky in my office. I need to let it air out," she replied.

"Go outside."

"It's snowing, numbnuts. Didn't you notice when you had your head stuck out the window?"

"Happy Hanukkah," Marc said for at least the twentieth time to her.

"Merry Christmas," Connie replied as she blew a stream of smoke out of the window.

"Speaking of which," she continued, "what are you and Maddy doing for Christmas? You should go somewhere."

"The kids are coming over Christmas Eve. Eric's bringing a girlfriend I haven't met. Jessie's bringing the guy I approve of, sort of. Maddy and I are flying out Christmas morning to Chicago."

"How's her dad?" Connie asked.

"It doesn't look good," Marc replied.

Maddy's father, an ex-Chicago cop, had been dealing with bladder cancer for two years. It was back and metastasizing.

"She's pretty worried. He's a young man yet. He just turned sixty and, well, it doesn't look good."

"I'm sorry. Is it okay to talk to her about it?" Connie asked.

"Of course," Marc said, "She's a big girl…"

There was another knock-on Marc's door and the subject of their conversation came in.

"Speak of the Devil," Marc said.

"What? Hi, Connie," Maddy said as she sat down.

"Hey, kid. We were just talking about your dad," Connie said.

"Yeah," Maddy softly said. "I don't think he'll see another Christmas. I love him and I'll miss him."

"Don't give up. We've all heard about people who were told they had little time left, then recovered. Hang on to hope," Connie told her then tossed her cigarette out the window and pulled it shut.

"Do you two want to be alone?" Connie asked.

"Here? Now?" Maddy replied. This eased the tension and brought a laugh.

"I have a list of witnesses for Flanders from Lake Country's mortgage department," Maddy said.

"Their mortgage department? What's that for?" Connie asked.

"We're having trouble coming up with a plausible substitute for the some-other-dude-did-it defense," Marc said. "Natalie Flanders was a vice-president at Lake Country. She headed up their foreclosure department. I guess she had a law degree. Anyway, Ms. Rivers came up with the idea that maybe it was someone the bank foreclosed on and he snapped, stalked Natalie and shot her."

"It's a theory," Connie agreed.

"Plausible," Marc said.

"They have hundreds of threatening letters from angry people. The problem is none of the letters were addressed specifically to Natalie Flanders. I have a dozen people to add to the witness list to testify about this," Maddy continued.

"When do you exchange witness lists?" Connie asked.

"The twenty-first," Marc answered.

"Tomorrow," Connie said.

"Uh, yeah, tomorrow," Marc said.

"Discovery?" Connie asked.

Marc shrugged and said, "I guess I have everything, but who knows? The Nazi has been known to, sort of, overlook some things at times."

While Marc was mentioning him to Connie, Jerry Krain, the Nazi, was at his desk reviewing a document. It was a ballistic report forwarded to him from the FBI through Krain's boss, Felicia Jones. It was the ballistic report for the gun found at the last Lake Country Federal robbery in Eagan. The one dropped by Jordan Simmons and left behind. The ballistics comparison came up a 98% match for the gun that killed Natalie Flanders.

Krain had read the report so many times he practically had it memorized. It was a Colt 9mm G10. Black with what are called Cherry

186

grips. A wood-style grain on the handle. The serial number had been removed, and the FBI tech was unable to recover any of it. It was the same type of handgun owned by Hal Flanders, but not exactly the same as Flanders' gun.

There were three or four raps on his door, then Jennifer Moore walked in. As she did so, Krain calmly, as natural as could be so as not to arouse suspicion, opened a desk drawer and put the report in it.

"I have the witness list ready. You want to look it over before I send it to Kadella?" Jennifer asked.

"How many names are on it?" Krain asked.

"Over two hundred, which is a childish stunt I don't approve of," Jennifer answered.

"I'll let you know when I care about what you approve or disapprove of," Krain said.

"What were you reading? It looked like a ballistics report from the FBI," Jennifer said.

"And?"

"I've seen enough of them," Jennifer replied. "Let me see it."

"It has nothing to do with the case you're working on," Krain lied.

"Then you won't mind if I look at it. Obviously, you didn't want me to see it."

"Mind your own business, Jennifer. Work your cases and don't worry about mine. Send the witness list any time you want. Thank you. You may go, I have work to do."

Marc jammed Maddy's suitcase into the plane's overhead then forced the lid to close. He looked down at Maddy, who was already seated at the window.

"Don't say it," she said. "I don't want to start a fight on Christmas morning. I just got a great gift from my boyfriend; I'm going to visit my family, and I don't want to fight."

"Fight about what?" Marc innocently asked.

"It saves twenty-five bucks, and the time it takes waiting for the luggage to be unloaded," Maddy said.

"Yeah, that fifteen minutes it takes to get your luggage delivered rather than dragging it through an airport makes all the difference. I told you, if we didn't have to wait for everyone to pull their stuff out of the overheads, we'd make up the fifteen minutes."

"Don't start, please," Maddy said. "It's Christmas. Let's just agree to disagree on this one."

"You're right, sorry. So, you like the gift?"

"Eight days in London? That's wonderful. Now I just need to decide who to go with," she laughed.

"I've been waiting for you to say that," Marc replied, shaking his head. "Be careful. I can still get most of it refunded."

Maddy put an arm through his, leaned her head on his shoulder and said, "Okay. I'll keep you around at least until then."

"Did I ever tell you I had a divorce client once who booked a weeklong cruise for him and his wife? A rekindle the marriage kind of thing," Marc said.

"Okay," Maddy replied.

"Anyway, they flew to Miami, got on board, and as soon as they got to sea, the very first day, she told him she wanted a divorce. They spent the entire cruise together not speaking."

"Oh my God," Maddy said. "Are you serious?"

"Yeah. He said it was even worse than you could imagine. They slept in the same bed, but most of the time they avoided each other."

"What was she thinking?"

"How should I know?" Mac replied. "You know men have no idea what women are thinking."

"And we're going to keep it that way," Maddy replied while poking a finger in his ribs.

"Good God," Marc whispered as he looked up the center aisle. A five-foot-tall woman that had to weigh at least two-fifty was coming at him eyeing up the empty seat next to him.

A moment later, Marc said, "Hello," as pleasantly as he could while she squeezed into that empty seat.

By this point, Maddy was staring out the window gently biting down on her left hand, trying not to laugh.

The two of them, pulling their luggage along, exited O'Hare at the passenger drop-off area. Maddy had called the ride—her brother Steve—who told her where he was.

As they approached Steve, Maddy could tell by the look on her brother's face, something was wrong. Steve normally wore a huge smile when he saw her, but today, he had a serious expression.

"What happened?" Maddy asked without even greeting him.

"Hi, Marc," Steve said as the two men shook hands.

"What happened?" Maddy asked again more insistently.

"Madeline!" Marc said.

"Something's wrong…"

"Dad's in the hospital. He collapsed this morning. Fainted. He's at Mercy now," Steve told her.

"Let's go," Maddy said, tossing her suitcase in Steve's trunk. She grabbed Marc's and threw it in on top of hers.

She slammed the trunk lid down, then began rushing toward the car door. Before she got there, Marc grabbed her, spun her around, held her by her shoulders and softly said, "Take a breath."

"My Daddy," she started to say with tears in her eyes.

Marc pulled her in and held her and repeated, "Take a breath. We'll get there."

"Okay," she replied. "You're right. Sorry."

As they pulled away from the curb, Marc, from the front passenger seat, asked Steve, "What did the doctors say?"

"Not much. They weren't sure. He's weak, and the chemo is really draining his strength. Plus, he's not eating enough."

"Steve, tell me the truth," Maddy said from the back seat. "Is today the day?"

"I don't know. He's not good, Sis," Steve said. "He needs to eat more to keep up his strength."

Marc swiveled around, reached back and took Maddy's hand, squeezed it lightly, and asked, "You okay?"

"Yeah, I am," she answered. "I don't want him to die on Christmas Day."

"Slow down. You're getting a little ahead here," Marc said.

They found Maddy's mother sitting at the side of her husband's bed. Her sister, Karen, was there also. Maddy hugged her mother and sister then looked at her dad.

"He's better," they both assured her.

"How are you feeling, Dad?" Maddy asked, taking his right hand.

"Okay," he said. "I don't know what happened. Fainted, I guess. I'm feeling much better now."

Every time she saw her dad, the big, strong, ex-Chicago cop, Maddy had to fight the tears. He was hairless from the chemo, his face bloated and pale. The cancer, a hideous disease, was eating him from the inside.

"What's this I hear that you're not eating?" Maddy admonished him.

"Here we go," her dad said.

"I warned you she would chew your butt for it," his wife said.

"Well?" Maddy asked.

"Hello, Marc," he said, ignoring her.

"Hi, Joe. It's good to see you again. How are you feeling?"

"A little better," he replied.

"Well?" Maddy said again.

"You might as well answer her," Marc said. "You know she won't drop it."

"Nothing tastes good, or even sounds good except chocolate milk. And it soothes my stomach."

A doctor walked in, saving him from further confrontation with his daughter. The woman greeted everyone, then stood at the foot of Joel's bed.

"We're gonna keep you overnight..." she started.

"Merry goddamn Christmas," Joel said.

"Joel!" His wife snapped at him.

"Merry Christmas," the doctor replied with a big smile. "Everything seems normal..."

"For a crabass old man," Maddy said.

"Yes, for a crabass old man," the doctor agreed. "We'll keep you overnight, by then I'm sure the nurses will insist you go home tomorrow."

"Is the cafeteria open?" Maddy asked the doctor.

"Of course. They're serving a turkey dinner for lunch. Take him down there and make him eat," the doctor said.

Two days later, as they were flying back to Minnesota, Maddy took Marc's hand, kissed his cheek and said, "Thank you."

"For what?"

"Coming with me. That dinner we had with the whole family on Christmas in the hospital cafeteria will be a great memory. Especially if it's the last one with him."

"It was nice, wasn't it? And the meal was quite good," Marc replied.

"I love you," Maddy told him.

"Does this mean you're not gonna dump me until at least July, after London?"

Maddy sat silent for a half a minute or so then Marc said, "Well?"

"I'm thinking," she answered.

THIRTY-SIX

"Does the state wish to make an opening statement?" Judge McVein asked.

Jennifer Moore stood and said, "Yes, your Honor."

"You may proceed."

"Thank you, your Honor."

Moore stepped out from behind the prosecution's table, took a few steps to get in front of the jury and stopped. Her hands folded in front of her, she took a moment to solemnly look at each juror including the three alternates. She then started by reintroducing herself and Jerry Krain.

Starting Monday morning, it had taken until 8:00 Wednesday evening to select the jury. Because the charge facing Hal Flanders was first-degree murder, jury selection was always slower. Each prospective juror had to be examined individually. First by the judge, then the prosecution and finally the defense.

Jury selection is always a contest among three competing interests.

The judge, assuming he or she is an objective, unbiased professional, is looking for a fair and open-minded jury. The defense and prosecution really do not want anything resembling an unbiased jury. Each side wants a jury totally slanted toward their point of view. Of course, if all three do their job, the jury, at least in theory, will be fair, unbiased and open-minded in theory.

In reality, the prosecution almost always has a huge advantage. People being people, it is rare that most of them do not have, at least a little, bias toward guilty. Why else would the defendant be sitting there if he was not?

During jury selection, the good defense lawyer will spend most of his/her time indoctrinating the jury, repeatedly asking each one if they believe in innocent until proven guilty, understand the burden of proof and the concept of guilt beyond a reasonable doubt. Then make each juror give you their word, in court, that they will do their duty, wait until all of the evidence has been submitted and then make a decision.

It was now Thursday morning. The jury had been sworn in, and Jennifer Moore would give the opening statement for the prosecution. Moore was an experienced and very good prosecutor. Marc believed she was better and more professional than Jerry Krain. In fact, he was glad that their immediate superior, Steve Gondeck, had assigned the case to Krain and not Moore.

Moore did an excellent job giving the jury a tour of the case against Hal Flanders. She thoroughly took them through what they would hear from the witnesses and the evidence they would submit. It did not hurt Jennifer's jury appeal that she looked and came across as the girl next door; a pretty blonde, blue-eyed girl Minnesota grows like a cash crop. One you would want your son to bring home.

As a conclusion, Moore explained the concept of a circumstantial case versus one with witnesses who saw the crime.

"There were no eyewitnesses to this murder," Moore told them. "You won't hear anyone point at the defendant and say, 'I saw him do it.' That's not unusual. What we have is evidence to show that everything points to one person and one person only."

By this point, she was standing in front of the defense table. She pointed a finger directly at Hal Flanders and said, "Harold Flanders stalked his wife to her new lover's apartment, waited for her by her car and in cold blood, deliberately and with premeditation, shot her in the back of the head with the intention of killing her."

Moore dropped her arm and said, "When this trial is over, and you have been given the case for a decision, you will find, beyond a reasonable doubt, that Harold Flanders is guilty of all of the crimes charged in the indictment."

She then turned to look down at Hal Flanders with a face full of contempt, looked back at the jury and then thanked them.

Some of what she did was objectionable as argument. Marc decided not to object because she did not overdo it and he did not want to annoy the jury with excessive objections. Besides, it would be a close call, and the judge might not sustain him. That would look worse.

Marc, as was his normal custom, deferred his opening until after the prosecution rested. He wanted to get a complete look at their case first.

The court recessed for lunch following the prosecution's opening statement. Before starting the afternoon session, McVein admonished the gallery about decorum then told Krain to call his first witness.

"The state calls Detective Marcie Sterling," Krain stood and solemnly said.

Since Marcie was the lead investigator, she was allowed to sit behind the prosecution's table in front of the rail. Marc had correctly assumed Krain would start with her. Establish the crime, the crime scene and fulfill a legal requirement. For a Hennepin County Court to have jurisdiction it must be factually proven the crime took place in Hennepin County.

Jerry Krain was a slow and methodical trial lawyer. Because the prosecution has the burden of proof, it is on them to submit courtroom testimony and evidence to prove each element of the crime.

Despite the fact that Marcie Sterling had testified many times, she was still a little nervous about it. It can be nerve-wracking even for someone as capable and professional as an experienced detective. Especially knowing no case is perfect, no case is ever without flaws, a good defense lawyer can exploit. For a detective, no case is ever perfectly investigated.

It was after 4:00 P.M. when Krain finished his direct exam. He had been very thorough, even putting up a reproduction to scale of the crime scene. Marcie, using a pointer, showed the jury the visual so they could see exactly how the murder occurred. One picture being worth a thousand words, the image of Natalie Flanders' killer waiting in the dark for her would be hard to shake.

By prior arrangement, Marc, being a defense attorney like most, had no qualms about trying to distract the jury. Reaching into his briefcase at the moment Marcie began to describe how the shooting took place, he pressed the send button on his phone to send a text to Maddy waiting in the hall. When every juror should have been watching Marcie, they were all distracted by the sight of Maddy strolling through the door. Even the women in the jury box watched as she walked up the center aisle, through the gate and sat down behind Marc.

Of course, Maddy was very displeased with Marc using her like this. He had done this before, and it always elicited an argument from her. Marc knew he would pay for it over the next several days.

"Your witness, Mr. Kadella," Judge McVein said when Krain finished.

"Detective Sterling, your testimony, and I'm paraphrasing a bit, was that you could find no evidence of anyone else having a motive to kill Natalie Flanders. Is that accurate?"

"Yes, I would say it is," Moore replied. She had known Marc for several years and had even been on the witness stand in front of him a couple of times. She knew him well enough to know he did not ask questions like that for no reason. He had something, and he was going to slap her with it. Verbally. Marcie could feel her abdominal muscles tightening in anticipation.

"What did Natalie Flanders do for a living?" Marc asked.

"She was, ah, vice president of a bank," Marcie answered.

"She was a vice president of Lake Country Federal, wasn't she?"

"Yes, that's correct," Marcie agreed.

"That's the same bank that has been hit with a rash of robberies in the past few months, is it not?"

"Objection," Krain stood and said. "Irrelevant and goes beyond the scope of the direct examination."

"A little leeway, your Honor. I'll get to it and show both the relevance and that it does not go beyond the scope of direct," Marc said.

"I'll overrule the objection, for now," McVein said. "Soon, Mr. Kadella. You may answer the question, Detective."

"Yes, I believe it is."

"And the gang of bank robbers has left behind a manifesto proclaiming a political purpose as their motive, is that correct?"

"Yes, I believe so."

"Did you investigate the possibility that one or more of this gang committed the murder of Natalie Flanders?"

"We had no reason to..."

"Non-responsive, your Honor," Marc said.

"Yes or no, Detective," McVein said.

"No, we did not."

"Isn't it true, Detective, that the manifesto that the gang left after robbing a Lake Country Federal branch in Grand Forks, North Dakota, included an admonition regarding homestead farm foreclosures by banks?"

This question caught Marcie totally off-guard. She sat silently for several seconds, uncertain of how to answer.

"Objection, your Honor. The..."

"Overruled," McVein said, not bothering to hear the reason.

"I'm not sure," Marcie finally said.

Perfect, Marc thought. He picked up copies of a document from the table and handed one to Krain.

"May I approach, your Honor?"

"Certainly."

Marc walked up to the bench, handed a highlighted copy to McVein and another to Marcie.

"I'm showing you a document entitled Defense Exhibit One. It is a copy of the manifesto printed in the Grand Forks Herald. Please, read the highlighted paragraph."

"Objection," Krain again jumped up and said. "Lacks foundation, your Honor and authentication."

"Mr. Kadella," McVein said.

"Detective, read the top of the page where it has the name and date of the newspaper's edition."

Marcie did this, then Marc said to McVein, "Your Honor, I have a complete copy of that newspaper I can submit. I have also been in contact with the editor and he is willing to appear and testify to the authenticity of Defense Exhibit One unless Mr. Krain is willing to stipulate to it."

"Mr. Krain?" McVein asked.

"The state will so stipulate, your Honor," he said with obvious reluctance.

"Please read the highlighted portion," Marc said again.

When Marcie finished reading the part about the cruelty of banks foreclosing on poor people, especially farmers, Marc moved to submit Defense Exhibit One into evidence.

"Would you agree, Detective, that this gang of bank robbers has a problem with Lake Country Bank and foreclosures?"

"Well, I, ah…"

"Yes or no, Detective," Marc said.

"I guess so," she said.

"Is that a yes, Detective?"

"Yes, they seem to have a problem with both Lake Country Federal and foreclosures."

"Objection," Krain stood and said again. "I fail to see the relevance."

Marc looked at Jennifer Moore whose back was to the jury. Good thing too, for she was giving Krain a look that could kill.

"Bear with me a bit, your Honor," Marc said.

"Go ahead," McVein replied while waving Krain to sit down.

"Isn't it true that Natalie Flanders was the vice president in charge of the foreclosure department at Lake Country Federal?"

Marc actually heard two or three jurors gasp when they heard this question.

"Um, I'm, ah, not sure," Marcie answered.

"You're not sure? Did you investigate this?"

"Um, no, we didn't think it was relevant given the evidence we had against the defendant."

This was both a good and bad answer for Marc. She admitted what he wanted, but because of the sloppy way he had asked the question, she was able to bring up the evidence pointing to his client.

Marc went back to his table and picked up an inch-thick stack of paper. He went back to the witness and handed them to Marcie. "These are just a sample of the letters the foreclosure department at Lake Country has received. There are many more. These are letters from angry customers making threats against Lake Country about property foreclosures. Did you investigate these?"

"Objection, authentication," Krain said.

"I can bring in a witness in my case-in-chief to authenticate, your Honor. Unless you want to recess, then I'll have her here tomorrow. Or, Mr. Krain can save the court some time and stipulate,"

By this point, Marc had walked back to his table, retrieved and gave copies to Krain.

"We were not given these during discovery, your Honor," Krain said.

"I guess that's my fault, your Honor," Marc said and turned to Krain. "I assumed your crack investigative team would have found them for you."

"Watch the sarcasm, Mr. Kadella," McVein said. "Will you stipulate to their admission subject to you being given an opportunity to review them?" he asked Krain.

"Yes, your Honor," Krain agreed.

"Do you have much more for this witness?" McVein asked Marc.

"No, your Honor. In fact, I'm finished subject to recall if I come across more evidence that was overlooked."

Marc got what he wanted from her. An admission that maybe the investigation was not as good as the prosecution wanted the jury to believe. And a piece to use for reasonable doubt.

By now, Marcie Sterling was staring laser holes in Marc's forehead.

Krain, much to the relief of Jennifer Moore, passed on redirect.

As Marcie walked past Marc's table—he had sat down by now—she tapped the tabletop with a middle finger. Marc saw it and tried not to smile.

While court was recessing for the day, Marcie Sterling almost ran across Fifth Street. She went immediately to Homicide, tossed her purse in her desk and stormed into Owen Jefferson's office. To her luck, Tony Carvelli was visiting her boss.

"I hate him! And I hate you, too!" she snorted, pointing a finger at Carvelli.

"Oh, oh," Carvelli quietly said. He knew what was wrong because Jefferson had mentioned she was testifying today.

"So, I take it everything went well," Jefferson said.

"I hate you, too! Marcie said to him. "In fact, I think I hate all men. We should keep a few for breeding and kill the rest."

By now, Carvelli and Jefferson were unable to contain their laughter.

"Come on, sit down," Carvelli said, patting the chair next to him. "Tell us what happened."

Marcie sat down, took a deep breath to calm herself, then told them what happened.

"Well, you overlooked something. It happens," Jefferson said. "Learn from it and move on. It's Kadella's job…"

"Don't tell me it's not personal. He was smiling when I left," Marcie said.

"You mean when you stormed out and flipped him off?" Carvelli asked.

"Shut up. I still hate you," she said.

"So, now would be a bad time to ask you out to dinner?" Carvelli asked.

Even Marcie had to laugh at that.

"I almost forgot. Right in the middle of my testimony, Maddy walks in, and everyone in the place watched her and paid no attention to me."

"He did that again?" Carvelli asked.

"Why does she let him do that to her?"

"She kicks his ass for it," Carvelli said. "I've heard him try to get her to dress like a hooker. Fishnet stockings, a leather mini-skirt, no bra."

"Stop," Jefferson said, "I'm gonna faint."

"Trust me, he won't bring that up again," Carvelli said. "Don't worry," Carvelli said to Marcie, "I doubt it was as bad as you think."

"Probably not," Marcie agreed.

THIRTY-SEVEN

Ben Sokol read the text message he had received while still on the plane. He was walking through the airport returning from his third paid speaking engagement, this one at Oberlin College in Ohio. The $25,000 was in his bank account.

The text was from his Uber driver who was at exit door number 5 waiting for him. Ben was feeling quite smug and self-satisfied. Three engagements at twenty-five grand each in less than a month. Life was about to become very sweet, indeed.

Ben found his driver waiting inside the airport entryway. He had neglected to check the weather report for Minnesota before leaving Ohio. A cold front had moved in yesterday, and it greeted Ben with a nasty slap when he followed the driver outside.

"Whoa!" Ben yelped when the wind hit him in the face.

"Yes, sir," the driver said. "It came in yesterday afternoon. It's still five below."

"It's four o'clock in the afternoon," Ben said. "How cold did it get last night?"

"Minus fourteen," the young man replied. "That's why I left the car running," he added while holding the door for Ben.

On the ride home, Ben checked the messages on his phone. His little band of save-the-planet gangsters had all called. Something was up but none of them said what. All Ben could think of was something must have happened regarding Jordan. Ever since her body was discovered, Ben had dreams, almost nightly, of the police kicking down his front door. These messages made the acid in his stomach start a mild fire. He decided not to wait until he got home. Instead, he called Luke and kept it cryptic.

"What's so urgent?" Ben asked.

"We need to meet. Where are you?" Luke replied.

"I'm in the Uber car on my way home. Is everything okay?"

"We need to meet," Luke repeated. "Tonight. Your place. Eight o'clock."

"Is that a good idea?" Ben cautiously asked.

"Yes, tonight. Eight o'clock, your place," Luke said.

"I'm not sure…"

"You be there," Luke told him. "I'll call everyone, and we'll see you then."

"And if I can't, then what?" Ben asked. Too late. Luke had ended the call.

Luke arrived a few minutes early and greeted Ben quite amicably. Almost deferentially as if nothing was amiss. By 8:15, all of the others had arrived. After removing their winter coats and hats, they all went downstairs. The first thing Ben did was to pass out beer to everyone.

"Have you been having a good time?" Sherry asked with a touch of malice. Ever since Luke had ordered Ben to break things off with her, she did not know it came from Luke, she was acting quite rude and a bit snippy toward him. A woman scorned.

"What's that supposed to mean?" Ben asked in return.

"We know you've been making big bucks on the lecture circuit," Luke answered.

"I wouldn't, ah, call it, you know, big bucks," Ben timidly replied unaware that they knew about this.

"Really? How much? Twenty-five, fifty grand a speech?" Sherry asked.

Recovering his composure, Ben said, "That's none of your business. This has nothing to do with any of you."

"If it weren't for us you would not have gotten this gig," Luke said. "We're the ones who've been out there sticking our necks out, and you're cashing in. Driving a new Beemer, hauling in speaking fees..."

"Spending our money on personal things," Sherry added with a knowing look on her face. "Don't lie," she said when she saw Ben was about to protest.

"We want to do a couple more jobs, and we want the money from them," Luke said.

"That's not why we're in this," Ben said. "Remember, climate change and social justice...."

"What a phony," Reese said.

"What I'm doing is very important. I'm out there selling our ideology. So, what if I get a little reimbursement for my time and expenses. I'm doing it for the cause!

"Did you recruit someone to replace Jordan?" Ben asked, looking at Luke, hoping to change the subject.

"Yeah, we did," Gary told him. "Donna Gilchrist. I started dating her again. She asked me if I was involved. She knows me pretty well."

"I vetted her myself," Luke said. "She's solid. What about the money?"

"You have another job in mind?" Ben asked.

"Yeah, we do. Another place up in Duluth. It's not a Lake Country branch. It's one of the Northland State branches. Reese and I scoped it out," Luke said.

"You think it's cold here, spend a few days up there," Reese said.

"It's perfect. Monday afternoon at two, they get a cash drop for the week. We went up and watched it three times. And it's laid out similar to the Lake Country branches. Two guards, three tellers and the branch manager's office right next to the vault," Luke told them.

"We can be in and out in under two minutes. In all the time we watched the place, not once did we see a cop. We can go east into Superior, north to Canada, south to the cities, west to Bemidji," Reese explained.

"Okay," Ben said. "When are you thinking to do this?"

"Today's Friday. If we work on the planning through the weekend, we should be able to go Monday," Luke answered.

"How much are you thinking this could get?" Ben asked.

"I don't know. We watched the delivery of cash three times. It took two armored car guards to carry it in," Luke replied.

"Maybe we should hit the armored car instead," Sherry said.

"No, no way," Luke emphatically replied. "There are four guards total. And they look like serious men. All armed, wearing bulletproof vests and two of them have automatic weapons. The last thing we want is to get into a gunfight with guys who look like they have Special Forces training."

Ben pointed to the easel standing at the head of the table with drawing paper on it. "Okay, lay it out for us and let's get to work. What about the new girl?"

"She can drive," Gary said.

"Let's see what you have," Ben said.

An hour after Ben Sokol's plane touched down from Ohio, Marc and the prosecution team were meeting with the judge. McVein had a few questions for Jerry Krain.

That day, Friday, Krain had only managed to get in the testimony of two witnesses. The medical examiner had taken up the entire morning and half of the afternoon. It was 1:30 before they could break for lunch. Krain's other witness was the ballistics expert. He testified about the bullet that was found in Natalie Flanders' head, the one that killed her. The significance of his testimony was that the bullet's lands and grooves, the identifying markings, were totally consistent with the type, make and model of the gun purchased by Hal Flanders, the missing 9 mm.

"Are you on track?" McVein asked Krain.

"Well, um…" Krain started to say.

"No," Jennifer Moore answered. This elicited a look from Krain that would have melted glass which Jennifer ignored.

Krain turned back to the judge and said, "We'll be caught up by Monday afternoon."

While this exchange took place, Marc sat passively hoping the judge would take a large bite out of Krain's ass.

"You need to do a better job of controlling your witnesses. The doctor took over and wasted too much time," McVein said. "We didn't need the history of forensic medicine, Mr. Krain. The victim was shot in the back of the head. Most jurors will get it that this is what killed her."

"Yes, your Honor," Krain replied.

"Monday morning. You're lucky I don't go through the weekend. I probably should. My mother-in-law is visiting," McVein added.

Marc was unable to suppress a laugh. Krain was too angry, and Jennifer smiled.

"I'll see everyone Monday morning," McVein said in dismissal.

A humbled Jerry Krain was up and headed for the door almost before McVein finished speaking. Marc and Jennifer walked out together.

"You want me to provide some cover for you with the Nazi?" Marc asked.

"I can handle him," she replied. "Have a good weekend."

"You, too."

THIRTY-EIGHT

Tony Carvelli woke up and laid in bed, staring at the ceiling. He had been out late the previous evening trying to track down a truckload of goods stolen from 3M. He knew who had done it; a man in their warehouse. Finding the goods had proven more difficult. Carvelli knew most places where something like that would be kept. When he finally found it, he contacted the Bloomington PD. The Bloomington cops had arrived at 2:00 A.M. with a search warrant. The truck had been sitting in an empty warehouse and was now being held as evidence. It was after 4:00 before Carvelli fell into bed.

He looked at his bedside clock. Seeing 6:55, he rolled over and closed his eyes. The pounding on his door must have been a dream. But then, it happened again.

Carvelli slipped into his usual pair of grey sweatpants to answer the door. He stopped in the kitchen to push the brew button on the coffee maker. He was reasonably sure who it was once again pounding on his front door on a dark, wintry morning.

"What is wrong with you?" Carvelli asked when he opened the interior door and spoke through the storm door. "Don't you ever sleep? And what do you want?"

"It's seven o'clock," Jeff Johnson said. "Get your ass out of bed."

Standing behind Johnson, Tess Richards was waving her hands back and forth, shaking her head and mouthing the words, "Not my idea."

"Can we come in?" Johnson asked. "It's freezing out, here."

"No shit, Sherlock. Minnesota. January. Do the math, genius. Why are you up and out in this?"

"Yeah, yeah," Johnson said as he opened the exterior door and pushed past Carvelli.

"By all means, Jeff, come in. Morning, Tess," Carvelli said, closing the door.

"They hit another bank," Johnson said, opening his overcoat and sitting down on the couch.

"I smell coffee," Tess said, unraveling her scarf.

"It'll be done in a minute," Carvelli replied. "Lake Country?"

"No, a branch of Northland State up in Duluth," Johnson said. "Yesterday afternoon."

"What day is it?"

"Tuesday," Tess said.

"How do you know it was them and I thought you were off of this?" Carvelli asked.

"They left their hug a tree, rob a bank and save the world from evil capitalists calling card. We're back on as of yesterday morning," Johnson answered.

"Coffee's done," Tess said. "I'll get it. You look tired."

"What happened to the other guys?" Carvelli asked referring to Special Agents Terrell Jones and Elliot Douglas.

"Jones is being wooed by the Democrats to run for Congress from Minneapolis. He's been too busy with that. The SAIC gave it back to us."

Tess Richards appeared with three cups on a small tray.

"Thanks, Tess," Carvelli said and picked one up. "That's all very enlightening, Jeff, but so what?"

"I told Swift you were a valuable asset, and I wanted to use you. She okayed it. We're on our way up to Duluth. We have a crime scene unit in place now. Thought you might like to ride along," Johnson said.

"I don't have a client," Carvelli replied.

"So, call Olson later. He'll put you back on the payroll."

"When are you coming back?"

"I have to be back for a three o'clock meeting with Swift this afternoon," Johnson answered.

"I could use the company on the ride up," Tess said.

"Sure, why not? I was only sleeping. I can do that after I'm dead," Carvelli said.

"That's the spirit," Johnson told him.

The three of them rolled into the parking lot of the Northland branch shortly after 10:00 A.M. It was even colder in Duluth; eleven below zero with a steady, twenty mile an hour wind blowing off of Lake Superior and a wind chill of minus fifty.

They ran with the wind inside and when they got there Carvelli asked, "Someone explain to me why we live here?"

"Keeps out the riff-raff," one of the FBI techs replied.

"I'm not sure it's worth it," Carvelli said.

For the next two-plus hours, they hung out with the crime scene techs. The techs filled them in on what little preliminary evidence they had and showed them the surveillance video of the robbery.

"This is the same guy that always grabs the manager," Johnson quietly observed while they ran the video.

"Yeah, the same walk. The same movements. Have your lab run a comparison, but I'm with you; it's him," Carvelli agreed.

"The ones taking down the guards, the tellers and the three customers are the same too," Tess said. "Except for this one. She's new. Probably replacing the Simmons girl."

"Looks like it," Johnson agreed. "The problem is no identifiable markings, no tattoos, no jewelry. Nothing really. They are very well covered up."

"What's the timing?" Carvelli asked.

"One minute, fifty-seven seconds," Johnson answered. "In and out with two bags of cash."

"That's different," Carvelli said.

"Yeah, it is," both Johnson and Tess agreed.

"Are they getting greedy?" Tess asked.

"Don't know," Johnson replied.

A new video scene was brought up on the office PC they were using. It was from two exterior cameras. The robbery crew threw the money, now in a large black plastic lawn garbage bag, into the back of a dark green Toyota RAV4.

"That's different," Carvelli said.

"The car was found a couple hours later in Superior," Johnson said. "It was reported stolen a half-hour after the robbery from a building's parking lot a mile from here."

"Lots of fingerprints from the owner, a sixty-two-year-old woman who works where it was stolen. The guys went over it for DNA, but good luck. She has kids and grandkids and their DNA all over the car. Plus, we're pretty sure granny's not in on it," Tess said.

Johnson shut down the computer after they watched the getaway three more times. He sat back and said, "At least no one was hurt this time." He looked at Carvelli and asked, "Anything else?"

"How much did they get?"

"They'll know for sure later today," Johnson said. "But they're estimating between two hundred and two-fifty. Maybe as much as three."

"I just thought of something," Johnson said. "How's your lawyer friend's trial going? The wife murder in Hennepin County?"

"I don't know," Carvelli said. "I haven't talked to him since before it started. He's usually pretty busy during a trial."

"I'm surprised that him finding out about the gun hasn't made any difference," Johnson said.

"What gun?" Carvelli asked.

"The gun used to shoot the wife. What's-her-name?"

"Natalie Flanders," Tess answered.

"Yeah, that's her," Johnson said. "Don't you know?"

"Know what?" Carvelli asked now becoming quite curious.

"The gun from the Lake Country branch in the Eagan robbery. Remember? One of them was hit by a guard and went down and we recovered her gun."

"Yeah, okay, I remember that," Carvelli said. "What about it?"

"We got a ballistics report on it. It's a match to the gun used to shoot the Flanders woman," Johnson said.

"Hell, I never heard a word about it," Carvelli said. "Marc would've jumped out of his ass for that. Are you sure?"

"Yeah, I saw it in the file. It was sent by email to the Hennepin County attorney herself. Jones?"

"I gotta see this," Carvelli said. "Let's go."

A minute later they were back in Johnson's Fed car. They went quiet while Carvelli sat in the back seat and read the ballistics report.

"This is pretty amazing," Carvelli said to Johnson when he finished. "A bank robber now murdered herself, probably by one of her gang members, had the murder weapon for Marc's case. Last I heard, and this was a couple days before trial, it was still lost. When did Swift send this to Felicia Jones?"

"I'm not sure. At least a month ago. In fact, I think it was in November," Johnson replied.

"I'll be right back," Carvelli said. He opened his door and the wind pulled it out of his hand and filled the car with cold air.

"Where you going?"

"To make a copy. Then I need to get back to Minneapolis."

"Shut the door!" Tess yelled from the back seat.

"Officer Tyler" Marc said, beginning his cross-examination of the police officer. Nathan Tyler was one of the two Burnsville cops who answered the domestic disturbance call at the Flanders' home in September. Hal's neighbor had called 911 when she heard arguing from the Flanders' garage.

Natalie came home and found Hal in the garage going through personal items. She threw a fit, they argued, with Natalie doing most of the yelling. When the police came, Natalie went to answer the door. Before she got there, she punched herself in the face to cause a bruise and tore her own blouse. She told the two officers Hal had done it, and they arrested him charging him with domestic assault.

Natalie was murdered before Hal was tried, but not before she obtained a restraining order against him. These things were being used by the prosecution to show a pattern of violence by Hal against Natalie.

"Isn't it true that it was at least four minutes from the time you arrived at the Flanders' residence then rang the front doorbell before Natalie Flanders finally answered the door?"

"Yes, that is true," he agreed.

"How many times did you ring the doorbell?"

"At least three or four."

"When you first arrived, did you hear the sound of people in the garage?"

"No, not all. The house was quiet."

"You went inside after Mrs. Flanders opened the door?"

"Yes, we did."

"And you testified your partner, Officer Tom Swann took Mrs. Flanders into the living room while you went through the kitchen to the garage, is that correct?"

"Yes, it is."

"How did you find the defendant? Was he upset, sweating, seem angry?"

"No, not at all. He was very calm."

"Did he cooperate?" Marc asked.

Marc heard the courtroom door open and turned his head enough to see Tony Carvelli come in. "Yes, he was very cooperative."

Carvelli handed a slip of paper to Maddy to give to Marc. On it he had written, *Urgent we talk now!*

Marc read it and looked at Judge McVein, "Your Honor, may I have a moment, please?"

"Sure.'"

Carvelli removed the folded ballistics report from his inside coat pocket. Standing on the gallery side of the rail, he unfolded it and showed it to Marc.

"I don't have time, what is it?" Marc impatiently asked.

"It's the ballistics report on the gun that killed Natalie Flanders. It was found on one of the Lake Country Federal robbers. The girl who was killed," Carvelli whispered.

"What?" Marc said loud enough for everyone in the courtroom to hear him. "Are you serious?"

"According to the FBI, yes."

Marc turned to McVein and said, "Your Honor, I have just received what may be significant evidence."

"Recess, fifteen minutes," McVein said.

"And according to Johnson, this was emailed to Felicia Jones in early November?" Marc incredulously asked. Marc and Carvelli were in a conference room attached to the courtroom.

"Yes," Carvelli replied. "When he showed it to me in Duluth, he wasn't sure. So, he called his boss, and she looked it up."

They heard a knock on the conference room door, then a court deputy opened it and stuck in his head.

"Mr. Kadella, the judge is asking for you."

"We need to see him in chambers," Marc told the deputy. "Right away."

"Okay, I'll tell him."

They went into the courtroom, and Maddy asked, "What's going on?"

"I, ah, look, baby, I'm gonna have to tell you later…"

"Mr. Kadella, the judge said everyone should come back," he heard the deputy say.

Marc looked at Maddy and said, "Oh, what the hell, come with."

When they were all seated, Maddy, Carvelli and Marcie Sterling on the couch, the lawyer's and Hal Flanders in the client chairs in front of McVein's desk, Marc began.

"Your Honor, this man," he said, pointing at Tony, "is Anthony Carvelli. He is a licensed private investigator currently working with the FBI on behalf of Lake Country Federal Banks.

"He received this document from Special Agent Jeff Johnson today," Marc continued handing his copy to McVein.

"What's in it?" Krain almost demanded.

"I have a feeling you know what it is," Marc said.

"Tell me," McVein said to Marc.

"It's a ballistics report from the local FBI crime lab. It shows a ninety-eight percent match to the bullet that killed Natalie Flanders to a gun found at a very different crime scene.

"You may recall, a couple of months ago, the Eagan branch of Lake Country Federal was robbed."

"Vaguely," McVein said. "I remember several were robbed by some environmental group. So?"

"This time, one of the robbers, a young woman by the name of Jordan Simmons, was shot by one of the bank guards. She was wounded in the leg. The other robbers got her out of there, and they escaped.

"But Jordan Simmons dropped her gun on the floor. It was recovered by the authorities and tested by the FBI. That is the gun that was used to murder Natalie Flanders."

"That's what this is?" McVein asked.

"Yes, your Honor. And the report was emailed to Felicia Jones by the FBI's Special Agent in Charge, Taylor Swift. This has been verified. That ballistics report has been in the hands of the county attorney's office this entire time and withheld from me."

Barely able to contain his anger, McVein looked at Krain and Jennifer Moore. "Well, what do you two have to say for yourselves?"

"May I see it, your Honor?" Jennifer asked.

While she looked it over, Krain mustered up his arrogance and said, "It is not exculpatory. I saw no reason to give it to…"

"It's not exculpatory? How dare you…" Marc almost yelled.

"No, it's not. It is the same type of gun, make and model of your client's missing gun. The serial number was scrubbed, and it was found long after the murder of Natalie Flanders. He still did it. He threw away the gun and this woman bank robber found it."

"I've never seen this before," Jennifer announced. "But apparently, you have," she said to Krain. "But he never showed it to me. Is this the one you quickly hid in your desk drawer when I walked into your office?"

"I don't know what you're talking about," Krain said. His nerves were starting to betray him.

"You got some kind of balls on you, Mr. Krain. Not only did you withhold evidence, important evidence…"

"It's not exculpatory," Krain said again.

"…from the defense but you even kept it from your own co-counsel," McVein said.

"How do we know this report has not been tampered with?" Krain tried next.

"Mr. Carvelli," McVein said.

"Yes, your Honor," Carvelli replied, standing to show his respect.

"Are you and Agent Johnson prepared to testify to this?"

"Yes, your Honor. What Mr. Kadella's told you is true."

"May I make a phone call, your Honor?" Jennifer asked, holding up her phone.

"To whom?"

"Felicia Jones," Jennifer replied.

"Good idea. Get her down here," McVein said.

Jennifer quickly told her boss they had a serious problem but did not tell her what. She only said the judge wanted her to join them.

The room went quiet for most of the two minutes it took for Jones to walk down the stairs and come into McVein's Chambers.

While they waited, Marc asked McVein, "How are you feeling?" McVein had a cold, and it was this that kept him from holding court on Monday.

"Lousy. I should still be home in bed. Hopefully, none of you will get it."

McVein looked up at his door as it opened to see Felicia Jones enter.

"How may I help, your Honor?" she asked as she walked toward his desk.

"Here, Ms. Jones, please take my chair. I think you'll need it more than me," Marc stood and graciously offered.

"It's Felicia," she said to Marc and shook hands. "And you must be Marc Kadella. I've heard a lot of cussing around my office about you from my lawyers," she said with a smile.

"I guess that's a compliment," Marc said.

"It is." She turned to McVein while Marc sat next to Maddy and asked. "Now, your Honor, how may I help?"

"Have you seen this?" McVein asked as Jennifer handed the report to her.

A minute later, after looking it over, Jones said, "It looks familiar, yes. I think it's a ballistics report emailed directly to me from the FBI, Taylor Swift, I saw the name Natalie Flanders on it and sent it to Mr. Krain. Is there a problem?"

"Mr. Krain stuck it in a desk drawer and hid it from everyone," McVein said.

"Again, in my opinion, it is not exculpatory. That is within my authority to determine and I…"

"Not anymore," McVein said while Felicia Jones stared daggers at Jerry Krain.

"Move to dismiss, your Honor. On top of this egregious, totally outrageous display of prosecutorial misconduct, the FBI has had the murder weapon for months. He stashed the report because he knew there was no way he could tie it to Hal Flanders. And a mistrial is not enough. The jury has been sworn, jeopardy has attached, and my client should be freed immediately," Marc stood and said.

"Can you tie the gun to the defendant?" McVein asked Krain.

"It's the same make and model…"

"Your Honor," Carvelli said. "I can testify as to where the gun originated. It was purchased illegally from a known criminal near Waseca long before Mrs. Flanders was murdered. Ms. Rivers and I investigated this along with a Waseca sheriff's detective named Tony Haig."

"You two are prepared to testify to this and Detective Haig?"

"Yes, your Honor," Carvelli and Maddy both agreed. "And I believe Detective Haig will drive up and testify also."

McVein thought it over for a minute then said, "Well, that won't be necessary. We're gonna go out and put it on the record. The jury has a right to know why the case is being dismissed,"

"Jennifer can handle this, your Honor," Felicia Jones said. "You and I have a meeting scheduled for right now," she told Krain.

THIRTY-NINE

Judge McVein fled immediately after he dismissed the case. It took almost ten minutes for the courtroom to settle down after the dismissal. Leaning over the bar railing, Hal Flanders was in a group hug with all three of his adult children. He was also sobbing uncontrollably.

A big hug and a kiss from Maddy was followed by Marc going to shake hands with Jennifer Moore.

"He didn't do it, Jenny," Marc said.

"I think you're right," she agreed.

"Whoever did it is still out there."

"Maybe. What about the girl, the bank robber who had the gun?" Jennifer asked.

"What's her motive? And who killed her? Find that, and you'll have your answer," Marc said.

"You're probably right," she replied.

"What's gonna happen to Krain?"

"I don't know, and if I did, I couldn't discuss it with you. We'll see. Congratulations, again."

Jennifer began to pack up and Marc turned back to his table. Hal Flanders was wiping the tears from his face, still with his kids. Leaning over the defense table was that annoying little man hitting on Maddy.

"Philo, you're not supposed to be inside the railing. I could have you arrested for impersonating a human," Marc said.

"What human? This is where lawyers hang out," Philo replied.

"Hey, watch it," Maddy snarled.

"Sorry. I didn't mean to compare you to lawyers," Philo said.

"Be careful with that," she replied.

Philo looked at Marc and said, "Hey, I heard a good lawyer joke the other day. You want to hear it?"

"No," Marc said.

"Yes," Maddy said.

"I knew you would," Philo said.

"A man was sent to hell for his sins. As he was led into the pits for an eternity of torment, he saw a lawyer passionately kissing a beautiful woman. 'What a joke!' he said. 'I have to roast in flames for all eternity, and that lawyer gets to spend it with that beautiful woman.' Satan jabbed the man with his pitchfork and snarled, 'Who are you to question that woman's punishment.'

"That's pretty good," Maddy laughed.

"Yeah, that's hilarious," Marc drily replied. "I've heard better than that."

"I want to know who the blonde is, and the lawyer better not be you," Maddy told Marc.

"Okay. After I die, I'll wait for you," Marc said.

"So, what happened here today? What evidence did Krain withhold that got the case dismissed?" Philo asked.

Maddy had answered her phone and before Marc could tell Philo what happened. Maddy said, "Just a second." She held the phone up to Marc and said, "It's Gabriella."

Marc took the phone, said hello and told her, "It's too late for your show."

"Don't give it to TV," Philo said, knowing who Gabriella was. "I was here first."

"How about tomorrow?" Gabriella asked.

"It's going to get out. I have Philo the Pitbull practically humping my leg right now."

"Now that's a disgusting image. I won't sleep tonight now thanks to you," Gabriella said.

Marc laughed, then said, "It's going to get out anyway. Jerry Krain is upstairs with Felicia Jones trying to get his nuts out of a meat grinder. I'll give it to Philo then see you tomorrow."

Marc covered the phone with his hand and said to the court deputy, "Give me a minute before you take him."

The deputy, minus the shackles and handcuffs, was about to take Hal Flanders for processing out of jail.

"I'll see you tomorrow what, ten o'clock?" Marc asked Gabriella.

"That'll be fine," she replied.

Marc shook hands with Hal, who was pouring praise all over him.

"The deputy needs to process you out. Have your kids wait then celebrate tonight. Call me tomorrow," Marc said.

"Thanks again, Marc, You too, Maddy."

Marc and Maddy brought Philo into the small courtside conference room. Philo recorded the statement.

The next day's Star Tribune had a blaring headline:

Prosecution Misconduct Loses Murder Case

By the end of the day, Jerry Krain was beginning a thirty-day suspension. It would be used to find a lawyer and begin preparing his defense before the Minnesota attorney's Office of Professional Responsibility. Because his record was clean except for complaints from defense lawyers, Krain would only get another thirty-day suspension. Defense lawyers' complaints about an overly zealous prosecutor held little weight with the OPR.

211

"Is Hal Flanders gonna pay up?" Connie Mickelson asked Marc.

Marc was back in the office after filming his guest appearance for Gabriella Shriqui's show, *The Court Reporter*. It would be aired later that afternoon.

"Always the practical Jewish Princess," Barry Cline kidded Connie.

The entire office was crowded into the conference room, enjoying a celebratory pizza lunch provided by Connie. Knowing this would happen after a big win in court, Tony Carvelli just happened to drop by.

"I talked to Hal a little while ago. He called me to let me know he's selling the house. He has a realtor who says it will sell quickly and he'll have me at the closing to get my check. I gave him a ballpark estimate of what the final bill would be. He said it was worth every penny. So, yeah, I'll get paid," Marc told her.

"So, who killed Natalie Flanders?" Carolyn Lucas asked.

Marc looked at Carvelli and said, "I'll let you answer that."

"We're not sure..." Carvelli started to say.

"Who's we?" Barry asked.

"Our pal, Tony, has gone over to the dark side," Connie said. "He's working with the Feebs."

"The FBI is letting you be involved in an active investigation?" Barry asked. "How'd that happen?"

"My client is Lake Country Bank, which reminds me, Ms. Maddy. Now that your trial is over, you want some work?"

"Sure," Maddy said. "Are they paying you again?"

"Yeah, and uh, Bob Olson would like to meet you," Carvelli sheepishly said.

Maddy narrowed her eyes, looked across the conference room table at him, and asked, "What did you tell him?"

"Me? Ah, nothing. Just that I have a female colleague working with me and he'd like to meet you. That's all."

"Who killed Natalie Flanders?" Carolyn asked again.

"The gun was found at one of the bank robberies, the one in Eagan a couple months ago," Carvelli began.

"Where the girl was shot by a guard? I remember," Carolyn said. "Wasn't she murdered by someone in the gang?"

"That's the theory," Carvelli agreed. "I'm not convinced she killed Natalie Flanders. It's likely others in the little gang had access to that gun. But what's the motive? What's the connection?"

It was Marc, the lawyer, who came up with it; Mortgage Foreclosures.

"Didn't you say their save-the-planet, down-with-capitalism manifesto included a shot at farm foreclosures from the Grand Forks heist?" he asked.

"You're right, it did," Carvelli agreed.

"Natalie Flanders was VP in charge of foreclosures at Lake Country," Marc said. "In fact, I have a stack of complaint letters containing a bunch of threats that were sent to the foreclosure department of Lake Country. You should go through them. See if anything jumps out at you."

"Are they signed?" Carvelli asked.

"Some are. Most of the worst ones are not," Marc answered.

"I thought you were a trained detective," Connie said. "Can't you deduce their identities from the writing, the paper or the scent on them?"

"You're right," Carvelli sarcastically said. "I should've thought of that, smartass."

"That's why you're always hitting on me, isn't it?" Connie shot back at him.

"No, dummy. It's your money," Carvelli said.

"Good luck with that," Barry said.

"I see it's time to consider the rent you're paying," Connie threatened Barry again.

"She's the most kind-hearted, generous person I know. She's like having a mom and Santa all in the same person," Barry said.

When the laughter died down, Barry said. "Tony, in all seriousness, she is the most kind-hearted generous person I know."

"Stop, you're gonna make me cry," Connie said sounding like a Marine Drill sergeant.

"I'll get the letters when the Comedy Hour is over, and you can go through them," Marc told Carvelli. "They have a lot more at the bank. I just took a good sample."

"We'll check them out," Maddy said.

"If we start with the premise that the guy down in Waseca that I talked to...." Maddy said to Carvelli.

"Wrangler," Carvelli added.

"Yeah, him. Anyway, if we believe it was him that sold the guns to the bank robbery crew, where did he get the gun that was used on Natalie Flanders?"

The two of them were the only ones using the law offices conference room. They had split up the stack of complaint letters to the Lake Country foreclosure department and were reading through them. Maddy needed a break from it.

"Good question, but why does it matter?" Carvelli asked.

213

"Because he sold them to a guy named Luke. We haven't found him. Is he part of this crew? We might be chasing our tails here. If somebody else provided the gun to this girl, Jordan, where did she get it? And, if it was part of the sale to the crew, who else had access to it? What if it's somebody in these letters and we're not seeing it?"

The two of them stared at each other thinking this over. Carvelli looked at the three stacks of letters he had made. One stack for 'maybes,' one for 'doubtful' and those still to read.

"A lot of cop work is chasing your tail," he said.

"True," Maddy replied. "Some of these people were really pissed."

"Yeah, but mostly what they're doing is venting. I've got four maybes, but they're all anonymous. What do you have?"

"Six, all anonymous," Maddy said.

"They're all stamped with the date received. We can give them to Randy Townes. He's head of security at Lake Country. They can go back and see if they match any foreclosures about that time," Carvelli said.

"Wouldn't they have already done that?" Maddy asked.

"Probably. But now that they're looking for something specific, a second closer look might find something," Carvelli answered.

"How is the homicide case of Jordan Simmons doing?" Maddy asked. "Does Minneapolis have it?"

"Let's find out," Carvelli said.

He found the number in his phone and called it. Owen Jefferson answered on the first ring.

"What's up, paisan?"

"You remember the girl who was a part of the bank crew they found in the woods?"

"Yeah, Jordan Simmons," Jefferson answered.

"You guys have it?"

"Well, yes, we do. Why?"

"What's going on with it?"

"You first," Jefferson said.

"We're back on the bank robbery case. Did you know the gun that was used to murder Natalie Flanders was the one she dropped at the Eagan robbery?"

"Is that why it got dismissed?" Jefferson asked, referring to the trial.

"Yeah, don't you read the papers?"

"Not usually, no," Jefferson said.

"The Nazi didn't disclose the FBI ballistics to Kadella. Your turn."

"Okay, yes, we still have Jordan Simmons case. The sheriff wanted it until they got a look at it. Then they decided not to take it. Why?"

"Where is it? How's the case looking?"

"The M and Ms have it and…"

"It's stuck on stupid and going nowhere," Carvelli said.

"I've been closely monitoring them. Be fair. Sometimes these things take time. They're doing everything that can be done."

"Spoken like a true bureaucratic ass-coverer. Mind if I take a look at the case file?" Carvelli asked.

"You got balls, Carvelli. You call me a bureaucratic ass-coverer then want a favor?"

"I'll bring Maddy," Carvelli said.

"Okay, then. I'll be here."

"See you in a half-hour."

"Hey, we're leaving. Can we take these letters with us?" Carvelli said, standing in Marc's office doorway.

Without looking up from the document he was working on, Marc said, "Don't lose them."

Maddy squeezed past Carvelli, tapped Marc on the shoulder and said, "See you later."

"Okay," Marc said, still not looking up.

"Do I get a kiss?"

"I'm kind of busy," Marc said as he continued to write.

"Excuse me!" Maddy said.

Finally getting it, Marc looked at Tony and said, "I said that out loud, didn't I? That was really stupid."

"Don't try dragging me into the middle of this," Carvelli protested.

Marc looked at Maddy who was scowling at him and said, "I'm really, really, sorry. Please, come here."

"Forget it, buster. Gonna be a cold night tonight," she said and started to leave.

"You mean I get a full night's sleep?"

"Keep talking, and you'll get a lot of full nights of sleep."

Smiling, Marc said, "Bye, baby. I'll see you later."

"You live recklessly," Carvelli said.

"Yes, he does," Maddy agreed.

She was almost out the door when she turned, went back to his desk, leaned down and kissed him.

"Love you," Marc said.

FORTY

On their way to MPD Homicide to review the file on Jordan Simmons, Carvelli made a stop at Lake Country Bank headquarters. They spent fifteen minutes with Bob Olson. Carvelli introduced Maddy, then brought Olson up to speed on the investigation. They received permission to go through all of the complaint letters sent to the foreclosure department. Olson also told them that copies of those letters had been sent to the MPD homicide department recently.

Olson also told them he was considering posting a $100,000 reward. Carvelli made the point that these things usually bring out a lot of false reports. Seeing Olson's look of disappointment, Maddy suggested he try it and see what happens anyway.

The bank would set up an 800 number to call. The information would go to his head of security, Randy Townes, who would have his people check them out. This plan drew Carvelli's blessing.

On their way to Jefferson's office, Maddy asked Carvelli, "You don't think much of this reward idea, do you?"

"I don't think I've ever seen one that led to an arrest," Carvelli replied. "Bob wanted to do it so, I'm glad you picked up on that. Randy Townes isn't gonna like it, but that's what he gets paid to do."

When the two of them entered the homicide squad room, they found Marcie Sterling with Jefferson. Carvelli had called to let Jefferson know they had stopped at the Lake Country offices. From there, it was a five-minute walk to the Old City Hall building.

Jefferson saw them coming across the room and waved at them. Marcie had her back to them, and when Maddy got inside the office, she stopped, concerned about Marcie's attitude.

Carvelli looked at Maddy, who was looking at Marcie with a concerned expression. "What's wrong?" Carvelli asked both women.

"Hi, Marcie. We okay?" Maddy asked.

"You and me? Sure," Marcie said. "I've got every cop in the metro area watching out for your boyfriend. I gave them the make and model of his car and license plate number. As soon as he's arrested, I'm to be notified," Marcie said.

Jefferson was wearing a huge grin while Carvelli stood with a puzzled look on his face.

"Marc, ah, kind of hammered her on his cross-exam during the Flanders' trial," Maddy told Carvelli.

"Ooops, that's right. I forgot how happy she was when she came back afterwards," Carvelli said then took the chair next to Marcie. He looked at Marcie and noticed the corners of her mouth slightly upturned.

"Don't you dare smile," Carvelli said. "Don't do it; you'll give it away."

Instead, Marcie not only smiled but could not help laughing.

"After Kadella embarrassed me…"

"Are you going to let it go?" Jefferson asked.

"No. Anyway, after Kadella embarrassed me on the stand, I contacted Lake Country to get copies of those letters. Of course, they had already sent them to us as they received them. We tracked them down this morning. The M and Ms are reading through them now," Marcie continued. "With the way those two move, this should take them until they officially retire. You think there might be something in there?"

"It's a place to look. Since Hal Flanders didn't kill his wife, who else had motive?" Maddy asked.

"Our little cult of socialist bank robbers had the gun," Carvelli said. "No doubt about that. Did the girl who was murdered…"

"Jordan Simmons," Marcie said.

"Did she do it? If so, why? Did other members of the cult have access to her gun? And why would anyone else kill Natalie Flanders?" Carvelli asked.

"Do you know that in their down-with-capitalist oppressors' manifesto that they left at the Grand Forks branch, they put wording in their condemning farm disclosures?" Maddy asked Jefferson.

"No, I didn't," Jefferson said. "Is that unusual?"

"Never did it before or since," Carvelli answered.

"Have you told the FBI this?" Jefferson asked. "About the letters?"

"Not yet," Carvelli said. "I thought we'd take a first look. But if it is in there, it's gonna have to jump off the letter and slap Menke or McNamee in the face for one of them to see it."

"I'd love to solve this before the FBI," Jefferson said.

"That will make the M and Ms happy," Carvelli sarcastically said.

"Yeah, I live to make them happy," Jefferson replied. "Speak of the devil," he looked up through his office window.

Jack Menke was hurrying across the room holding, a sheet of paper in his hand. Before he reached Jefferson's door, the lieutenant waved him in.

As Menke closed the door behind him, seeing Carvelli and Maddy, he hesitated.

"Hey, Tony, how you doin'?" he asked.

"What do you have?" Jefferson said.

217

"I may have found something in one of the letters the bank sent over," Menke replied. "Can I say it in…"

"Yes, they know," Jefferson told him.

"Good, okay. Isn't there a Luke-somebody maybe involved in this?"

"What did you find?" Carvelli quickly asked.

"I got a letter here from someone who gave his name as Luke. He didn't sign it just said his name was Luke and he was writing to the bank angry about his grandpa," Menke replied, handing the letter to Jefferson.

"And?" Carvelli impatiently asked.

"And Lake Country foreclosed on grandpa's farm, and the old guy committed suicide," Jefferson said while reading the letter.

"The letter itself is kind of mild," Menke said. "Most of them are a lot worse than this. It's hardly threatening at all."

"Mostly just says they killed his grandpa, broke the kid's heart and he would never forgive them," Jefferson said.

He had finished reading and reached across the desk to hand the letter to Maddy. Carvelli looked over her shoulder while they both read it. It was only a couple of paragraphs long, and when she finished it, Maddy gave it to Marcie.

"It might be something," Menke said.

"Yes, you're right, Jack. Good catch," Carvelli said. He looked at Jefferson and said, "Now we need to search farm foreclosures with a suicide in the period before this letter was written.

"I can get the information from Lake Country about farm foreclosures quicker than you guys," Carvelli told Jefferson.

"Doesn't say when or where," Marcie said referring to the letter. "Could be a dozen or more depending on how far back this happened. Plus, this could be a kid who might be ten years old. But, it's a solid lead."

"I don't think it's a young kid," Maddy said. "It's too well written. Grammar and punctuation are both good. Plus, look at the margins. This was done on a computer using Word, and the margins are neatly squared."

"College kid?" Jefferson asked. "How are you gonna run this down? We have tech people who can do that."

"Um, yeah, ah," Carvelli started to say.

"He knows someone who might not be totally legitimate who can do it faster," Maddy said.

"Oh? What does that mean? Not quite totally legitimate?" Jefferson asked.

"Ask me no questions, I'll tell you no lies," Carvelli answered.

Jefferson slanted his head to his left, then silently stared at Carvelli for ten seconds. He finally said, "You're probably right. The less I know, the better."

"Will we be able to use this in court?" Marcie asked.

"Marcie, right now that's the least of our concerns. We need to find this guy then put a case together," Carvelli said.

"Good point. In the meantime, we'll keep looking through the letters and let you know if we find anything else," Jefferson said.

"You want what from how far back?" Bob Olson incredulously asked Carvelli.

Carvelli and Maddy were outside the Old City Hall on the sidewalk of Fifth Street. He was on the phone with his client at Lake Country.

"Hang on," Carvelli said into his phone. "There's a train pulling up."

The light rail train came to a stop, and Carvelli continued.

"We need every farm foreclosure you guys did from a year ago last October for three years," Carvelli said.

The train started up again, and Carvelli told Olson to wait. When it was far enough away, he heard Olson ask, "Why that date?"

Carvelli explained the letter that was found and the date the bank received it.

"Do you know how many farm foreclosures there were during that time?" Olson asked.

"I don't know, a couple hundred?"

"Try a couple thousand, at least. We are the largest holder of farm mortgages in the country. In a three-year period, we could have several thousand of them," Olson said. "I don't even know how many there could be."

Carvelli told Maddy this who said, "Maybe go back just one year to start."

Carvelli relayed this to Olson who, much relieved, agreed to get it for them.

"If we don't find what we're looking for, we'll need more. But we'll start with that. How long?"

Olson said, "It's too late today. The computer can spit them out, and I'll get you copies."

"Can you just put them in a file and email them?"

"It will be too much for one file. I'll have them do it by month and separate emails. What's your address?"

Carvelli gave him his email address then ended the call. By now, it was pushing 6:00 P.M. Unlike most normal people, it was not quitting time.

219

"Should we call Jeff Johnson?" Maddy asked.

"Not yet. What do you say we go canvas some local dirtbags and see if they got a sniff of who these guys are?" Carvelli asked.

"Sure. I should call Marc and let him know. And I want to tell him what Marcie said," Maddy answered.

FORTY-ONE

Ben and Luke were working on stacking the cash from the Duluth bank while the others waited. They were in Ben's basement and a sharp, short argument had burst open between Sherry and Neil. They had growled at each other over the money, how much to distribute to themselves and how much to donate to various causes. Sherry, who was originally totally committed to the cause, was becoming a little too self-interested. Neil had as well, but not to the same level as Sherry.

"Enough!" Luke snapped at the two of them. "First things first. We need to launder this," Luke said while Ben passed out the money.

"How much was it?" Reese asked.

"Two-twelve," Luke answered.

"Two-twelve what?" the new recruit, Gary's on-again girlfriend, Donna Gilchrist, asked.

Being new, Donna had been assigned a simple task. She had waited at the rendezvous in Superior with her car for those who went in the bank. She then drove straight back to the Cities with Sherry and Cindy.

"Two hundred and twelve thousand," Gary told her.

Luke went around the table, placing a single sheet of paper in front of each of them.

"This is a list of casinos to use. Gary, you go with Cindy and take Donna along. Show her how it's done. The rest of you have enough experience to do it yourselves. That way it gets done faster," Luke said.

"Illinois," Gary said looking at his list. "We're going to Illinois?"

"Yeah, we have to branch out farther," Luke said. "I'm going to Missouri. Sherry's going to Deadwood, South Dakota. We're all going farther. Everybody has forty-two grand to get clean."

"Do we all have clean, new phones and everyone has each other's numbers?" Ben asked.

They all acknowledged they did.

"Where are you going?" Sherry asked Ben. Ever since Ben had broken things off with her, Sherry treated Ben with little deference, at least in front of the others.

"It's not important," Luke quickly told her.

"Oh? Mine is not to reason why?" Sherry snidely asked.

"Get over yourself, Sherry," Luke said. "Stick with the gig. We're supposed to have a purpose here, remember?"

"Do you two?" Sherry asked looking at Luke and Ben

Luke stared harshly at Sherry, and after three or four seconds of it, she quietly backed down and said, "Sorry."

Gary, with Donna in the passenger seat, Cindy behind them, were cruising east on I-94. They were in Gary's newer, two-year-old Ford SUV heading toward Illinois. Since leaving St. Paul, none of them had spoken a word. As soon as they crossed the bridge over the St. Croix River into Wisconsin, Donna turned to Gary.

"What happened to Jordan?" she asked.

Caught off guard by the question, Gary's head turned to Donna, then Cindy, finally snapping back to look at the road.

"Um, why do you ask? I mean, I don't know what you mean," Gary said.

"Don't bullshit me, Gary," Donna replied. "I've known you too long. I know Jordan. Not very well, but I know who she is. I heard those two guys, Reese and Neil, whisper her name. Then they both looked around as if someone might be listening."

"Oh, that. Well, you know how guys talk about girls. They were just..."

"I said don't bullshit me, Gary. Something in your merry little group is wrong. That's not the first time I heard people whisper her name. What happened to..."

"She's dead," Cindy abruptly said. "Don't you watch the news?" Cindy said from the backseat.

"What? What do you mean, she's dead? What happened to her?" Donna asked, looking back at Cindy.

"She was kidnapped and murdered," Gary told her.

"No, she wasn't," Cindy said. "You may as well know the truth. She was wounded in a robbery, the bank in Eagan. That night, while they were trying to decide what to do with her, someone shot her in the head."

Donna, looking horrified, stared speechless at a very calm Cindy. Donna turned to Gary who refused to look at her, then back to Cindy.

"What the hell is wrong with you people? Stop the car! Stop it right now! I want to get out!"

"I can't stop here on the freeway," Gary said.

"I don't give a damn! Stop the goddamn car now!" Donna screamed.

"Donna," Cindy calmly said. "Calm down and we'll talk about it."

"No! I won't calm down."

"You need to. It's best if you do, please," Cindy said.

Donna held her hands up, palms out, then took several deep breaths. Not a word was spoken while Gary continued to cruise along at 65 mph toward Illinois.

"Okay," Donna finally, quietly said. She again looked back at Cindy and said, "So, tell me."

When Cindy finished telling her what had happened and who she thought did it, Donna turned to Gary.

"Why didn't you tell me? I would never have…"

"How could I tell you that?" Gary asked. "Sorry, but when we got back together, you knew what I'd been doing."

"I didn't know," she said.

"You guessed, and you wanted to help. Well, you're in, and this is what we do," Gary said. "I tried to talk you out of it, remember?"

"Yes, yeah you did," Donna sadly agreed.

Not another word was spoken for almost forty-five minutes. Near Menomonie, Donna saw a sign for a rest area. She asked Gary to stop so she could use the restroom.

They all got out, and Cindy took hold of Donna's arm. "Give me your phone," she said.

"I'm not going to call anyone," Donna assured her.

"Not if I have your phone, you won't."

"I'm in. I just wish I had known. It's still a worthy cause and I'm in."

"Phone," Cindy said, holding out her hand.

Donna handed her both the burner and her personal phone before they got inside.

As they were pulling out of the rest area, Donna asked Cindy, "Now what?"

Despite Donna's assurance, Cindy had still followed her into the women's restroom. On their way in, Donna again told her she was over it and okay.

"Now we go first to the Rover's Casino in Des Plaines," Cindy said.

"It's near Evanston, northeast of Chicago," Gary said.

Over the next five days, they visited four casinos. The first was in Des Plaines, then Joliet, Aurora and finally, Rock Island. Rock Island is across the Mississippi from Davenport, Iowa. By then they were down to less than five thousand dollars to launder.

Right away, Donna got into it. The gambling was fun, and she even had a bit of luck. By the time they headed north out of Davenport, she had won over two-thousand dollars. Of course, she was not at all pleased when she had to put her winnings in with the rest of the money. The three of them, along with the others, would be back in Minneapolis that evening.

"These numbers don't match what I have," Luke told Ben.

223

The two of them were in Ben's kitchen going over the totals from all of the bank robberies, the amounts donated to various groups and their own expenses. Before leaving to wash his share of the Duluth money, Luke had reminded Ben he wanted a complete accounting. Now that he was back, Ben gave him the same list he would show the others.

"What do you mean? What are you implying?" Ben said, trying to act indignant.

"I'm not implying anything," Luke said. "I'm saying your numbers don't match mine. There are sixty-seven thousand dollars and change unaccounted for. Did you think no one else would keep track?"

Luke was sitting on one side of Ben's kitchen table, Ben directly opposite him. Close enough so Luke could reach across the table and grab him. While Luke stared straight into Ben's eyes, Ben had trouble returning the intensity.

"Okay," Ben finally said. "I admit I've done some skimming. So what? The whole thing was my idea. I figured it out. I set it up, and I have the most to lose."

Instead of responding, Luke simply continued to stare. A bead of sweat broke out on Ben's forehead, and he began to fidget with his hands.

"And, there's something bigger coming up. Much bigger. I was going to talk to you about it today, anyway," Ben said while Luke continued to stare.

"This thing I've been doing, these lectures," he began. "That's barely the tip of the iceberg. I'm getting in with some very rich and powerful people: billionaires, politicians, political heavyweights. Luke, what we're doing is peanuts. These people have a long-term plan in mind. They're going to remake America and with it, the world. No more wars, no more poverty, racism, or injustice. And we are about to get in on the ground floor."

"Tom Breyer's group. They're backing that fool Jacob Trane. How naïve do you think I am?" Luke asked.

"They're using Trane," Ben said. "He attracts the kids, the future. It won't happen overnight, but it will happen a lot faster with them than the way we're doing it."

"That's great, Ben," Luke drolly said. "In the meantime, you need to do a little skimming for me."

Luke slid a piece of paper across the table with two sets of numbers on it. "Here's the bank account to use. I'm not greedy. I'll settle for the same sixty-seven grand you took."

Ben looked at the note and said, "It will take a couple of weeks."

"Okay. Now fix this and make it something we can show the others," Luke said, handing the accounting document back to him.

"Why is everybody so quiet?" Neil asked.

He was in the backseat of Gary's Ford SUV with Cindy and Donna in the front on their way to Ben's house. Unknown to the four of them and the others, it was an hour after Ben and Luke met in Ben's kitchen.

Everyone was back from their money-laundering trips. Tonight, was the time for accounting and delivery. They would present cashier's checks and washed cash for deposit and re-routing. In another two-three weeks it would be safe to use the money.

"Why is everyone so quiet?" Neil asked again after no one answered the first time.

"We told Donna what happened to Jordan," Cindy said.

"Oh, shit," Neil said. "You okay?" he asked Donna.

"No," she glumly said. "But it's too late now."

"And," Cindy continued, "we're getting screwed over on the money. Ben, for sure is skimming and if he is, then Luke is too."

"Are you sure? We need to be sure before we accuse them of it," Neil said.

"Sherry said Ben is," Gary said.

"And she should know," Cindy added. "She was screwing his brains out."

"Seriously?"

"Come on, Neil. Take notes, keep up. We talked about this. Remember?" Gary said.

"Yeah, I guess I didn't want to believe it," Neil replied.

"I think we tell them we want to split the Duluth money up and keep it ourselves," Gary said.

"You bring it up, and we'll back you," Cindy told Gary.

"Deal," Gary said.

The cash and checks were neatly stacked on the table in front of Ben. He had made a list of the amounts everyone turned in and then compared the net total to the expenses.

"Best job, yet," Ben announced. "The net was a hundred ninety-six thousand, eight hundred and forty-seven dollars. Congratulations. We're going to make some of our comrades very happy."

Gary, with Cindy looking over his shoulder was using the calculator on his phone. When he finished, he looked at Ben and Luke.

"Yeah, we are and I'm one of them. We each get twenty-eight-thousand, one hundred and twenty-one dollars. Except you, Ben, you've already taken out at least that much," Gary said.

Ben sat speechless, his mouth hanging open, his eyes locked on Gary, uncertain of what to say.

225

"Sounds about right to me," Sherry said. "And don't bother to deny it, Ben. It's time we got paid. We've earned it."

"Are we forgetting why we're doing this?" Luke asked.

"The only reason I'm cutting you in is because I don't know how much you already got," Gary said.

"When did you take over?" Luke angrily asked.

"We're all in this together," Sherry interjected. "At least we're supposed to be."

"Reese, where do you stand on this?" Ben asked, finally finding his voice.

"I'm with them," Reese said, addressing Gary and the others as if they were mutineers. "It's our asses on the line. We're doing the work; we deserve more than just a little of it here and there. But I don't see why Donna should get a full share."

"Because she's in," Gary hotly defended her.

The bickering continued for another few minutes with Sherry taking a clear shot at Ben. She flat-out asked him to deny taking the money and how much. He stuttered a bit then admitted it was about as much as they were now demanding.

The temperature of those at the table finally went down. It was even agreed that Donna, although only involved in one job, would get a full share.

When that was settled, Luke announced he had scouted a new bank on his way back from Missouri. It was in Ames, Iowa. Ames is a college town where Iowa State is located. Luke saw it as very similar, almost identical to the setup in Grand Forks, North Dakota. It was agreed that Luke and Cindy would go down to Ames and do a thorough recon.

"Damn, it's cold out," Neil said as he and the others piled back into Gary's SUV after the mutiny meeting. Gary started the engine, and while he let it run for a minute to warm up, they talked about the meeting. It was generally agreed it did not go too well but ended well.

"I feel guilty," Donna said. "I don't think I deserve a full share. Plus is this what I signed on for?"

"Yes, you do deserve it," Cindy said. "And we all can use some money. Saving the world will wait a while."

"We need to talk," Ben said to Luke. "Things are getting out of our control."

"Relax," Luke told him. "They were right. They deserve more than just a pat on the back."

"I didn't tell you this before, but my contact with Tom Breyer and his people called me after Duluth. He was pretty pissed. They want us to stop."

"Tell your pal, Webster Crosby, when they start paying us, then they can tell us what to do," Luke replied.

Ben looked at Luke with surprise on his face.

"What, you didn't think I knew what you were doing with Webster Crosby?"

FORTY-TWO

Tony Carvelli tossed back his bed covers and rolled out of bed at the crack of noon. It was the first time in more than a week he had slept in. Normally Carvelli was the consummate Night Owl. Twenty plus years with MPD and another decade as a PI, night work was the norm.

Carvelli sat on the edge of his bed, looked at his clock then picked up the bottle of water he kept on the bed stand. He took three or four swallows from the bottle and put it back. Because the first look he gave the clock had not registered, he checked it again. The shades over the windows were drawn, but he saw sunlight along the edges.

"Must be noon and not midnight," he muttered to himself. "I guess I can get up."

Tossing the gray sweatpants he normally wore in the morning over his shoulder, he headed for the bathroom. A couple of minutes later, he was in the kitchen. After turning on the coffee maker, he checked the messages on his phone. There were seven of them, including one from his "friends with benefits" pal, Vivian Donahue. He owed her a call and a night out. There was one from Bob Olson of Lake Country Banks inquiring if he had received the complaint letters. He had, and at two o'clock in the morning last night, Carvelli had forwarded them to his computer hacker contact to get started looking for the mysterious Luke.

Maddy had called twice; once shortly after 9:00 A.M. and again twenty minutes ago. The second message was her wondering if he was alive; a not so subtle way of telling him to call back pronto.

"Well, you are alive," Maddy said. "I was beginning to wonder."

"You were not," Carvelli replied. He had redialed on his way to the living room with his first cup of coffee. He sat in his favorite chair and took a sip.

"Are you just now getting your ass out of bed?"

"I was up until…. never mind. I was up late. The stuff came in from the bank and I forwarded it to Paul," Carvelli replied, referring to his hacker, Paul Baker.

"That's why I called. To see if you had heard from the bank," Maddy said.

"Yeah, I got it late last night, after you left," he replied.

The two of them had spent the previous evening talking to local criminals including Noah Hemmer, Carvelli's fence snitch. Maddy grew a little tired and bailed out at midnight because they were getting nowhere.

"Did he give you an estimate of how long it would take him?" Maddy asked.

"No. It doesn't matter. He always lies about that to jack up the price. Then he gets it done early and expects a bonus. I'll let you know as soon as I get something."

"When do I get to meet this mystery computer whiz?" Maddy asked.

"I'm not sure you really want to. Paul's a little, um, out there, would be a good way of putting it."

Maddy laughed, then said, "Of course he is. He's a computer, techie geek. They're all like that. That's why they're computer geeks. They don't deal well with humans. I'll bet Paul's interesting in an oddball sort of way and I'd like to meet him."

"He is that, interesting in an oddball way," Carvelli said. "I suppose I could warn him. Tell him to open some windows, air the place out and take a shower."

"It's January, Tony. Opening windows to air the place out isn't a good idea."

"I'll check with him after I clean up. You want to get lunch or breakfast?"

"You buying?"

"I'll meet you at Jack's in a half-hour," Carvelli said.

"You're buying," Maddy said again, only this time it was not a question.

"Hey," Maddy said, greeting Carvelli as she slid into the booth opposite him.

Before Carvelli could reply, the waitress was at their booth.

"Hi," Maddy said, "I would like a BLT on wheat, no mayo and a Diet Coke, please."

"That was quick," Carvelli said after giving the waitress his order.

"I'm hungry, and a BLT sounded good," Maddy said.

"Paul called. He's got some stuff for us," Carvelli said.

"Already? How...?"

"I don't ask. I told him I was bringing someone, and he needed to clean up his act. You've been warned," Carvelli told her.

"Did you tell him you were bringing a girl?"

"Yeah, that will make him even more nervous. We'll eat and run over there."

"Are you gonna make me sit in back with a hood over my head?" Maddy asked.

"Very funny, smartass. Although, maybe I should check with Paul. I'll warn you now; we'll have to sit through a long explanation of how he came up with what he did. He likes to impress. And inflate his bill."

Maddy parked behind Carvelli's Camaro while watching Carvelli get out of his car. The temperature was a balmy plus five degrees. With no wind, it was the warmest day for a week.

Maddy joined Carvelli on the sidewalk in front of the brick and vine-covered house. She had enough sense to be wearing a warm, knit hat, gloves, scarf and a winter coat. Carvelli, ever the tough guy, had on his usual leather jacket, no gloves, no hat and certainly no scarf.

"What's wrong with you?" Maddy asked. "It's freeze-your-ass-off real winter."

"It's nice out, today," he replied. "Listen, I should warn you, Paul is an indoor guy. He's always dressed in a ratty-ass, terry cloth bathrobe, white t-shirt and boxers. And, the robe is usually open. Oh, and of course, flip-flops."

"He rarely shaves and the last time he bathed was during the Clinton Administration," Maddy said.

"Pretty close," Carvelli replied.

When they reached the door, it opened before Carvelli knocked even once. There stood a man, clean-shaven, wearing a sweater, clean jeans, socks and loafers.

"Who the hell are you?" Carvelli asked. "Do we have the right house?"

"Very funny, Tony. Hi, you must by Maddy," Paul said as he stood aside to let them in.

They went into the living room, and Carvelli stood sniffing the air.

"What are you doing?" Maddy asked.

"What did you do with Paul Baker?" Carvelli asked. He looked at Maddy and said, "An alien life form has taken over Paul's body."

"Don't be an ass," Maddy told him. "It's nice to meet you," she said to Paul.

Carvelli was looking around the downstairs, then said, "Did you get a cleaning crew in here? What the hell is going on? I feel like I've stepped into an episode of the Twilight Zone!" he yelled.

"You have. I'm having you for dinner later," Paul said with an evil look which made Maddy laugh. "You will go well with a nice Chianti and fava beans."

"You'd have to tenderize him for a week first. He's tough as shoe leather," Maddy said.

"Very funny," Carvelli said.

Tony and Maddy sat down on the couch, and Paul began presenting his findings.

"I found over eighty suicides, eighty-three to be precise, after farm foreclosures during the time frame you gave me," he began.

"Eighty-three! Seriously?" Maddy said.

"Lake Country handles mortgages nationwide. There were more than three thousand by them during the time period you gave me," Paul explained. "Of the eighty-three, I found nine with a grandson with the name Luke or Lucas. It's a fairly popular name.

"I boiled it down to these three," he said, turning on the big TV. Side-by-side pictures of three young men came up—all in their early to mid-twenties.

"Right age group and two in Minnesota, one in Wisconsin."

"There he is," Carvelli said, pointing at the TV.

"The one in the middle," Maddy agreed. "That looks like our picture."

"You have a picture?" Paul asked.

"A composite drawing from the Waseca cops," Carvelli said.

Maddy had carried a leather satchel along with everything they had in it. She quickly found the drawing and gave it to Paul.

"Yeah, that's pretty close. Why didn't you give me..."?

"Because I didn't want to influence you. I wanted you to cast a wide net. But I think you have him," Carvelli answered him.

Paul handed the drawing back to Maddy and said, "There are reports on all three of them in front of you." He was referring to the documents on the coffee table.

Carvelli picked them up and started reading through the one who most resembled the drawing. Maddy looked over his shoulder and read along.

"Say, um, Maddy, you wouldn't happen to have a sister with a thing for slightly demented computer geeks, would you?"

Maddy smiled at him and said, "Sorry, she's married to a very normal dentist in Chicago."

"My luck holds," Paul said.

"Print off all three of those photos on good photo paper for me, will you, Paul?" Carvelli interrupted by saying.

"Will do," Paul said then went upstairs to his workroom.

"We need to make a run back to Waseca," Carvelli said.

"And see the hot, biker dude," Maddy said. "Wrangler."

"Hot?"

"It's the bad boy thing," Maddy said.

"And yet you fell for the least bad-boy guy I think I've ever known," Carvelli said.

"Marc's a bad-boy, sort of," Maddy said. "In a buttoned-down, tight-ass sort of way."

Carvelli stared at her while he pulled his phone out of his coat. He dialed a three-digit number, continued to stare at her, then said into the phone, "Waseca, Minnesota Police Department."

While he waited to get the number, he told Maddy, "See, this is why men don't try to figure you people out. It's hopeless."

"Good."

"Detective Tom Haig, please," Carvelli said when his call was answered.

Haig was in, and Carvelli explained what he wanted. Haig told him he would be happy to help them. They set a time and told him they would be there.

A couple of minutes later Paul came back with the photos printed off.

"I'll drive," Maddy said as they walked toward their cars.

"Don't say it," Carvelli said. He knew she was about to say something disparaging about his driving.

As she pulled away, Carvelli said, "I should call Owen Jefferson and let him know what we have."

"What about Jeff Johnson?" Maddy asked.

"He can wait," Carvelli replied.

He found Jefferson's personal number on his phone and called it.

"Hey, we got something," Carvelli said.

"What?" Jefferson asked.

Carvelli explained to him that they had come up with a Luke they thought was a possible match. When he finished, the line went silent.

"You still there?" Carvelli finally asked.

"Yeah. Listen, I shouldn't do this, but I'm gonna ask you two to run with this and keep in touch with me, for now. We're up to our ass in alligators because of last night."

"What about last night?" Carvelli asked.

"Don't you watch the news or read the papers? Although, I guess it isn't in the papers yet," Jefferson said.

"What?"

"A triple homicide in Kenworth last night. You didn't hear?"

"No," Carvelli said. He covered the phone and asked Maddy if she had heard about it. She shook her head and said no.

"Three people. A married couple and the wife's mother. All tied up and murdered."

"No shit? Okay, you're busy…"

232

"It's worse. The husband was the mayor's brother," Jefferson said. "It's a giant political shitstorm around here. Everybody's on it. So, go ahead and see what you can find out in Waseca. Stay in touch!"

"Will do. Good luck. These are serious assholes that need to be put away," Carvelli replied.

"The mayor's brother?" Maddy asked when Carvelli finished telling her.

"Guess so," Carvelli replied.

"They are up to their ass in alligators," Maddy said.

At 4:30 P.M., the three of them, in Tom Haig's car, pulled into the farm where they had met Kenny Wrangler the first time. Haig had called ahead and told them he was coming. Wrangler reluctantly agreed to see them.

By the time they pulled up to the house and parked, Wrangler and two of his friends were waiting for them. Despite the snow and cold, all three men were dressed as if it was summer—white T's under leather vests, boots and jeans.

"I'll talk to the chick," Wrangler said, pointing a finger at Maddy.

The two of them walked off out of earshot range of the others while Wrangler's goons stared down Haig and Carvelli.

"How you guys doing today?" Carvelli asked. "Little cool out here, don't you think?"

Neither of them even flinched.

"How about those Timberwolves? Suck again, don't they?" Carvelli asked.

Again, no response.

While Carvelli was being a smartass with Wrangler's guys, Maddy showed Wrangler the three photos. The entire conversation lasted less than a minute.

When Maddy walked past Tony, she quietly said the word, "Bingo."

"Nice chatting with you guys," Carvelli said and waved. "Hope to see you soon."

"Don't come back," Wrangler said as the three of them got into Haig's car.

"It's him," Maddy said. "He picked him out immediately."

"Now we have to find him," Carvelli said.

FORTY-THREE

"Hello," the harried-looking woman cheerfully said from her desk. She stubbed out her cigarette, got up and hurried through the office door into the reception area.

"You look like a nice couple. Interested in an apartment?" she asked Maddy and Carvelli who were standing at the office's counter.

"Sorry, no," Maddy sweetly replied. "We're trying to find a tenant of yours."

"Oh, well, what's the name?" the woman answered now obviously annoyed with being disturbed.

"Luke Hanson and…"

"What do you want with that deadbeat bum?" she asked.

"So, you know him," Maddy said.

"Sure, he skipped out owing three months' rent. Packed up in the middle of the night about a year ago."

"So, he owes you money?" Carvelli asked.

"What's it to you?"

"Well, you could be in luck. We are investigators with a law firm, and he had an uncle die and left him a bunch of money."

"How much?" she eagerly asked.

"Well, I can't tell you that, but I'm sure it's more than the rent for three months. Any idea where he went?" Carvelli asked.

"Not a clue," she replied.

"Do you know where he works?" Maddy asked.

"He was going to school somewhere. And he was working at a grocery store somewhere. A Cub, I think," she replied, referring to a local grocery store chain.

"Do you still have his rental application?" Carvelli asked.

"Yeah, but I don't think I can show it to you. Legally I mean," she said.

Carvelli unfolded two twenty-dollar bills, slid them across the counter toward her and said, "Would two pictures of President Jackson clear your conscience?"

The woman looked at the bills and said, "You know, I've always had a high regard for Ben Franklin. Got a picture of old Ben to add to those pictures of Jackson?"

Maddy held back a laugh while Carvelli found the hundred-dollar bill for her. She snatched up the money and said, "Be right back."

Two minutes later she came back holding a single sheet of paper.

Carvelli held it while the two of them read through it. Most of the questions on the application were left blank.

"Not much information," Carvelli said. "Did you do a background check?"

"Don't think so," she replied. "We were in a hurry to rent the apartment."

"Could we get a copy of this?" Maddy asked.

The woman looked silently at her with an expectant expression.

"Would another picture of Andrew Jackson cover the copying expenses?"

"Tell you what. I'll get you a copy for another Jackson if you promise to get me paid if you find him and he gets the money."

"Deal," Carvelli said then handed over another twenty. "How much does he owe you?"

When they got back to Carvelli's car, he said. "Seven hundred bucks a month for this dump? What is this place, part of the witness protection program?"

"We got his old address and the Cub he worked at," Maddy said.

"We got his social security number," Carvelli said.

"If it's real," Maddy replied.

"Yeah, if it's real," Carvelli agreed as he placed his phone to his ear.

"Paul, I got a job for you. An SSN to run down for Luke Hanson."

Carvelli handed the phone to Maddy as he drove away. Maddy read the number off of the application to Paul.

Carvelli was taking his turn doing surveillance duty looking for Luke Hanson. He was parked on North Seventh Street in Minneapolis about a mile from Target Field, the baseball stadium for the Twins. He had been there for an hour, the car's engine shut off and the cold creeping in. A running engine was a little too conspicuous for a stakeout, especially in the winter with the exhaust it created.

Carvelli was watching the building where Paul's search of Luke's social security number gave as his employment; Nieman Containers, LLC. A box and industrial container manufacturer. He had a clear view of the back door to the parking lot, but unfortunately at quitting time, 5:00 P.M. it was already quite dark.

The back door burst open, and a line of people came streaming out. Carvelli picked up his camera with a 300mm lens. With the help of the parking lot light, he had a clear view of faces.

One of the men caught his attention. He looked nothing like the drawing or any of the photos, but the height, size and facial features were right, except he was placing a stocking cap on an almost bald head. He was also wearing tinted glasses and sporting a moustache, goatee and a gold stud earring. But there was something about him. Carvelli had seen him two days ago for the first time when he first noticed it.

Once again, he was with two other young men. Carvelli got at least a dozen fairly good photos of all of them while the three of them entered a car, engine running and waiting for them. He also got a close up of the car's driver, a young woman that one of the guys kissed after getting in the front seat.

She drove her car out of the lot less than thirty feet from Carvelli, turned right, away from him and as he watched her taillights go down the street, the memory clicked in his head.

Carvelli quickly started the Camaro and took off after him. As he did, he quietly said to himself, "I've seen that guy walking before. Many times. It's him. I'm sure of it." While he drove, he jotted down the car's license plate number on a notepad.

Keeping a reasonable distance, Carvelli easily followed the car. Traffic at this time of day was heavy and slow which was both a help and a hindrance. With Carvelli's experience, he kept them in sight without being noticed.

It took almost an hour for the normally twenty-minute drive. Carvelli was hoping the driver would drop each of them off at their own home. Instead, she pulled her car into an underground garage of a high-rise apartment building, one of three in the apartment complex. It must have been her place since she used a keycard she had to enter the garage.

Carvelli waited in the parking lot for twenty minutes—engine running to keep out the cold—deciding whether to stay or go. He had the girl's license plate number and address. He also made a note of which apartment was hers when he saw the lights go on. While he waited, a pizza delivery car drove up. The driver checked in with the security guard at the front desk. A few minutes later, the girl showed up in the lobby and paid for the pizza.

"Pizza and beer," he quietly said. "They could be in there for hours."

Before leaving, he made two calls—the first to Maddy to let her know what happened. Then one to Paul Baker to run the address and license plate number.

Carvelli was less than ten minutes from where Paul lived. On the way, he called Maddy back and asked her to meet him. By the time he got there, Paul had the information for him. Maddy arrived a few minutes later.

"Hi," Maddy said to Carvelli as he opened Paul's front door for her.

"He's upstairs printing off some material for us," Carvelli said explaining why he answered the door. "Actually, I think he's getting dressed. I told him you were coming."

Maddy sniffed the air as they went to the living room.

"I haven't smelled this much weed since college," she said.

"Sorry about that," they heard Paul say from behind them. "I was ah, you know, relaxing when Tony called."

"It's okay," Maddy said as she sat down. "I just don't want to walk out of here lightheaded, giggling and hungry."

"What do you have?" Carvelli asked.

"Donna Marie Gilchrist," Paul said, handing each of them several sheets of paper. "Brown hair, brown eyes. Five-foot seven. One hundred thirty pounds, or so it says on her driver's license."

"What girl would lie on her license about her weight?" Maddy asked.

"Good point. Same address as you gave me. No criminal record except for a minor in possession of alcohol a couple years ago. She turned twenty-one last year."

"Okay," Carvelli said as he looked over the documents. "Now what?" He absently asked.

"And she's a student at Midwest. I didn't have time to dig further for grades and family."

"Check that out," Maddy said. "I bet you'll find she's taking liberal arts, social justice type courses."

"Look into her family, too," Carvelli said.

"Give me a half-hour and I'll have that for you," Paul said, secretly hoping to impress Maddy.

"Go ahead," Carvelli said. "I'll wait."

"Me, too," Maddy concurred.

Fifteen minutes later, Paul was back downstairs with more to report.

"Okay," he said as he walked through the living room opening. "Here's her transcript and family."

"Tell me," Carvelli said, holding the papers Paul gave him.

"Good student, good grades. She's carrying a three-point four GPA. But you were right," he said, looking at Maddy. "A lot of liberal arts courses. Not exactly knock yourself out-degree of difficulty. I could get a four oh taking these courses and sleep through all of them."

"She have a job?" Carvelli asked.

"Not that I could find," Paul said. "No student loans, no debt of any significance."

"How does she do that and drive a two-year old Lexus?" Carvelli asked although he knew the answer.

"Mommy and daddy are loaded," Paul said. "Or at least mommy is. She's a member of the Drew family. As in Drew Investment Funds. The whole family is wallowing in money."

"Why live here?" Maddy wondered.

"As opposed to New York?" Paul replied.

"Never mind. Good point," Maddy said.

"So, she's on the 'social justice,' 'down with capitalism' crusade while mom picks up the tab for her and capitalism pays for all of it," Carvelli said.

"Maybe," Maddy replied. "We don't know if these are even the right people."

"Damn, I'm an idiot," Carvelli declared. He stood and started for the door.

"Don't leave, no one's arguing with you," Maddy said.

"I'll be right back."

Carvelli came back in carrying his camera. He pulled up the photos he wanted on its screen and scrolled until he found the one he wanted.

"Here," he said, showing it to Paul. "I want you to do a facial recognition program on this guy. Compare him to Luke Hanson. See if it's a match."

Ten minutes later, Paul was back with the results. "It's him," Paul declared. "Ninety-nine point three. It's him."

Carvelli looked at Maddy and she said, "It's them. It's gotta be."

"Well, we're gonna find out," Carvelli told her.

FORTY-FOUR

Maddy shut off her headlights and slowly came to a stop. She was at a residential intersection a couple of blocks from the Midwest State campus. She watched the car she had been tailing come to a stop after turning left at the corner where Maddy now waited and watched.

There were two people in the car. One was the owner, Donna Gilchrist. In the passenger seat was a young man—her boyfriend—Paul had identified through Carvelli's photos. His name was Gary Weaver.

While Maddy followed them, even at a discreet distance, she could see the two were arguing all the way here. Watching them walk down the sidewalk verified it. Donna was six steps ahead of Gary walking fast and ignoring him. Despite the dark, the ambient light was sufficient for Maddy to see which house they went in. She turned her headlights on again just as another car drove past from her right. Her headlights lit up the car's interior just enough to give her an excellent view of the driver. It was Luke Hanson, shaved head and goatee, driving a late model SUV. Instead of pulling away, Maddy shut her lights off again and watched him. He parked two houses behind Donna's car, then hurried to the same house.

Maddy thought for a moment about calling Carvelli. Instead, she waited two more minutes, then drove down the street where they parked. Slowly driving past Luke's SUV, she jotted down his license plate number. She looked to her right to get the house number they went in. Unfortunately, there were no lights on in front and she could not read the numbers.

Disappointed and determined to get the house number, she drove a half a block farther along and parked. Despite the cold, which makes most people walk faster, Maddy casually strolled back to the house. When she got there, she took a quick look around then ran up the front walk. When she reached the front steps, she saw the house's numbers at the same time, the front door opened.

"Can I help you?" Luke Hanson asked, stepping onto the stairs' platform. He wore a very serious expression on his face with his right hand behind his back. Obviously holding a gun. Caught.

Feeling almost naked, Maddy very quickly said, "Yeah, um, is this Susan and Doug Collins home?"

"No," Luke brusquely said.

"Oh, gosh. Sorry to have bothered you," she said, taking a couple of steps back.

"What address are you looking for?" Ben Sokol asked. He stepped out of the house and stood to Luke's left. He was smiling and looked far less threatening.

Thinking very quickly, Maddy gave him a house number close to his and the name of a street she had driven past.

"That's a couple blocks south," Ben said.

"Oh, gosh, ditzy me," Maddy said, playing the flaky woman act. "I guess I got turned around a bit. Well, thanks. Have a nice night," she added and quickly fled.

The two of them stood on the stoop, watching her walk away. While they did, Luke said, "I don't like it. We should've got some ID."

"What were you going to do, force her into the house at gunpoint? Relax, she's too good looking to be a cop," Ben said.

"What do you think? Did they buy it?" Carvelli asked Maddy.

She was back in her car, heading home. As soon as she could, she called Carvelli to tell him what happened.

"I don't know," Maddy answered. "I played the ditzy female and don't say it," she said.

"Say what?" Carvelli tried to answer innocently.

"Anything about me being a ditzy female," Maddy said.

"That's the last thing you are," Carvelli said. "Except for maybe your taste in men. I mean, a lawyer?"

"Shut up," Maddy said. "Anyway, I got the house address and Luke's license plate number. Send them to Paul."

Maddy repeated both for him as he wrote them down.

"I think there's some kind of meeting going on at that house," Maddy said.

"I'm leaving now," Carvelli replied. "I'll tail…"

"Don't bother," Maddy said. "At this time of night, when she leaves, she'll go home. I'll pick her up in the morning."

"You think he was holding a gun behind his back?" Carvelli asked.

"He was holding something. Most likely a gun."

"We're up to about ninety percent these are the guys we're looking for," Carvelli replied.

"When are we going to let Jeff Johnson know?" Maddy asked.

"I don't know. Anytime now, I guess. I don't need the Feebs pissed at me."

"How about I take a run at Donna tomorrow? Poor little rich girl is in this up to her ass and she needs to have her eyes opened," Maddy said.

"Okay, look for an opportunity to get her alone. Then go at her."

"Will do. Goodnight, paisan."

"Hey, be careful. They've already done one murder," Carvelli said.

"You, too."

The next morning Maddy was on station at 6:00 A.M. The apartment complex where Donna lived was large and expensive; three twelve-story buildings, each with heated underground parking. Directly across the street from the entrance to Donna's parking garage was an upscale, trendy, boutique mall. Even at this early hour, there were enough cars in the mall's parking lot for Maddy to hide in.

There was a Starbucks located on the first floor of Donna's building. Maddy watched for a couple of minutes then went across the street and inside. During the night, a warm front moved in and the temp was already almost thirty degrees. Balmy.

When she left the Starbucks, Maddy sneaked down the ramp into the parking garage. To her relief, she found Donna's car parked in its reserved spot.

Surveillance is normally boring and in the winter, even worse. With the engine off, the cold creeped in and made it even more uncomfortable. Along with her latte, Maddy had purchased a breakfast croissant and a paper. It could be a while sitting in the cold.

A few minutes past eight, Maddy saw Donna's Lexus drive out of the garage exit. Donna was driving and Gary, who apparently spent the night, was in the passenger seat.

"Must not be fighting anymore," Maddy whispered to herself.

"That's not the way to the school," she said when she saw which way they went.

Maddy followed them for about fifteen minutes and saw Donna pull into a Dunkin' Donuts and park next to an SUV. While Gary got out of Donna's car and into the SUV, Maddy checked the license plate number. It was Luke Hanson's.

Without waiting, Donna drove off. Maddy thought about following Luke then realized her job was to get Donna alone.

Donna drove to the Crosstown Hwy 62 ramp and took it to 35W heading south. Maddy fell in a safe distance behind her.

Traffic heading south out of the Cities was fairly light and moving briskly along. When they reached Lakeville twenty miles south around 8:45, Carvelli called.

"Bad news," he told her.

"What?"

"The SUV is registered to our guy, Luke Hanson. But he gave them the same address he has on his driver's license."

"The one, the apartment with the crabby bitch we had to bribe?" Maddy asked.

"Crabby bitch? You're gonna lose your PC card," Carvelli replied. "Yeah, that's the one.

"There is good news," Carvelli continued. "The house you spotted last night belongs to a professor at Midwest State. The guy's name is Ben Sokol."

"Where have I seen that name before?" Maddy asked.

"It's in the report from the MPD on the murder of Jordan Simmons. They interviewed Gary Weaver, checked his phone records and found a dozen or so calls to this Sokol guy."

"What's he got to do with this?" Maddy wondered out loud.

"He could be the guy calling the shots," Carvelli replied.

"Or they could've been there for a study group," Maddy said.

"With our boy Luke holding a gun behind his back when he caught you sneaking around? I don't think so," Carvelli said.

At that moment, a familiar-looking SUV drove past her. Maddy looked and saw Gary in the passenger seat and was pretty sure Luke was driving. There were two people in back.

"What the hell is going on?" Maddy said mostly to herself.

"What?" Carvelli asked.

Maddy told him where she was, what she was doing and what just happened.

"Stay with Donna," Carvelli advised.

"I will," she replied. "I'll keep in touch."

Three hours after starting out, Maddy followed Donna into a rest area in Iowa. They were 50 miles north of Ames. Maddy parked a dozen cars past Donna toward the rest areas exit ramp. She watched as Donna walked toward the building with the restrooms and decided to chance it. Plus, the coffee she had drunk was forcing the issue.

Maddy followed Donna inside and used the stall next to her. Donna finished first and forced Maddy to hurry. If Donna took off ahead of her, she might lose her. Instead, Donna got back in her car and went nowhere. In fact, she looked at the entrance several times as if waiting for someone.

Twenty minutes later, a shiny, black BMW sedan pulled in next to Donna. The driver got out and walked toward the building. Maddy recognized him immediately. He was the man who came outside with Luke, the previous night. Probably Ben Sokol.

While she waited and watched, he came out of the men's room after a couple of minutes. When he got back to the Beemer, Donna exited her car and got in his. It took about three more seconds for the light to go on in Maddy's head.

"Answer your damn phone," she impatiently said into her telephone. The voice mail came on, and she hurriedly said, "Hey, call me right now. I think they're pulling a job in Iowa. Probably Ames or Des Moines."

For the next hour as cars came and went, Maddy waited for Carvelli to call back. It finally occurred to her to try Marc.

As she was explaining things to Carolyn Lucas, one of the secretaries, Carvelli finally called.

"It's Tony, Carolyn. I gotta take this.

"Hey, where've you been? Never mind," she quickly said when he started to explain.

"You think they're doing a job?"

"I don't know what else to think," Maddy said. "Why else are they down here and she's sitting in a rest area?"

She quickly filled him in on everything and when she finished, Carvelli agreed.

"I called Jeff and Tess. The calls went to their voice mails. I don't know what else to do," Carvelli said.

"You know anyone in Iowa?" Maddy asked.

"No, I don't. You think Ames?" Carvelli asked.

"Probably Des Moines," Maddy said.

"I'll call, but I don't know what they can do."

"Call Ames and the Iowa state people, too," Maddy said. "If you have to, call Owen Jefferson and have him call."

"Will do," Carvelli said.

"Call me back," Maddy replied.

A half-hour later her phone rang with Carvelli's return call.

"Hey, what did they say?"

"They weren't impressed," Carvelli said. "The information we have is pretty vague. I'm not sure what they can do."

"What about Jeff or Tess? Did they call back?" Maddy asked.

"Not yet."

"The BMW is pulling out. Donna got out and is back in her car. Should I try to go after her inside her car?"

"No. If they are doing a job, she probably has a gun. She might use it. Stay with her. Is she leaving?"

"No, she's still sitting."

"Goddamnit," Carvelli yelled.

The line went silent between them until Carvelli said, "Stay with her. Just follow, for now. Don't go barging into the middle of a bank robbery. I'm very fond of you. Stay with the girl."

"Besides we aren't sure what they're up to," Maddy said.

For the next two hours, Maddy sat in her car watching Donna. Donna had fallen asleep shortly after Ben Sokol drove off, which helped Maddy remain inconspicuous. At three o'clock, a car pulled up with three people in it: two men and a woman. One of the men, in the front passenger seat, was Gary Weaver. The woman, identity unknown to Maddy but was Sherry Toomey, got into Donna's car. Before she did, Maddy got her picture. The other young man was Neil Cole. His picture and ID they had from the photos Carvelli took at the container company where they work.

Both Gary and Neil got out and walked off toward the men's room. As they did, Donna pulled out and drove off. More convinced than she was before that they had robbed a bank, Maddy decided it was best to follow Donna.

FORTY-FIVE

"Damnit, Carvelli, the next time you get information like this, you make sure I get it!" Jeff Johnson yelled, glaring down at Tony who was calmly letting the FBI agent vent.

Carvelli was sitting in front of Owen Jefferson's desk at the MPD Homicide Division. A steaming mad Jeff Johnson, with Tess Richards, had barely closed Jefferson's door when he let loose at Carvelli.

Finally fed up with Johnson's tirade, Carvelli snidely said back at him, "Oh, well sure, Jeff. Next time you don't answer your phone, I'll just drive around looking for you until I track you down. Not a problem."

"Jeff, stop!" Tess said, stepping in front of him.

The FBI agent looked at the MPD lieutenant, who said, "He did what he could. Let it go, Jeff."

Johnson inhaled heavily, looked at Carvelli and said, "I just had a large piece of my ass bit off by Taylor Swift. I guess I needed to vent on someone, sorry."

The two FBI agents found chairs, then Johnson said, "Okay, what happened?"

Carvelli went over the entire chain of events with them. How Maddy and he had found what were now suspects. He told them about Maddy's late-night adventure the previous night and the events of today. He also told them their suspicions about another robbery, Carvelli's attempts to alert the FBI and the Iowa cops.

"They hit the Farmers and Mechanics Bank in Ames while Maddy was fifty miles away sitting on one of them. We tried to alert the appropriate people, Jeff. Sorry," Carvelli said.

Johnson leaned forward in his chair, clearly angry again and said, "You knew about these people for how long without contacting me?"

"We didn't know anything about these people until today," Carvelli shot back. "And we still don't, not for sure. You have any evidence they robbed the Ames bank? Do you even have probable cause for a search warrant, let alone an arrest warrant?"

Seeing the look on Carvelli's face, Tess quickly said, "Don't say it, Tony. Please."

"Say what?" Jefferson asked.

"These aren't Republicans for you to go after. We need real evidence," Carvelli said.

Jefferson burst out laughing, Tess just shook her head and even Johnson had to smile.

"How did you find them?" Tess asked.

"I'm not saying," Carvelli said. "At least not yet."

"You used your off-the-books hacker to come up with a list of Lukes whose grandfather committed suicide after his farm was foreclosed," Johnson said.

"Ask me no questions, I'll tell you no lies," Carvelli said.

"Good work," Johnson sincerely replied. "But you're right. We really don't have anything we can use to get a warrant. We have the video from Iowa coming, but that will probably show us nothing we don't already have."

"We do have a tie between the murdered girl, Jordan Simmons, and this guy, Gary Weaver. And the Weaver kid ties in with all of the others," Carvelli said.

Johnson looked at Tess, who shrugged her shoulders. Johnson looked back at Carvelli and said, "That's a maybe, at best."

"What about the guy who sold him the guns?" Jefferson asked.

"We could force him," Jefferson said. "Give him immunity on the gun sale and if he refuses to testify, hold him in contempt."

"He'd laugh at you, Jeff," Carvelli said. "He's done plenty of time. Contempt isn't gonna scare him."

"Where's Maddy?" Tess asked.

"That's our best bet," Carvelli said. "Let her go after this girl, Donna. If Maddy can get her to flip, then we'll have something."

At that moment, the object of the conversation in Jefferson's office was, again, parked across the street from Donna's building. Maddy had followed Donna and the other girl back to the Cities. When Donna dropped Sherry off, Maddy called Carvelli. He had just arrived at Owen Jefferson's office, and Maddy quickly brought him up to date.

Maddy then watched while the two girls spoke in Donna's car. Sherry then got out and went to a bus stop shelter while Donna drove off. Disappointed she would not be able to get an address for the second girl, Maddy continued following Donna.

At 7:00 P.M. Carvelli rapped a knuckle on Maddy's passenger window. She let him in, and he handed her the bag from Chick-fil-A.

"Oh, man that smells good," Maddy said, her face inside the bag. "I'm so hungry I was thinking about eating a shoe."

"That is hungry. You, destroying a shoe?"

"Shut up," Maddy snarled then took a large bite of her sandwich.

While she ate—gobbled ravenously would be more accurate—Carvelli started to speak. Maddy held up a hand to stop him. He chuckled and waited for her to finish. In less than two minutes, she had devoured the sandwich, a large bag of fries and most of a Diet Coke.

"I'm proud of you. You ate that like a man," Carvelli said, laughing.

"Shut up. I was hungry. I hadn't eaten since breakfast. I had a candy bar a couple of hours ago when I went to the gas station to pee. That's been it."

"Are you sure she's still home?"

"Yeah, that's her light on in that corner window on the fourth floor. I checked for her car. It's still there."

Maddy slumped over against her door, leaned her head on the window and said, "I feel so much better. Thanks. How much do I owe you?"

"Nothing. It was worth the price just to watch you scarf that down," Carvelli replied.

"Be nice. I was hungry. How long should we stay tonight?"

"Go home. I'll sit for another hour or so then take off if she doesn't go out. I don't think they'll do anything with the money, tonight. Johnson and Tess are sitting on the professor's house," Carvelli said.

"What do you think?"

"I don't know. I'm up to ninety-seven percent this our gang. But we have no evidence."

Carvelli shifted in his seat to look at her and said, "When you confront her, make sure she understands that if she goes to these guys and tells them you went after her, they'll kill her."

"I know, Tony. We went over this already."

"You sleep in tomorrow. I'll be here by seven and take the first watch," Carvelli said.

"You're getting up that early?" Maddy asked. "You got a deal. In fact, I think I'll call Marc and go there tonight. It's, ah, been a while."

"I don't want to hear it."

The next morning, Maddy hurried across the parking lot at Midwest State toward Carvelli's Camaro. It was a gray, cloudy, wet day with a smell of snow in the air. She was wearing a coat with a hood on it which she used to cover her head. Not for the weather, but to avoid being identified by Luke or Ben if they happened to see her.

"Good, morning," she said, getting in next to Carvelli.

"Hey, kid," Carvelli saw. "Have a good night?"

"Ah, sort of. Marc's in trial and…"

"Say no more. He was busy all night."

"Yeah, but it was still nice to see him. What's up here? I see her car over there," Maddy said.

"According to her schedule, she only has one class today. We'll see what happens."

Carvelli looked at his watch and said, "Fifteen minutes. Maybe she'll go somewhere for coffee or something."

Ten minutes after the top of the hour, they saw Donna walking toward her car. Maddy waited until she drove off before going back to her car. Carvelli stayed with Donna and kept Maddy up to date on the phone.

Donna was headed in the direction of her apartment when she pulled to the curb. There was a Caribou Coffee on the corner.

Carvelli pulled over and watched her go in. He told Maddy and held the parking space for her.

Maddy went in and spotted Donna. She bought a latte for herself then went to Donna's table. Donna had a textbook open and was reading, a large cup on the table.

Maddy sat down without asking and Donna looked at her slightly annoyed, "Please, have a seat," she told Maddy.

"Thanks, Donna. I will."

The intrusive woman's use of her name froze her for several seconds. She stared at Maddy, who calmly sipped her beverage while staring back.

"How do you…"

"I've decided not to play games with you. Instead, I'm going to get right to it," Maddy said. She leaned forward, looked Donna right in the eyes and continued. "You are in very serious trouble, young lady."

When she said this, Donna closed her book as if to leave.

"I'm here to save your life," Maddy said.

"I don't know…" Donna stammered but remained seated.

"My name is Madeline Rivers. I'm a private investigator working with the FBI. Are you getting it now?"

Donna did not say a word. She sat with her back straight, tears forming in her eyes. The use of the initials FBI having scared her to her core.

"Luke, the professor, Benjamin Sokol, your boyfriend, Gary Weaver, Neil Cole and a couple of others are playing a very dangerous game. When, not if, but when you are tried and convicted, your pampered, privileged life will be over. You may get out of prison in thirty years or so, but this will be over.

"No career, no money, no husband, no kids, no family, no life. That's what you're looking at. And don't tell me you care so much about climate change, social justice, socialism and the rest of the garbage those professors are feeding you to spend thirty years in prison."

"I didn't do anything. I only drove a couple of times. Please, you have to believe me," she whispered, whined and pleaded.

248

"Wait you want me to turn them in," she said before Maddy could respond. "I can't do that. I won't do that," she defiantly said.

Maddy sat back, looked across the small table and said, "Okay, I'll get one of the others. It doesn't matter. All they need is one. And by the way, if you tell anyone about this, they'll kill you like they did Jordan Simmons."

"I don't know anything about that," she pleaded again. "I wasn't with them, then."

"Doesn't matter. You're with them now," Maddy said.

"I can't do this to Gary. I love him and…"

"Gary's my next target. You think he's strong enough to say no?"

The tears started to flow, and the sobbing began. So far, the two of them were quiet enough to avoid drawing attention. With the crying, several patrons turned and watched as Maddy let her go on crying for almost a minute.

"You have ten seconds to make a decision, then I'm leaving," Maddy said.

Donna used her napkin to wipe her eyes and blow her nose. When she had gathered herself sufficiently, she quietly asked, "What do you want me to do?"

"Atta girl," Maddy said.

"I want a lawyer," Donna said. "Someone to help me."

"It's your lucky day. I know just the guy," Maddy replied.

FORTY-SIX

"She's in," Maddy said into her phone.

Maddy and Donna were still at the table in the coffee shop. Donna was still fighting back tears while Maddy phoned Carvelli. Maddy explained how it went.

"How's she doing?" Carvelli asked.

"She'll be okay if I can get her to stop crying. She's pretty upset."

"She should be," Carvelli replied.

When he said this, he heard Maddy say to someone, "Can I help you with something?"

"Yeah, maybe you oughta lighten up on her," Carvelli heard a man say.

"Who's that?" he asked Maddy.

"Some do-gooder sticking his nose in where it doesn't belong," she said into the phone while staring at the man.

The customer who was butting in was two tables away. He was a good-sized man in his late twenties. He heard Maddy call him a do-gooder which pricked his male ego. Putting on his best tough-guy face, he stood up and started toward her.

"This idiot's coming over here," Maddy said to Carvelli.

"Maddy! Don't do it. Please."

"Hey, look, it's not what you think," Maddy told him as he approached.

"You think you're pretty hot shit, don't you, bitch?" he said. "I didn't like the do-gooder crack."

If he had not used the 'B' word, it would have been okay. Calling her that was like waving a red flag at a bull.

She hung up on Carvelli, set her phone on the table and looked up at the intruder. By now, Donna was done sobbing and had slid down the bench seat away from them.

"Look, tough guy," Maddy said not even bothering to get up. "Run along, and there won't be any problems."

He bent down. Pointed his right index finger at her and started to speak.

It took her less than two seconds. Maddy grabbed his right hand with her left, pulled his arm straight and bent his wrist back. As she did this, she slammed the palm of her right hand under his elbow. As he howled from the ligament damage in his elbow, she drove her right foot into the inside of his right knee. His knee started to collapse, and as he started going down, she kicked him squarely in the chest. He went backwards into an empty table, cursing at the truck that just hit him. Maddy did all of this without even getting out of her chair.

"Be thankful I don't charge you with assault. I know every cop in Hennepin County. Next time someone tells you to mind your own business, remember this," she told him.

By now, the entire restaurant was hovering around. No one said a word, uncertain about what had just happened.

Maddy looked over the crowd and said, "We had a misunderstanding, and he came after me. A girl has a right to defend herself, doesn't she?"

The door opened, and Tony Carvelli came hurrying in. He politely shoved his way through the spectators then shook his head when he saw what happened.

"Come on fella," Carvelli said, helping the man to his feet. "You okay?"

"No! That…" he said almost calling Maddy a bitch again.

When he did, Maddy jumped to her feet, stuck a finger in his face and snarled, "Call me that again, and I will really hurt you this time."

Carvelli put the man in a chair and checked him out. Maddy had actually pulled her punches a bit. The man's ego and pride would take longer to heal than his injuries.

"Let's go," Carvelli quietly but forcefully said to Maddy.

When they got outside, Carvelli asked, "I take it he called you a bitch?"

"Yeah," Maddy said.

"I'll never call you that," Donna said. "That was awesome."

"He's lucky he didn't use the 'C' word. We'd be waiting for an ambulance," Carvelli said.

"Cool," Donna replied, truly impressed.

Tony introduced himself and showed Donna his PI ID. When they reached Donna's car, he explained that they would take her to see a lawyer.

"Have you talked to Marc?" he asked Maddy.

"No, I haven't had a chance. He's in trial anyway," Maddy said.

"Try him. They might be on a break," Carvelli said.

As he said this, the man who had confronted Maddy was hobbling out the Caribou Coffee door.

"Have a nice day," Carvelli said. It was the only thing he could think of.

The man was going in the opposite direction. Without turning around, he raised his good arm and gave them a middle-finger salute.

"Okay," Carvelli heard Maddy say into the phone. "We'll meet you at the office."

"They took a plea on his case," Maddy said as she put her phone away. "He's wrapping up and, on his way back."

Carvelli looked at Donna and said, "He's a great lawyer. You may have heard of him. Marc Kadella."

"I don't pay much attention to lawyers," she replied.

"You okay?" Maddy asked her.

"I'm really scared. I can hardly sleep, eat or study. Am I gonna be okay?" Donna replied.

"If what you say is true, you only drove for a couple of them, yes, you should get through this and have your life back," Maddy said placing a comforting hand on her shoulder.

"We're on your side, Donna," Maddy continued, "believe me. But, the most important thing for you to do, starting right now, is to tell the truth. And all of it. Especially to Marc."

"I will, I swear. I haven't slept since I got in this. I thought it was an adventure. But it's not. It's totally serious."

"Yes, it is," Carvelli said. "I'm in the black Camaro," he continued pointing at his car parked down the street. "I'll pull up. You follow me and Maddy will follow you."

Marc entered the office, and when Carolyn saw him, she silently pointed at the conference room. Marc looked through the room's window and saw the three of them seated at the table. They were seated together on the exterior window side, away from the door. Donna was sitting between Maddy and Carvelli looking very nervous.

Marc went in, tossed his coat on a chair, placed his briefcase on the table then reached across to shake Donna's hand and introduce himself.

He sat down directly opposite from Donna, gave her his best, comforting smile and said, "They tell me you've gotten yourself into a bit of a jam and would like to get out of it."

"Yes," Donna very quietly said.

"The first thing I want you to do is take a deep breath.

"Go on, do it," Marc said when she hesitated.

"Again," he said.

She did it again, and when she exhaled, he said, "Feel a little better?"

"Yes, I do."

"Good. First thing, none of us are going to judge you. Whatever you did, we're here to help you get through it, okay?"

"Yeah," she said as Maddy placed a hand on the back of her neck and squeezed a little bit.

"Rule number one, you have to be totally honest and tell me everything," he said and held up a hand to stop her from speaking. "Let me finish. If you lie or hold anything back, it will come back to haunt you. Don't leave anything out even if it is embarrassing or you feel stupid or ashamed of it. Trust me," he continued looking at Carvelli, "we all do stupid things from time to time."

"Hey, don't look at me, talk to your pal about the new friend she made at the Caribou a while ago," Carvelli said.

"Now what?" he said looking at Maddy.

"Nothing," she said, waving a hand as if chasing off a fly. "I defended myself a little."

Marc looked back at Carvelli and asked, "Hospital, broken bones, anything I should worry about?"

"He'll be limping for a while, but he should be okay. We didn't have the cops get involved, and they didn't get our names," Carvelli said.

"See? A minor misunderstanding is all," Maddy said.

"Are they always like this?" Donna asked.

"Not always," Marc answered. "Sometimes they're worse."

"You're gonna regret that statement," Maddy said.

"My trial's over," Marc said.

"Oh, that's right. Never mind."

"You two are an item," Donna said. "That's cool."

"Let's get back to it," Marc said. "Do you know what attorney-client privilege is?"

"I think so. Anything I say to you is confidential, right?" Donna answered.

"Right. And it also covers people who are not lawyers but are working for me on your case—specifically, anyone in this office including Ms. Rivers and Mr. Carvelli. You can speak freely with them also.

"That reminds me," Marc said, looking at Carvelli. "As of this moment, you are no longer working for Lake Country Bank or the FBI. Agreed?"

"Yeah," Carvelli said,

"In fact, I'm going to record this, and we'll make a record of that. Then you're gonna call whoever you need to at the bank and the FBI. Don't explain anything, yet. They'll find out soon enough what's going on."

He looked back at Donna and said, "We're going to record your statement, too. Then we'll decide the best way to proceed."

Two hours later, with Marc asking questions to lead her through it and going over it multiple times, they were finished. Marc shut off the recorder and asked Maddy and Carvelli if they had any questions for her. Both declined, although Maddy did raise an issue.

"She can't go home," Maddy said.

"No," Marc agreed.

"Why?" Donna asked. "I have to go home."

"Sorry, no. These people have already committed one murder. You believe this Sherry did it?"

"That's what Cindy told me. I believed it, too. Sherry is tough. She could do it," Donna said.

"If they get even a whiff that you're cooperating, don't you think they'd do it again?" Maddy asked.

"Yes, I think they would," Donna agreed.

"How many phones do you have?" Carvelli asked her.

"Two," she replied. "a burner phone from them and my own iPhone."

"Let me have them," Carvelli said. "I need to take the SIM cards out. They could track you with them. We'll get you another burner, but you can't call any of them with it."

While Carvelli was disabling her phones, Donna looked at Marc and sadly said, "It was supposed to be about doing good. Climate change, social justice, helping people. I don't understand what went wrong."

"Everybody likes what money can do," Marc said. "Speaking of which, do you have any?"

"Not really. I have a trust fund, but I can't get at it until I'm twenty-five. My parents have money. I'm not sure I can go to them, though."

"There's the reward money," Maddy said. "The bank put up a hundred grand. She should get it."

"Now comes the big question," Marc said. "Do you want me to represent you?"

"Well, yeah. I mean, I thought that's what this is about," Donna said.

"We need to be clear about it, Donna. I kind of need you to say it," Marc said, smiling at her.

"Wait, I do have the money from the Duluth robbery," she said.

"How much?" Marc asked.

"I have a little over twenty-eight thousand. It's in cash. I didn't spend a dime of it. I was too afraid I'd get caught. I can give that to you."

Marc laughed a little bit and said, "I can't use that for fees. It's an interesting thought, but I can't do it. You need to bring it in. I'll hold it here. Connie, my friend and landlord, has a safe we can put it in. It has to go back to the bank."

"I just remembered," Donna said. "We're supposed to meet at Ben's tonight to get the money from Ames, Iowa divided up to launder."

"What time?" Carvelli asked.

"Nine o'clock," Donna answered.

"Call Jeff Johnson," Marc said. "Get one of the U.S. Attorneys on this. We'll get her full immunity, and they can arrest them tonight."

"We need to find a place for her to stay," Maddy said.

"And some bodyguards," Carvelli muttered while scrolling through his phone. "We can get some of our guys and Sherry Bowen," he added as he put the phone to his ear.

"Jeff? It's Carvelli. I'm going to drop another one in your lap."

FORTY-SEVEN

The elevator bell dinged, and Marc looked to see what floor they were stopping on. The doors slid open, and both Marc and Tony Carvelli walked off. They stepped up to the glass-enclosed reception desk where an armed guard was seated. It was after-hours, past 5:00, so the normal receptionist was gone.

"Can I help you?" the young man behind the bulletproof plexiglass asked through the speaker.

Marc had already retrieved his attorney license card. He held it up against the glass while saying, "We're here to see Special Agent Jeff Johnson. They're expecting us."

Marc placed the card in the extended metal tray for the guard. Holding it up, the guard made a call. When he finished the call, he placed the card back into the tray, then buzzed them through a door. Once inside, they saw Jeff Johnson coming toward them.

After the three men shook hands, Marc said, "I'm always amazed that we make government buildings and police departments more secure than we do our schools. And the government offices have armed, trained guards in them."

"It's not my idea," Johnson said. "If it was up to me, I could make our schools secure in a heartbeat. Come on in," he continued as he held open the door to a conference room.

At the head of the table, a very young-looking, demure, black woman was seated. On the opposite side, away from the door was Tess Richards. Introductions were made and everyone sat down. Before anyone could say anything, Marc jumped right in.

"Is this it? Is this all the people you're going to involve in this?" Marc said, looking at Johnson. "Do you understand what we have here, Agent Johnson?"

"We can get as many people as we need…"

"Excuse, me," Marc said, cutting him off. He looked at the Assistant U.S. Attorney, Delia Ferguson, and said, "Please don't be offended but you look very young. May I ask how long you've been with the DOJ?"

"I'm not offended," she replied. "Almost a year."

"Right out of law school?"

"Um, yes," she hesitantly answered.

"Let's hear what you have to say, Tony," Johnson said to Carvelli.

Carvelli pointed a finger at Marc and quietly said, "Talk to him."

"Do you understand what we have? We have your bank robbery case. All of it. The entire crew."

256

"Okay, let's hear it, counselor," Johnson said, getting a touch annoyed.

"We have a witness, a client. This person is on the inside. This person wants, demands, complete immunity for any and all crimes committed by my client or anyone associated with the bank robberies involving this gang..."

"I'm not sure we can give you that," the AUSA replied.

"Then get someone in here who can," Marc said.

"Jeff," Carvelli leaned forward and said, "it's the real deal. And you can have them tonight."

"I'll give you this much, Jeff," Marc interjected. "My client is a very minor player. Never went inside a bank, never held a gun, never hurt anyone."

Johnson looked at Delia Ferguson, nodded his head and said one word, "Yes."

"Where's your client, now?" Tess Richards asked Marc.

"With Maddy. I can have them here in twenty minutes," Marc replied.

Ferguson opened a file she had on the table and withdrew a two-page document. She handed it to Marc while saying, "I think this should do what you want. It's pretty standard."

Before Marc started reading, he asked, "Does it include witness protection?"

"Yes, again. Standard. Do you want it?" Ferguson replied.

"Probably not," Marc quietly said as he started to read.

While Marc read, the room went silent for a moment. The silence was broken when Johnson said while he looked at Carvelli, "I'm sticking my neck out trusting you."

"Have I ever let you down?" Carvelli asked.

"Yes! Many times," Johnson said. "But he hasn't," Johnson continued pointing a finger at Marc.

Marc finished reading the document and placed it on the table in front of him.

"Do you guys get the most anal legal writing teacher there is to write this stuff for you?" Marc asked.

"I didn't write it," Ferguson said with a big smile. "It is pretty convoluted."

"It's almost indecipherable," Marc replied. "Are they still teaching this in law school?" he added. Before she could answer, Marc looked at Carvelli and said, "Call Maddy, please."

"Yes, they are," Ferguson said.

"They started this because lawyers used to get paid by the word. They can stop teaching this any time," Marc said. "Where did you go to school?"

"Stanford," she replied.

"They'll be here in ten minutes," Carvelli said as he put his phone away.

"Okay," Marc told Carvelli. "Good school," Marc said. "Is there a coffee pot around here somewhere?"

While they waited for Maddy to arrive with Donna, Johnson called for a video tech. They arranged the seating so the guest of honor, Donna Gilchrist, would be seated at the head of the table. The videographer set up the camera at the other end. Marc would be seated to Donna's right, Maddy to her left and Carvelli next to Maddy. Delia Ferguson, two seats down from Marc with Tess to her right. And Jeff Johnson was two seats down from Carvelli.

Maddy and Donna arrived, escorted back by the front desk guard. When everyone was seated, Jeff Johnson tried to get things started. Marc quickly cut him off.

"Don't turn that on just yet," Marc told the camera tech. "I need to tell my client something."

He turned to Donna and said, "Before we get started, you need to be told something. I have read the immunity document. It's fine; you get a complete walk with no charges. But you need to be fully cooperative and completely honest."

"I understand," she said.

"Let me finish," Marc said. "If you hold anything back or they find out you've lied to them, the deal is off, and they can prosecute you for everything they believe you were involved in."

"What if I forget something or, I don't know, am not quite right about something, something I didn't mean to hold back but comes up later?" Donna asked.

Marc looked at Delia who hesitated, uncertain how to answer. It was Tess Richards who spoke up and answered.

"As long as it is in good faith, it won't be a problem. But, if it is something you did that you are trying to keep from us, that would be a problem."

"I'll want that on the record," Marc said, looking back and forth at the three Feds. They all nodded in agreement, and Marc again spoke to Donna.

"They want to make a video of this. I'm okay with that, and we'll get a copy. They will reduce your statement to writing and want you to sign it. We'll get a chance to review it before you do. We'll also be able to make minor corrections before you do. Are you okay with that?"

Donna stole a quick glance at Maddy, who smiled and slightly nodded her assent.

"Okay," Donna quietly agreed.

"We're going to get started now…" Marc began.

"Would you like some water?" Tess asked.

"Yes, please."

"I'll get it," Tess replied.

Apparently, it had been decided that Tess would be the good cop, Jeff Johnson the bad cop. Marc looked at Johnson who had an expression of indifference on his face while staring intently at Donna.

"I'll warn you right now, Agent Johnson," Marc said. "If you try to intimidate my client, you'll live to regret it."

"I don't know…" Johnson sputtered.

"Good, then don't try it," Marc said.

Looking up at Donna again, Marc continued. "We'll get started now. First, there will be some preliminary things said for the record. Things like today's date, time, place and we'll all identify ourselves. Then we'll get started. Just tell them what you know the same way you told it to me in my office. Go slowly. There's no hurry.

"There will be questions. If you get confused, uncertain, want to talk to me alone or just need a break, say so. It'll be all right. Okay?" Marc finished by giving her hand a little squeeze.

"Okay. Once the camera starts, is it okay if I say something?"

"Of course," Marc said. "Wait until it's your turn, to start."

Tess arrived with a half-dozen bottles of cold water and gave one to Donna. The camera started, and Jeff Johnson took over. When the preliminaries were finished, including reading Donna the Miranda warning, Marc told Donna to begin.

"First, I want to say, I have never been in any kind of trouble before. And I'm terribly sorry about what happened."

Because Donna was a latecomer to the cult, her knowledge of its origins and early activities was quite limited. A significant amount of what she told them was hearsay; things she had been told, especially by her boyfriend, Gary Weaver and things she overheard from others.

Her full statement, with very few interruptions, took less than forty minutes. Her personal knowledge about the bank jobs and money laundering she did was very accurately described. She even remembered the names of every casino she had helped launder money through.

The videographer packed up his equipment and left to make copies of the disk. When he did, everyone looked at each other, waiting for someone to say something.

"You say they're meeting this evening at Sokol's home tonight to divide up the money from Ames, Iowa for laundering in casinos?" Johnson asked.

"Yes, nine o'clock," Donna said.

"She should go to this meeting," Johnson said. "If she's not there it will raise suspicions."

"No," Marc emphatically said. "They've already made one sacrifice, committed one murder. I'm not letting her go back to them. If they get a whiff, they'll kill her. You know who they are. Get your warrants, make your arrests."

"She said she'd cooperate," Johnson angrily said. "The deal's off!"

"What?" a panicky Donna yelled.

"Nice try," Carvelli said, staring down his FBI friend.

"No, no," Delia Ferguson said. "They're right. We have enough for search and arrest warrants. We'll have them by nine and execute this evening. The deal is still on. Cooperation does not require this young woman to risk her life."

Ferguson, finally realizing she should be running this thing, looked at Donna and said, "Text him back and tell him you can't make it. Tell him you got your period, you feel like hell and you're staying at your mother's.

"In the meantime," Ferguson continued rising from her chair, "I'll get going on the warrant for this professor's place. Get his address for me," she said, looking at Johnson.

While they were riding down in the elevator, Marc asked Maddy, "Where are you taking her?"

Just in case the elevator was bugged—this is the federal government—Maddy covertly answered, "Our friends on the lake."

Understanding immediately she was referring to Vivian Donahue, Marc replied, "Good choice."

It would be after 9:30 before all of the arrest warrants and search warrants were ready. They even did one for Donna just to provide a little cover for her with her radical little cult members.

Despite Jeff Johnson's and Tess Richard's years of experience, they made a mistake. The two of them discussed it but decided not to do it. They did not want to scare them off if they were discovered. They

260

agreed not to put a surveillance team on Ben Sokol's house ahead of time.

FORTY-EIGHT

Gary Weaver was fifteen minutes late and the last to arrive. He descended Ben's basement stairs and found the others already seated at the table. The cash from the Ames, Iowa robbery neatly stacked in equal piles in the middle of the table.

"Thanks for showing up," an annoyed Luke sarcastically bit into him.

"Hey, fuck you, Luke. I'm getting tired of your 'everything revolves around me' attitude," Gary quickly snapped back. "I got hung up a little bit."

"Whoa, stop. Easy guys," Reese interjected. "Chill out. We're all in this together, remember?"

"Yeah, okay," Gary said. He took his seat while Luke followed him with his eyes, clearly not pleased with the insubordination.

"Where's Donna?" Luke asked.

"She's not feeling well. It's that time of the month. She went to her mom's house for a day or two."

"Good, well, let's get started," Ben said, trying to lighten the mood.

"Something's wrong," Luke said. "I can feel it. Something's not right. First, you're late and now Donna is missing. When was the last time you saw her?" he asked Gary.

"Down in Iowa. What are you getting at? Are you accusing us of...what exactly?" Gary replied.

"You're being paranoid, Luke," Sherry said.

"Maybe, but a little paranoia is a good thing. Sorry," he said, looking at Gary. "It's just, I don't know, a feeling. Something's wrong tonight."

Luke looked at Ben and said, "We need to call this off tonight. Get out of here. Throw the cash in a bag. Get the guns, anything that might be incriminating."

"You think, what?" Ben asked.

"I don't like it that all of a sudden the newest member doesn't show up. Let's just get out of here for tonight and meet again in a couple of days," Luke said.

The room went silent for a moment, then Gary said, "Donna wouldn't..."

"I don't know. I don't think she would but let's not take any chances," Luke replied.

"Okay, let's do it," Reese said. "Go through the house. Anything the cops might find has to go."

There was not much. The money, the paper wrappings and bags from the Ames job, guns and even the easel went into the back of Luke's SUV. Luke knew of a Dumpster he could toss the bank money wrappers and bags into. In fifteen minutes, the house had been thoroughly cleaned.

Before he left, Luke convinced everyone else to stay. If the cops did show up, all they would find was a group of students at a professor's house. They even decided to claim they were having a group discussion on the virtues of socialism versus the failings of capitalism—a great story about a police raid for the newspapers.

While the little band of social justice cultists was loading Luke's SUV, the FBI was getting ready to leave. It is not as easy as TV makes it out to be to obtain search and arrest warrants. Especially from a federal judge who takes his or her job seriously. As almost all of them do.

First, Delia Ferguson had to find her boss who was at a Democrat fundraiser. While she was doing that, her assistant was typing up affidavits and the warrants to present to a judge.

While that was taking place, Jeff Johnson was putting together the entry team. The warrants called for Johnson to knock on the door, give warning and identify himself before entering. This would be a formality. The door would be crashed.

It was almost ten o'clock by the time everyone, including Tony Carvelli, arrived at Ben Sokol's house. According to Donna, the others would be meeting in Ben's basement. Because of this, little attention was paid to a stealth approach to the house. Carvelli waited in the street leaning on his car watching from a couple of houses down. The D-Day Normandy landings could not have been much more obvious than what he was witnessing.

There were more than twenty SWAT cops in full gear surrounding the house. Johnson led three of them up to the front door with Tess Richards trailing behind with six more. Johnson rapped once on the door while one of the men swung a steel battering ram at the door handle. The door exploded inward and within seconds there were a dozen fully armed cops swarming through the house.

Once inside, Johnson and his support crew found a mild-looking, fifty-something professor seated in the living room along with five college students. All were face down on the floor, secured with zip tie plastic handcuffs, within thirty seconds. And all completely terrified. While they laid there four SWAT team members with automatic rifles stood over them. The six suspects would stay this way while the house was completely searched.

While waiting outside for the entry team to finish, Carvelli walked up and down the street to keep warm. Before the search was completed, Tess Richards came out and joined him.

"Nothing," Tess said when she got to where Carvelli was waiting.

"What? What do you mean, nothing?" Carvelli incredulously asked.

"I mean, nothing. They were sitting in the living room having some kind of discussion circle-jerk when we blew the door in. We covered every inch of the place including the attic. Nothing, nada, zilch. No money, no guns, no evidence of anything."

"They knew," Carvelli said.

"Or, they guessed when Donna didn't show up," Tess said. "I knew we should've sent her in there and act like nothing was going on."

"She wouldn't have been able to pull it off," Carvelli said.

"Probably not," Tess agreed. "That's another thing. No Luke, either. We asked where he was, and they sounded like a flock of owls. Who? Who? Who? He's the one that guessed it and then set us up."

"Do owls travel in flocks?" Carvelli asked.

"You know, I'm not sure," Tess said. "Never thought of it before."

"Here we go," Carvelli said, looking down the street in the direction they had come from.

"Oh, shit," Tess replied. "Just what we need. The media shows up."

"I know him," Carvelli said watching the reporter come toward them, a cameraman in tow.

"You want to talk to him?" Tess asked.

"Sure," Carvelli replied. "But he's a bit of a bulldog. He'll see all of these FBI vests and he'll want to talk to Jeff. Go in and warn him while I head him off."

"Hey, Carvelli," Philo Anson said when he saw Tony approaching. "What's going on?"

"Nothing for a hotshot who wants to win a Pulitzer," Carvelli replied.

The two of them were standing in the middle of the street one house down from Sokol's. Carvelli was trying to block the cameraman's view, to no avail.

"Bullshit," Philo replied. "There are more cops here than a donut shop. And the FBI, too. What gives?"

"Why are you here?" Carvelli asked instead of answering.

"I got an anonymous tip. Someone called in, asked for me. Said the FBI was pulling a raid and it might have to do with the Lake Country Bank robbery gang. The enviro gang."

"I don't know anything about..." Carvelli started to say while thinking, *Luke*.

"Hey, why are you here? I heard you were working for Lake Country. This must be about that," Philo asked Carvelli.

"You use my name and I'll have Maddy Rivers hunt you down and beat the shit out of you," Carvelli seriously told the reporter.

"Oooo, that would be worth it. How do you spell your last name?" Philo asked, holding his notebook and pen.

"Keep my name out of it, and I'll see if I can get the Feeb who's running this thing to talk to you. And no film of me, either."

"Deal," Philo said.

For a half-hour, after he drove off from Ben Sokol's house, Luke drove aimlessly around the streets of South Minneapolis. Satisfied that he was not being followed, he found the Dumpster he wanted and got rid of the evidence that he could. Then he decided to risk the temptation to drive back to Ben's.

Luke stopped at the intersection a half a block from Ben's house. He expected to see the cops and FBI but was still shocked with what he saw. In the light from the streetlamps, he had a clear view of the activity in front of Ben's house. There were at least six squads of various types with lights flashing and a number of armed officers coming and going. Luke watched for maybe two or three seconds before driving off. Despite the coolness of the winter night, a steady stream of sweat ran down both sides of his face.

He had driven a half-mile on the same residential street before he was breathing calmly again. Then the realization of what was going to happen began to set in. Up until this very moment, it had all seemed like a game. A game, due to their superior intelligence, they were winning they convinced themselves. No longer.

With armed police officers and probably FBI agents staring them down, one of his fellow cult members would crack and sing like a canary. When that happened, all of them would spend the rest of their lives in prison. It was with that realization that Luke made his decision. But first, he made the call to the reporter for the Star Tribune.

When Luke reached his apartment, he drove around the block three times to check the cars in the street. Seeing nothing unusual—it was a low-income neighborhood, and his was the newest car to be found— Luke decided to chance it.

He parked in the alley behind his building. Having made a mental list of what to take, Luke went in and was back out and driving off in under ten minutes. He had filled a gym bag with clothes and personal

265

items, grabbed the money stashed in the closet and combined it with the Ames money. Luke was saying goodbye and was going to run. At this point, he was not even sure where.

I-35W was barely a mile away. He drove five blocks south to 42nd Street, turned left and was almost there when his carelessness caught up with him. While his mind was occupied with deciding where to go, he blew through a red light at 2nd Avenue and 42nd.

A Ford pickup, doing ten miles over the limit, T-boned him at the driver's side passenger door. Both vehicles began to spin around, and Luke's hit the curb sideways and flipped on the passenger side.

The seatbelt and airbag saved his life, but he would wake up two days later in Hennepin County Medical Center. An IV tube was stuck in his left arm, his right wrist handcuffed to the bed's railing and a uniformed MPD cop sitting in the hall.

FORTY-NINE

"Good morning, Jeff, Tess," Ethan Pace said. "Want some coffee?"

Both FBI agents answered in the affirmative and greeted Delia Ferguson. Delia was seated at a table in the corner of Pace's office, and Johnson and Richards joined her.

Ethan Pace was a twenty-year veteran prosecutor with the U.S. Attorney's office. He was Delia's boss, and this would be his case to prosecute. It was 7:00 A.M. the morning after the raid on Sokol's house.

"Have you seen the morning Strib?" Pace asked the agents after pouring coffee for them.

A copy of that morning's Star Tribune was lying face down on the table. Pace handed the A section to Johnson. The left-hand column headline read:

FBI/Police Raid College Study Group.

The byline was Philo Anson who made the authorities look, at best silly, at worst like Gestapo Storm Troopers. He even used the word socialism to describe the study group.

"Well, that was fair and balanced," Johnson said when he finished reading the article.

"Where are these people and what are we holding them on?" Pace asked.

"Two are in isolation at Hennepin County, and the other four are at the ICE detention facility," Johnson answered.

"Actually, they are all on their way here. We'll put them in separate rooms for interviews," Tess said.

"The main guy, Luke Hanson, wasn't there. We believe they either found out we were coming...." Johnson started to say.

"Unlikely," Tess said.

"...or they got nervous and emptied the place before we got there. We got a BOLO out on Hanson and his vehicle. He'll turn up," Johnson said.

"We're holding them on suspicion of bank robbery and interstate flight for the Ames job," Delia said.

"Will it hold up?" Pace asked.

"Uncorroborated accomplice testimony is all we have so far," Johnson replied.

"So, no, it won't hold up. How good is your witness?" Pace said.

"She's good, honest, but young," Delia answered.

"So, any good defense lawyer will turn her into a puddle on the witness stand," Pace said. "Speaking of which, have they called lawyers?"

"We were told no, they haven't. The kids called their parents..." Johnson replied.

"Who will get lawyers this morning," Pace said. "I won't even arraign them on what we have, Jeff."

"I figured as much."

"What are we gonna do today?" Pace asked. "You want to make a run at them before their lawyers get here?"

"That's the idea. We know these are the right people. The kids are seeing the inside of a jail cell for the first time. We'll see how committed they are to their 'save the world from the evil capitalists crusade' now that they know what jail looks like."

Pace's desk phone rang, and he went to answer it.

"Which ones?" the others heard him ask. He wrote down two names on a notepad then said, "We'll be right there.

"Gary Weaver and Cindy Bonn are here. Who first?"

"Weaver," Johnson said. "That's the boyfriend of our snitch."

"Who I want to meet," Pace said. "Where is she?"

"Her lawyer has her under private protection. Marc Kadella. You know him?"

"We've met," Pace said. "Okay, let's go."

The four feds filed into the interrogation room where Gary Weaver was being guarded. Weaver was shackled to a table with several chairs around it. Johnson and Pace sat down directly across from him. The first thing both noticed was how calm the young man looked.

"Lawyer," was the only word Weaver said.

"Did you contact one?" Pace asked.

"My parents are getting one. My dad has plenty of money. He'll get a good one."

"Nice to have a successful, capitalist dad when you need one," Johnson said.

Weaver looked as if he was about to say something then stopped, pulled back and again said, "Lawyer. I'm not talking to you or answering any questions until he gets here."

"We're not going to question you. You have the right to remain silent. The agents read you your rights, did they not?" Pace asked.

"Yeah," Weaver reluctantly admitted.

"Good. That doesn't mean we can't talk to you," Johnson said, taking over the conversation.

"There are seven of you, we picked up your girlfriend, too. Donna. Eight when we find Luke Hanson. It looks like he took off on you. I'll bet he has most of the money with him."

When Hanson did not say anything, Johnson continued.

"Anyway, every one of you is in very deep shit. We're going to convict you and when we do, you will spend most of your life in prison."

Johnson paused, leaned forward, forearms on the table, looked directly into Weaver's eyes and said, "When I say prison, I mean a real prison. A stay-out-of-the-shower federal prison. The boys are gonna love you."

"And after we're done, with you," Tess Richards said, "the state of Minnesota is going to want you for first-degree murder in the death of Jordan Simmons."

"I had..." Weaver blurted out then caught himself before he said more.

"You had what? Nothing to do with that? So what? You're a college boy. You know that won't matter. First-degree murder in Minnesota gets you another thirty years. You're gonna be back in diapers before you get out," Johnson shot back at him.

"Lawyer," Weaver said although this time with noticeably less confidence.

"Unless we decide to make her death part of an ongoing federal criminal act in which case, we can ask for the death penalty," Pace said.

The room went totally silent for a minute while everyone stared at Weaver as he absorbed that bit of news.

"Unless," Johnson said, "and we're only giving out one of these, you're the one who jumps on the immunity deal we're gonna offer. But only one of you gets it. And you know what that's for. You switch teams and work with us. Testify against your pals."

"We're going to offer this to each one of you. How long before one of you grabs it?" Pace interjected.

There was a knock on the door, and a guard opened it. The four feds stood up to leave Weaver alone. As they filed out, Pace turned and said, "Talk to your lawyer."

In the hall, the guard let them know all six of the cult were in separate rooms. Johnson looked at his watch and realized they had to hurry before the lawyers started showing up.

"Let's split up. Ethan, you and Tess go see the next one and Delia and I will take one. Give them each the same 'Come to Jesus' talk. These are not tough, street kids. They need to have reality shoved in their face."

"After their lawyers get here, we'll have to kick them loose. The lawyers will figure out that we don't have much," Pace said. "We'll have to show them the search and arrest warrants. They will know about your snitch and who she is."

"Yeah, I know. Scaring the hell out of them is what we have," Johnson said. "We'll do what we can. When we get our hands on Luke Hanson, I'm betting we'll have more evidence."

By 9:00 A.M., the fed team had spoken to all six defendants. Each had a lawyer on hand by then, along with several sets of very distraught parents.

Quick discussions were held with the lawyers during which Pace assured them their clients had been read their rights and made no statements. By ten o'clock they were all released to go home. The lawyers made it absolutely clear the parents were not allowed to ask them anything. If the parents were told something incriminating, they could be forced to testify about it.

"Okay, thanks, Jeff," Carvelli said into his phone then ended the call.

Carvelli was on a couch in the library of Vivian Donahue's mansion on Lake Minnetonka.

Vivian Donahue was the matriarch of one of the wealthiest and most prominent politically connected families in Minnesota. She had come to know Marc, Maddy and Tony following the murder of a nephew several years ago. Maddy had become the daughter she never had and Tony—Anthony she called him—was her friend with benefits.

"Jeff Johnson?" Marc asked. Marc was there along with Maddy, Vivian and Donna Gilchrist.

"Yeah," Carvelli acknowledged. "They had to kick them loose. But, before they did, they had a little chat with each of them. They told each of them that there is one get-of-jail-free card on the table. First come, first served."

"What does that mean? What happened?" Donna anxiously asked.

"They had to let them go," Carvelli said.

"Why? Don't they believe me?"

"Yes, they do. But you're an accomplice, and they need more evidence than just your statement," Marc told her.

"Don't worry, they'll find it," Maddy assured her.

"Did they execute the search warrants on their homes?" Marc asked Carvelli.

"Yeah. Nothing. These kids, for all their inexperience, are pretty smart and very careful.

"Luke Hanson's missing," Carvelli said to Donna, "Any ideas where he might be?"

"No," Donna said, shaking her head. "I don't even know where he lives. I knew Luke before this. He always seemed like a nice guy. Now, he's gotten, I don't know, cold, even a little hard. A little scary."

"You think one of them will flip?" Vivian asked.

Carvelli looked at her and said, "You've been hanging around too many cops and criminal lawyers. Flip?"

"Anthony," she replied and looked at him like an annoyed mother.

"Yes, dear," Carvelli said to Vivian. "These kids are smart but they're not street tough. One night in jail should be enough to scare them."

"They're still committed to their cause," Donna said. "They might even see themselves as martyrs."

"God, how tragic," Marc said. "To throw your life away for this nonsense."

"It's not nonsense, Mr. Kadella. We believe it's our future. Our responsibility to save the planet for future generations," Donna said.

"Donna, the planet will be just fine without a bunch of naïve kids going to prison," Marc said. "That would be tragic."

"Jordan Simmons was murdered," Maddy reminded him.

"Yeah, you're right," Marc agreed. "Now what?" Marc asked Carvelli.

"Now, we wait," Carvelli answered. He looked at Donna and said, "They'll find more evidence. Now that we know who, for sure, the FBI will dig and come up with it. They're good at that."

"And what do I do in the meantime?" Donna asked.

"You can stay here as long as you need to," Vivian said.

"And we can protect you here," Carvelli added.

"Can I at least call my mom?"

"Yes," Marc said. "Just don't discuss what you're up to or where you are."

FIFTY

Webster Crosby took off his Wayfarers and placed them on the table. He was in Cancun on what should have been a brief, five-day vacation. A quick break from winter. Webster checked his watch, mostly from anxiety, and saw the time was 11:15 A.M. His watch also gave him the temperature in both Fahrenheit and Celsius. Already it was 85 and 29 and not a cloud in the sky.

He re-lit his Cuban, puffing hard to get it going again. Webster appeared a lot more relaxed than what he was. He glanced at his phone next to his sunglasses, half-expecting a hand to jump through the screen and slap him.

Twenty minutes ago, out of habit if for no other reason, he had used the phone to check the news in Minnesota. It was becoming an almost paranoid obsession to do so. To keep an eye on Ben Sokol's little band. This time, what he saw soured his stomach. The entire bunch, it appeared, had been rounded up the previous evening by the FBI. Crosby spent five minutes debating whether or not to call Tom Breyer. He finally realized Breyer would find out and call screaming sooner or later. Better to call, tell him what he found online and get it over with.

Crosby had left a message with Breyer's latest plaything/assistant. He had been waiting for the eruption ever since. Of course, it was Crosby's fault because he had convinced Breyer not to eliminate Sokol, and his cult several months ago. That course of action was still a bridge too far as far as Crosby was concerned. Crosby was starting to regret it.

"Hello, Tom," Crosby said into his phone. It had been ringing for less than three seconds when he answered it.

"They've been released," Breyer said without even a hello. "Apparently, there are no charges against them. Something happened, though. The FBI got wind of them somehow."

When Crosby answered his phone, he was holding his breath. Instead of a tirade, Breyer was quite calm about it.

"From what I found out," Breyer continued, "they raided your professor pal's house and found nothing."

Crosby cringed at Breyer's use of the term "professor pal," but his overall relief was almost palpable, so he let it go. Crosby knew there was a "but" coming and he knew what it was.

"But, this needs to be dealt with. Do you understand?"

"Yes, sir," Crosby replied.

"We're, at most, a few weeks away from scoring the largest green energy, taxpayer-subsidized deal in history. The government is practically giving us five thousand square miles of ocean zoned area for a huge wind farm. And, they're paying us ten billion to make it happen. We could sell it off for double that and walk away. I cannot let these idiots in Minnesota be tied to us. Do you understand?"

"Yes, sir," Crosby said.

By this point, Crosby was not even listening. His end of the wind farm deal was 10%. If Breyer was right, he was about to become a billionaire. With that kind of money, he could walk away from this socialist, save-the-planet crusade and never look back.

"And the wind farm is just the beginning. Green energy will get us Bezos money. Are you with me?"

"Yes, sir. Of course," Crosby said, swallowing hard at the comparison to the richest man alive.

"And think of the good we'll do for the environment," Crosby managed to mutter.

Breyer laughed, then said, "Not likely. All of this green energy staff comes with serious costs of its own. But who cares? The media doesn't report any of it. And that won't be our problem."

"What are we gonna do about the socialist?" Crosby asked referring to Jacob Trane. "Have you reached a decision?"

"As long as he remains useful, he's right where I want him. And you, the smooth-talking TV star. You've done great work. Keep it up. The taxpayer gold vault is about to open up. I'll be in touch."

Crosby had been lying on a chaise lounge, poolside chair under an umbrella, With the news of his green energy riches about to come true, he sat up, leaned forward and took several long breaths of air. His head was literally spinning with the thought.

When he finally calmed down, he looked out onto the Caribbean and quietly said, "Sorry, Ben. But then, I never liked you anyway and besides, you were warned."

"Tell me about this professor, this Ben Sokol guy," Marc told Donna.

After Carvelli had spoken with Jeff Johnson and received the news of the little gang's release, they were tossing around ideas of what to do next. Some of the gang were vulnerable to go after, but who should be next was the question.

"Ben? He's a great guy. A really smart teacher and has a lot of influence on students," Donna said.

"What does he teach?" Maddy asked.

"Well he's in the history department," Donna said. "I've had a couple of classes from him and I learned a lot."

"Like what?" Maddy persisted.

"Ah, a lot about progressivism. He's pretty much a socialist. He taught us about the origins of it. How it came about because of the inequalities of capitalism and how terribly destructive and unfair it is."

Marc stole a quick glance at Vivian, a card-carrying member of the super-rich capitalist class. To her credit, she was watching and listening with an impassive yet interested expression.

"I shouldn't say this," Donna continued, "and I don't really agree, but he really hates Jews. I have heard him say that socialism and antisemitism go hand-in-hand. That socialism began in Europe because the Jews controlled the entire economy and wouldn't share it with the workers."

"Do the others agree with him?" Marc asked.

"Gary pretty much does. We've argued about it. He thinks Jews have too much money and power. They all support Palestine," Donna said, clearly embarrassed.

"Gary told me Ben's making money by giving speeches about socialism and the oppression by capitalists on other campuses," Donna added.

"How did he get into that?" Maddy asked.

"Another professor he knows. That's what Gary told me. I'm trying to think, to remember his name," Donna said. "I'm pretty sure it was Webster something."

"Webster Crosby?" Vivian asked.

"Yes! That's it. That's the guy," Donna quickly answered.

"Do you know him?" Marc asked Vivian.

"I know of him," Vivian said. "He's connected with Tom Breyer. The guy from California who made his fortune from coal and wall street. Now he is invested heavily in green energy. I think he's a complete con artist."

"I've seen him on TV," Marc replied. "So, you think this Professor Sokol might be involved with Webster Crosby and Tom Breyer?"

"I don't know," Donna said. "Gary does. Can I ask something?"

"Sure," Marc replied.

"What about me, now? Is my deal still good with the FBI? I told them the truth," she asked, tears glistening in her eyes, nervously rubbing her hands together.

"Everything is still in place," Marc said, trying to reassure her. "And you can still stay here if you're okay being surrounded by capitalism."

Donna smiled, looked down at the floor then up at Vivian and said, "I'm sorry. I didn't mean to insult you. I'll stay as long as I can."

"I'm not offended," Vivian said. "You can stay as long as you like."

"They're going to turn on her," Carvelli said to Marc. "They'll know it was her, they'll get together and turn on her if they have to. Right now, they're sitting pretty smugly thinking they have the Feebs fooled."

"That won't last," Marc said.

"No, it won't," Carvelli agreed. He turned to Maddy and said, "You want to go after Gary, or you want me to do it?"

"Your turn," Maddy said.

"I'll talk to Paul and have him pull up everything he can on Sokol, this Webster Crosby guy and his pal, Tom Breyer," Carvelli said.

"Be careful. Breyer has a lot of money and he has connections with the naïve children running the social media tech companies. He may find out someone's poking around," Marc said. "What about Luke Hanson?"

"He's the key. Not much anyone can do until they hunt him down," Carvelli said. "Unless we can get Gary to flip, too."

Carvelli looked at Donna and asked, "If he wants to see you, do you want to meet with him?"

"Of course," she eagerly agreed.

FIFTY-ONE

Jeff Johnson and Tess Richards hurried past the nurses' station. The room they were headed toward was on the lockup floor of the Hennepin County Medical Center. The one they wanted was obvious. There were three plainclothes MPD detectives and two uniformed MPD officers in the hall in front of the room peering through the window.

Lt. Owen Jefferson was the senior officer. He greeted Johnson and Richards and introduced them to the other two detectives. They were the M & Ms, Jack Menke and Cliff McNamee. It was the M & Ms who had made the connection with the arrested car accident victim and the bank robberies.

"Good catch," Johnson told both Menke and McNamee.

The five of them crowded together in front of the window looking into the room. They stared quietly at the unconscious figure lying shackled to the bed.

"So, that's the infamous Luke Hanson," Johnson said still while still looking into the room. "What are the doctors saying?"

"He'll make it, but they can't say when he'll come to. I guess he got hammered pretty good. T-boned going through a red light," Jefferson said.

Johnson led them away from the window and the uniformed cops to have a little privacy.

"We found a bag of guns, almost three hundred grand in cash and a bag of clean clothes," McNamee told the FBI agents.

"He was running while we were busting his friends," Tess said.

"Looks like it," Jefferson agreed.

"How many guns, what type and have they been tested?" Johnson asked.

"Nine handguns. All nine millimeters of various models. All with the serial numbers burned off. And, they're with ballistics now," Menke answered.

Johnson asked Owen Jefferson, "Do you have the juice with ballistics to put a rush on it? We need to check for a match with the Simmons girl."

"Already done," Jefferson answered.

"Jeff," Tess said, "didn't Maddy and Carvelli say that guy down in Waseca claimed he sold him an even dozen guns, all nines?"

"Yeah, I think you're right. Let me check," Johnson said.

He pulled his phone, found Carvelli's number and dialed it.

"Is this a beautiful blonde calling to come over and jump my bones?" a groggy Carvelli answered without saying hello.

276

"You'll never live that long," Johnson replied. "Get your ass up. I got a question for you."

"What time is it?"

"Almost nine."

"What's the question?"

"That biker down in Waseca, didn't he say he sold a dozen guns to Luke Hanson?" Johnson asked.

"Yeah, an even dozen. Why?"

"I'm looking at Luke Hanson as we speak," Johnson said.

"Where? How?" a now wide awake Carvelli asked.

Johnson took a minute to explain the accident and what the MPD responders found in Hanson's SUV.

"There were only nine guns in the car. We have one. The one found at the Eagan Lake Country bank…"

"The one used to kill Natalie Flanders," Carvelli said.

"Yeah. They're in being put through ballistics now. I'm betting the one used on Jordan Simmons is one of the missing ones," Johnson said.

"Plus one more," Carvelli said. "Where are they?"

Before he could answer, Johnson heard Tess Richards say, "Is he waking up?"

She had moved to the window and was watching Luke. His head was moving, and he appeared to be trying to wake up.

Johnson joined Tess and the others at the window. As Tess yelled for a doctor, Johnson spoke to Carvelli.

"He might be coming to."

"I'm on my way. I'll call Maddy and we'll be down. Don't leave," Carvelli said.

"We won't. Listen, I'll call downstairs to security and have them let you come up. You know where it is?"

"Sure, I'm on the way."

Thirty minutes later, his hair still damp from the shower, Carvelli and Maddy hurried down the hall toward the gaggle of cops. They joined them outside Luke's room where they all watched through the window as a doctor, and two nurses attended to him.

"Have you talked to him?" Carvelli asked no one in particular.

"Not yet, no," Johnson replied.

"He looks awake," Maddy said seeing Luke move his head to look out the window at them.

The doctor straightened up and spoke to his patient. Luke barely nodded his head then said something back to the doctor. The doctor looked at the people watching through the window, spoke to Luke again and, along with the nurses, exited the room.

"Who is in charge here?" the doctor said with just a slight Indian accent.

"We are," Johnson said indicating himself and Owen Jefferson.

"He's too tired to talk to you now," the doctor told them.

"Will it cause him any medical problems to talk to us?" Jefferson asked.

"Well, um, I think not but he…"

"Too bad," Johnson said then stepped past the doctor to the door.

"We'll keep it down to just the two of us," Johnson said to all of the others.

The doctor looked at Jefferson who said, "Suspicion of murder."

"I see. Well, all right. Just two of you."

"I'm not saying a word," Luke said to the two men.

"Shut up, asshole. You're in enough trouble," Johnson said.

"You have the right to remain silent…" Owen Jefferson began as he read Luke his Miranda rights from a card.

"Do you understand these rights as I've given them to you?" he asked Luke then put the card up against the window so the others could witness it.

"Yes. Lawyer," Luke said.

"Be quiet," Johnson said. "Just listen. We got the guns, the money, your clothes, your car. We will find prints and DNA. Your ass is mine. And when we tell your pals that you were running out on them, how long before at least one or two starts singing? You think that bunch will hold out?"

"Lawyer," Luke said, only this time a little less forcefully.

"You want to get your own lawyer, or do you want me to get someone from the public defenders' office?" Owen asked.

"I'll get my own," Luke replied.

"Okay, we'll let you make a call to a lawyer. But we will monitor who you call. You're not calling any of your friends. You have the right to an attorney. You do not have the right to communicate with any of your co-conspirators."

"I was gonna call my Mom. I don't know a lawyer. And I don't know what you're talking about. What's a co-conspirator?"

Jefferson handed him the room's phone and said, "Go ahead, call your mother."

Luke looked at Owen and Johnson then said, "Go ahead and get me a public defender. Now Get out."

As Owen unplugged the room phone, he said, "There will be a cop outside. Medical personnel and the lawyer only. No visitors."

While Jefferson took the phone to the nurses' station, Johnson talked to the others in the hall. He quickly told them what happened.

"We can hold him on suspicion of bank robbery for seventy-two hours. We'll need evidence to charge him, which we have."

"Now we need to round up the rest of them, again," he continued.

"Wait until you hear back from ballistics and see if they turn up fingerprints," Carvelli said.

"Yeah, I suppose. We did print them the last time, but we didn't get DNA," Jefferson said.

"Let's take a run at Donna's boyfriend, Gary Weaver," Maddy said to Carvelli.

"I should be there," Johnson said.

"With you there, anything he says will get suppressed 'cause he has a lawyer. We can go as reps of Donna, working for her lawyer," Carvelli said.

"Is that Kosher?" Tess asked.

"I don't know," Carvelli answered. "It sounds good. The worst that can happen is anything he says we can't testify about."

Johnson looked at Tess who simply shrugged her shoulders and held up her hands, palms out.

Johnson turned to Carvelli and said, "Go ahead. See what you can do."

"If he won't flip, we go after the girl, Cindy Bonn," Maddy said.

"And there he is," Carvelli said. "Right on time."

The two of them were in Carvelli's Camaro parked on the street near the container factory. Gary came out of the employee exit by himself. Carvelli and Maddy watched him as he hurried through the cold parking lot to his car.

"I'll follow you," Maddy said. She got out and went back to her car parked two cars back of Carvelli.

When Gary pulled out of the lot, Carvelli and Maddy fell in line behind him. In the dark and with the traffic, he was easy to follow. Fifteen minutes later he pulled into the lot of a Buffalo Wild Wings in Edina.

"We're with someone," Carvelli said to the hostess.

It was early enough, so Weaver did not have to wait for a table. When the two PIs got inside, he was already seated in a booth by himself.

Carvelli slid onto the same seat as Gary while Maddy sat across from them. Carvelli pushed the smaller, younger man all the way over until he was up against the wall.

279

"What's for supper, Gary?" Carvelli asked. "I don't eat here very often. Are the burgers good?"

So far, Gary had not said a word or taken a breath. He knew this had to be something to do with the robberies.

"Ah, um," he tried to say. He cleared his throat, wiped his forehead and finally croaked, "Who are you, and what do you want?"

"No, wait, forget that," he continued finding a little courage, "I don't know you and get lost."

"You gonna call the cops?" Carvelli asked.

"They have Luke," Maddy said.

Gary went silent again, then finally stuttered, "Luke? I don't know any Luke."

"And we have Donna," Maddy added.

"Don't insult us by saying you don't know her," Carvelli said. "We're not cops. We work for a lawyer. Donna's lawyer."

"Whatever she's telling you is a lie," Gary said.

The waiter showed up with a tall beer which Carvelli took from him.

"Nothing for us just yet," Maddy said to the young man while he stared at her.

While Maddy dealt with the waiter, Carvelli downed half the glass of beer.

"I needed that," Carvelli said as he handed the glass to Gary.

"Here's the deal," Carvelli continued. "You're being given a chance to have a life. They're not going to promise no prison time, but you can help yourself. There's room for one more person to testify against your little band of do-gooders..., shut up!" Carvelli quietly barked when Gary started to speak.

"Just listen. Donna wants it to be you. We can take you to the same lawyer who represents her, and he'll work a deal for you. But you don't have much time."

"Your pal, Luke, was in a car accident. He's in a hospital with police guards. He was running, Gary," Maddy said. "He got caught with guns, money and a suitcase full of clothes. He was running with the take from Ames, Iowa."

When Maddy mentioned Ames, Iowa she watched his eyes carefully. She also paused for a reaction. When there was none, especially no denial, she continued.

"Luke will end up making the best deal he can. The feds have him by the balls. You need to decide what you're going to do right now," she told him.

"You're looking at a minimum of thirty years," Carvelli said. "If the feds roll in Jordan Simmons murder, they can charge everybody with conspiracy and seek the death penalty…"

"I…" Gary started to say then clamped his mouth shut.

"You had nothing to do with her murder," Maddy said. "So what? You're part of the total package."

"I got a good lawyer. A new guy from L.A. I didn't do anything, and I don't know what you're talking about. Donna? Who's Donna?"

"Okay," Carvelli said as he slid out of the booth.

"Thanks a lot," Maddy said, looking at Gary. "I thought you were smarter than this." She handed Carvelli a five-dollar bill and said to Carvelli, "You were right. He is the stupid one."

"I knew it just looking at him," Carvelli said as he took the bill and shoved it in his pocket. "He thinks he's a tough guy. The boys are gonna love you in prison."

"Literally," Maddy said as she slid out of the booth. She removed a business card from her purse and placed it in front of Gary. "I want to win the bet. Call me, but you better make it quick."

They left the restaurant and walked out to their cars. Carvelli's was closer to the door so they reached his first. As he was getting in, Maddy placed a hand on the door to stop him.

"What?" he asked.

Maddy held out her hand and said, "My five bucks. We didn't really bet, you know."

"Oh, oh. I must be getting old. I thought we did," Carvelli said.

"Nice try. Hand it over," Maddy said while he retrieved the bill from his pocket.

FIFTY-TWO

"What's up?" Carvelli said into his phone.

"Are you out of bed?" Jeff Johnson asked.

"It's after ten. Even I'm not always that bad," Carvelli replied.

"I thought you might want to hear the latest," Johnson said.

"Okay," Carvelli replied.

"We had a meeting at the hospital this morning. Me, Tess and Ethan Pace, the AUSA handling this," Johnson said. "Owen Jefferson was there and Steve Gondeck from Hennepin County."

Steve Gondeck was the head of felony prosecutions for the Hennepin County Attorney's office.

"Hanson's lawyer was there. A guy from LA. A heavy-hitter named Jonah Cliff," Johnson said. "Ever hear of him?"

"No, have you?"

"Yeah, I have. He's a heavyweight who handles mostly high-profile white-collar crime almost exclusively in federal courts."

"How's Hanson paying for him?" Carvelli asked.

"What?" Maddy asked Carvelli. They were doing surveillance in Carvelli's car.

"Is that Maddy? Say hello," Johnson said.

"Johnson says hello. I'll tell you in a minute," Carvelli said.

"What are you two doing?"

"We're sitting on one of the girls. Cindy Bonn," Carvelli said.

"Seriously? Can you see a sedan that looks like it might belong to the U.S. Government?" Johnson asked.,

"Yeah, there's one in the apartment's parking lot. I can't see from here if anyone is inside, though."

Carvelli heard Johnson say something to someone but could not make out what it was.

"I just told Tess to call him and tell him to take off. FYI, he checked in a couple hours ago and said he saw her go in, this Cindy Bonn. She's in there. I'll let you guys have her."

"Maddy's gonna take a run at her. Give her a 'come-to-Jesus' talk to see if she'll flip. What happened at the meeting?"

"We met with the doctor at HCMC. Hanson's okay. No serious injuries, no broken bones or internal bleeding. The airbag punched him in the face and gave him a broken nose, a couple of black eyes and a slight concussion. They want to keep him another day, but they think he can get kicked loose tomorrow.

"His lawyer is insisting we either charge him or release him. I recorded his voice this morning, Hanson's. We got a warrant and

282

recorded him before the lawyer showed up. He had a fit when he found out. Ethan says it's valid and this guy can go screw himself.

"You remember the Eagan bank job? One of the customers had her cell phone on and got a clear recording of him speaking..."

"You're just telling me this now?" Carvelli asked.

"You're not official, Tony. We are. We don't have to tell you dick. Anyway, we'll have our techs check it out to see if there's a match. If so, that will get us an arrest for sure."

"What about Donna's statement and what was found in his car? Isn't that enough?"

"Yeah, buts it's a little thin. We can't tie the guns to the robberies and none of the cash we found. We've got forensic accountants on it, but it looks like they did a good job of washing it through the casinos. No matter what, we're gonna charge him but we don't have enough for a conviction. He'll make bail."

"Who's paying for this lawyer?" Carvelli asked again.

"Don't know and they don't have to say. All of them have new high-priced lawyers. We need another snitch. Someone else to flip. You don't think Gary Weaver will?"

"Doesn't look like it. At least not yet. Your guy's leaving," Carvelli told him when he saw the dull, nondescript Chevy sedan drive off.

"The lawyer says he's got both a federal and state court judge coming to the hospital at one o'clock. We have to charge and arraign him or kick him loose. Ethan's putting together enough facts to at least charge him."

"But he'll make bail," Carvelli said.

"Oh, I almost forgot. Seems that professor's prints are on file from some protest thing back in the eighties. His prints are on some of the bills."

"Is that enough for a conspiracy charge?"

"Conspiracy to do what? Handle money? We need another snitch. Someone with more detailed information."

"There she is," Maddy said.

"Speak of the Devil," Carvelli said to Johnson. "She's coming out and heading toward her car. I'm willing to bet Maddy will do better with her than we did with Gary Weaver. Gotta go. We'll talk later."

They followed Cindy to a nearby Target store. Carvelli found a place to park almost directly across from her. They waited until she was in the store before following her. Maddy spotted her in the personal products area. Cindy was looking at hair coloring products when Maddy caught up with her.

"Coloring your hair won't be much of a disguise, Cindy," Maddy said to her.

Maddy expected shock or at least a little surprise from her as a reaction. Instead, Cindy very calmly replaced the product on the shelf, looked to her left to see Carvelli then looked at Maddy.

With an almost relieved inflection in her voice, Cindy said, "I've been wondering when someone would confront me. Who are you?"

"My name is Madeline Rivers," Maddy replied. She waved to Carvelli to join them while she retrieved her PI license. "I'm a private investigator…"

"You're not a cop?"

"No. The police can't talk to you without your lawyer. We're not working for the police so we can," she lied. "This is Tony Carvelli," she said, introducing him. "He's also a private investigator."

"Hi, Cindy," Carvelli said with his best innocent, harmless smile.

"Hi," she replied. "So…?" she continued, looking at Maddy.

"We work for a lawyer, Marc Kadella. Donna Gilchrist's lawyer," Maddy told her.

"Really? How is she? Is she all right? Can I…."

"Let's grab a cup of coffee and talk," Maddy said.

They found a booth in the Starbucks within the Target they were in. While Carvelli stood in line to order for them, Maddy and Cindy went to the booth.

"Are you helping Donna? Can you help me? I'm so scared I can barely function," Cindy blurted out too fast.

Maddy reached across the table, took her hand and said, "Whoa, slow down. Take a breath. Donna's fine. I think you'll see her soon. Is she a friend?"

"Yes, I mean, well, we became friends. I knew her before all this. Then when Gary brought her in, we became friends. Neil. Neil's another one who would like to, what do you call it, snitch? At least I think he might."

"One thing at a time," Carvelli said as he sat down next to Cindy. "You need to think about yourself, first."

"You've thought about this and want to cooperate?" Maddy asked.

Cindy emphatically nodded her head and replied, "Yes, ever since they killed Jordan. She was my friend and a sweet person. She just wanted to help save the environment and help people."

"Who killed her?" Carvelli asked.

She started to speak then said, "I'm not gonna say until I'm sure you are who you say you are, and I know you guys can help me."

Maddy looked at Carvelli and said, "Smart girl. Fair enough. Let me call Marc and see if he can see us."

While Maddy spoke to Marc, their order came up. Carvelli went to get it, and when he came back, the women were getting ready to leave.

"Let's go," Maddy said as she took her latte. "I'll ride with Cindy. She'll follow you."

After introductions were made, Marc led the three of them into the office conference room. Before they were seated, Connie Mickelson joined them. Connie's presence almost always helped with nervous, first-time clients in serious trouble. Marc had asked her to join them.

"This is my mom," Marc told Cindy. "Actually, her name is Connie, she's also a lawyer and I asked her to sit in with us. Are you okay with that?"

While Marc said this, Carvelli had moved to hold a chair for Connie. Connie sat down and said, "It won't work, Carvelli. I'm too much woman for you."

"Another broken-hearted dashed dream," Carvelli said as he sat down.

"How come you never hold a chair for me?" Maddy asked Marc.

"Now you want to discuss this?" Marc asked.

"We'll talk about it later," she replied.

"See what you started?" Marc asked Carvelli. "Thanks."

"Are you guys always like this?" Cindy asked. She was smiling when she did.

"It's our way of putting people at ease," Marc said. "Before we go any further," Marc continued getting down to business, "you need to know that whatever is said in this room will stay in this room. Even if you decide you don't want my help…" Marc said, holding up a hand as Cindy started to speak. "Just wait. Even if you don't want our help, we are all covered by attorney/client privilege. Do you know what that is?"

"Yeah, I think so. You can't talk about anything I tell you without my permission. The other lawyer, Mr. Garrett told me."

"What's his first name?"

"Paul, Paul Garrett," Cindy said.

Marc picked up the conference room phone and punched two numbers.

"Jeff, I need you to drop what you're doing for a few minutes. I need you to find a lawyer, Paul Garrett. See if he's local," Marc told Jeff Modell.

"There may be more than one," Jeff replied.

"Likely. It's not an uncommon name. See what you can find and come in with it."

"I don't even know who he is or where he came from. All of a sudden, he shows up and tells me he's my lawyer. He came with the others when we had a meeting at Ben's after we were arrested. They all knew each other, all the lawyers. They all talked to each other as if they were all together. Each one was there for one of us. There was one extra one who kept asking about Luke. Wanted to know where Luke was. None of us knew. I heard he's in Hennepin County Medical Center. He had an accident with his car."

"He's in HCMC and he was in an accident," Carvelli told her. "The cops and FBI have him. They have the guns and the money too.

"I heard from Johnson. I'll tell you later," Carvelli told Marc.

"He was running," Carvelli told Cindy. "He had his clothes in his SUV, three hundred grand in cash, the guns and was heading out of town while you were downtown with the others."

"I'm not surprised," Cindy said. "We were all told to shut up, not talk to anyone. Stick together, and the lawyers would get us off. I don't believe it. They wanted to blame everything on Donna. Including killing Jordan. I don't trust them. I can tell I already feel more comfortable with you."

There was a knock on the door, and Jeff Modell came in.

"Oddly enough," he said, handing Marc several sheets of paper, "I only found one. He's with Jonah Cliff and Associates in L.A. Mostly white-collar crime."

"I've heard of Jonah Cliff," Connie said. "Very expensive. One of those assholes that makes sure every hair is in place for the cameras before he does anything."

Marc finished scanning through the pages, looked at Jeff and thanked him. As Jeff was closing the door to leave, Marc slid the papers across the table to Carvelli.

"Have your pal dig into this and find out everything he can. I want to know who's paying for this," Marc said.

"The feds will be interested, too," Carvelli said. "I'll get it to him today."

"Mr. Kadella…"

"Marc," Marc said to Cindy.

"Marc, okay. I've been thinking about this. Am I going to prison?" she said as several tears trickled out of her eyes.

"I can't promise you you're not. A lot will depend on what you did. You not being there when Jordan was killed is a plus. We'll see about the rest.

"Let me ask you, when did your involvement begin?"

"At the very beginning," she replied, wiping her eyes with her hand.

"So, you know a lot. That's good."

"I know it all," she said. "And, I have it all written down. Everything. Every date and time of everything we did. Including dollar amounts from every bank."

"You have it all recorded?" Marc asked. "All of it?"

"They think I'm just a ditzy chick with nice boobs. I'm not. I started right away, keeping track of things…"

"Excuse me," Maddy said. "Nice boobs? What does that have to do with anything?"

"I, ah, used them sometimes to distract the bank guards. You know, unbuttoned my shirt a bit," she reluctantly said.

It took a full minute for the laughter to die down. Finally, Maddy said to a red-faced Cindy, "I'm sorry. We didn't mean to embarrass you."

"It's okay," Cindy said. "It is kind of funny."

"Actually, it sounds like a stunt Marc would pull during a trial," Connie said.

"Hey, that's not a bad…"

"No!" Maddy said.

"Okay. It was just a thought. So," Marc finally said to Cindy, "you have it all written down?"

"Yes, including the money laundering. At least as much as I know. I don't know all of it, but I know a lot. I want, what do they call it, immunity?"

"If what you say is true, they'll give it to you. But, the one thing they're going to want, two things really, is you give them everything and no lying. I'll warn you, now. If they catch you in a lie, all bets are off."

"Marc, I'm so scared I just want this over. Even if I have to do some jail time. It started off as almost a game. Robinhood kind of deal. Steal from the rich and give to the poor. We were gonna do such good things. Then it all went to hell. They, me too, started doing it for the money. We got greedy."

"The important thing is, you weren't there when Jordan was killed," Marc said. "Tell me now if that isn't true."

"No. I was not there. I wasn't even in the bank when she was shot by the guard. I swear. I drove Luke's van after, but I wasn't there when Jordan got shot. Neil was there. He said Sherry shot her later that night. She shot her in the head through a pillow. I believe it, too. That crazy bitch could do it. Sorry."

"Call Vivian," Marc said to Maddy. "See if she'll put up another guest for us. Then we'll go out there."

After Maddy called Vivian, it was decided, at Vivian's insistence, to go there for dinner. When the conference room emptied, Connie told Marc to stay for a discussion.

"You may have a conflict going here," Connie told him.

"I've thought of that," he replied. "I think I'll be all right as long as there is full disclosure. I'll write up something, go over it with both of them and have them sign it. I think that will be okay and if it becomes a problem, I'll get out."

"What about this firm, Jonah Cliff and his ass-kissers?" Connie asked.

"I don't know. We'll find out who's paying. That's who they're really representing," Marc replied.

"And it's not these misguided, nitwit kids," Connie added.

FIFTY-THREE

Marc, alone, sat patiently in the reception area of the U.S. Attorney's office in downtown Minneapolis. His right leg casually crossed over his left, a leather folio in his lap.

The previous evening had been spent in private conversation with Cindy Bonn. They were in a rarely used study of the Corwin Mansion on Lake Minnetonka. Just Marc and Cindy. Unusually for this time of year, the Corwin family matriarch, Vivian was in residence. She was also delighted to have these particular guests arrive.

Marc and Maddy had delivered Cindy to the Corwin home while Tony Carvelli made a stop at his computer hacker's house. After dinner, Marc and Cindy had adjourned to the small study. For the next two hours, Marc interviewed her without recording Cindy's story. When he finished, he called Ethan Pace at home requesting an early morning meeting. With Marc's assurance that it was well worthwhile, Pace agreed.

At 8:00 A.M., Marc took a seat in the reception area where he now patiently, waited for Pace. The wait was less than two minutes.

"Morning, Marc," Pace said when he came out to get him. The two men shook hands, and Pace escorted him back.

When they entered Pace's office, as Marc expected, waiting for them were Jeff Johnson, Tess Richards and the other AUSA assigned to the case, Delia Ferguson. They were all seated at a table in the corner with two more empty chairs.

"Look at this," Marc said to Pace as he checked out the office. "Two large windows for your office. You're moving up in the world, Ethan. The last time I was here, you were in a broom closet-size office."

"That's mine now," Delia said.

"You need to do more federal stuff. Get a better class of clients," Pace said.

"Right," Marc said with a touch of sarcasm, "Drugs and interstate sex traffic."

"Very good," Pace laughed. "Well, what brings you here this bright and early on this lovely winter day?"

"You got to Cindy Bonn," Johnson said, a statement not a question.

"No comment," Marc said. "Not yet at least. Yes, I, or should I say Tony and Maddy…"

"Is it true," Pace interrupted him, "you and the lovely Ms. Rivers are…?"

"Very friendly," Marc replied.

"He's head over heels," Tess said with a big grin. "You should see them together. He's like a lovestruck puppy."

"Moving on," Marc said a little more loudly than necessary.

"Hey, I don't blame you," Pace said.

Marc looked at Pace and repeated, a bit more emphatically, "Moving on. Yes, we flipped another one. Or I should say, I have another client. This one has the goods. Or, at least most of it. This person," he said looking at Johnson and deliberately avoiding the use of the pronoun, she, "has been involved from the beginning. And this person, kept a ledger. Of everything. Dates, times, places, the involvement of everyone. Meetings, money laundering, amounts…"

"Was she involved in the murder of Jordan Simmons?" Johnson asked.

Marc looked at Johnson and replied. "All right, Mr. Persistent G-Man, no, Cindy Bonn was not there. She heard, was told, it was Sherry Toomey."

"Who was there?" Pace asked.

"You guys taking the murder charge?" Marc asked.

"Yes, we are. We discussed it with Hennepin County, your pal Steve Gondeck, and he agreed we have the better case. We'll roll the murder into everything else and threaten them all with the death penalty," Pace said.

"You know, Ethan, there are people who consider that to be torture. To threaten someone's life to get a confession," Marc said.

"That's nice," Pace said. "I tell you what, I promise not to beat them…"

"Although if their parents had when these spoiled brats were growing up, they wouldn't be in this mess now," Tess said.

"Who was there when Jordan Simmons was murdered?" Pace asked again.

"Neil Cole was for sure," Marc said. "He's the one who told Cindy what happened. Or, so she claims. The others were Luke Hanson, Ben Sokol and Sherry Toomey. They did it in Sokol's basement."

"We didn't find any evidence," Johnson said. "Nothing. A lot of DNA but no evidence of a homicide."

"Then we're down to hearsay. No gun, no forensics, no eyewitness," Pace said.

"She thinks Cole will flip for a decent deal," Marc said.

"Why don't we just deal all of them?" Pace sarcastically asked.

"Do you really want to put all of these kids in prison for the rest of their lives?" Marc asked. "This isn't the Manson Family. These are a bunch of idealistic kids likely led astray by this loser professor."

"Do we give Cindy Bonn immunity?" Pace asked the others.

"We don't need to," Johnson said. "We should have enough now for indictments. Did you get the voice comparison of Luke Hanson from the recording in the bank?"

"Yeah, late yesterday. Check your email. The best they could do was a seventy-eight percent match," Pace said.

"That's not good enough. A decent lawyer will punch enough holes in that to make it useless," Marc said.

"Exactly. So, that leaves us with the money and guns found in Hanson's car. And unless we can trace the money back to a bank, we don't have any way to tie it to a robbery," Pace told Johnson.

"What about the testimony of the two girls?" Johnson asked.

"Right now, you only have one," Marc reminded him.

"We can grab Cindy Bonn and sweat her," Johnson said.

"She's represented by two very good lawyers. One of whom is sitting in this room," Tess said.

Pace looked at Marc and said, "Same deal as Donna Gilchrist. She gets a walk with full cooperation and total honesty if she has this ledger and she was not at all involved in the murder of Jordan Simmons."

"Agreed. Write it up," Marc said.

"I already did," Pace replied. "I used the same document as Donna's and just changed the name."

"We were pretty sure it was Cindy," Tess said to Marc.

"But," Pace said, "we want her to stay inside the gang. We want the evidence about the murder of Jordan Simmons."

"Hold it," Marc said, leaning forward and looking at the others one at a time. "Nothing was said about this."

"We're saying it now, Marc. Or, she can take her chances. Nothing that was said in this room will be used against her. We will make the case, eventually. You know that. And she will do time. Probably a lot," Pace said.

"Do they know where she is? Do they know she has contacted you?" Tess asked.

"I don't know," Marc said. "I know I don't like this. She could get killed. They already have one murder on their hands."

"She took the risk when she signed up," Johnson said.

"Shove your cynicism up your ass, Agent Johnson," Marc snarled. "This is a young girl's life we're talking about!"

Before Johnson, whose face was quite red by now, could reply, Pace stepped in.

"We'll monitor her. We'll put round the clock surveillance on her. We'll wire her and monitor everything. If she wants out, if she wants a walk, this is what she agrees to."

"I don't like this one bit," Marc said, obviously annoyed.

"Tough shit," a still angry Jeff Johnson said.

To stop him from saying more, Tess Richards calmly said, "We'll make the case. We know who did these robberies. We got that from Donna. She gets a walk because she gave us a lot of valuable information…"

"So will Cindy," Marc said.

"And she was in on it from the beginning," Pace said. "She'll get a walk same as Donna, but she has to earn it. If she had come forward sooner, but she didn't. Now, we want her to stay in. Look, Marc. If she truly gives us a good faith effort, she'll get her deal. But we need to make an effort to nail down who did the killing."

"Right now, you can't make a case for the murder at all," Marc said. "At best a very weak circumstantial case these lawyers will tear to shreds."

"You're right. No, to be honest, we can't make a good case for the murder. That's why we need her to take a shot at it. To get us something," Pace admitted.

"What about Neil Cole? What if he talks?" Marc asked.

"He was there. He was directly involved. I don't think I could give him a complete walk for it," Pace said.

"Unless Cindy can't get it for you," Marc said.

"We'll see," Pace said.

"I want two things. I want a separate written statement signed by you about this good-faith effort business. And, I want Maddy Rivers and Tony Carvelli to monitor your people. To make sure, they're really covering Cindy," Marc said.

"No way," Johnson said.

"Jeff, calm down. If it wasn't for them, you'd still be walking around with your dick in your hand trying to break this case," Marc said.

"He's got a point," Tess said. "They handed us this case."

"And Damone Watson," Pace added referring to a huge drug and corruption scandal.

"Okay, I can deal with Tony and Maddy," Johnson agreed.

"If she agrees, I'll have her down here at two o'clock this afternoon," Marc said.

"With her ledger," Johnson said.

"Yes," Marc said. "She'll have to go through it with you. She wrote it in some kind of personal code."

"Have you seen it?" Pace asked.

"No, I haven't. She explained it to me." Marc turned to Tess and said, "She's taken to Maddy like a duck to water. Let Maddy deal with her as much as possible."

"Will do and thanks," Tess replied.

Johnson stood up and said to Marc, "No hard feelings?"

"I'm a defense lawyer, Jeff. That little row we had is nothing. Don't worry about it."

FIFTY-FOUR

Marc sat next to Cindy while going over the immunity agreement. They were in a conference room, along with Maddy and Tony Carvelli at the U.S. Attorney's office.

"I can't do that, I can't do that," Cindy protested for at least the fourth time. "Wear a wire when I meet with the guys. I'll be scared to death."

Maddy was sitting opposite Cindy. She got up and went around and sat next to her. Maddy had become the strong, big sister to both Donna and Cindy. She took Cindy's hand and gently rubbed the back of her neck.

"Relax, sweetie," Maddy said. "No one's done anything yet. And having gotten to know you, I know you're strong enough to do this.

"Before you do it, we'll practice it. You'll see. It's not a big deal. You'll be comfortable with it. And I'll be monitoring every bit of it," Maddy assured her.

"Okay, I'll try. Promise me you'll be close by if something goes wrong," she told Maddy.

"Absolutely," she answered.

"Did Luke have all of the guns with him when he left the night the feds showed up?" Carvelli asked.

"I think so. At least as far as I know. I don't think anyone kept them. We always had to turn them over to Ben to store them after each job. They were all at his house that night, and Luke took them and anything else we had."

"What were the easel and the large pad of paper for that was found in Luke's truck?" Carvelli asked.

"Whenever we did a job, we always sent in a team to check out the bank. Then we'd draw it on the paper to plan the robbery. We always wanted to plan it to go in when there weren't a lot of customers there. We didn't want to hurt anyone."

"So, what do you think," Marc asked. "Feel a little better about this?"

"No, maybe a little."

"Cindy, I hate to be the bad cop..." Carvelli started to say.

"No, you don't, you're perfect for it," Maddy said which got a laugh and broke some of the tension.

"Okay, smartass," Carvelli said. "And, I don't mean to sound like your dad. But you got yourself into this mess. This is what you need to do to get out of it."

"I know, okay, you're right," she replied. "Now what?" she asked Marc.

"Sign these," he said then began showing her where on the immunity agreement.

While they did this, Carvelli received a text. He read it then put his phone away.

"From Johnson. They found Luke's, Ben Sokol's and of course, Cindy's fingerprints on the money you were holding for her," Carvelli told Marc.

"That ties them to that cash, but it still doesn't tie that cash to the Ames, Iowa robbery," Marc said. "Although they are building a pretty good circumstantial case. They can take what they have to a grand jury and get indictments. A trial where the burden is beyond a reasonable doubt, that's still pretty iffy."

"What about me and Donna? What about what we say?"

"Two scared girls willing to say anything the feds want to stay out of prison," Marc said. "The defense lawyers will try to eat you both."

"What they need is to trace the money," Carvelli said.

"The feds are pretty good at that," Marc said.

"I know someone even better," Carvelli replied with a sneaky smile.

"We don't have a lot of money in the girl's defense fund," Marc reminded him.

"Ah, it's about time he did little pro bono for all the times he overcharged us."

"What are you talking about?" Cindy asked.

"Nothing for you to know, just yet," Marc said. "A friend of Tony's."

Marc stood and went to a credenza along the front wall. There was coffee and water on it, and he poured himself a glass of water. There was also an office phone. He punched two numbers and told Ethan Pace they were ready.

While they waited, Cindy received a text. Carvelli had her phone and he read it out loud.

"A meeting tonight at the music room," Carvelli said. "Ten o'clock."

"Oh, boy, they're gonna want me there wearing that wire, aren't they?"

"Yes," Marc quietly replied. "It will be all right. Where's this music room?"

"It's on campus. I'll show you. You can park really close and listen in," Cindy said.

"Good," Maddy replied.

Without bothering to knock, Johnson, Tess Richards and Pace entered the room.

"We all set?" Pace asked.

"Yeah, here're your copies," Marc said, handing him copies of the immunity agreement.

For the next half-hour, Pace walked Cindy through the process of a formal statement of cooperation. He also recorded it and would have it transcribed for signatures.

When that was finished, Maddy pulled out Cindy's ledger detailing the entire criminal enterprise. Without recording it, Johnson took over, and the group spent another two hours going through the ledger while Cindy explained the codes that she used.

"I have to tell you, Cindy," Johnson said to her when they were done, "I am very impressed. You did an amazing job."

"Thanks. I just wish I knew more about the banks Ben used and the names of the companies he set up to launder the money. And, like I said, those are just a couple of the groups we sent money to. I'm sure there were others."

"Over a million dollars. We'll track this down," Tess said.

"You think Neil might turn on them and testify about Jordan Simmons?" Pace asked.

"Yeah, he um, well, he has a thing for me, I'm pretty sure. He was there. I don't know exactly what happened. He would never talk about it except once when he admitted Sherry did the shooting. But I know he was there," Cindy answered.

"She got a text. There's a meeting tonight at ten at a place on campus," Marc said.

"Interesting," Pace said. "I have news. Luke Hanson made bail. I don't know how. He assured the judge he was not a flight risk and the judge bought it. He doesn't even need to wear a monitor."

"That's what the meeting's about," Marc said. "Luke's back."

"She knows she'll be there wired up?" Johnson harshly asked Marc, referring to Cindy.

"I'll take care of it," Maddy said. "Cool it, Jeff."

"Just wondering," he backpedaled.

"She knows, I'll take care of it. We'll take her through it and practice. Tess and I can handle that," Maddy said, giving Johnson a subtle, back off look.

Cindy took one of the metal folding chairs stored in the music room and placed herself in between Neil and Reese. Including Ben, who always arrived early for these meetings, they were the only ones here.

"You want a beer?" Reese asked. Cindy was looking at both his and Neil's when he asked.

"Yes, you have one?"

"Sure, here," Reese said, handing her a can from his twelve-pack.

"Thanks," she said, then popped it and drank off half of it in one shot. Both Neil and Reese almost laughed while watching her do it.

"You okay?" Neil asked.

"No! Luke got busted and let out right away. How do we know he's not working with the cops? How do we know they're not waiting for everyone to get here then kick open the doors and drag us off in handcuffs again?"

"He isn't," Ben said to her. He pulled up a chair facing the three of them.

"How do you know?" Cindy asked after another long swallow from the can.

"Because the lawyers would know. They're all working together to keep us out of jail. The cops found some cash and guns, but nothing that ties Luke or us to anything," Ben said, popping open a beer.

"What about...?" Cindy started to say.

"What?" Ben asked.

"The gun that was used to kill Jordan?"

"What gun? What are you talking about? Jordan died from being shot by a bank guard. It was an accident. None of us had anything to do with that."

Maddy, Carvelli and Tess Richards were in a van parked in a school lot two hundred yards away. All three were wearing headsets listening to the conversation from inside the music hall room.

"Damn," Tess quietly said. "He almost admitted they were involved in the bank where the Simmons girl was shot."

"Back down, Cindy," Maddy said. "Ben's a little suspicious."

"Why are you worried about Jordan? It was terrible when we found out about her, but we had nothing to do with it," Reese added.

Neil was avoiding eye contact while they talked about Jordan. He sipped nervously at his beer and looked around the room.

"Was Luke taking off on us?" Cindy asked, hoping to change the subject.

"Why would you ask that?" Ben asked.

"Because my lawyer had a copy of the police report. He let me read it. Luke was two miles from home, a block away from a freeway that he could have got on and been gone in half an hour. Plus, in the police report, he had most of his clothes and things in his truck."

"Did she really see a copy of the arrest report from her lawyer?" Tess asked.

"Yeah," Maddy said. "Unfortunately, it was Marc who showed it to her at your office today."

"Luke is always running around with things in his truck," Reese said.

"Let it go, Cindy," Ben firmly told her.

"Okay," Cindy said. "I was just wondering. I'll let it go. Sorry, I'm worried."

The exterior door opened—Sherry had a key—and Sherry, Luke and Gary Weaver came in.

The four of them stood up to greet the others, then Ben asked Gary, "Still no word from Donna?"

"No, sorry, no," Gary weakly said.

At least a couple of the others had let their disappointment be known to Gary about Donna. She was his girlfriend, and he had brought her in.

"She's flipped," Reese said. "She's gone to the cops."

"Maybe she's just hiding out," Cindy said. "Maybe she went to a lawyer or someone who told her to get out of town."

Ben looked at Cindy and said, "Could be. Let's hope so."

"What about you?" Neil asked, looking at Luke. "You turn Judas on us?"

"Hey, fuck you, schoolboy!" Luke yelled. He then did something foolish. Luke went after Neil.

Neil Cole was generally the quietest one of the group. A natural follower, not a leader. His outburst at Luke, the real natural leader, came as a surprise to everyone.

Neil did not look it, and he almost never acted or talked like it, but Neil was a strong, tough guy. He had been a conference champion wrestler in high school and continued to lift weights daily.

Luke rushed Neil with his hands out front expecting to be able to push Neil to the ground. Instead, it took Neil less than two seconds to have Luke face down on the concrete. While Neil straddled Luke's back, he asked the question again.

"No, goddamnit. I'm not working with the cops," Luke managed to say.

"Come on, Neil. Get off him. Let him up," Ben said while everyone else stared in shock.

"That's it, boys," Carvelli said in the van, "Start pointing fingers at each other."

"Keep the suspicion off Cindy," Tess added.

Neil stood up, and Ben helped Luke to his feet. While Luke brushed himself off, Neil decided not to let it go.

"Strip," Neil said. "I want to make sure you're not wearing a wire."

"Screw you," Luke said only much more passively. "I'm not wearing a wire."

"How did he get out so easy? Twenty grand bail. Who paid that? Seems pretty cheap. How can we trust him?" Neil said.

"And he was running," Cindy said.

"You're right, I was," Luke said, looking at Cindy. "I panicked and thought about taking off. Then, while I was driving, I was thinking about that instead of paying attention. That's what caused the accident. I changed my mind."

"Nice face," Sherry said, causing the room to lighten with laughter.

Luke was still sporting two nasty looking black eyes and a taped-up nose. The cost of being hammered by an angry airbag.

"Why are we here?" Reese asked.

"My lawyer suggested it," Ben said.

"Speaking of lawyers," Luke said. "Where did they come from and who's paying them?"

"A benefactor," Ben told them. "For now, that's all you need to know.

"He just wanted to make sure we're all on the same page. He's very experienced. He knows the cops, especially the FBI and Justice department, will do whatever they have to against us. Including using us against each other with lies."

"Does he know where Donna is?" Gary asked.

"He hasn't heard a word about Donna," Ben answered. "But he assumes she is talking to them.

"The main thing is that we don't have anything to worry about. Let the lawyers handle this. They don't think there's much of a case. Everybody stay calm, stay together and don't talk to anyone outside this room. Except, of course, the lawyers."

Once outside, Cindy sought out Neil. She caught up with him, looped her right arm through his left and asked him to buy her a drink.

They found a table for two in a bar off-campus filled with students. It was crowded and noisy making it almost impossible for Cindy's friends in the van to listen in. Something that did not occur to her.

Two tall beers accompanied by two shots of Jägermeister lubricated Neil's tongue. His conscience had been bothering him ever since it happened, and he finally spilled it all. By the time he finished, Cindy had every detail of Jordan's murder. Unfortunately, Maddy and company did not hear much of it. Bits and pieces, an intelligible word here and there was the extent of it. Mostly the bar noise drowned it out. Even the techs at the FBI in Washington, and they gave it their best effort, would not get it cleaned up sufficiently.

While they listened, all three of them believed they were hearing a confession. Mostly from the questions Cindy asked. Being much closer to the mic, more of what she said came through. But without hearing what Neil said, it was useless in court.

Carvelli finally gave up. He removed the headset and threw it on the floor. Angrily, he said, "She should've taken him home and got him in the sack. He would have confessed to anything."

"The mic's between her boobs," Maddy said. "I think he would have noticed."

Tess, mocking the sound of Neil, said, "Hey, look what I found."

This at least, made them laugh.

The three of them stayed with it until after 2:00 A.M. It was then they saw Cindy put Neil in an Uber and send him home. She ran to her car and immediately called Maddy.

"Did you get it? He told me everything," Cindy excitedly asked.

"Sorry, no. Too much bar noise."

"Damnit!"

"Listen," Maddy said. "We'll escort you home. When you get there, write it all down yet tonight while it is still fresh. Every word. At least then we'll know what happened."

"Okay."

"Ask her if he said anything about Natalie Flanders," Carvelli said.

Maddy did that, and Cindy simply said no. She said she even asked Neil about her.

"You shouldn't have done that," Maddy said. "Let's hope he was too drunk to remember. Let's call it a night."

FIFTY-FIVE

Tony Carvelli shut the door on his Camaro, stuffed his bare hands in his coat pockets and hurried along the sidewalk. It was January 30th, a Saturday and the last weekend of the month that was normally the coldest. As usual, the Gods of Winter were howling this weekend. It was almost noon, and the temperature was still a crisp minus 14. There was a steady twenty mile an hour wind gusting to thirty pushing wind chills as low as fifty below zero.

"Freeze-your-ass-off Minnesota cold," Carvelli grumbled as he hurried up to the house. "Why the hell do we live in this fricking ice world?"

Before he even raised a hand to knock, Paul Baker opened the door.

"Where's Maddy?" Paul asked, looking past Carvelli.

"Not here. Get out of the way. It's cold out here."

When he got inside Carvelli looked over Paul and said, "So, if I tell you I'm bringing Maddy, you'll clean up and look presentable?"

"Well, no. I mean, I don't know…" a slightly embarrassed Paul muttered.

"Look, she's seriously with someone and," Carvelli hesitated, "a bit out of your league. But you do clean up okay. If you want to get out and meet a girl, I can help. In fact, I know a really cute FBI agent…"

"Shove it," Paul said, then walked past him into the living room.

"I was being serious," Carvelli protested following behind.

"An FBI agent? I'll end up in prison if it doesn't work out."

"Yeah, that could happen," Carvelli said from the couch. "So, what did you find out?"

"This law firm, Jonah Cliff and Associates is very well connected," Paul said.

"To the mob?" Carvelli asked.

"No, I didn't see any of that. I meant connected to rich people, especially Hollywood type celebrities. And these lawyers seem to be good at making problems go away. You remember that hotshot producer who found his wife in the sack with another guy and shot both of them? Killed the guy but only wounded the wife?"

"About four years ago?"

"Six. Merriman was the producer's name. Anyway…"

"He got off on a temporary insanity type plea," Carvelli said. "I remember Marc talking about it. Shocked everyone."

"It shouldn't have," Paul said. "I found something very interesting. I came across a trail of money, half a million bucks to guess who?"

"I'm not very good at that, Paul."

"Four jurors."

"Seriously? Jeff Johnson will…"

"Statute of limitations is up," Paul said.

"I'll tell him anyway."

"I found something, or I should say, someone, more interesting than that. You ever hear of a guy by the name of Tom Breyer?'

"Yeah. He's some rich, billionaire asshole out in California. Always preaching to the rest of us about the environment, social justice and other causes. Telling the rest of us to drastically change our lives and lifestyles to save the planet. Of course, this is really telling the rest of us what we have to give up, so he and his celebrity do-gooder pals don't have to give up anything."

"That's pretty good, Tony. In fact, that's spot on. Anyway," Paul continued, "I saw some emails between Breyer and this Jonah Cliff. Breyer is picking up the tab for the attorney fees for your little band of bank robbers."

"Really? Why?"

"Well, I don't know except Breyer is hot to keep them out of jail. Especially that professor, Ben Sokol."

"What's in it for him?" Carvelli wondered.

"Don't know yet. I started digging around in Breyer's business. Sokol's name came up, but I didn't find out why. Breyer seems to have a pretty sophisticated computer security system. I was in on him for maybe five minutes then, guess what happened?"

"I told you, I'm not very good at that," Carvelli impatiently said again.

"I had a typed, live message show up on my screen warning me to get out of what I was doing."

"No kidding. Live?"

"Yeah, it wasn't some canned thing. It was someone in real-time."

"Now what?" Carvelli asked.

"Now, I'll take it as a challenge. I'll find a way around his security and find out what he's trying to hide," Paul answered.

"Be careful. Don't let them trace you back to here."

"No problem."

"Hey, don't get cocky. Those people are probably very good."

"I know. I'll be careful."

"I have something else for you," Carvelli said then removed an envelope from his coat pocket.

"What is it?"

"It's a list of bank robberies with actual dollar amounts. There are also names of casinos where the money was first washed. It was then sent through the internet into Bitcoins and other cryptocurrency, whatever that is, then withdrawn into bank accounts. The money was deposited into fictitious company accounts and then withdrawn and turned back into cash. See if you can trace some of this and where it ended up."

"That will take some time," Paul quietly said while scanning though the pages Carvelli gave him.

"Don't pad your bill on me by blowing smoke up my ass," Carvelli said.

"Would I..."

"Yes." Carvelli jumped in with.

"This is complicated. Some of these banks are internet banks. Who do you think did it?"

"I'm not saying. I know, but I want you to track it and tell me."

"Okay, will do."

That same Saturday, in the evening, Ben Sokol was attending a Midwest State cocktail party. It was a more or less—more rather than less—mandatory appearance. Ben had dreaded the thought of going. Ever since the FBI raid on his house, he had kept a very low profile on campus. He was uncertain of how his peers would respond and treat him.

Ben need not have worried. He was there less than ten minutes when it was clear he was the toast of the entire Midwest State faculty and administration. They could not get enough of him. Mild-mannered Ben had made the mighty FBI look like fools. A university staff's wet dream.

Ben arrived at 8:00 and enjoyed the adulation until almost midnight. He played the part of the harassed academic to perfection. Basically, repeating the mantra that academic freedom will not be intimidated or hampered in any way by the jack-booted thugs of a repressive government. It was quite a display coming from a man whom many of these people considered a mediocrity, at best.

Around 11:00, he received a text message: *I'm waiting*. He knew who it was from. His trysts with Sherry Toomey had never really stopped. They had simply become more discreet. This suited Ben just fine. He had no real emotional feelings for her. In fact, he considered her to be a bit of a simple-minded fool. Sherry's only real significant attribute was a great body and a passion for fellatio. And she was quite good at it.

Ben would have let his lust lead him out the door then, except for the Dean of Students. Lauren Smothers was a fifty-something married woman. Rumor had it that her husband was quite openminded and Lauren was reputedly very available. She was still an attractive woman and Ben had been rebuffed by her on a couple of occasions. Thanks to his newfound notoriety, she was apparently seeing Ben in a new light and reconsidering. Ben had fun and a bit of an ego boost playing along with her. The thought of Sherry's decades younger and firmer body was an image Ben did not want to shake.

Practically begging off from the woman's obvious advances, Ben was able to escape. He had to promise a future engagement with her. This was an opportunity he decided he would keep.

Before leaving, he made his way around the room to receive a few more 'atta boys' from the crowd. With his head swollen enough to barely get it through the door, he left and hurried to his car.

For almost four hours, the man waiting for Ben sat in his car, mostly very uncomfortable from the cold. A half-block ahead of him parked on the same side of the street was another car with a cold occupant; only this one was a little careless. To fight off the cold, the person inside ran the engine a little too often for a little too long. A cop or Feeb and an unprofessional, impatient one, the man believed.

He finally saw the pudgy, little professor come out and scurry to his car. It was parked two spaces in front of the cop. Sure enough, when the professor drove off, the cop followed.

Keeping his distance and routinely turning his lights off so as not to be noticed, he followed the two cars. Before they had gone very far, he knew Sokol was heading home. The professor's house was less than ten minutes away on the other side of the campus. When they got there, the cop following Sokol did not even bother to stop. Sokol turned into his driveway, and the cop drove past. *A perfect opportunity*, the man thought.

Ben hurried through the bitter cold from his unattached garage to his back door. Fortunately, the wind had died down, but the night air was still minus twenty, and the snow made frozen, crunching sounds as he walked over it. Having grown up on the East Coast, January was still too much for Ben to take.

Inside, the house was dark except for a light above the stove. It was also very quiet. Likely, Sherry had fallen asleep waiting for him. This had happened before. He would have a short cognac, go upstairs and wake her.

Ben went into the living room, turned on a lamp then stood for a moment at the bottom of the stairs, listening. Hearing no sounds, he hung his overcoat up in the foyer closet. He stopped again at the foot of the stairs believing he had heard a noise. Satisfied, he went across the living room to the dry bar for his nightcap. Holding the brandy snifter to his nose, he enjoyed the pleasant aroma of the Courvoisier.

"Good evening, professor," he heard a man's voice say from behind. The words the man spoke shattered the silent room and a terrified Ben wheeled around and almost dropped his glass.

The intruder was staring at Ben while holding a silenced gun in his right hand. The lamp Ben had turned on was a reading lamp next to his recliner. The man stepped over to it and turned the lamp, so the light was in Ben's face. Standing behind the lamp, Ben's assassin was a silhouette in the dark.

"Who, who…who are you and what do you want?" Ben was barely able to croak. "If, um, ah, you want money. I'll get it. Please…"

"Don't take this personally," the voice came from the dark. "I'm here on behalf of your acquaintance, Tom Breyer. He wants me to remind you that you were warned to cut out this silly, bank robbery, nonsense. You didn't listen, so he sent for me. I'm sort of a, um, problem solver. A permanent problem solver."

"Please, I swear…" Ben started to say.

Instead, he was stopped by the sound of a loud, "foomp" coming from the silenced handgun.

Ben instinctively ducked and stood frozen in place, his head tucked into his shoulders, still holding the glass. He stared at the silhouette of the assassin, not comprehending why he was not dead or at least in pain from being shot by the man. Instead, the intruder, gun still in his hand, slowly fell forward, face-down onto the rug in front of Ben's chair. Behind him stood Sherry Toomey holding a bloody letter opener she had used to stab the man through the spine where his head and neck met killing him instantly.

The sudden impact of the blade severing his spinal cord stem caused him to reflexively squeeze the trigger. Fortunately for Ben, his aim was off just to enough to blow a small hole in the wall and not him.

Sherry had been sleeping in Ben's bed with the door open. She was a light sleeper and had awakened when Ben got home. Hearing the talking, she had silently made her way in the dark down the carpeted stairs.

Knowing Ben kept a sharp, bone-handled letter opener on a small table by the front door, she found it. Sherry crept up behind the killer, listened to the threat to Ben then calmly stabbed the man in the back of his neck.

An hour later, with the body wrapped in the rug he conveniently fell on, Ben and Sherry found a suitable dumpster. They were in a dark alley in North Minneapolis. This was several miles from Ben's house in a neighborhood heavily populated with African Americans. Even if the body was found, tracing it to Ben would be next to impossible.

Ben had driven his car with the carpet covered corpse in the trunk. Sherry had found the man's car keys and discovered his rental a half a block away. The car was left a mile from where they tossed the body in a dumpster.

The big question for them was: now what? Tom Breyer was likely to try again.

FIFTY-SIX

Marc, Maddy, Tony Carvelli, and Donna Gilchrist were sitting around a conference room table in the U.S. Courthouse. With them was Waseca County Sherriff's investigator Tom Haig. Across the hallway was the federal grand jury room.

Marc looked at his watch and said to no one in particular, "He's not gonna show."

"He will," Carvelli replied. "I told you when Tom served the subpoena, I made it clear if he doesn't show, I'll track his ass down and he'll go to jail. Then I'd put it out on the street that he was a federal informant. He'll show."

They were referring to Kenny Wrangler, the biker crook who sold the guns to Luke Hanson. Wrangler had been given a complete grant of testimonial immunity. Anything he said, anything he testified about, could not be used against him. It was not Wrangler and his bunch of drooling, knuckle-draggers the Feds were after. At least not yet. They wanted Wrangler to identify Luke Hanson and the guns.

Ethan Pace knocked once, then entered the conference room. It was 1:15. Time to get the show started.

The grand jury was made up of 23 jurors chosen for six months. They met once a week, more often if necessary, to hear cases presented by the U.S. Attorney's office. Their job was to look at the evidence, listen to the witnesses and determine if there was probable cause to believe a crime was committed. If so, was there probable cause that the subjects of the hearing were the ones who committed the crime. The defendants may be allowed to testify, but it would likely be foolish to do so. It is not the grand jury's job to find guilt beyond a reasonable doubt. There is an old saying that a good prosecutor can indict a ham sandwich. The reason for that is because the threshold for an indictment, probable cause, is extremely low.

"Okay, let's get started," Ethan told the group. "I want Donna first. If it will make you feel more comfortable, I'll let Marc sit in. He can't ask questions or participate, but he can watch."

"How about Maddy? I'd rather have her," Donna said.

"No, sorry, she's a witness. I shouldn't let Marc sit in…"

"I'll be okay," Donna said. "He should stay outside."

"If you want to talk to him about anything, you can just tell me and I'll take a break, okay?"

They all filed out of the conference room into the hall. Ethan Pace conducted the hearing and was very prepared. Donna's testimony lasted the longest. She was followed by Carvelli, then Maddy. When Maddy came out, the elevator doors opened, and Kenny Wrangler, accompanied by three of his pals, stepped off. He also had a lawyer with him. A man Tom Haig knew well.

Haig even introduced the lawyer to everyone. His name was Malcolm Butters and he was a Waseca County institution.

"My client is willing to cooperate," Butters said. "I've gone over the immunity document, and it has a flaw. Nothing he says can be used against him, but it does not cover anyone else. So, I've added an Addendum," he continued as he handed it to Ethan, "to cover others as well. You could take his testimony, use it against someone else then induce that person to well, maybe come up with things not discussed in front of the grand jury to use against Mr. Wrangler. Nothing he says can be used against anyone."

"Deal, as long as he fully cooperates and doesn't lie," Ethan quickly agreed then signed the Addendum. When that was done Ethan said, "I'll take him next. We're mostly looking to have him identify the guns and the guy who bought them from him."

"Yeah, okay, let's go," Wrangler said.

As he walked toward the door, his posse started to go with him, except the lawyer.

One of them, clearly annoyed, said to Wrangler, "Dude, you sure about this?"

Wrangler shrugged and said, "What do I care about these college kids. I'll be right back."

Wrangler did exactly as expected. In fact, he made a very credible witness. Looks sometimes are deceiving. He was clear, articulate and convincing.

When Wrangler was finished, he joined his pals in the hall. Tony Carvelli was leaning against the wall opposite the grand jury room. As Wrangler and company walked back toward the elevators, he looked at Carvelli. Tony was staring back with a smartass smirk on his face. Wrangler curled up his upper lip and flipped him off with both hands eliciting a short laugh from Carvelli.

An hour after Tom Haig testified, the grand jury voted a multi-count indictment against all of the members of the little cult, including Cindy Bonn. Cindy working on behalf of the Feds had not been discussed. Being included in the indictment would lend credibility that she was still one of the cult members.

There was only one glitch, but it was significant. The grand jury refused to include any charges related to the murder of Jordan Simmons. The only evidence presented was Donna's hearsay. No witness, no gun, no forensics tied to anyone. The bank robberies, lesser gun charges and only the money laundering that Donna participated in herself were considered.

By the time the grand jury handed down its bill, Marc and all were gone. Instead, Jeff Johnson and Tess Richards had replaced them waiting in the hall. Ethan Pace had the two agents follow him into the conference room that his witnesses had used.

Ethan went over the indictments with the agents. When he finished, he asked Johnson, "Is the surveillance in place?"

A few days ago, it had been decided to put a net on all of the cult member suspects. To put around-the-clock surveillance on seven people required a lot of agents. The FBI has a lot of agents. It took a couple of days to get it completely set up, but it had been in place for two days. They knew where all of them were, including Cindy, twenty-four hours a day.

"Okay, get your teams together. I want them all arrested tonight. Early morning," Ethan said.

"The plan is set, and we're ready to go. Get us the arrest and search warrants and we'll go tomorrow morning, five A.M." Johnson replied.

"Without the homicide indictment, they'll make bail," Tess said.

"Yes, I'm sure they will," Ethan agreed. "We can ask for monitoring ankle bracelets. I'm not sure we'll get them. These kids are gonna look like a church choir sitting in court. Their lawyers will argue they are not a flight risk and an ankle bracelet hinders their right to participate in their defense."

The next morning at precisely five o'clock, seventy FBI agents, local cops and SWAT members made their move. Ethan Pace's boss had made a foolish decision from which Ethan could not dissuade him. There were news camera crews at every location the Feds hit. The film went nationwide and made the Feds look like the Gestapo. Six college kids and one short, pudgy, pathetic looking professor, were rousted out of bed. All were handcuffed and each held by two large men in FBI vests as they were paraded before the cameras. If that was not bad enough, it was still very dark out, cold and there looked to be an invasion of cops at each place. The media had a field day.

Ethan Pace's prediction turned out to be accurate. The lot of them were arraigned later that day, some still in pajamas and nightclothes before a displeased woman magistrate. Bail was set at ten thousand dollars each, passports were ordered to be surrendered but no other restrictions put in place.

At four o'clock, Tony Carvelli and Maddy Rivers entered Jeff Johnson's office. Of course, they had called ahead so Johnson and Tess Richards would be waiting.

Carvelli was carrying a leather, locked briefcase and set it on Johnson's desk. He worked the lock, opened it and pulled out a four-inch stack of paper.

"Here you go. Here's a road map all spelled out for the money," Carvelli said, handing it to Johnson. "Bank accounts, casinos where they went, amounts washed. My..." Carvelli paused searching for the right word, "...friend even traced it through the internet, Bitcoin and other cryptocurrency funds whatever that is, and through PayPal. My friend thinks it's all there."

"Is any of this admissible?" Tess asked.

"If you can't scare the hell out of at least one of these kids, then..." Carvelli started to say.

Carvelli was still standing in front of Johnson's desk while Johnson riffled through the stack of paper. Maddy had taken a chair next to Tess.

"Go after Neil Cole," Maddy said.

"We tried," Johnson said. "We can't get past his lawyer."

"Cindy can testify to what he told her about the murder of Jordan Simmons. We have enough now to go to Ethan and tell him we're going to pull her in," Tess said.

"Isn't that hearsay?" Carvelli asked. "I mean Cindy saying what Neil told her."

"Ethan says it's a statement against interest. A hearsay exception," Tess said.

"Marc said so, too," Maddy added. "He said it's an exception because Neil was there when it happened. He participated and could be charged as an accomplice. Admitting it is a statement against his own interest. It's admissible in court but likely only against Neil."

"We gotta bring in Cindy," Tess said.

Johnson picked up his desk phone to call Ethan Pace while saying, "I'll call Ethan, then we'll go get her."

While Johnson did this, Carvelli sat down and said, "My, ah, friend is still tracing the money. He's not sure..."

"He?" Johnson asked, holding the phone.

"Yeah, okay, he," Carvelli said. "Anyway, he's traced it to these environmental, save-the-world groups, but he's not sure the money these outfits bring in go to where they claim. He thinks because these groups are do-gooder types, the IRS never checks up on them. The government just accepts whatever bullshit they submit. He's now following the money of those groups."

310

"Okay," Johnson said. "Let us know if he comes up with anything."

"Wait, Jeff," Maddy said. "Before you go after Cindy and bring her in, let us take a shot at Neil. He's the one you guys need."

"I'm not that crazy about another immunity deal," Johnson said. "Especially for someone who was involved in the Simmons girl's murder."

"Cindy swears he didn't pull the trigger. You read her statement. These are high-buck lawyers they have. Neil could nail it down," Carvelli said.

"Okay, I'll give you one more shot at him," Johnson agreed.

"His lawyer might make the same deal," Tess said.

"Not a chance," Carvelli told her. "They're all with the same firm and working together. They aren't gonna let anyone take a plea and flip."

"Good point," Tess replied.

"If you're gonna send Cindy to go after Neil, she needs to be wired."

"No," Maddy said. "If she's wired then their lawyers can say we're working for you. Let's try to get him to flip by coming to his senses. No wire."

"I don't like it," Johnson said.

"We really don't need your permission, Jeff," Carvelli said. "Maddy will get him then you'll have the whole package."

FIFTY-SEVEN

"What?" Maddy asked.

She and Carvelli were walking toward their cars when Carvelli's phone buzzed. He was receiving a text and stopped to read it, which piqued Maddy's curiosity.

"It's from Paul," Carvelli replied. "Says he's found more information for us. Wants to see you and me right away."

"You go. Marc's expecting me," Maddy said. She had called Marc from inside the courthouse building.

Maddy arrived at Marc's office, parked in back and saw Cindy drive into the small lot. The two of them went up together. They entered as the staff was getting ready to leave.

Connie came out to the reception area, leaving a window open and her door closed to air it out. The other two lawyer's doors were closed indicating they were working. Marc was out to greet Cindy right away.

"You want one of us to stick around for a while?" Carolyn Lucas, the senior staffer, asked.

"I can," Sandy quickly volunteered. "I have some work I can do anyway."

"Thanks, Sandy, but I don't think we'll need you. Get out of here on time for once," Marc said.

"Let's go in here," Marc said, referring to the conference room.

Connie joined them, and they took seats at the table.

"You remember my mom?" Marc said, referring to Connie.

"Hi, Cindy," Connie said and shook her hand.

"You're not really his Mom, right?" Cindy asked.

"No," Connie said with a smile. "I'm his landlord, and it is time for a rent increase, and he's trying to suck up to me. It won't work."

"You want me to call Neil and see if I can set up a meeting?" Cindy asked.

"Yes, that's what this is about," Maddy said. "You okay?"

"Sure. What kind of a deal do you think you can get for him?" Cindy asked. "These other lawyers, they got us all together and told everybody they can get us off. That the FBI doesn't have enough evidence. That if we all stick together and keep our mouths shut, we can beat this at trial."

"I'm not gonna lie to you," Marc said. "That could happen. And then every one of you will have to live with what you did. Including Jordan Simmons."

"I can't live with that now. Luke can, and Reese maybe and Sherry, too. Probably Ben. He's become an ambitious, greedy little prick. And he's so angry at the world," Cindy said.

"Call, Neil," Maddy said. "Meet him someplace quiet. Then we'll come in and talk to him."

"Can I have a cigarette?" Cindy asked Connie. "I can smell it on you. Would it be okay? I'm getting nervous and…"

"I didn't know you smoked," Maddy said.

"I don't unless I need to calm down."

"Here, hon," Connie said, handing her a cigarette and lighter. "Oh, shut up, Mr. Health Nut," she said to Marc. "Nothing worse than an ex-smoker," Connie grumbled as she opened a window.

"You want one?" Connie asked Maddy, another ex-smoker.

"No, Mom. Only when I'm drinking beer. Even then, I don't indulge," Maddy said.

"Call Neil," Marc said. "I need to get you away from the bad influence of this office."

Cindy walked through the entrance of Joe Senser's, a sports bar on the I-494 strip in Bloomington. Being a weekday evening, the restaurant was less than half-full.

Anxious to see Cindy alone, Neil arrived ten minutes before her. When he saw her, he almost jumped out of the booth. He frantically waved at her, and she turned to her left, saw him seated along the wall, waved back with a smile and hurried to join him.

Cindy sat down in the booth, her back to the door, reached across the table and took both of Neil's hands. Seated at a table facing Cindy, three tables away were Marc and Maddy.

"Hi," Cindy said, holding Neil's hands.

Her hands were warm, and Neil, his heart thumping in his chest, felt a tingle run up his arms. The shy, insecure, small-town boy had a crush on this city girl since the first time he saw her.

"Neil, I have to tell you something," Cindy began.

She had rehearsed her opening with Maddy until they got down exactly what she should say. At first, Marc had wanted her to just come right out and tell him. Tell him she was working with the feds. The women, always the more subtle of the species, knew how to reel in a smitten male.

"What?" Neil asked, still holding her hands.

"Well," she started to say. A waiter appeared, and Cindy pulled her hands slowly back. She ordered the same beer Neil had but in a small glass.

"Um," she continued when the server departed, "I don't trust our lawyers."

"Why?" Neil asked, a startled look on his ace. "I think they're great..."

"They're not being straight with us. Where did they come from? Who's paying them? Why are they all working together? Something is wrong," she said.

"Yeah, that stuff has been bothering me, too," Neil said. He had not actually given it one second of thought, but he wanted to agree with Cindy.

"I don't believe for a minute we're all gonna get away with this and not go to jail. That scares the hell out of me," she said.

"So, what can we do?" Neil asked

When he used the word "we," he signaled that he wanted her advice. Maddy had told her this. Using that word would be the signal that she could pull him away from the others.

"I talked to Donna," Cindy quietly said then watched his eyes for a reaction.

"How is she?" Neil asked, sincerely concerned.

Perfect, Cindy thought. "She's fine."

"Is she working with the cops?"

"Yes," Cindy answered.

"Are you? Are you wearing a wire?"

"No, I'm not wearing a wire. I'm trying to decide if I should save myself. Donna says they know pretty much everything. We're not gonna get away with it. We were idiots to think we could."

Neil went silent thinking for a moment. He was not a stupid kid. His grades reflected that. Neil Cole was a little naïve and a little in love with this girl across from him.

"How could they know everything? Donna doesn't know much..."

"Because they're the FBI, Neil. They are going to pull us apart. We need to think about ourselves and our future," Cindy said.

Using the term "our future" almost made Neil melt. A future with this girl was the answer to his dreams.

"I'll do what you think is best," he said. "I think we should go to the cops but tell me what you want."

"I want you to meet someone," she said. She took ahold of his hands again and said, "Two people. One is a lawyer. A really good lawyer. He can help us."

"Okay," Neil agreed. "When?"

"Now," Cindy said then waved at Marc and Maddy who quickly joined them.

Cindy moved over to Neil's side of the booth. With her right leg pressed against his left, he was having a difficult time paying attention to Marc. They ordered a round of small domestic beers. After the waiter brought them, Marc explained to Neil who he was and how he could help him. When that was finished, they adjourned to Marc's office.

It was almost midnight by the time they were done. Marc had Neil tell his story three times before he decided Neil was telling the truth. There was just enough deviation in each to give him credibility. Neil did not have his story memorized.

Finally, going slowly and taking more than an hour, they recorded it.

"I'll have it typed up tomorrow," Marc said. "Then, before we go to the Feds, you can read it over and make any changes, corrections or additions. I'll make an appointment with the Assistant U.S. Attorney handling this case. Before you sit down with him, we'll have a deal in hand."

"What do you think?" Neil, as does every client no matter what the case involves, asked Marc. "Will I have to do time?"

"Neil, I can't say. I'd love to sit here and tell you no, I'll make sure you get a walk. But I can't promise that.

"What will cause us problems is that you were there. You didn't pull the trigger to kill Jordan, but you were there. And you helped hide the body. I'll push for a complete walk, but we'll see."

"I was scared to death. Sherry is nuts and had a gun..." Neil started to protest.

Marc, having heard this several times already, held up a hand to stop him. "I know and I will make sure he knows. We'll see."

"What are you thinking?" Maddy asked Neil. "How much time are you willing to do?"

Neil looked at Marc, shrugged and quietly said, "You know, this has been eating at me ever since it happened; ever since Sherry pulled that trigger. I feel better just getting it off my chest. I'll do whatever they want. I'll testify and do all the time they say. I'm just glad it's coming to an end."

"They need you," Marc said. "The defense lawyers are really good. Even if they get convictions for all of the bank robberies, the defense can play the 'misguided kids trying to do good' card. The government needs the murder conspiracy conviction. You can give it to them."

"I feel bad for Ben," Neil said. "He's such a great man."

"Let me tell you who Ben Sokol is," Marc said. "He's a pathetic little social misfit who's pissed off at the world. When Ben Sokol looks in the mirror, he sees unappreciated greatness. Unrecognized brilliance.

And he's angry that the world has not showered him with money, adulation and accolades.

"When I was in college and law school, the professors in the business school and law school were mostly quite good. But then, they were teaching things that were actually useful. The ones in liberal arts and humanities were the biggest pack of mediocrities you'll ever find. There wasn't one that couldn't be replaced in ten minutes by any number of teaching assistants. And these are the ones that are pumping kid's heads with the wonders of socialism and how evil America and capitalism are.

"When these people talk about how great socialism is, they're not talking about the wonders of socialism for themselves. Not a chance. They're talking about socialism for you."

Marc looked at Maddy and asked, "What is that old fools name? That cranky old congressman..."

"Trane," Maddy answered.

"Yes, that's it. The senile socialist dreaming of a socialist paradise where everyone but him lives at the same level of squalor. And that's your pathetic little loser, Ben Sokol. If it weren't for this cushy gig he got for himself in academia, Sokol would be holding a 'will work for food' sign.

"Don't weep for the Ben Sokols of the world. Start thinking for yourself."

"That was quite a speech," Maddy whispered to Marc.

Cindy and Neil had left to go to Cindy's apartment. Marc and Maddy were in bed.

"I get a little wound up about these mediocre, pathetic professors filling these kids with garbage," Marc replied. "Sorry, I didn't mean to get that fired up."

"Oh, I agree with you," Maddy said. "In fact, it kind of turned me on."

Maddy sat up and pulled the T-shirt she was wearing over her head. She tossed it on the floor and laid down on top of Marc.

"Enough talking for today," she said.

"Why, madam, are you trying to have your wicked way with me?" Marc asked while Maddy planted kiss after kiss on his face and neck.

"By the way, little Mr. Woody is starting to stir, I can tell it's working," Maddy purred.

While Marc and company were hearing Neil's story, Tony Carvelli was being given a lengthy lesson on tracking money. He was sitting in

Paul Baker's living room impatiently listening to Paul. It lasted over an hour, and they went through two beers each before he got to the point.

"So, let me see if I understand this," Carvelli said when Paul finished. "You traced the money our cult of bank robber nitwits scored, to a dozen socialist, social justice and climate change nonprofits. Then you traced their money and found that around seventy percent of it…"

"In some cases, even more," Paul corrected.

"… is being funneled overseas and either directly or indirectly into the pocket of this Tom Breyer guy. Is that correct?"

"Yeah. No doubt. And there are millions, even hundreds of millions, more from the government and other philanthropy type groups donating also. This guy has made at least a billion dollars fleecing these people," Paul said.

"How the hell is he getting away with it? Doesn't anyone pay attention to what is happening with this money?"

"No, they aren't. Look, if you're on the PC side of the political spectrum, nobody looks. Nobody is watching this let alone auditing any of it very carefully. These nonprofits spend just enough on their crusades to look legitimate. They file tax returns that come from Breyer's accountant signed by someone else and the IRS and government oversight people in Congress don't pay any attention to it. They believe the lies because they want to, and there is plenty of cash being spread around. I suspect there are people in government, especially Congress, who know what's going on and likely prospering from it."

"I need a road map for Jeff Johnson. A report, complete with charts, diagrams and amounts," Carvelli said.

"I'll need a couple days. I haven't slept much for, I'm not even sure, three or four days," Paul replied.

"Okay. Two days," Carvelli said.

"Say, ah, Tony. Um, how am I, ah, getting paid?"

"I have no idea. With civic pride? I don't know how anybody's gonna get paid. We'll see."

"Great," Paul grumbled.

As Carvelli was leaving, he turned back and said, "Hey! I almost forgot. Include all that stuff you found about the California lawyer bribing jurors for that producer killing his wife."

"Will do," Paul said.

FIFTY-EIGHT

Luke Hanson looked longingly at the bottle of cheap whiskey sitting on his coffee table. It was now five days since they were arrested. Their lawyers had convinced the magistrate to set a very low bail which was promptly posted by the lawyers themselves. Why they were doing this, Luke could only guess. Someone or some group in the climate change community was helping them, but whom? Right now, Luke did not much care.

Since returning home, Luke had not gone outside. Not even for a minute. The weather for February was quite gentle. He simply had no reason to leave. Luke had not communicated with any of his co-cultists. The first three days were tolerable. Of course, he had enough liquor on hand to get him through. His drinking was becoming more and more of a problem, and he was down to his last quart of cheap booze. And the walls, due to cabin fever, were starting to close in.

Luke was also suffering from depression. He was out of money, food, booze and alone. The robberies had been the best thing he had ever done. The planning, leading them and executing the plan was a high he wanted again. Except he was being watched and he knew it.

Luke's couch was in front of his apartment window overlooking the street and a small apartment parking lot. He had the curtains drawn closed. Sitting on the couch, he used two fingers to open the curtains enough for a peek. The car was easy to spot. The only one out there with someone in it. As if they wanted him to know.

He let the curtains fall back to fully closed, retrieved the bottle from the coffee table and took a short swallow. Holding the bottle up, even though he believed the apartment was wired, he said out loud, "This has got to stop. I have to do something." Except the apartments were not wired. It was only Luke's drinking and paranoia that led him to believe it.

After capping the bottle and putting it under the kitchen sink, he went into the bathroom. Luke had his burner phone and was going to make a call with the water running. Like he had seen in the movies. Deciding against it, instead, he went into the interior hall outside his apartment and walked up two flights.

"Hey," Luke said, greeting the man he had called, "it's me."

"It's about time. I was beginning to wonder if you're okay," Reese Fallon replied.

"I'm not okay, and I need to do something about it. But, listen, be careful what you say. Your apartment is probably wired by the FBI."

"Okay. What can I do?"

Reese was a follower and a puppy when it came to Luke Hanson. He had made it clear to Luke on more than one occasion; he would follow Luke anywhere.

"Okay. Just say yes or no. Think about your answer first. Can you sneak out and get a car? The cops and FBI are watching all of us."

"Yes," Reese promptly answered.

"Are you sure?"

"Yes," he firmly said again.

"Good. There's a gas station a couple blocks from me. A BP station. Do you remember it?"

"Yes."

"Okay. When you get the car, call me and I'll meet you there."

"Yes," Reese said again.

Luke had to smile at the simple, one-word answers Reese was still giving him. Reese was not a deep thinker, but he was a loyal friend.

Standing in the bathroom preparing to shave, Luke could literally smell himself. He had not shaved, showered or put on clean clothes since he was bailed out.

After shaving, while standing in the shower, he again thought of his narrow miss attempting to escape. Fool's luck, he had told himself. Today would be different. Today he would be careful and pull it off. Reese could come with him. He would make a good companion. But, first, they needed money.

The Twin Cities Metro area is so covered with trees that, outside of downtown, there was a wooded area within easy walking distance of everyone. Luke's apartment was no exception. Most of these places were municipal parks.

When he was ready to go, a go-bag packed and at the door, Luke took another peek at the cop. Still there and probably mightily bored.

He slipped on his winter coat, grabbed the go-bag and went out the door. Within two minutes, he had gone down to the basement and used the connecting, underground tunnel to the building next door.

Luke's destination was a park three blocks away. Half-way there, he got the call from Reese. Reese had a car and would meet Luke at the nearby BP station.

Once in the park, empty thanks to winter, he quickly found the place he wanted. Among several barren lilac bushes, he knelt in the snow and removed a tool from his bag. It was a climber's ice axe. He found the spot and was through the frozen turf in under two minutes.

Still, there were two guns and two extra magazines in a large, zip-lock plastic bag, nicely protected and preserved from the weather.

Before Luke had reached the park and found the hidden handguns, Jeff Johnson had answered a phone call. It was from the FBI agent who had been watching Reese.

The team in the parking lot watching Luke was deliberately conspicuous. They wanted Luke to know he was being watched. This had been Tony Carvelli's idea. Sit on Luke until it drives him to do something rash. Maybe.

"Fallon's on the move," the woman agent sitting in the car in back of Fallon's apartment told Johnson.

"How's he moving?" Johnson asked.

"On foot. At least so far. Mike's on him on foot. I called him first, then you."

"Good. Call Mike back and have him keep in touch with you, Liz. You stay in your car and cruise along at a distance. If Fallon gets in a car, go with him," Johnson told her.

"I know what to do, Jeff," she replied. "Where are you?"

"I'm at the office, but Tess and I are on the way. I'll call Greene and tell him to go in and see if Hanson is home."

By the time Johnson and Tess were in their car, Agent Scott Greene, the man who had been watching Luke, was calling back. Johnson took the call while Tess drove.

"Okay, Scott. Call Liz and find out where they are. Then move after them," Johnson said into his phone.

"Luke's not in his apartment," Johnson told Tess. "He must have gone out through the basement of the building next door."

"What's he up to?" Tess rhetorically asked.

"Don't know," Johnson said. "But he's up to something. I think he has guns and money stashed and he and Fallon might try to take off."

"Are you with me?" Luke asked Reese.

They had met up at the BP station ten minutes ago and were driving around. Just in case they had not slipped away unnoticed, Reese was looking for a tail. Except they were being followed by professionals and Reese was not one.

"Hell, yeah," Reese said. "I'm just glad you called me."

"Spending most of my life in prison is not what I signed up for. Sooner or later, the others will fold if they haven't already."

"You mean like Donna?" Reese asked.

"Yeah. I was already being careful about what I said around Gary. Whose car is this anyway?"

"My sister's. She lives a couple blocks from me. I called and told her I need it for errands. She wasn't happy, but she told me I could use it.

"What's the plan?" Reese asked.

"After, we drive like hell up to Alexandria. We dump the car and steal another one…"

"You know how to steal a car?"

"A Ford van like my old one, yeah. There's nothing to it. Anyway, we go up to Alex to make the cops think we're running to Canada. Instead, we go straight south to Mexico."

"Okay. Sweet and simple," Reese said.

"And your sister gets her car back, eventually. Turn left up here. It's a block down. It will be on our right at the corner. Pull up in front and we go in."

"Where are they?" Johnson said into his handheld radio. Now that there were multiple agents involved, he was reluctantly using a radio.

"On forty-second heading west about a half-mile west of thirty-five W," Liz reported back.

"Wait a minute," she continued. "They're pulling over and stopping. Holy shit. They're stopping in front of a Lake Country bank branch. They're going in! They're going in! Forty-second and Donald. Hurry!"

The bank branch they went in was one Luke had cased before. It was rejected as a target because it was too close to home. Since their arrest, Luke figured, correctly, that security would be relaxed.

Luke went in first and went directly past the tellers and into the manager's office. Reese waited a couple of seconds then followed. He found two tellers, a guard and one customer only. While Reese got them on the floor and covered them, Luke went into the vault with the manager.

Liz pulled her car at an angle in front of Reese's sister's car. She had it effectively blocked in from the front. Within a few seconds, Scott Greene pulled up behind the sister's car, blocking it from behind. He jumped out of his car and joined Liz, guns drawn, using the hood of Liz's car as a shield.

The bank was situated on the corner, the front door facing the middle of the intersection. Johnson and Tess arrived while their quarry was still in the bank. Seeing Liz and Scott Greene, Johnson pulled his car around the corner to cover that part of the street.

It was only ten seconds after Johnson arrived, drew his gun and leaned over the car's trunk that Luke and Reese came out each carrying a bag of money. They began to turn toward their car. When they did, Liz started yelling for them to put down their weapons. Reese dropped his gun, threw up his hands and went to his knees. Luke did not.

Luke turned back and was looking directly at both Jeff Johnson and Tess Richards. Johnson immediately, quietly said the word no. He could see it in Luke's eyes, even with the mask, that Luke was not going to cooperate.

"Luke! Don't do it," Johnson yelled, almost pleading.

Instead, Luke raised his right arm, pointed the gun toward them and was hit center mass with three quick shots. Two by Johnson, one by Tess.

Pointing his gun at Luke, lying on his back on the sidewalk, Johnson went right at him.

"Call it in! Call it in! Ambulance," he yelled several times.

By this time, Greene was on Reese who was face down on the sidewalk. Liz was on her car radio calling for help and an ambulance. Tess was right behind Johnson and both were kneeling next to Luke.

"Hang in there, hang in there, Luke," Johnson was pleading. "Help's on the way. We can get you…"

"No," Luke was able to say. "Not gonna make it."

"No, no, no," Johnson pleaded some more, yelling in Luke's face.

"Jeff," Tess quietly said, "easy."

"Gotta tell you. Gotta tell you," Luke said, tears trickling out of the corners of his eyes. "Sorry. Catholic. Gotta confess. It was me. Alone. No one else. I killed Jordan. Shot her through a pillow, then I buried her up by Aitkin. I had to. She was dying. I had to. That's the gun I used," he said, turning his head toward the gun lying nearby on the sidewalk.

Luke's eyes rolled up in his head, and he was gone.

"Shit, goddamn, sonofabitch!" Johnson yelled.

FIFTY-NINE

While Luke Hanson was pacing about his apartment formulating his future plans, Marc Kadella was meeting AUSA Ethan Pace. They were in Pace's office. Marc was in one of the client chairs patiently waiting while Ethan read a transcription of Neil Cole's statement.

When Ethan finished, he set it aside, looked at Marc, smiled and said, "So, there we have it. Except I distinctly noticed the name of the interviewee is missing and it's not signed. I assume it's Neil Cole…"

"We'll get to that," Marc said.

"I can't give him a complete walk, Marc. He was in on everything from the beginning. He was even there when the Simmons girl was murdered. He helped wrap her up in plastic and bury her up in Aitkin."

"He was terrified. Psycho Sherry was holding a gun on him. She had just committed one murder. You don't think his fear was reasonable?"

"Doesn't matter. He can't get a walk. I can't give him a walk. I already gave them to the two girls. My boss will have my ass."

"Bull," Marc said. "You're a civil servant. She's a political appointment. You can do it and you know it. Besides, Neil only went in a bank once. Otherwise, the most he did was drive and…"

"…help hide a murder."

"Psycho Sherry. Gun. Do you really want to try him for it? He's giving you the shooter and the two leaders of the gang who were the most responsible for all of it. Otherwise, you roll the dice with hearsay coming from two, scared, very pliable young women. You know what this defense team will do to them."

The two men went silent for a very long minute while Ethan Pace thought it over. In both his head and his heart, he knew Marc was right. He had what he needed to wrap up a notorious, highly publicized string of bank robberies. He would convict the main principals for that and a murder. It was likely the best he was going to get, and he would not get that without Neil Cole. At least, it would be much more difficult.

"All right. I'll give it to him. I want to record his statement here, in my office, now. Is he available?" Ethan said, caving into Marc's complete immunity demand.

"I can have him here in ten minutes. Write up the Grant of Immunity, sign it and I'll call them. After they get here, you'll find out what else they have."

"Would you leave the room for a few minutes, please?" Marc asked the video tech when he finished setting up his equipment.

The tech looked at Ethan who shrugged and looked at Marc.

"We have something to tell you, but it's not going to be filmed," Marc said.

Ethan looked at the video tech and nodded. When the man was gone, Ethan turned to Marc and asked, "What?"

Marc looked at Cindy, who was brought along by Maddy with Neil and said, "Go ahead."

"Marc told me I need to tell you this even though it has nothing to do with the bank robberies or Jordan's murder," Cindy began. "Jordan told me that she shot a woman to impress Luke. Jordan had a big crush on Luke. He told her, all of us actually, that a woman who worked for Lake Country bank was responsible for his grandfather's death. She, the woman, was the head of the bank's foreclosure department. They took his grandpa's farm, and his grandpa hung himself because of it."

The light went on in Ethan's head. He looked at Marc and asked, "Natalie Flanders?"

"Yep," Marc said.

"That was the gun recovered from the Eagan robbery," Ethan said. "Jordan was shot and dropped it."

"Jordan sneaked the gun out. She told me she found out where this woman lived and followed her. She followed her a couple of times to some guy's apartment. Then, one night, she waited for her and shot her in the back of the head."

"Why didn't you come forward sooner?" an angry Ethan Pace asked.

"I don't know…I guess, I just…, well because Jordan was my friend and…"

"I could charge you…"

"With what?" Marc asked. "Being told of a crime? Jordan's lawyer would have had her deny it and the county would be nowhere. I've already spoken to Steve Gondeck at Hennepin County. They won't prosecute. No one else was involved. Only Jordan is tied to the physical evidence. They cleared a homicide. The Flanders family can now be told what happened. You can't punish Jordan. Move on, Ethan."

The video tech was brought back in along with a stenographer. She would make a written record of Neil's statement. Having told the story a half dozen times already Neil was quite prepared. With questions asked to clarify certain points, the statement took about an hour. As soon as she could, Maddy hustled both Cindy and Neil out of there to take them to Vivian's for safekeeping.

The stenographer and videographer had also packed up and left, leaving Marc and Ethan alone.

"They'll keep their mouths shut until we round up everybody and make arrests?" Ethan asked.

"Maddy's got it under control," Marc replied.

Before either man could say anything else, Ethan's desk phone rang.

"We weren't to be disturbed..." he started to say to his assistant.

"It's Agent Johnson and he says it is extremely urgent," the man replied.

"Okay, put him through," Ethan said. He looked at Marc and mouthed the words 'Jeff Johnson' at him.

"What's up?" Ethan asked.

"Got really bad news," Johnson said.

For about a minute, the AUSA listened while the FBI agent told him about the bank robbery and shoot out.

While this was taking place, Marc also received a call. It was from Tony Carvelli.

"Did you get it?" Marc asked.

"Everything," Carvelli answered. "At least enough to get warrants."

"Where are you?"

"About fifty feet from the courthouse door where you are," Carvelli said.

"I'll have Ethan call the receptionist to let you in. Come on up."

"Will do."

When Johnson finished telling him about Luke's death and confession, all Ethan Pace could say was "thanks" as he hung up the phone.

"Tony Carvelli's on his way up. He has a case for you. A corruption case that will make you a deputy attorney general."

"I hope so. Otherwise, after what Johnson just told me, I'll be looking for a job next week," Ethan glumly said.

"Why? What?" Marc asked.

"I guess I may as well tell you," he said as he called out front to leave instructions about Carvelli.

"Luke Hanson's dead," Ethan told Marc.

Three minutes later, Carvelli arrived and joined the two lawyers. Ethan had just finished telling Marc the story about Luke Hanson's death and confession. Carvelli sat down, and Marc told him. When Marc finished, he turned back to a distraught looking Ethan Pace.

"Your murder conspiracy just blew up," Marc said.

Ethan nodded as Carvelli asked, "Why?"

"Because," Marc began, "he has two conflicting stories. One from an eyewitness with a motive to lie and one from a dying man who the law presumes is telling the truth. A dying declaration, a confession made by someone who believes he is about to die, is an exception to the hearsay rule. And given a lot of weight.

"He can have Neil testify, but Luke's confession will be allowed in. Ethan will have to give it to the defense lawyers. These guys will eat it up. Luke just created reasonable doubt about who killed Jordan Simmons."

"Why did he do that?" Carvelli asked.

"Don't know," Marc said.

"To royally screw me" Ethan replied.

"Cindy said he was pre-law. Taking a lot of legal courses. Especially criminal stuff. Maybe he knew. Plus, Cindy told me he was hot for Sherry, but she was sleeping with the professor. You tell me, why did he do it?"

"Our immunity deals are off," Ethan angrily said. "Obviously all three of our clients lied. The deals are off."

"Nice try, Ethan," Marc said.

Marc took out his phone and called Maddy. Speaking to her so Ethan could hear him, Marc said, "Ask Cindy and Neil if they are willing to take a polygraph, a lie detector test."

Maddy was quickly back and emphatically said, "Yes. Both. No problem."

"Now tell them this. Luke Hanson tried to rob a bank today with Reese Fallon. Reese is fine, but Luke was shot to death. Before he died, he confessed to killing Jordan Simmons. Then ask again about the polygraph."

Marc could hear Maddy speaking to them and came back and again said, "Yes, again. They both insist Luke was lying."

"Bring them back. We'll do it now," Marc said.

Under normal circumstances, Marc would never let a client take a polygraph test. This situation was hardly normal. If Ethan went ahead and tried to tear up the immunity deals, Marc needed to be able to negate the grounds for it.

Maddy was babysitting Cindy in a separate room while Neil took the test. Marc had explained to him exactly what to do. Remain calm, think about the question, answer only the question with one word and do not anticipate.

Marc, Carvelli and Ethan Pace sat in a separate room watching the test on a video monitor. When it was over, the technician joined them while Neil waited.

"Passed with flying colors," the tech told Ethan. "He's telling the truth. No doubt about it."

"Thanks, Clark," Pace said.

Marc asked, "You still want to test Cindy?"

The phone on the table rang, and while Ethan answered Marc's question in the negative, Carvelli beat him to the phone.

"FBI torture chamber," Carvelli said into the phone.

"Give me that!" Pace yelled as he jerked the phone away from Carvelli.

Pace heard the receptionist tell him Jeff Johnson was calling with more urgent news.

"Let's hope this is better," Pace said. "Put him through."

Johnson had barely started speaking when Pace said, "What! Say that again."

He listened for almost two minutes, slumped in a chair next to the phone. The news was anything but good.

"Are you serious? Of course, you're serious," Pace quickly said before Johnson could reply.

"Today must be the day I put the gun in my mouth and put an end to it. I'll talk to you later, Jeff."

By now the technician had left to unhook Neil from the machine. Marc and Carvelli were impatiently waiting.

Still seated next to the phone, Pace looked at the two men, took a deep breath and said, "Johnson got a call from Minneapolis. Owen Jefferson. Ben Sokol didn't show up for the classes he was supposed to teach.

"A secretary finally got worried and sent a teaching assistant to his house to check on him. The secretary had a key.

"The kid got there and found the professor and Sherry Toomey in bed. Both dead with what looks like a couple of shots to the head."

"Whoa," Marc said. "Where did this come from? Your guys were sitting on everybody. We had Neil, Cindy and Donna and..."

"This sounds professional," Carvelli said.

"That's what the MPD people think, too," Pace said.

"Breyer," Carvelli replied. "You got my guys' report. Who else had motive? Put your people on it."

"We will. We'll get him. We can claim we simply did what your guy did and tracked the bank money to Breyer. But, I'm not sure we can get that law firm for jury tampering and bribery. It's too old and how do we explain it? We had no probable cause to even look into it. And a judge would raise hell if he or she believes we investigated the defense attorneys on this case while the case was ongoing."

"Leak it to the media. Some blogger. Put it out there. You might get their license," Marc said.

Ethan Pace looked at Marc and said, "That's an idea. What do I have left?"

"Not much," Marc said. "Cindy, Neil and Donna have immunity. Luke, Sherry and Sokol are dead. Reese Fallon and Gary Weaver. That's it.

"From what Neil and Cindy told me, they were not exactly the masterminds of any of this," Marc continued. "My advice let it go quiet then give them an offer they can't refuse. Minimal jail time at a minimum-security prison. Probation would be more appropriate. Do those two really deserve to be the only ones to do time? Close it quietly and go after Breyer. If you get him, you'll likely get a bunch of others who fed him money without getting too curious about what he was doing with it."

"That's probably the thing to do," Ethan agreed.

"Ethan, you and the FBI solved this case and put a stop to it. Your career will be fine," Marc said.

SIXTY

Tom Breyer had waited a full twenty-four hours before sending a second hitman—in this case, a woman—to Minnesota. The first one—the one Sherry Toomey killed with a letter opener—had a sterling reputation. His professional name was Pete Gilbert. Breyer did not know the man's real name and did not want to know it. When Gilbert missed a routine check-in time, Breyer knew something was wrong. Having used the man twice before, this had never happened.

On top of that was the news that someone out there had hacked through his security. This someone had spent a lot of time going through Breyer's business. And his people had not been able to track him down. That news had come to him two days ago and completely negated the news he received that Ben Sokol had been dispatched.

Breyer was lounging on his 800 square foot deck overlooking the estate's swimming pool. The pool was on a cliff one-hundred feet above the Pacific Ocean. The view Breyer was looking at was majestic. Even the one in the pool.

Her real name was Melanie, but her Hollywood wannabee name was Tiara. She was blonde, five-foot-eight and beautiful, doing laps in the nude and completely boring Tom Breyer. He was making a mental list of things to do, and she had moved up to number one. The only question was, could he send her packing for only five grand in cash or would he need ten? That problem, along with many others, was about to resolve itself.

Breyer's personal phone rang. He looked at the ID and answered.

"It's worse than we thought might happen," Breyer's main lawyer Jonah Cliff abruptly said.

"Tell me," Breyer replied.

"The FBI hit a dozen of the nonprofits first thing this morning. They shut them all down and grabbed everything. Files, computers, desks, paper clips, you name it. It will take a few days for them to get through it, but the party's over, Tom."

Breyer could feel the blood rushing up into his face. He looked down as his naked blonde playmate climbed out of the pool. She waved up at him, picked up a towel and wrapped herself in it. All the while, the controlled fury Breyer was feeling had him thinking about strangling her just for a release.

"Tom, are you there?"

"Yes, I'm still here. Just thinking," he calmly replied. "Anything else?"

"Isn't that enough? What happened out there on the tundra of frozen ass flyover Minnesota is what triggered this. I'm sure of it," Jonah said.

"Where are you?" Breyer asked.

"L.A. and I'm not going back to Minnesota. No need to," the lawyer answered.

"I need to make some phone calls. I'll get back to you," Breyer said.

"Tom, they're going to trace it back…"

"I know what to do," Breyer said then abruptly hung up.

Tom Breyer had a contingency plan in place for this occurrence. With one phone call, he would trigger a fire sale of his assets, turn everything into cash and move it to safe havens. Even after the losses were factored in, he would still have over two billion to live on. Everything was set. Being a practical man, Breyer knew it had to be done.

The bimbo, now in a bikini, appeared on the deck. She walked over practicing her FM look and walk and kissed him on the cheek.

"I have to leave for a couple of days. Something has come up," Breyer told her.

Without meaning it, in fact quite relieved to be rid of the fat old man for a couple of days, she stuck out her lower lip and said, "Oh, I'll miss you."

She would even wait to call her life-guard boy-toy until after he was gone.

"Just a couple days," he repeated.

Leaving her on the deck, Breyer went inside. He made two calls. One to a trusted executive at a large, New York brokerage. This would start the fire sale. The other call was to a connection who would contact the woman who had hit the idiot professor and his girlfriend. Within an hour, Tom Breyer was in his private G650 flying over the Pacific.

Four days later, Tony Carvelli called Marc Kadella at Marc's office.

"What's up?" Marc asked.

"I just got a call from Jeff Johnson. You remember that guy, that professor who was sort of connected to Ben Sokol?"

"No," Marc answered.

"Sure you do. Webster Crosby," Carvelli said.

"Yeah, okay, now I remember. What about him?" Marc answered.

"He was on TV a lot hustling money. Johnson tells me the Feebs had linked him to the money going to these phony nonprofits. They also have him involved with the missing Tom Breyer.

"Webster Crosby was found in a cheap motel in Del Rio, Texas lying on the floor with two neat, extra holes in his forehead," Carvelli reported.

"Wow! No kidding," Marc said.

"Johnson thinks it's a loose end Breyer cleaned up before he took off," Carvelli said.

"Any sign of Breyer yet?" Marc asked.

"Nah, he's gone. Probably to some nonextradition country. The feds are finding out he sold off everything he could and bailed. How are the kids doing?"

"My kids? They're great."

"No, the cult kids."

"They're good. Hopefully, they learned their lesson. I talked to Ethan and he told me he has offered probation to both Gary Weaver and Reese Fallon. Getting a murder conviction for Jordan Simmons was not going to happen. Putting these two in prison when everyone else walks or is dead, well the U.S. Attorney's office thinks that would be a waste of taxpayer's money."

"I agree. What are you and Maddy up to Saturday night?"

"I don't know. Dinner and a movie. Date night. Why?"

"Um, Vivian has this thing, a fundraiser. I don't know, saving chipmunks and other assorted endangered vermin. I'm not sure. Anyway…"

"No," Marc emphatically replied.

"Hey, I could go to Maddy and ask or have Vivian do it. Please? Please don't make me sit through this by myself."

"You're going to beg?"

"If I have to, yes,"

"You're not very good at it. Try harder," Marc teased.

"Pleeeeease!"

"God, that's lame. You really suck at begging. No wonder you're twice divorced. Tell you what, tell Vivian to get two more tickets for Connie and the judge. But I want you to call Maddy and practice your begging."

"When have you ever had to beg Maddy for anything?"

"We're not talking about me we're talking about you. You need the practice."

THREE MONTHS LATER

"Maddy's on the phone," Carolyn told Marc through the intercom.

331

"Hey," Marc said after answering the call.

"Have you seen this morning's paper?" Maddy asked.

"No, I haven't," Marc answered. "Why?"

"I'll read the headline. Frontpage. Billionaire fugitive believed dead. Tom Breyer," Maddy added.

"No kidding?"

"Nope. Apparently, an accident scuba diving in the ocean off the Maldives. The Maldives just happens to be a nonextradition country."

"You don't suppose our government had anything to do with it, do you?" Marc asked.

"I certainly hope so," Maddy answered.

Thank you for your patronage. I hope you enjoyed Cult Justice.

Dennis Carstens

Email me at: dcarstens514@gmail.com

Also Available on Amazon
Previous Marc Kadella Legal Mystery Courtroom Dramas

The Key to Justice

Desperate Justice

Media Justice

Certain Justice

Personal Justice

Delayed Justice

Political Justice

Insider Justice

Exquisite Justice

Made in the USA
Las Vegas, NV
06 October 2021